The Rabbit Hunter II
The Battle of Crete

The Rabbit Hunter II
The Battle of Crete
~ CHRISTOPHER WORTH ~

First published in 2024 by Renaissance Publishing
www.renaissancepublishing.co.nz

Copyright © 2024 Christopher Worth

The author asserts his moral right to the work.

ISBN: 978-0-473-70426-1

A catalogue record for this book is available from the
National Library of New Zealand

Cover design: Nick Turzynski, www.redinc.co.nz
Text design: Julie McDermid, www.punapub.com
Front cover images: © Crown copyright
Imperial War Museums
Back cover: © Alexander Turnbull Library

Printed in New Zealand

For my brother, Geoffrey Noel Worth,
31 July 1950–20 October 1984
A gentle giant, victim of someone else's war.

Contents

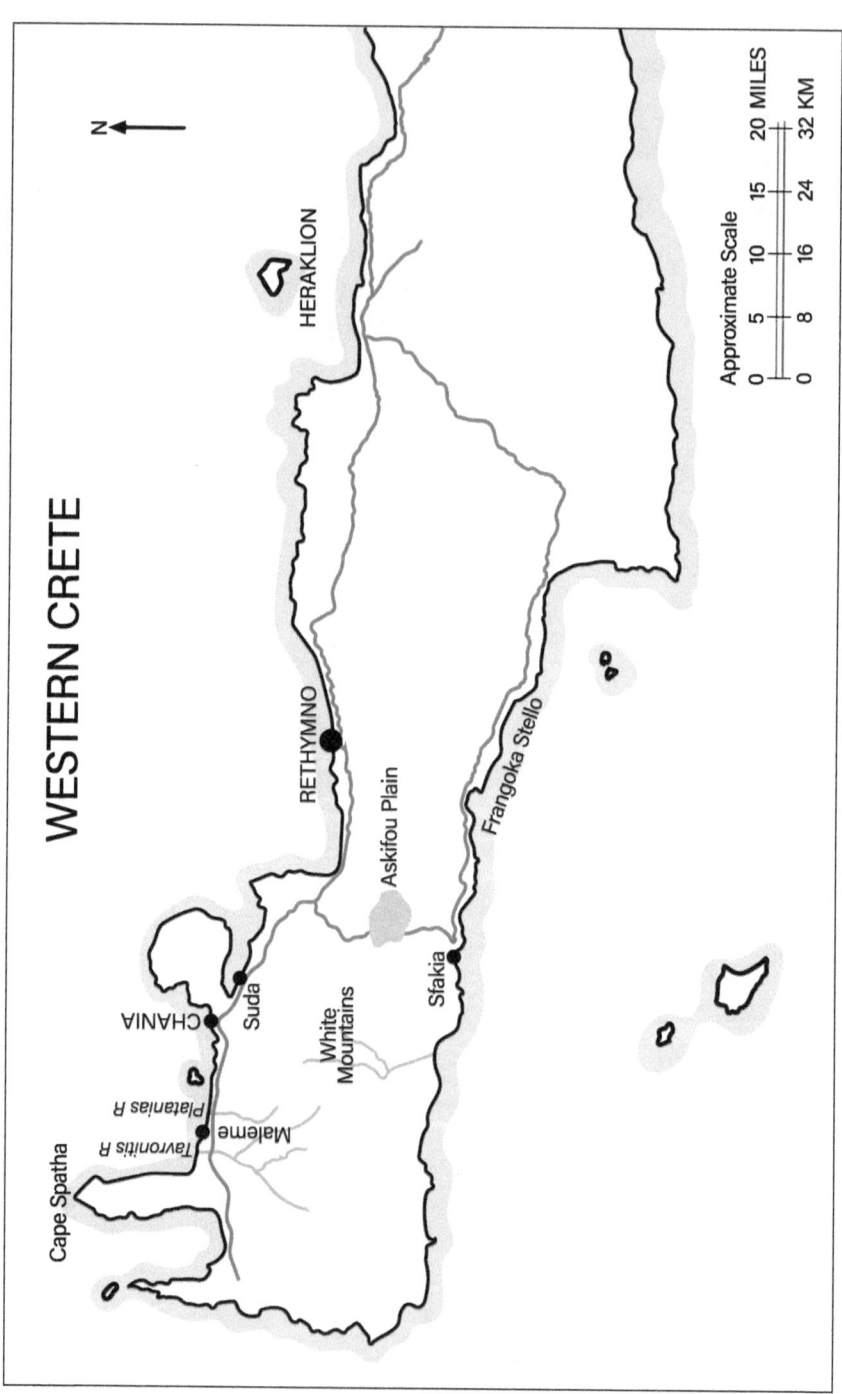

WESTERN CRETE

N

Cape Spatha

Tavronitis R

Platanias R

Maleme

CHANIA

Suda

White
Mountains

Sfakia

Askifou Plain

RETHYMNO

HERAKLION

Frangoka Stello

Approximate Scale

0	5	10	15	20 MILES
0	8	16	24	32 KM

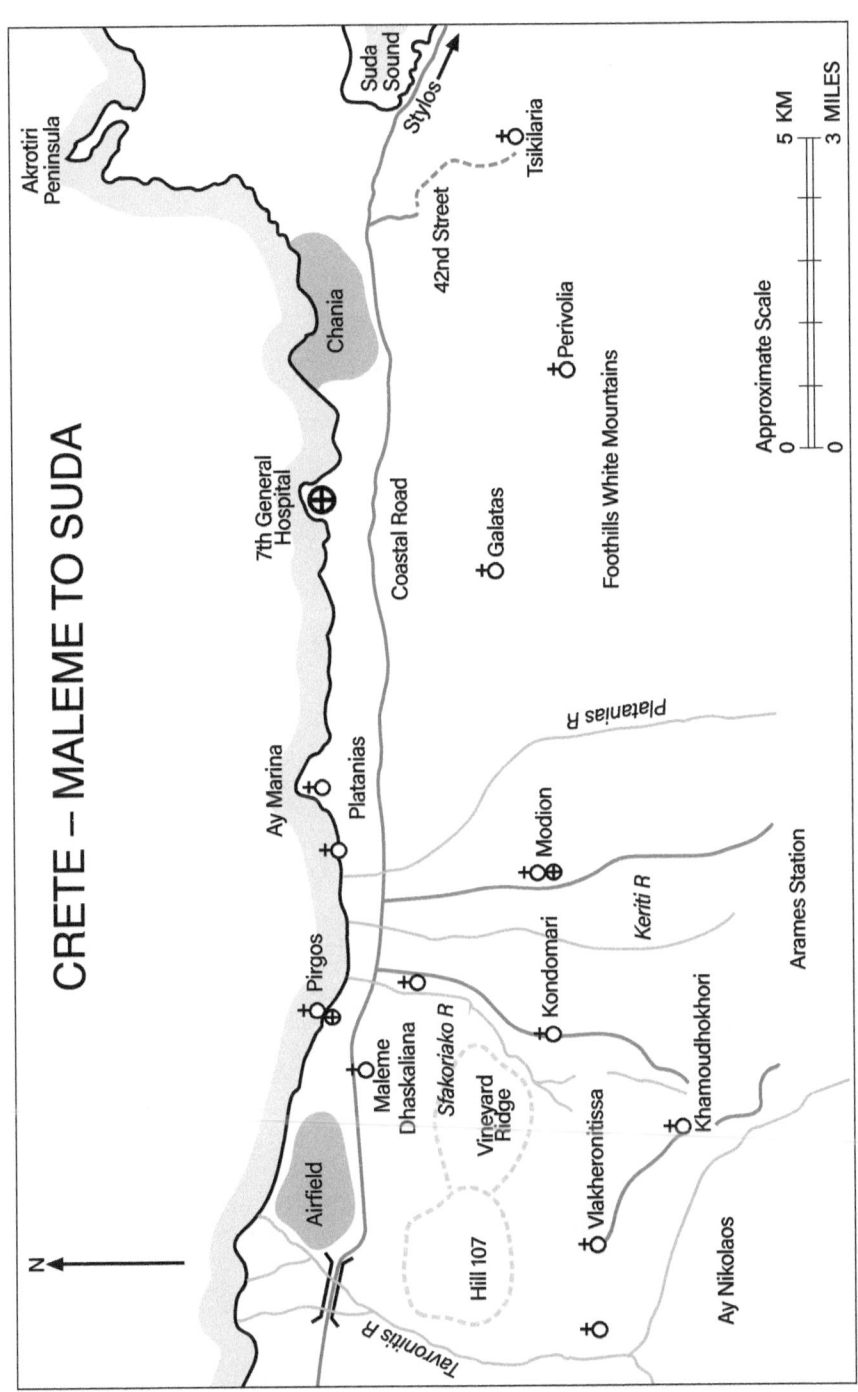

CRETE – MALEME TO SUDA

N

Akrotiri Peninsula

Suda Sound

Stylos

Chania

42nd Street

♂ Tsikilaria

7th General Hospital ⊕

Coastal Road

♂ Perivolia

♂ Galatas

Foothills White Mountains

Ay Marina

Platanias R

♂ Platanias

♂ Modion ⊕

Keriti R

Arames Station

Pirgos

♂ Kondomari

♂ Khamoudhokhori

Maleme

Dhaskaliana

Sfakoriako R

Vineyard Ridge

♂ Vlakheronitissa

Airfield

Hill 107

Tavronitis R

♂ Ay Nikolaos

Approximate Scale

0   5 KM

0   3 MILES

PART ONE

INTO THE LABYRINTH

CHAPTER ONE

Welcome to Crete, 2 May 1941

THE BLUFF STEEL bows of Tank Landing Craft A6 shouldered aside the long, low Mediterranean swell. Neither graceful nor agile, she lumbered across the silent, starlit sea, leaving a trail of bubbling phosphorescence and oily fumes in her wake. To those aboard her, however, she was the most beautiful vessel afloat. Astern, Greece and the volcanic pimple of Monemvasia receded to a dark and dangerous smudge across the broad horizon.

Leaning against the wire-rope rail strung along the narrow catwalk above the vehicle deck, Second Lieutenant Neil Rankin was lost in thought. He had a lot to reflect upon. They had made it aboard a ship out of Greece by the skin of their teeth. But made it to what, and to where? In barely more than a month, they had arrived in Athens, fought the invading Germans on the flanks of Mount Olympus, and then been chased the length and breadth of Greece. Hitler's Wehrmacht seemed unstoppable. His Luftwaffe, which controlled the skies, harried them at will.

Rankin's fingers went to his chest, subconsciously feeling the layers of dressing through the tattered and stained fabric of his shirt. A reminder of the morning they had arrived at the Corinth

Canal, just in time to be savagely bombed and then assaulted by German airborne troops. The following firefight had left Rankin battered and sore – and ensured that their little convoy had been the last of the Allied traffic to escape encirclement and capture on the wrong side of the canal. To cap it all, they had had to fight a vicious little battle in an obscure fishing village near the bottom of the Peloponnese Peninsula to make sure of their place on the very last boat out of Greece.

The hectic British evacuation of Monemvasia concluded when the two tank-landing craft cleared the stone-built harbour mole for the open sea. A6's well deck, built for vehicles, was a mass of sprawling, squatting and smoking humanity. Many of the troops vociferously complained that they were like sardines packed into a tin can, especially when trodden on or doused in something unpleasant. Their fellow passengers just as loudly reminded them how lucky they were to be there at all, and not waiting to be marched off to captivity like the thousands of disillusioned and resentful men who had been left behind. It was true: many owed their escape to the fact A6 was no doubt carrying many more passengers than her designers had intended.

The ship had no facilities. Men who needed to vomit, defecate or urinate had to do so from the narrow, elevated catwalk along the ship's sides. The Navy, ever considerate of its landlubber passengers, had thoughtfully rigged wire railings to stop them falling overboard or tumbling onto the deck six feet below. Some had dysentery, or at least diarrhoea, and those vulnerable even to the gentlest sea-movement became seasick almost as soon as the ship butted into the open sea. Their need to make use of the rudimentary facilities was neither uncommon nor without difficulty. They were barely out of port when the first seasick soldier needed to vomit over the side, soon followed by the diarrhoea cases.

The sailors had shouted in no uncertain terms to use the lee-ward – pronounced "looward" – side of the ship. The nuances of nautical terminology were quickly impressed upon anyone seeking relief; the unfortunates who chose the wrong – windward – side of the ship soon realised their error when their offerings to Neptune blew back over them and down onto the crowded deck below.

If the night had seemed long, the day that followed was longer. The ship's captain, a Naval Reserve sub-lieutenant named Johnny Hutton, extended to Rankin, as the sole army officer aboard, the limited hospitality at his disposal.

Rankin contrived to wash and shave in the tiny basin in Hutton's diminutive cabin. It was an opportunity to inspect the damage: the filthy, stained bandage wrapped around his forehead and the livid black and yellow bruises around his eye and across his chest, brought back vivid memories of the events of the last several days. The memories brought with them hot pricking tears. Steadying himself on the little handbasin, he allowed the memories to recede. "Jesus," he breathed, shaken. If it was a relief to be clean; it was a much greater relief to rid himself of his battered uniform with the stain left by the former occupant of the 15-hundredweight truck in Ariana, whose place Rankin had taken in the frantic assault to dislodge the Germans from the town.

After washing his uniform and hanging it up to dry he borrowed a clean khaki shirt and shorts from his host and then joined him on the ship's tiny bridge. Hutton grinned, eyeing his own clean shirt. "You managed to get rid of the other chap, I see."

Rankin smiled wanly, pointing to A4 ahead of them. "Is it my imagination, or is the other boat getting away from us?"

"With every passing mile, old chum," Hutton said, picking up his binoculars.

Rankin looked at him blankly.

"Engine trouble," Hutton said. "Only reason we came back at all last night. We should be safely tucked up in Suda by now. We've got a buggered bearing or an inflamed big-end or some such. Whichever it is, it's kept us at the princely speed of six and a half knots. Slow enough to give us a sporting chance of having another crack at the enemy."

Rankin stared at him, the unwelcome knot of fear hard in the pit of his stomach.

———

HUTTON'S PREDICTION WAS not an idle one. The open Mediterranean provided no place to hide. Early in the afternoon a pair of Messerschmitt 109s appeared and strafed the ship, wounding half a dozen and killing one. The soldiers brought every weapon they could to bear and using the catwalks as rests, they made a lot of noise which probably did more for morale aboard ship than damage to the Germans. A lucky shot from one of the ship's two single-mount 2-pounder pom-pom guns, one on each side of the bridge, sent them on their way – one trailing smoke – to wild applause from the well deck.

Towards evening A6 was bombed by a flight of Stukas. Providence intervened in the form of two naval Gladiators, which arrived from Maleme airfield, on Crete. The antiquated-looking biplanes forced the dive-bombers into a defensive circle and shot one down, but not before several bombs landed close enough to send tons of water aboard, soaking everyone, and peppering the sides with splinters, causing more casualties.

After nightfall, the signalman brought Hutton orders from Suda Shipping Control to proceed direct to Chania. "That's uncommonly considerate," he remarked to Rankin, smiling broadly and brandishing the flimsy page from the pad on which the signaller had laboriously transcribed the dots and dashes in his earphones to coded letters which he then translated into plain text. "If we fetched up in Suda, you'd only have to walk all the way back again."

Rankin took the few steps from bridge wing to the cupboard that served as a chartroom behind the bridge where he bent over the chart on the table. "The Navy's not usually that obliging," Hutton said, pointing out the distance from Suda Bay, the naval base, to Chania.

"Nor is the army," sighed Rankin.

It was near midnight when A6 picked up the coloured lights, the "leads" Hutton called them, that led them to the harbour entrance. She rounded the mole, its Venetian lighthouse passing abeam almost unseen in the pitch black and slipped into the port. Moored alongside the stone quay were several landing craft, patrol boats and small coastal ships. The scene was one of feverish activity, starkly illuminated by floodlights rigged along the quay.

"Welcome to Crete, old boy," Hutton said, laughing as he rang "finished with engines" on the telegraph. "Don't forget to pick up your laundry on your way out, or you might end up taking her back to sea on her next cruise."

"Thanks very much for the lift, I'm sure. Not as I have always imagined a Mediterranean cruise, really, but we're all very grateful to you, and for your providential bung bearing."

Rankin's platoon sergeant, Sandy Nicholson, and the other NCOs began the task of forming the men up on the quay as they staggered off the landing craft, flexing muscles and stamping feet to restore circulation.

"How was your Mediterranean cruise, then, Nick?" Rankin asked, eyeing Nicholson's stoop, which seemed more pronounced than he remembered.

Nicholson's expression under the harsh lights was uncharacteristically sour. "I never want to see another boat as long as I live. Standing room only, like catching the New Brighton tram at the weekend and getting covered in other people's muck while you're at it." Nicholson wrinkled up his nose as he flicked something off his shirt. "And no blimmin' grub. I've gone right off the Navy."

Rankin laughed and clapped him on the back before heading off in search of someone who might be able to tell them where to go next.

"Who the hell are you, and what the bloody hell are you doing here, sport?" The voice with an unmistakeably Australian drawl came from a lanky figure that strode out of a dark recess into the pool of light where Rankin stood. The Australian's slouch hat was pushed well back from his forehead, he was dressed in a grubby singlet and shorts, and his face and arms glistened with sweat. The appearance of hard-grafting toil was completed by the glowing stub of a cigarette hanging out of one corner of his mouth.

Rankin shielded his eyes from the painful glare of the lights above. "I have a party of evacuees from Greece."

"Stone the bloody crows. Another lot," the man grumbled.

"Shift yer arses so's we can turn these boats round before the fuckin' Luftwaffe comes back."

He must have seen Rankin's expression.

"Try that little buildin' over there, mate." He pointed towards a low building on the other side of the road. "Only you'll need to get these clowns off the bloody wharf quick-smart," he said jerking his thumb at the straggling assembly alongside A6.

Rankin avoided a three-ton lorry rumbling along the quay and opened the door to see several harassed-looking naval and army officers, all hatless and in their shirtsleeves, working around a desk littered with ashtrays, coffee cups and papers. The room was lit by several hurricane lamps. A thick blue haze obscured the far wall, and the place stank of tobacco and sweat.

One of the officers looked up from the desk and said testily, "If you're looking for the hospital, it's about five miles down the road." He turned back to his papers.

"Actually, sir, we've just arrived. From Greece. Wondering if someone might tell us where to go," Rankin said.

The man's head jerked up, and he fixed Rankin with an unblinking stare. "I'll tell you where to go alright. Who's 'we'? The Shah of bloody Persia? Every other bugger's turned up here, all looking for ways to get their 'special packages' out." He leaned back in his chair and lit a cigarette, studying Rankin all the while. "Special packages, my arse. Didn't bring a boatload of floozies with you, did you?"

"Er, no, sir. About three hundred men from Monemvasia – on the Greek mainland."

The officer sat upright, narrowing his eyes. "I know where it is, son. Closed to traffic several nights ago. Occupied by the enemy now. You'll have to do better than that."

"We caused the Hun some grief at a little port they held, just north of Monemvasia. We were the last to get clear, in two landing craft."

They all stopped what they were doing and looked up at him.

"You don't say. What ship was it that you came on, then?" the officer asked, leafing through some papers, and spilling the contents of an overflowing ashtray in the process. "Oh, bugger!"

"A6 landing craft – Sub-Lieutenant Hutton. We were strafed on the way here. We'll need some ambulances, too."

"A6? *A6?* She was bombed and sunk. You can't have got here aboard her." The man's exasperation increased to petulance; next could be a full-blown tantrum. They all seemed to be cut from the same mould, these port officers.

At that moment, Hutton himself stepped through the door. "Oh, I see you have met Lieutenant Rankin. I have just landed him and nearly three hundred like him. Refugees."

"And who the bloody hell are you, Sub?"

"Hutton, Sub-Lieutenant, A6, sir."

"If I may, sir." An army officer hastily rose and stood beside the desk. His tidy uniform, neatly trimmed moustache and soft-spoken accent evoked Salvation Army for Rankin.

"I am Captain Sanderson, Service Corps, assisting the Port Officer and naval supply branch," he said. "Now, gentlemen, we heard that A6 had been bombed, and sunk, so if you would care to enlighten us as to the precise circumstances ..."

"Bombed, but not sunk," Hutton said gaily. "Saved by the Navy's gallant flying Gladiatorial cavalry, from Crete. My privilege to deliver these fine chaps to Chania, from Monemvasia, as instructed by Shipping Control at Suda."

The Port Officer harrumphed. "Pity they didn't bloody tell us."

"Someone seemed to be expecting us," Hutton continued airily. "Light signals, berth, sweating Aussie coolies on the quay, all laid on."

Rankin, watching the exchange, wondered idly how the Australian stevedore gang might feel about being labelled "coolies".

Sanderson stepped in before the naval officer suffered from apoplexy. "Well now, Lieutenant, what was your cargo?"

"Three hundred pirates, hale and hearty – armed to the teeth, mi-lud," said Hutton. "And now that they're all ashore, I need permission to get cracking round to Suda for some TLC for my TLC."

They all looked at him blankly. "Tender loving care for my tank landing craft, sir. Rather clever, don't you think?"

The seated naval officer lit another cigarette, no doubt to soothe the vein throbbing in his temple and slumped back in his chair. "For Christ's sake! Bloody public schoolboys!"

He turned to a couple of naval ratings sitting at another table equipped with several telephones and barked some instructions. He then turned to yet another table, half hidden in the haze, and shouted, "Call the army office in charge – what do they call themselves? Creforce Evacuees or some such. Tell 'em we've got three hundred new arrivals and ask them what the bloody hell I do with them!"

Sanderson, whose job it seemed to be to pour oil onto waters troubled by the unnamed port officer, asked Rankin which unit the men came from.

"Any unit that went to Greece. The one criterion was that they're armed. They attacked Ariana."

"You're wounded, young man. You need an ambulance, you say?"

"Not for me, sir. We had about a dozen wounded in air attacks at sea."

A naval rating brought a signal to the port officer, whose eyes lit up as he scanned it. "That's more bloody like it. Fast destroyer *Nizam* an hour out with eighty-five tons of small arms ammunition and two hundred and fifty royal marines. Can we turn her around before 0400? Of course, we bloody can. Suda has a problem with a wreck, apparently. Bloody harbour's full of 'em."

"I see," said Sanderson, looking back to Rankin with a worried frown. "Most enterprising. Good show. Now, I believe when Creforce directs you to your new home, which will be one of the transit camps established to act as reception and re-equipment centres, they will ask you to hand in your weapons as you leave the port. This is so we can take a census of chaps and equipment available. Weapons will be redistributed, shared out to all, don't you see?" Sanderson's worried frown transformed into a beaming smile, like a Sunday school teacher leading a class of heathen children into the sunlit uplands. "Save you from carrying them away with you, what?"

"I see, sir," Rankin said. "Not bloody likely," he thought to himself.

Nicholson was standing outside by the door, waiting for him. He handed Rankin his helmet, commenting that the lights were a bit hard on the eyes.

"Thanks." Rankin nodded, adjusting the angle of his head so that the helmet rim blocked the glare from the floodlights. "I hope the Luftwaffe's nowhere close," he said, examining Nicholson. "You seem to have hoisted yourself up to full height while I've been gone."

"Like a spring released, now that I can feel what's inside my boots again. Made me realise my stomach thinks my throat's cut, too. Anyway, they're all formed up. But some of the unattached blokes and small units have gone walkabout, Neil. A couple of them said they'd find their own way to their outfits, taking in some of the sights on the way."

Rankin nodded. "None of our lot?"

"No blimmin' fear."

"Right oh, can't be helped. I doubt they can get into much trouble here. Now, I've just been told they might ask the boys to hand in their weapons, so that they can be 'redistributed' later," Rankin said.

Nicholson started bolt upright, eyes wide. "No bloody fear!"

———

WHILE THE MEN waited on the quay, the sweating teams of wharfies dealt with A6, a caique moored in front of her and a small coastal trader behind. The air rang with the noise of their activity, and their none-too-gentle instructions to Rankin and Nicholson and their lot to park themselves somewhere out of the bloody way. The troops dumped whatever they carried in front of the buildings lining the quay and sat down for a yarn and a smoke.

After what seemed an eternity, a despatch rider rode into the port with a tall man riding pillion. Getting off, he tapped the rider on his helmet, looked about, and strode towards the men lounging on the quay.

"Who's in charge here? Good God, Neil, is that you?"

Rankin recognised the voice. "William, William O'Rourke! I'll be buggered," he exclaimed, standing up to shake the proffered hand. "You all buggered off out of Thebes, left Boney and me to it, you shit!"

O'Rourke took off his steel helmet, wiped his forehead with his handkerchief and smoothed his jet-black hair with the heel of one hand. "We all thought you'd bought it, old boy," he replied, peering at Rankin's face. "Jesus, what the hell happened to you? Have a run-in with the schoolteacher's husband?"

"Ha, ha. Very funny, William."

"You should get that looked at," O'Rourke said, examining the bruises around his eye and the dressing showing under Rankin's helmet. "We were just following orders, Neil. We all thought you were goners when you never turned up at the evacuation beach. Then Boney turns up this evening, large as life and twice as obnoxious, and now you." He fitted a cigarette into its holder, surveying the surroundings as the match flared. "Boney only came back with his own platoon. You seem to have come back with half the bloody army."

"It's a long story. They're not all mine, although they sort of were for a day or two."

"Well, get them on their feet. We've got a few miles' march before they can knock off for the day."

Rankin raised his eyebrows. "Jesus, that'll please them. At least it's dry land, and doesn't feel like a whole lot of drunks swaying on a camel. Where's the transport?"

"Where do you think, you daft bugger? Lining miles of Greek roads. Along with everything else: everything down to the bloody dixies and spoons, it seems. I'll give you a bit of advice," O'Rourke said quietly as the NCOs got the protesting men to their feet, their gear on their backs and lined up to march out. "The Redcaps will try to tell you that orders are to surrender your weapons, and these will be redistributed according to need. Don't believe a bloody word of it. A couple of the early battalions in here fell for it, and now they've got half what they brought back from Greece, and a quarter of their establishment. And a full complement of very angry chaps."

"Thanks, Will. I wasn't born yesterday," said Rankin.

Nicholson came up to them. "Nice to see you again, Mister O'Rourke," he said, handing Rankin his pack and weapons. "Company formed up in column of threes, ready to move off, Mister Rankin." He took a pace back and saluted them both.

O'Rourke smiled as Rankin returned the salute and told his sergeant to carry on before putting on his own kit and slinging the German weapons over his shoulder.

"You seem to have become more military, Neil. Being a company commander obviously suits you." He stepped back and exaggeratedly appraised Rankin. "I see you're not exactly short when it comes to offensive capability."

"Oh, we picked up a few bits and pieces as we went along. Previous owners had no further use and all that," he replied as orders rang out and the column set off along the quay.

The noisy illuminated stone quay ended abruptly in blackness. A gate house at one side of the road and a barrier arm blocking the entranceway to the port were dimly visible beyond the pool of light cast by the floodlights. Several trucks had just passed through the gate and could be heard grinding their way up a hill in the dark as the column marched up to the lowered boom.

The military police corporal, whose job it was to check the drivers' papers, marched up to Rankin and shone his torch over him, then over the men behind, as they came to a halt.

"No contraband here, Corporal," said Rankin.

The torch lingered over Rankin's rifle and Schmeisser. "Orders are to collect weapons from men returning from Greece for redistribution." The light moved up to shine directly into his face.

Rankin's eyes hurt. He couldn't see the man's face, but he could guess. A short man, peaked cap pulled down over his eyes, precisely clipped moustache, ramrod stiff bearing, older than himself. His arrogant tone and working-class British accent told him all he needed to know: a jumped-up little twat. All Rankin could see was the painful glare of the torchlight.

"I didn't come down in the last shower, Corporal," he sighed. "Please lower your torch, you're shining it right in my eyes."

"I have orders to collect weapons from men returning from Greece. For redistribution... sir."

The delay in using his title was not lost on Rankin. He clearly thought himself as a British MP to be a cut above an officer from the colonies.

"I have orders to kill Germans ... Corporal. So do these blokes. Damned difficult without weapons, I would suggest."

"You all right there, Corporal?" A voice from the gate house.

"Under control, Sergeant. Evacuees from Greece." The torch did not waver.

"Get a move on, Corporal. There's a shipment of small-arms ammunition to be dispersed. It'll be along in a jiffy."

"Yes, Sergeant," the corporal said over his shoulder. "There's a compound by the gate house, Lieutenant. You can deposit your arms and ammunition there and the Sergeant will give you a receipt for them."

"I'll do no such thing. I've already asked you once: put the bloody torch down."

The light in his eyes had galvanised his headache.

"Orders, sir, are orders. The weapons are needed to arm others on the island." Rankin noticed the torch waver, then drop from his eyes at least. The man still held him in its glare, though.

"Orders are indeed orders, Corporal. My orders were to bring out able-bodied, armed men – which I have done. Nothing about laying down arms. Quite the opposite to what I was instructed. Without an original order signed by the General himself, I will not be asking my men to relinquish anything. Now, I suggest you move aside so we can all get on with our jobs."

"I must insist, sir," said the policeman, moving the torch back to Rankin's unblinking eyes.

Rankin felt his blood pressure and temper rising. "All right, Dad, you've done your job. Your sergeant can write out a receipt for anything he likes, and say he distributed them back to their rightful owners. Now, piss off. Get back to playing with your trucks."

As soon as he uttered the words, he regretted them. Malice radiated from the other man.

"Look," Rankin said soothingly. "The last MP I saw was dead. He had done a fine job guiding transport over the Corinth Canal all night long, but he didn't last a minute when Jerry got there. His pistol, you see, was no match against one of these." He swung the Schmeisser machine pistol forward on its sling. "He was riddled with bullets, not an hour after he'd marshalled us across the bridge," Rankin sighed, indicating the column waiting behind him. "I'm not taking the risk of leaving these men waving a piece of paper, like your Mister Chamberlain, at another bloody German parachutist!"

Rankin was aware his voice had risen; he was breathing hard. The silence behind him was tangible. His eyes hurt, his head felt it was about to explode, every breath hurt his chest.

The man was not going to give up. He turned and called to the sergeant in the guardhouse to make a phone call. He turned the torch back onto Rankin. Muttering rose from the ranks behind.

Rankin ostentatiously pulled back on the Schmeisser's cocking handle. "Did you not hear me, Corporal? Killed by a German paratrooper who took no notice whatsoever of the wee pistol the policeman had been given to defend his bridge." He jabbed the man several times in the chest with the barrel of the Schmeisser, ensuring the safety was engaged with his thumb as he did so.

"These men have seen their friends killed. They've sacrificed their personal kit to bring their weapons with them. I am not going to ask them to forget that and put them in a position where they cannot defend themselves against the enemy." He emphasised the last words by poking the man's chest. To his credit, thought Rankin, the man did not back away. Behind him, he sensed the column becoming restless. He heard the snick of a bolt.

"I must insist, sir," the MP repeated. Rankin felt his hackles rise even further. "Orders are to surrender weapons for redistribution."

Rankin sighed. Tiredness threatened to overwhelm him. His head ached fearfully. "Our orders are to kill Germans – unlike yours, which seems to be to get in the bloody way!" Rankin shouted, shoving the barrel of the Schmeisser into the man's chest so hard he stumbled a pace backwards, dropping his torch. The falling light showed fear flash across his face.

Nicholson stepped up and laid a restraining hand on Rankin's arm. More than one man moved behind him. More weapons were cocked.

Not shifting his eyes from the corporal, Rankin said over his shoulder, "Clear this obstruction out of the way, and open the boom." Boots crunched on the gravel, the corporal was hoisted bodily off his feet, and the boom swung up. "Now, we must get on, we've had a very trying couple of days. Good night, Corporal."

Nicholson ordered the column to resume its march.

O'Rourke guffawed with laughter as the company marched briskly away, elbowing the protesting policeman aside in the process. "My gosh, Neil, quite a speech. Was he dead? The last MP you saw?"

"Yes, he was. Nice young bloke. Turfed out of his post like a dog's turd. The buggers set up a machine gun in it."

"I see," said O'Rourke.

Rankin looked at him in the low light. "I doubt that." How could anyone imagine Charlie Temple, arms flailing grenades right and left, running at the gun post? He was suddenly overwhelmed, his knees on the verge of buckling, tears pricking his eyes. "I say, Will, I'm awfully tired. Can you carry the Schmeisser for me, please?"

O'Rourke glanced at Rankin, nodded, and took the weapon. "Yes, of course. Glad to help, old man," said O'Rourke, examining the Schmeisser.

"They won't do it again," Rankin said absently. O'Rourke gingerly turned the gun over in his hands. "It's not loaded, Will."

They marched along in silence, boots ringing on the cobbles. Soon they were stamping in unison along a paved road, and finally crunching on gravel. Rankin's head was pounding; his temple throbbed in time with his footfalls.

O'Rourke finally asked, "So, what did happen after we pulled out of Thebes?"

"I'm sure you've heard the story from Boney. Where did you get evacuated from?"

"Marathon, or rather a beach nearby called Porto Rafti."

"Oh," said Rankin. "Sounds nice. We got a bit held up – had to by-pass Athens and Marathon. How long have you been here, then?"

"Since a couple of days after Anzac Day. The battalion has moved to a place called Platanias. We officers have a roster to help meeting and greeting the waifs and strays. My turn tonight."

"Anzac Day …" Rankin said softly. It seemed an age ago, and far, far away.

"Did you really fight the German paratroopers? They're supposed to be their elite. What are they like, Neil?"

"Just like the rest of us, Will. Hit 'em in the guts hard enough, and they go down like a sack of spuds."

————

THE TRANSIT "CAMP" turned out to be an olive plantation ranging up gentle slopes on either side of the road. Several hurricane lamps suspended from trees at the roadside and a loose line of sentries marked it out as a camp. Although it was long after midnight, a reception committee comprising the camp commander, his adjutant and sergeant-major, and some cheering and clapping earlier arrivals turned out to greet them.

At the first sight of lights, the crunch of boots on the gravel road fell properly into step. Rankin felt the backs around him straighten, heads lift and free arms swing. Rankin halted them in the road, turned them to face the waiting officers, saluted, and presented them: "The Monemvasia Evacuees Composite Company, sir!"

After the formalities, the men were stood easy, and the commandant climbed onto an ammunition box so that he could be seen and heard by all.

"Welcome to Crete, chaps, to Transit Camp B. This is the Perivolia Olive Plantation. You chaps must be amongst the very last evacuees, and we know you've had a hard time of it. This is not a holiday camp" – to which a groan and cry of "shame" went up – "but you will find duties light for a day or two. We need to sort you into your respective units and make arrangements for you to rejoin them. You will receive an issue of much-needed kit to replace some of what you have lost. But first, when I dismiss you, please form two lines to pass by the tables down the road, where you will pick up something to eat and a hot drink, and then you'll be shown where to bed down for the night.

"There are no tents, chaps; you'll be sleeping under the trees. But I'm sure that's nothing new. I'm afraid there aren't blankets for those who don't have their own. Reveille is at 0530," which elicited a loud groan, "to enable breakfast to be distributed before the Luftwaffe arrives. They generally arrive between 0700 and 0800 hours. The Luftwaffe's activities have been increasing in the last day or two, so we must keep out of sight during daylight hours. I'm sure you don't need reminding about staying under cover. I must stress to you all, in case you've forgotten, do *not* on any account fire at passing aeroplanes!"

Rankin fell out with the rest of them and, gasping for a drink, moved to join the queue at the tables. As he joined the line, he heard a shout and raised his head to see Boney Anderson, his oldest friend, striding forward holding out his hand.

"What ho, Neil, welcome to Crete. Good to be back on terra firma, eh?"

Rankin felt the tiredness and strain wash over him, and his shoulders slumped. "I could murder a mug of tea. No bloody catering on our boat, and we had to fight off a couple of air attacks." Anderson's face shone, freshly washed and shaved. His eyes were bright; he looked the picture of health. "You look like you've been here for weeks. I suppose you got here completely unscathed, no trouble, with luxurious accommodation?"

Anderson looked affronted. "I wouldn't say that. Those landing craft will never catch on. Bloody uncomfortable, especially for steerage-class passengers. Standing room only, you know. Bloody senior officer snaffled the captain's cabin. I never got a look-in."

"Oh, God, how awful for you, Boney," Rankin laughed, looking at the little patches of light spread over the hillside. "Lanterns on the hillside. How romantic, they look like fireflies in a grotto."

"It's going to take Jerry a week or two to work out where we've gone. We should have time to do some exploring," enthused Anderson. "Crete is the home of the Minotaur! We could look for the Maidens' Grotto in his Labyrinth, Neil. We could make archaeological history. The Cretans would be forever in our debt." Anderson's eyes shone brightly. "Who knows, there might still be maidens in it."

"I think you've been touched by the sun," said Rankin. "Right now, Boney, I'd trade the lot of them for a cup of tea and a bully sandwich."

CHAPTER TWO

Perivolian Sojourn,
the Calm Before the Storm

DAYLIGHT SAW THE cooks struggling to prepare breakfast over cut-down petrol drums and four-gallon tins. Rankin and Anderson, as new arrivals, reported to the camp office located in a basement at 0830. Arrangements would be made, they were informed, to post their men back to their units; or where their units had not come to Crete – "or had ceased to exist for some other reason" – decisions would be made as to "how best employ them or detail them for onward movement". It was clear it would be some time before everyone could rejoin their units.

The first days followed a relaxing routine: parades were held for every conceivable purpose. New khaki drill shorts and shirts and "Indian pattern" boots were issued. Walks were organised to break in the new boots. Route marches were pleasant strolls in the countryside followed by swimming parties to the beach to cool off. The English contingent named themselves the Perivolian Rambling Association. The colonials substituted the words "Tramping Club".

All activities proceeded on foot as there was no motor transport, but this was a minor inconvenience. The days dawned clear and bright, and the nights were mild. The road through the plantation was flanked by stone walls with all routes passing through fields and vineyards – many being worked by waving, cheering locals. The men soon became familiar with the countryside, dotted with whitewashed churches, villagers' houses and farm buildings. The hills rising to the south, some terraced, were cut through by dry, stony riverbeds in narrow defiles. The beautiful, balmy clear days, with birds chirping in the trees and bees and cicadas buzzing in the oleander bushes, made it possible to forget the war for a while.

Sunday 4 May brought a battalion church parade, the first since the Olympus Pass. What a difference a month makes, thought Rankin. They had all turned out as well as they could, but lost kit was evident in the assortment and variety of dress on parade. Everyone had a head covering, be it helmet or field service cap, but not everyone had matching uniforms, web kit, or regulation boots.

The padre spoke of the sacrifice made by the nation, paying tribute to those of the battalion who would forever be part of Greece, and the anguish of those languishing behind barbed wire, separated from their kith and kin, for who knew how long, like Christians of old in a heathen empire. He honoured those who stood ready to face the next challenge, personal and collective, however and whenever it might come. He told them of the confidence of the government and people to acquit themselves with honour in this new challenge, and that their performance would be surely known unto themselves and to God, whatever happened.

General Freyberg also attended, speaking warmly to the

assembled officers and NCOs afterward of their performance in Greece, the skill and audacity they had displayed in conducting a fighting withdrawal in the face of superior enemy strength, and maintaining good order and discipline in the trying and worrying circumstances of a sea evacuation. The situation in Crete was serious, and he stressed that the island would be held in spite of an aggressive and well-equipped enemy. Invasion was imminent, but he had every confidence in the men under his command to deliver a swift and paralysing knock-out blow by destroying the enemy wherever and whenever he landed. He finished with pride, declaring he had never commanded better troops, and that they had won his total confidence.

The battalion marched off to its new positions, occupied only the day before, around the town of Dhaskaliana. A beautiful hillside terra cotta tile and whitewashed village they were assured, making Rankin and Anderson even more disconsolate as they marched their two platoons in the other direction, to resume their residence under the olive plantation in the Perivolia Valley.

The setting sun found them sitting under an olive tree on the slope above the camp.

"I wonder how long we'll be stuck here," Anderson fumed. "How long does it take to draft an order for us to rejoin our own unit, for Christ's sake?"

"You know the army, Boney. We can do the impossible in minutes, but simple things take weeks." Rankin picked a grass stem to chew. "I can't help wondering what's happening at home."

Anderson poured him a tumbler of raki. "Same as usual, I s'pose. The old man will be complaining that we haven't tanned their hides yet. 'Sittin' around under the bloody trees? Wouldn't have happened in my day'."

"They probably don't even know we're alive. For all we know, we were posted missing when we didn't get here with the rest."

"Probably not." Anderson sighed and downed his glass.

"It can't be easy. Worrying all the time."

"No. I sent a field postcard when I got here. By the time they get it, I could be dead."

"Me, too. Everyone knows someone whose last letter turned up after the telegram boy."

"You can always say 'wish you were here', Neil. I'm sure my father could give Gentleman Jim the benefit of his advice. To say nothing of the Dimwit," he said, reaching for the bottle.

"I haven't told you, Boney," Rankin said, nearly draining his glass. "Hamilton said something very odd when he was shouting at me in Thebes and covering my face in spittle. He told me I'm just like my father, 'a disloyal shit', or words to that effect." He grimaced and shuddered as the spirit coursed down his throat.

Anderson sat bolt upright and turned to face Rankin. "Good lord. Are you sure?"

"Of course I'm bloody sure." Rankin chewed on his grass stem, the memory raw. "He was wild – it just came out." He emptied the glass, eyes watering. "I got the impression he instantly regretted it."

Anderson was staring at him, mouth open. "How could he possibly know your father?" He poured another measure into his glass and put the bottle down.

"I have no idea." Rankin's answer was distant, deep in thought. "He's never said anything before."

"Jesus, Neil. You'd better pull your head in from now on."

"You can talk."

———

THOSE WITH AILMENTS and injuries, including Rankin, were ordered to attend the Seventh General Hospital. It was several miles' walk along the coast, a delight on a beautiful sunny morning. Rankin was placed in the care of a Greek nurse named Despina, who massaged olive oil into the dried blood-encrusted dressing around his forehead. Eventually, the dressing was eased off and the evil smell was out. The wound was a mushy, jagged slash from just above his eyebrow to well beyond his hairline, bisecting his forehead. It exuded a greenish-white vile-smelling ooze, which looked for all the world like thick leek and potato soup. No wonder it throbbed, he thought. The area surrounding it was red and angry, the skin hot and taut.

A young doctor came and looked into his eyes, held a finger up in front of him and made him follow it to the edges of his vision. He listened to Rankin read the letters at the bottom of the eyechart, gave him some simple arithmetic problems to solve and recite the alphabet backwards from "H". He poked and prodded all over his black and yellow chest, whistled at the livid stripe across his ribs, examined the puncture under his armpit, made him breathe in and out while listening front and back, tested his reflexes and listened intently to the sound made when he tapped him on the back. Finally, he made Rankin lock arms in front of him, flex his arms over his head and grip them behind him.

He stood up. "You'll do. Sulphanilamide powder in the wound, dress it again, and come back in two days. With any luck we'll be able to stitch it up. Once it's stitched, saline bathing – swimming in the sea to you – after a few days is recommended."

"Sounds good to me, Doctor. Light duties?"

"Ha, what would you classify as light duties, Lieutenant?"

"A day off, no Luftwaffe, a good night's sleep, followed by a couple of afternoons at the beach, and an evening or two over an ice-cold beer," said Rankin.

The doctor scribbled something on a form. "Wouldn't we all, my good man. Give this to your commanding officer then. I'm sure he'll arrange it."

"You don't know my commanding officer," said Rankin.

———

ANDERSON AND RANKIN were summoned to Battalion at 1000 the morning Rankin's wound was stitched. They walked together the six miles or so via the hospital in the glorious early morning air, avoiding the attentions of several low-flying aircraft. The turquoise Mediterranean sparkled to their right and the sun shone brightly on the low-lying green of vineyards and orchards between the sea to their right and the dry brown hills inland. The warmth on their backs put a spring in their step.

"I didn't think much of that hospital," remarked Anderson as they passed workers in a field, waving at them enthusiastically.

"Why ever not, Boney? It's a field hospital." Thay both waved back at the men and women amongst the vines.

"Yes, but the only reason I came with you was to gawk at the nurses. You never told me they were almost all blokes!"

Platanias turned out to be a typical seaside village, with houses and shops strung along the coastal road, those nearest the beach virtually backed into the grassy sand. The ground sloped gently to the beach, while inland the low coastal hills rose abruptly out of the plain no more than half a mile away.

Battalion headquarters had been set up in the village school. There was a lot of catching up to do as for many in the battalion there had been very little opportunity to talk to friends and acquaintances and hear the stories of the fighting in Greece and the evacuation. It was also sobering to note that so many familiar faces were conspicuous by their absence, either casualties or prisoners.

When the meeting was called, the officers filed into the school room and stood to attention as Colonel "Acky" Falconer[1] entered and waved them to sit.

After the squealing and scraping of chairs on the floor, Falconer began. "Good morning, gentlemen. The Battalion is now complete," he said, nodding at Anderson and Rankin, "after the miraculous return of D Company's rear-guard detachment. I can inform you of our present situation. Nothing that is said here will leave this room, as the enemy is expected to have a presence amongst sympathisers on the island.

"Before we continue, however, let us stand and remember all those who are not here with us, and whose absence is sorely missed by us all."

Chairs scraped again and boots shuffled. Everyone stood, heads bowed, in absolute silence. Rankin thought of Patterson, crumpled and small, leaning on his telephone pack; Simpson, smiling thinly through his agony, begging for death; and Temple, etched into his soul by the brand across his own chest left by the bullet that had killed Temple and pummelled the air out of Rankin himself. It had very nearly killed them both.

---

1   Colonel (later Brigadier) A.S. Falconer, Dunedin tobacconist and secretary; born Mosgiel 4.11.1892; Otago Regiment 1914–19, CO 23 Battalion May–Aug 1940 and Mar–May 1941.

"Be seated, gentlemen." Falconer looked out into the room. "Creforce Operational Order Number 3 records that General Freyberg was appointed commander-in-chief of the island's defence force by C-in-C Middle East Command yesterday."

Cheering and clapping greeted this announcement.

"I don't need to tell you that the appointment of our commander makes this a 'New Zealand show'," Falconer continued when the hooting and cheering died away. "The honour and reputation of the Battalion, the Division, the entire country, will be forever linked to what happens here. The name of this island, Crete, is a name that will be bound to that of our own islands for generations to come."

Falconer's briefing covered the difficult geography of the island and the way it had been divided into operational sectors centred on the three airfields along the northern coast. It became clear just how much they lacked. All heavy equipment had been left behind, along with trucks and carriers, communications, and in many cases, weapons. He went through a list of the advantages they had and the disadvantages they faced; it was apparent to all that the list of disadvantages far outweighed the advantages. The only advantage with the defenders, it seemed to Rankin, was that they would occupy prepared positions. On the other hand, there was precious little to prepare them with, and only the enemy knew where the axe would fall.

Seeing the dismay written on their faces, Falconer appealed to their ability to harness their own inventiveness and ability to make do. After all, he reminded them, they came from a pioneering people, used to making do, and practically every trade or profession was represented among the ranks.

The key sector in the whole island was the Maleme sector,

he continued, which had been allocated to their own 5 Brigade. Maleme boasted the only operational airfield on Crete, which operated both Royal Navy and Royal Air Force squadrons. There followed a detailed description of the tasks and allocations of each battalion.

"We have been given a two-fold task, gentlemen. The first is holding the coast in this sector, along here," he said, sweeping his pointer along the coast from a town called Modhion to another called Pirgos, a distance of at least two miles, "while acting as mobile reserve, available to counter-attack the Hun on the airfield, should he gain a foothold there."

The room sat up as one man: the dropping of a pin would have roused the dead. They stared at the map, along the length of coast they were required to defend from prepared, static positions, then gaped in disbelief at their commander, the question written in their faces: how is it possible to provide static defence while acting as mobile reserve?

———————

AFTER THE BRIEFING, Rankin and Anderson reported to Captain Hamilton, and were told to return to their platoons, which would be sent for in short order. The battalion was to be centred on a town called Dhaskaliana, with D Company occupying a position astride a watercourse with its front on a canal, about half a mile back from the beach. They arranged to make a reconnaissance visit to Pirgos and meet the other subalterns there.

"We need to solve the transport problem," said Rankin, as he and Anderson walked into Pirgos to the café in the town square after the day's work.

"Well, I'm out of gorgeous Greek schoolteachers who just happen to own a motorbike at the moment," said Anderson.

Rankin's face burned red.

"And I bet you haven't written to her either, you cad. You've had plenty of time since you've been here."

"Idiot. She lives in occupied territory. How would a letter from a serving officer on the other side go down, do you think?"

Anderson turned to look at him, his eyes twinkling. "Gosh, Neil, you know, I hadn't thought of that."

Rankin fumed inwardly, knowing he'd walked straight into another one of Anderson's traps. "Oh, shut up, Boney."

The sun was setting over the little village of Pirgos as the two men arrived. Pirgos was like a thousand other Greek villages: a town square shaded by plane trees, a whitewashed church and a medley of shops and houses built of stone and plaster, strung along the main road into and out of town. A café in the square was full of old men playing chess, drinking raki and coffee, and complaining about the price of goats and the prospects for the harvest.

The village houses were two-storeyed and would afford a view across the surrounding vineyards and fields. Each featured shuttered windows, awning-covered roof terraces, and many had animal enclosures out the back. Pirgos was the last village on the main road to Maleme Aerodrome; both were overlooked by a high hill less than a mile inland.

There were a few Cretan civilians sitting at the café's tables in the square, and several officers and others from 22 Battalion, who were in the process of taking over responsibility for the airfield and its defences. The elderly Cretans, all dressed alike in dark blue trousers, high black boots, black shirts and embroidered waistcoats, got to their feet, raised their glasses or coffee cups, and saluted the newcomers.

Robertson, O'Rourke and Pyne were already seated at a table, waiting for them. After greeting the other New Zealanders present, Rankin and Anderson joined them and ordered coffee, wine, ouzo and raki, after having established that there was no beer.

"Well, that's a bugger, I must say," said Robertson, commander of D Company's third rifle platoon. As usual, he looked harassed and put-upon. "I never really developed the taste for ouzo. God knows what this stuff will be like."

"You look like a man under the cosh, Nellie, if you don't mind my saying so," said Anderson. "Still running around after the Old Man trying to get his returns right?"

Robertson's expression indicated it was a good thing Anderson was sitting across the table, out of range.

"You can mix ouzo with orange juice, Nellie," said Pyne hastily, stepping into the breach. "Tastes like orange aniseed sweets, wards off both scurvy and colds, all handily packaged with a king-sized hangover."

"Pyney's patent remedy, for all ailments including Jerries!" laughed Anderson.

"What exactly are you and Pyney doing, William," asked Rankin, "now that all your anti-aircraft stuff and his carriers are still in Greece? Who's going to take care of the Luftwaffe and cart us honest foot-soldiers around now?"

"We have reluctantly joined the ranks of the honest foot-soldiers, have we not, Pyney?"

"Yes, and I'm working on a jingle about Indian pattern boots. They could be a goldmine after the war," said the former shoe shop manager from Timaru, to hoots of derision.

"I say, William, have you still got a bottle or two of your vintage Hymettus Camp retsina? Neil has on many occasions expressed the wish to reacquaint himself with the sophisticated nuances of that particular elixir five thousand years in the making."

They all laughed at the memory of the night in Athens before they entrained for the Olympus Line. It seemed an aeon ago.

"Made me toss it over the side when we got on the boat, more's the pity," said O'Rourke, carefully fitting a cigarette into his holder. "Along with all the other non-essential paraphernalia that went in the drink."

"Not your cigarette holder, though, Prof," Anderson said as O'Rourke struck a match.

"I say, Boney. There are limits, you know."

"We're here with less than half our kit," said Robertson sourly. "God knows what we're even doing here. We were supposed to go back to Egypt." He looked at O'Rourke. "Nothing on God's earth would induce me to drink that stuff again."

"How *do* you like your new Indian boots, Pyney?" asked Rankin. "I see you got brown ones."

"Very comfortable, so far," he replied, stretching out his long legs and admiring his shiny new boots. "Narrower, more in the Aussie stockman style, with Malay rubber soles. Just the thing for leaping in and out of carriers."

"Pity we haven't got any," Anderson observed.

They watched with the usual child-like fascination at how the ouzo went cloudy, then white like milk, as they added more cold water. Thick black coffee and raki came and went, along with the only snack food the café could offer: some baked flatbread triangles brushed with salt and olive oil.

Anderson decided to try the wine, which was plentiful

and cheap. "It tastes a bit resinous." He looked accusingly to O'Rourke. "Less so than that ghastly stuff you bloody nearly poisoned us with, William."

Gazing about the square, taking in the locals and the few pools of light from lights outside the café and across the square, Rankin sighed. "It seems our little holiday might soon be over. Sounds like we're coming to rejoin you any day," he said.

"Well, you might at least sound enthusiastic about it," Anderson said.

Robertson stood up and raised his glass: "Let's raise a toast: the Battalion!"

They stood and downed their drinks, then poured themselves another from the flasks on the table.

"I wonder what our strength is," said Anderson. "We went to Greece with about eight hundred and fifty."

"I think we came here with about six hundred," said Pyne. "Worst off is 21 Battalion. They landed with fewer than four hundred, less than half strength, I understand." The others stared at him.

"Shit," Anderson said softly. "I came back with twenty-eight, including me."

"Twenty-five for me," said Rankin, "plus one stray Scot."

"To the lost and missing, then," said Robertson, standing again.

They stood and raised their glasses. "To the lost and missing."

"Virgins. That's what we are," said Anderson, as they sat down. They all looked at him, eyebrows raised.

"Virgins. Sacrificial bloody virgins. Tied to a stake. At the mouth of the Labyrinth. Waiting for the bloody Minotaur to come and devour us all."

The others looked at him, aghast. "It's not as bad as all that!" cried Robertson angrily.

Blurry faces swam behind Rankin's watery eyes.

––––––

RANKIN AND ANDERSON walked back to the transit camp after they farewelled the other three where their ways parted.

"Robertson seemed a bit out of sorts," said Anderson. "I hope he's not heading for a crack-up."

"You always manage to wind him up. Virgins waiting for the Minotaur? For fuck's sake, Boney."

"We're not tied to a stake, Boney. Some of us, at least, can shoot back."

"He's a sensitive lad. I don't have to try to ruffle his feathers, it just happens. Same with you, Neil."

Rankin raised his hand, as if to clout him.

"Being tied to Dimwitty's apron strings morning, noon, and night would be depleting, to be fair," said Anderson, fending him off with the half-empty bottle of wine they had taken from the café.

"'Depleting': that's a good word for it."

"The briefing went well, I thought," continued Anderson airily. "When Acky got to the bit about combining fixed area defence with mobile reserve for the airfield, you could have bowled them all over with a feather duster. Ingenious. Clearly no one else had thought of such an efficient use of manpower."

Rankin searched Anderson's face in the low light. Was he being sarcastic? "Everyone certainly sat up and took notice. I'm not sure how we're supposed to be in two places at once."

"That's why it's genius, Neil. Jerry'll never think of that," he said, taking a swig from the bottle. "Jerry's much more likely to follow traditional military doctrine. No imagination."

Rankin scoffed. "On a serious note. The main target is the aerodrome, Boney, so why does it form our flank? Along a riverbank, I grant you, but there's five miles of undefended open ground beyond. To assemble in."

"Precisely. You do realise the river is dry, don't you? Hardly a tumbling alpine cataract to sweep the nasty Germans into the sea." Anderson waved the bottle in the air. "How can Freyberg not see this as a problem?"

"Perhaps he wasn't able to alter things."

"What's the fucking point of being commander-in-chief if you can't change things?" Anderson shouted. He stopped in the middle of the road and turned to Rankin. "If you're coming by air, what d'you need? An airfield," he cried, raising both arms. "There's only one in working order on the whole bloody island." He paused, fixing Rankin firmly in his gaze, and wagged his finger at him. "That airfield is the key to everything. Yet it's on our flank, next to five miles of undefended country. It's a bloody gift to Hitler!" His arms flopped down by his sides.

"Steady on, Boney, that's a bit strong!" Rankin took the bottle from Anderson's hand and helped himself. "There's also the matter of invasion by sea, don't let's forget. We have to have forces available to foil seaborne invasion."

"We have, Neil, we have," Anderson sighed, taking the bottle back. "It's called the Royal Navy. The only arm of the services who have done anything with panache and, consequently, success. Everything else has been half-arsed, half-baked and half-brained."

"Oh, come off it, Boney."

"It bloody has! We're paying for it in lives. Half of 21 lost. For what?"

"You know what, Boney. And while we were holding them back, we proved ourselves as good as them, man for man. And we learnt a lot."

Anderson stood facing Rankin, bottle in one hand. He leaned forward and jabbed him in the chest, emphasising his words. "Yes, Neil, *we* learnt a lot. The men learnt they're as good as them."

Rankin took a step back, protecting his chest. "Jesus, watch it, Boney, that hurts. I'm injured, you know."

"Sorry." He seemed to deflate, took a drink and passed the bottle to Rankin. "Ask yourself, what have the high-ups learnt, Neil? We're in for another bloody hiding. Another bloody fiasco." Anderson gazed out over the dark sea, shoulders slumped. "And our blokes'll pay for it."

"Jesus, Boney, I was feeling good until now," Rankin said, lowering the bottle from his mouth. He put his arm around his friend's shoulder. "Watch what you say, for Christ's sake, Boney." They stood there, watching the gentle luminescent swish of the wavelets on the beach. "You've got a bloody nerve to call *me* a Jonah."

They walked on in silence. Anderson finished the bottle and left it sitting on a stone wall.

"You know, Boney," Rankin said eventually, "I never did hear what happened to that Jerry armoured car on the top of the escarpment."

"Just goes to show Jerry can fuck it up with the best of us," Anderson replied morosely. "Backed straight over the cliff at the first whiff of trouble." They walked on in silence for a while. "Anyway, it wasn't an armoured car. It turned out to be one of those little staff car things. What are they called? Kub-wagon?"

"Kubelwagen," Rankin laughed, picturing the little car roaring backwards over the cliff.

They continued along the road, each alone with his own thoughts. The smirk soon froze on Rankin's face as the knot in the pit of his stomach reasserted itself: what was happening in Greece? With a jolt he realised he would never know what became of Dada in Thebes.

CHAPTER THREE

The Gathering Storm, 7-13 May 1941

THE PLATOONS PARADED in full kit: clean new shirts and shorts, narrow Indian-pattern boots, head covering, web and packs if they had them, and weapons. Every man was armed. Rankin's main concern was ensuring anything that could have been deemed "excess" was out of sight.

Having been ordered to parade the whole group that had returned from Greece, Rankin thought they formed a rather smart company, even if uniforms varied considerably. Some of the Indian boots were brown, like those of Australian issue, some black, more like their own, but at least the pairs matched even if some units now had mixed-colour footwear. The same applied to headwear; every conceivable head covering provided by the army was on display somewhere in the ranks, although the majority wore helmets, with or without covers.

The parade was inspected by the Camp Commandant, the Brigade-Major of 4 Brigade, and Brigadier Hargest[2], commanding

---

2   Brigadier J. Hargest, born Gore 4.9.1891, farmer, Otago Mounted Rifles 1914–20, CO 5 Brigade May 1940–Nov 1941.

5 Brigade. After a few encouraging and congratulatory words and a quick walk around with stops to chat to random men, asking them how they came to be there and what they'd done along the way, the brass were off, and the parade fallen out.

Rankin heaved a sigh of relief. No one had mentioned "surplus" weapons, or even the fact that none had been handed in, and there had not been a single comment about the variability of kit.

"Enjoy the beauty parade?" Anderson asked as the staff car disappeared in a cloud of dust.

"I wonder what that all meant," Rankin said, staring down the road after them.

"You know the Army, Neil. They won't tell you until it's all gone wrong, and then they'll say it's your fault."

"That's cynical, Boney, even for you."

"Doesn't make it not true, old son."

———

"SIR, ME AND some of the boys have been talking."

Rankin, sitting under his tree, looked up from Nicholson's laboriously completed returns to see the driver, Graham, holding his cap in front of his belt, a picture of nervous concentration. Graham had driven Rankin's truck in the assault on Ariana. Nicholson called him "rough as guts", but Graham, as promised, had stuck by Rankin's side "like shit to a blanket", earning his ticket out of Greece as a combatant.

"Our outfits don't seem to have turned up here or haven't got a proper job to do. We want to be part of the action. The boys have been told they'll be going to a Composite Company of non-infantry blokes, but they're shit-scared they'll get officers put in charge who haven't got the foggiest fuckin' clue – if you'll pardon the expression, sir – about fightin' as infantry." He shuffled from foot to foot, looking at the ground. "It's not the Jerries that worry us, sir, if you get the drift."

Rankin concentrated, searching the face of the man who was doing the talking. Rough and ready he might be, but Rankin saw concern plain on his face. "You see, sir, the boys think we've got a better chance of doin' our bit an' stayin' alive with an officer we already know, and who knows what he's doin'…" Graham's voice tailed away.

"That's very flattering, but I can't just sort of appropriate you into my platoon. There are proper channels to go through."

"We know that, sir, but the whole thing's a bit of a shemozzle at the mo', sir – sayin' it how it is. We thought if we could tag along with you when you move to Battalion, we'd have a chance of stayin' with your outfit long enough for the Jerries to turn up before the army catches up with us."

Rankin laughed. "I admire your spirit, Grazer, but there are all sorts of practical things, like rations, which depend on allocations. I can't pretend you're men who've already been lost, if that's what you hope."

"No, sir!" Graham looked indignant. "We don't want to take their places by pretending to be them. But you're short-handed because they're not here and we would be bringin' ya back up to strength."

The logic was undeniable.

"Alright, Grazer, give me a list of names and I'll make appropriate application when we rejoin Battalion. In the meantime, you'll have to stay here. Sorry."

"Very good, sir." He could not hide his disappointment. He

put his hat back on, made what could have passed for a salute, and turned on his heel.

"What did he want?" asked Nicholson none too gently. Nicholson must have been nearby, but not close enough to intercept Graham before he approached Rankin.

"To join us and our merry band of warriors, Nick."

"He's run out of trucks to wreck, I suppose," said Nicholson. "I hope you didn't say yes, Neil," he added, looking alarmed. "We're not short of difficulties of our own."

"Well, nevertheless, we need a new signaller, and Reilly would appreciate being relieved as batman. That young Scot, McIntyre, is as keen as mustard. Can handle a rifle, too, he told me – comes from some mountains in the Highlands. God knows where the rest of his lot might've gone."

———

THE PLATOON HAD been back with the company several days. A silent, dispirited audience had watched from under the olive trees as they formed up on the roadway. Rankin could feel Graham's eyes boring into him as they swung down the road and out of Transit Camp B.

Work consisted of strengthening the areas occupied by the company, setting up perimeters, company facilities, strong points (houses and other buildings with a view of the surrounding countryside), company headquarters and office, and some rudimentary catering and sanitation facilities. Billets were found in the village for about half the men at any one time, and the rest camped under trees and grapevines. Each company kept one post manned and alert at all times during the day.

Work was frequently finished early in the afternoon when the troops were released for swimming parades and sports.

"It feels like a holiday, Mick, but I'm sure it won't last," Rankin remarked to a corporal signaller while in company headquarters one day. Company HQ was in a little house, requisitioned for the duration. The signals detachment was trying to connect a phone line, by the sound of the conversation emanating from outside.

"Parsons, is there any sign of that wire we were promised?" The irritable query addressed to a clerk came from Hamilton, the company commander, standing in the doorway of his office. Hamilton's uniform looked immaculate; Rankin marvelled. He wore a polished Sam Browne belt, whereas everyone else on the island below the rank of brigadier made do with webbing. Hamilton's eyes fell on Rankin. "Oh, Rankin. I need to talk to you."

Rankin raised his eyebrows at Parsons as he followed Hamilton into his office.

"Shut the door, will you?"

Rankin stood in front of the makeshift desk. The owners' belongings were piled up behind Hamilton. The tiny window was open, but it was stifling and dusty in the room.

"You just can't help yourself, can you, Rankin?" Hamilton muttered, leafing through a sheaf of paper on the pile of boxes that passed as a desk.

"I'm not sure what you mean, sir."

"I have received a complaint from the British Military Police authorities in Chania. It took me a while to work out who they were complaining about. But then I interviewed O'Rourke, who was on reception duty in the transit camp that evening, and of course, it had to be you."

"I see, sir. Lieutenant Anderson and his platoon arrived the same night, sir." Rankin waited for Hamilton to finish reading the close-spaced typed paper in his hand. Hamilton looked more annoyed and agitated the further he read.

"You apparently threatened a military policeman with a loaded weapon, Rankin, after refusing his request to hand in your surplus weapons in accordance with standing orders."

"A bit of an exaggeration, sir. I was merely showing him. He expressed an interest. And I told him that none of our weapons were surplus to our own requirements."

Hamilton's face paled, and his mouth begin to twitch.

"You thrust the weapon at the man, beat him, and threatened to shoot him with it for God's sake!" he screeched, the typewritten pages crackling in his shaking hand. Rankin marvelled at the effort this must have taken; to make it all up, find the right forms, and no doubt to type the bloody thing in triplicate, facing the threat of imminent invasion as they were.

"He must have misinterpreted my action, sir. I may have bumped him, perhaps. After all, he was shining his torch directly into my eyes, sir. I was completely blinded."

Hamilton looked up at him. He opened his mouth, then closed it. He told the corporal clerk sitting at the other desk to leave the room. They both waited, staring each other in the eye, while a chair scraped on the bare boards and boots clumped to the doorway. "And shut the door behind you," shouted Hamilton.

Rankin's heart was pounding so loud Hamilton must be able to hear it. His throat was parched, like a wadi in the dry.

Hamilton rose, leant on his knuckles, his face bent close to Rankin's.

"The corporal who made the complaint has a witness, his

sergeant, to back him up. You won't get away with this, Rankin!"
Rankin could feel little spots of saliva pepper his face,

"Impressive, sir. One witness. I have three hundred."

Hamilton reared up to his full height. "You're a smart arse,
Rankin. A disrespectful, disloyal smart arse! I will see to it that
you are held to account when we get back to base. Don't you
dare try and justify threatening a British soldier – a soldier of
the Imperial power in the King's service, for God's sake – with a
loaded weapon. I'll see you disgraced and serving out your time
as a senior officer's batman when we get back," he hissed, more
spittle flecking from his lips.

"Be careful what you wish for, sir," said Rankin.

Hamilton jerked back, as if he had been punched, pale blue
eyes like iced water.

Rankin's heart pounded in his chest. His mouth was so dry
he had trouble forming the words. Pain seared through his
head. "What happened between you and my father?" he asked.
"Bearing a personal animosity against me because of something
that happened between you and my father in the past would be
of great interest to the prisoner's friend in a court martial – as I'm
sure you're aware, sir." Rankin's chest was tight, his eyes fixed
on Hamilton's. Was that a shadow of doubt that flickered for an
instant behind the pupil? "As would the question of desertion of
your command in the face of the enemy at Thebes."

Hamilton rocked back on his feet, the colour completely
drained from his face. It took him several moments to regain
control, mouth working all the while, like a stranded fish.

"How dare you?" he hissed, the tremor in his face causing his
mouth to twitch and his eyelid to quiver. "How dare you question
my fitness for command? Your father put you up to that, didn't

he? The disloyal bastard. You're your father's son, alright. I'll see to it that you serve out the war in a punishment centre, you arrogant little shit. Now get out of my sight!"

"This is probably not a good time to ask you about requests I've received for non-combatant troops to join my platoon and temporarily make good the losses we have suffered, then, sir."

Hamilton spluttered and gasped. Hate radiated from his baleful eyes. "Get out! Get out of my sight! So help me God, I'll swing for you, Rankin."

Rankin saluted, turned about, and marched across the tiny room, all the while holding his breath.

Outside Hamilton's office, Rankin stood shaking for a moment, leaning against the door post, trying to regain control.

"Are you alright, sir?" enquired the corporal clerk.

Rankin nodded, not trusting himself to speak.

On his way out he bumped into Captain McKenzie coming in.

"Ah, young Rankin, good to have you back in our gallant company, lad. Come into my parlour for a moment," he said cheerfully, opening the door to a room that might have passed for a large wardrobe.

"Now, let me see, you've put in for some replacement picks and shovels. We're a bit short at the moment." He leafed through papers on an ammunition box.

"I just asked Captain Hamilton about a request I've received: to have a number of non-combatants who travelled back from Greece with us join my platoon and make up the deficit in numbers," Rankin said, feeling the tension subside. "They tell me their own units either aren't here or they'll be drafted into a composite battalion, where there may be an overall lack of combat experience."

"I see," said McKenzie, the piece of paper in his hand forgotten. "And how did that go down?"

"Not well, sir."

"You can vouch for these men? They'd become your responsibility, you know."

"Yes, sir. I have seen them perform under very trying circumstances. Some of them may be rough around the edges, but they do not lack aggressive spirit."

"Hmm. Leave it with me and I'll see what we can do. Lord knows, we could do wi' some aggressive spirit around here, lad."

———

"I SAY," SAID O'Rourke as Rankin arrived at the Pirgos café that evening. "What's different about you today, Rankin?"

"No bandage round his noggin, Prof," replied Anderson. "Instead, we have El Zorro come amongst us."

"Stitches out today," said Rankin. "More importantly, Despina, the nurse, sold me a bicycle for a hundred drachmae."

"Bargain," said Anderson.

"We could start a bicycle corps," offered Pyne. "Like in the last war."

"Dream on, Pyney," muttered Anderson.

"They didn't have the Luftwaffe in the last war, old son," said O'Rourke, forming his mouth into an "O" and attempting a smoke ring.

They were seated at the little Pirgos café in the cool before sunset. Having tried the other establishments within easy walking distance of Dhaskaliana, they'd gone back to the café with a radio where sometimes they could listen to Lord Haw Haw if the pretty waitress was on. The usual groups of old men sat around the tables in the square, along with servicemen from 22 Battalion and other units based around the airfield.

Robertson was like a cat on hot bricks, hardly able to contain himself. "I was up at Battalion HQ today," he said.

"Yes, so?" they all chorused.

"The Intelligence Officer said he'd been busy reconnoitring the route from Dhaskaliana to the aerodrome. Said it shouldn't take long to get between the two."

"Easy for him to say," muttered O'Rourke. "He won't have to lead a platoon when the muck's flying thick and fast."

"The Intelligence Officer reconnoitred the route?" asked Anderson, his drink halfway to his lips. "Surely to God that's something we should be doing. Practising it. Company strength, at night. It'll be our job to work out where we're going when we need to move sharpish to pull these poor blokes' nuts from the fire," he said, gesturing at the 22 Battalion tables. "In the middle of the bloody night, if things run true to form."

"He must know what he's doing, Boney," said Rankin. "He's another good Otago man. Rhodes Scholar to boot."

"Knowing your iambic bloody pentameters from your isosceles bloody triangles doesn't mean to say you know sod-all about an air invasion. He made Herculean efforts in Greece, though, I hear, to give him his due."

Pyne leant closer to the table, and spoke in a low voice, "There was an all-in brawl between some blokes from the 21st and 22nd."

"Boney told me the other day that 21's under a cloud," Rankin replied. "The story's going round that they cocked up badly in the Pinios Gorge."

"That'll be it. The 22nd blokes poked the borax and the 21st took exception," Pyne said. "Had to be separated. There were several black eyes and a few teeth knocked out."

"There's a story going round that one of their sergeants was run over by a tank and lived to tell the tale," O'Rourke chipped in, smoke curling up from his cigarette in its holder.

"Yes, I've heard that," said Robertson eagerly. "Apparently got up and ran after it, throwing grenades and yelling like a maniac."

"That's just bullshit, Nellie. You shouldn't listen to fanciful rumours, man of your standing in headquarters," O'Rourke scoffed. "He was run over by a tank, not swatted by a feather bloody duster." He held his cigarette holder in one hand while he sipped his drink, the others all agog for more information. "By all accounts he was lucky to be picked up and put on a carrier as they pulled out. Dislocated all his ribs and broke his pelvis. Got sent down to Athens. Sounds much more likely. God knows where he'll be now, poor bugger."

"'Sent down'... Sounds like he was sent home for bad behaviour," laughed Anderson.

"Well, being run over by the enemy *is* terribly poor form, Boney," O'Rourke replied.

"God, spare us your university in-jokes, you blokes. Getting back to Davin,[3] what else did he say, Nellie?" Pyne stared at him intently. "What's the gen on the war effort? General Wavell must've recognised my talent by now. I could coordinate his carrier forces."

---

3 2nd Lieutenant D.M. Davin, born Invercargill 1.9.1913; mentioned in despatches, wounded Crete May 1941.

They all laughed and drained their drinks.

"Tiny Freyberg needs HQ staff since all his buggered off to Cairo on holiday," Pyne continued thoughtfully. "What's puzzling is that 6 Brigade and Divisional staff went to Egypt while we came here."

"The answer to that is obvious, you twit. We'll be slaughtered to a man, and they'll rebuild the division from Cairo," Anderson said, nose in the air.

The others howled him down.

"Well, ask yourself this: why is Gentleman Jim's Brigade HQ five miles away from the airfield? The main objective? Force, Division, even his own Brigade orders all emphasise mobility. Counter-attack is our key role. How's he going to direct it from there?"

"Obvious," said Robertson. "Keeps a strategic view and his powder dry for the sea landings."

Anderson opened his mouth to say something, but was cut off by Pyne.

"Lord Haw Haw sends greetings to all us Kiwis ensconced beneath the olives. Apparently, he's invited us to enjoy our little holiday, for beneath the olives is where we'll stay."

The table erupted in noisy derision, cut short by a loud bang which echoed off the nearby hillsides. A string of bark-like pops was drowned out as a Dornier 17, bomb doors open, hurtled overhead, going full bore and making a mighty racket. The café patrons hurled themselves to the ground, scattering tables and sending glasses to smash on the cobbles.

An old man in baggy trousers and knee-high boots stood defiantly in the square, shaking his fist and hurling abuse after the departed bomber as they sheepishly got to their feet, dusted themselves down, and picked up the tables and chairs. In the distance, a cloud of smoke rose above the airfield.

"Bugger me," said Pyne, looking around foolishly. "I'd just about forgotten them."

"Not good form to have a war without them, Pyney," said Rankin, brushing his hands together to wipe the dirt from his palms. "Need a baddie to play against, don't you see."

The waitress, daughter of the proprietor, a smiling girl with a thick rope of jet-black hair plaited down her back, came out of the café and swept up the broken glass. She smiled demurely at each in turn, as they held up their chairs while she brushed under them.

Replacement flasks of raki, wine, ouzo and water appeared, and when they protested, she smiled again and nodded at the old man who had shouted at the departing bomber. He was pulling a black, fringed bandana onto his head and puffing on a large cheroot.

He stumped his way over to them, stood as erect as his arthritic body would allow, and saluted their table. He stalked off to the next table and repeated the gesture, saluting all the military personnel before marching off down the road.

"Please, dear God," muttered Anderson, "please don't let this be another bloody fiasco like the last one. For their sake, if no one else's."

———

RANKIN HAD BEEN summoned to the company commander's office. Fearing the worst, he stood rigidly to attention in front of Hamilton sitting behind his desk.

"Rankin, against my better judgement, I have agreed to detail your platoon to fill a request we have received from Brigade to transfer a platoon to 22 Battalion to bolster the airfield defence. You are to take up a position on the Tavronitis riverbank, south of the road bridge. You will hold 22 Battalion's flank, near the village of Vlakheronitissa."

Rankin felt a surge of excitement, tempered with astonishment and apprehension. Why did he choose me? "Yes, sir. Very good, sir. Thank you, sir."

"I am entrusting you with this assignment, despite my grave misgivings, because both Captain McKenzie and CSM Clutterbuck recommended you and your platoon." Hamilton looked up from his makeshift desk, eyes narrowing as his brow creased; Rankin felt the sheer malevolence radiating from him, as he articulated every word with heavy irony: "Your platoon appears better armed than most; and with additional support from some fools who have volunteered to join you, it will be nearly at full strength, it seems."

"Thank you, sir."

Hamilton's gaze did not waver from Rankin's face, as if he was trying to fix him in his memory. He lowered his voice to continue: "Don't think this lets you off the hook for one minute, you cocky little shit," he hissed. "I intend to have you up on a charge when we get back to Egypt. Now report to the adjutant and get your orders."

Rankin took a pace back, put his service cap on, and saluted. "Yes, sir. Thank you, sir."

He turned smartly about and marched the three paces to the door, feeling the man's eyes boring into his back.

Captain McKenzie beamed when he saw him outside his

office. "Aye, do come in, my boy. Now, here we are then," he said, looking through a neat pile of papers on his table, "orders for this wee job. The CSM and I persuaded the old man that you were just the chap for the task. Previous experience against Huns falling down from the sky and all that. And it seemed a pity not to make use of a fine aggressive talent when we're short-handed."

"I'm very grateful to you both, sir. I think."

"Ah hah, you are right to be dubious. Could be quite a hot spot. Now, look here at the map," he said, unfolding a large map of the airfield and seafront, covering the area from west of the Tavronitis to Suda in the east.

"This is the position you are to take up, Rankin, here," he said, pointing to the flank of Hill 107, south of the bridge. "The position is strategic. It covers access to this valley and its road." He traced his finger along the line of the track. "From the village of Vlakheronitissa to Khamoudokhori, here, to the radio station and the rear of 21 Battalion's position." He pointed to the summit of Hill 107.

"HQ, 22 Battalion. Colonel Andrew's[4] job is to hold this hill, overlooking the airfield." He stabbed the map. "Crucial. You provide flank cover. You have neighbours, D Company, 22 Battalion, is dug in further along the riverbank to the north," he said, stabbing the map again by the bridge.

"This position may form the nucleus of a battalion position in the event of a counter-attack on the aerodrome, to force a way north along the riverbank. In any event, if the aerodrome is seriously threatened or overrun, this route is the one that will be

---

4 Brigadier L.W. Andrew VC, Wellington, regular soldier, born Ashhurst 23.3.1897, CO 22 Battalion Jan 1940–Mar 1942.

taken by 21 Battalion coming from their position on this ridge, here." He pointed to another ridge, known as Vineyard Ridge, above the village of Khamoudhokhori.

"You will see, lad, that 23 Battalion" – he tapped the map at Dhaskaliana – "could also swing up the Sfakoriako River valley and over this saddle here, and then through Vlakheronitissa to the rear of Hill 107, and to the aerodrome, as an alternative to a frontal assault through the villages of Maleme and Pirgos." The place names were emphasised by more map tapping. He looked Rankin in the eye. "Your position preserves these options. Don't stuff it up, laddie."

Rankin felt the weight of the entire defence of Crete fall on his shoulders. The position, he saw, was the exposed southwestern flank of the whole Creforce position. It must be the first place a substantial attack would fall once the forces that would surely land in the undefended area west of the dry water course had a chance to assemble and organise themselves.

It was crystal clear why Hamilton had agreed to his platoon taking the job; he expected Rankin to be killed in the first five minutes, along with most of his platoon.

"I have requisitioned additional rations. One reason you got this job is that your platoon came back with more weaponry than most," the wily old Scot said, looking meaningfully at Rankin. "There's no point asking for more; there isn't any. But you already know that," he smiled, albeit a humourless smile, then looked stern. "I had a run-in with the bloody Sassenach Redcaps in the last war. Mindless bullies, the lot of 'em. However, just like maggots and leeches, they have a role to play in the proper ordering of God's universe. Don't forget it. Now, I have a transfer order here for you to pick up your additional personnel, if they're still available. I've left spaces for you to fill in the details. I'd skedaddle back down to the transit camp to see if they're still there, if I were you."

On his way out, Rankin bumped into the tall, spare frame of Bernard Clutterbuck, the company sergeant major, looking irritated as he leafed through a sheaf of papers in his hand.

"Hello, Bernard. I'm off to move my platoon to the comely leafy banks of the limpid Tavronitis. I have you to thank for this great honour, I hear."

"I did lend a hand there, young Mister Rankin, true enough." He looked around to make sure no one was in earshot, raising his finger to his lips like a theatrical conspirator. "His Nibs let slip you should be languishing in the field punishment centre. A little misunderstanding to do with handing in weapons on arrival, I gathered. Unless they decide to invade the prison, I thought it a bit of a waste. Had a word with Captain McKenzie."

"Well, I'm very grateful, Bernard. When we are ensconced under the shade of the coolabah trees by the graceful, languid flow of the leafy Limpopo, I shall invite you to a cream tea, and be the first at our home-warming party."

"Don't take the piss, Mister Rankin. I suggest you get your arse up there on the double and out of the way before His Nibs changes 'is bloody mind," said Clutterbuck, face creased by a mirthless grin. "And keep out of bloody sight. Intelligence says air raids can be expected to increase dramatically any day now."

"I shall be the soul of discretion, as always, Bernard. Your confidence in me is not misplaced."

"Fuck off, Mister Rankin, sir, if you don't mind," he said waving his papers in Rankin's face. "Some of us have got a proper job of work to do."

RANKIN ISSUED THE order for the platoon to move as soon as he got back. Half of them were away on a conditioning march with Corporal Lawrence, and the other half was working on wiring and preparing positions in and around Dhaskaliana under the supervision of Corporal Johnstone. Rankin took Nicholson to look over their new position. They spent an hour clambering about the lower southwest slopes of Hill 107, a task interrupted by a twin-engine German fighter roaring low overhead and spraying the hilltop with cannon shells. Rankin's excitement grew along with his sense of foreboding. The way the position had been prepared perhaps pointed to its intended occupants being a force considerably larger than a platoon, especially a much depleted one. The trenches dug were all on the terraces that stepped up the hillside. Some of the slit trenches were in good cover but others not; the position as a whole extended over 200 yards from flank to flank.

Leaving Nicholson at Dhaskaliana to make the arrangements and organise packing up, clearing billets and getting ready to move that evening, Rankin got on his bike and pedalled as fast as he could down the road towards Chania and the transit camp. Nicholson stood staring after him as Rankin pedalled away, looking none too happy. He had made his thoughts clear on the matter of contaminating his platoon with riff-raff.

The transit camp was still populated with men who had not yet found their units or some other home to go to. Some were awaiting transport to Egypt, and for them the waiting must have seemed interminable. Their days were filled with walking, swimming, being picked up for work parties out of camp, fatigues in camp, and getting into trouble. The service corps commandant beamed from ear to ear when Rankin turned up to take another dozen or so men off his hands. If he could find them.

Rankin left a message written on a page from a signal pad for Driver Graham to assemble his nominations to transfer to Rankin's platoon. He could take a maximum of twelve. They had to be men Graham trusted and have an instinct for a fight. Rankin would interview them next morning after stand-to.

The platoon marched to their new position as evening fell. There was barely time before dark to identify trenches and weapon pits dug by a previous tenant, possibly the Welch Regiment. Most of them were too wide and too shallow to be proper slit trenches, but some were well sited and well dug, which was fortunate since their digging tools were limited to their helmets, bayonets, and one shovel.

Terraces bordered by earthen embankments and the occasional stone retaining wall climbed the hillside and ran along the length of the position parallel to the riverbed. The first of these, covered in olive trees, was about 50 to 70 feet back from the track; those above were planted with oranges, vines, and mandarins as well as olives. Irrigation water came from a canal at the northern (aerodrome) end of the hill.

At the southern end of the slope the hillside curved round into a shallow valley where mainly grapevines grew. The lower parts of the position were densely foliaged, which provided good cover from the air, but obscured the view along the hillside. The higher slopes were more open, allowing some observation over the otherwise dead ground beyond the Tavronitis River. Bamboo clumps and scrub grew along the opposite riverbank, and a spur coming down off the main hill to the north obstructed the view to the airfield or the neighbouring platoons from 22 Battalion.

22 Battalion's HQ was above Rankin's platoon on the summit of Hill 107. The hilltop was peppered with weapon pits and surrounded by wire. About 500 yards north along the riverbank from Rankin's platoon, 22 Battalion's D Company was digging in on the slopes above the key junction of the coastal road (which crossed the river on a concrete bridge at that point, before continuing east around the perimeter of the airfield) and the riverbank track, which ran south past Rankin's position towards Vlakheronitissa.

As dusk turned to night, Rankin made his rounds. The positions were makeshift and required work, but that could wait until tomorrow. There was plenty to do. Rankin stopped by a pit occupied by Smith, the Boys rifle anti-tank gunner, who was surrounded by some of the older hands, smoking and yarning.

"Well, boys, what do you think?"

"Beats hanging about in that olive orchard, Skipper. Too many bloody officers coming and going there, if you know what I mean," said Mitchell.

"Too right," said Smith. "And that town we were just in, Dezzy-what's-it. German bombers far too interested in it. Out of sight, out of mind here. Bloody well done, Skipper."

"Trust you to think of that, Smithy," said Duggan. "Comes from years of practice, keepin' out of the way of the missus."

They all burst out laughing. Rankin left them to it, happy in the knowledge that morale was high and whatever the future had in store, they would face it head on.

———

NEXT MORNING, THEIR first on the Tavronitis, numerous low-flying German fighters and bombers strafed the airfield and anything that moved along the roads nearby. Ominously, aircraft paid considerable attention to the crest of Hill 107, directly above, roaring over their position.

With breakfast over, Rankin pedalled back to the transit camp where Graham was waiting for him. "Just like you said, Skipper, I have selected some additions for your platoon," he said, indicating the group of men clustered behind him.

"Have you indeed, Grazer? That's very presumptive of you. I might not like the look of them."

While they were parading near the road, a few curious men came up to them to see what was afoot and then clamoured to be included. Rankin told them to apply to join the New Zealand Composite Battalion, which was forming as part of the new 10 Brigade, under Brigadier Kippenberger, who, they need have no fear, "is a proper infantry officer".

Rankin spent well over an hour interviewing his applicants. He told each of them that he would not tolerate any out-of-line behaviour; discipline was paramount, along with aggression, flair, the ability to think for themselves and move undetected. Men with hunting and stalking experience were especially valuable. He needed all men under his command to be capable of undertaking independent action in case "anything happens to me or the NCOs". They also, he emphasised, needed to be able to kill when the time came, and not turn into blubbering wrecks. Above all, they had to look after the next man, but continue to function if their friends were hit.

After they'd all nodded gravely, he moved on to test their awareness of the general situation and the landmarks. He made them draw diagrams in the dust of named points, describing what lay on all sides and to give their own idea of the advantages and disadvantages of such a position. Rankin was eventually convinced that for men who had no fixed appointment, who paraded each morning in case they were needed for a work party that day, they had kept their eyes and ears open and gleaned a great deal of useful knowledge.

"It's like seagulling on the bloody wharves, mate," one of them said to him. "Waiting for the bloody boss to pick you out of the beauty parade for a day's work or go home with nothing if he doesn't like the look of yer. Wears you down."

They looked tough, resilient, fit, with a sense of purpose and they held their own opinions. Equally important, they still had the weapons they brought with them from Greece, concealed from prying eyes.

Finally, Rankin looked at the 16 men standing in front of him and said, "I can only take twelve of you. You're all capable, but you will have to choose for yourselves."

He signed 12 movement orders and said they were to be presented to the transit camp commandant before making their way to the position on the banks of the Tavronitis in ones and twos. "Do not make a spectacle of yourselves. Above all, keep out of sight of aircraft, and for Christ's sake don't shoot at anything!"

He rode his bike back to "their" hillside. As he rode, he wondered how he was going to break the news to Nicholson.

———————

NICHOLSON WAS NONE too impressed. Roughly a third of the platoon would now be made up of ring-ins. "For God's sake, Neil, they're from all over the place – hardly a South Islander among them. Half of them haven't fired a weapon since basic training. Misfits, cooks and stewards, I shouldn't wonder. What do you expect me to do with them?"

"You'll turn 'em into first-class infantrymen, Nick, I know you will," Rankin replied, laughing.

Nicholson's response was masked by furious pipe puffing. He became practically apoplectic when 16 men marched up next day, not the 12 he was expecting.

"Graham," Rankin shouted, "what is the meaning of this?"

"They were keen as mustard and didn't want to leave their mates behind, sir. I didn't have the heart to say no," said Graham, standing rigidly at attention.

"All very well, Graham, but how am I going to feed them? I now have rations for fewer men than I've got," said Rankin.

"It's all fixed with the Quartermaster's Department," said Graham in a conspiratorial whisper.

"Jesus Christ Almighty," shouted Rankin. "How in God's name have you done that?"

"Better you don't know, sir," Graham whispered back. "I helped him fix a little two-up problem he had."

"God in bloody Heaven," Rankin muttered, dismissing the parade. "Whatever bloody next?"

———

"THINK OF IT this way, Nick," Rankin said in what he hoped was his most conciliatory tone, "we've now got an over-strength platoon instead of an under-strength one."

"So long as they don't do more damage to our boys than

Adolf's," fumed Nicholson.

Nicholson's wrath had been blunted by a delivery of precious mail, held for the time they had been in Greece, and the latest edition of *Crete News*, the Creforce paper. The men who received mail avidly read and re-read the letters from home, full of news of children, family and friends. Rankin hid his bitter disappointment at the absence of any letters for him as he distributed the mail to the fortunate, who rapturously received their letters and parcels.

On Tuesday, 13 May, Brigadiers Hargest and Puttick[5] – with Puttick now acting commander of the Division after Freyberg's elevation to Commanding Officer Creforce – made a flying visit. Hargest's round, florid face and chubby geniality beamed out over the assembled platoon. Rankin and Nicholson showed them around the perimeter, trench system and weapon pits, not all of which were yet dug to their own satisfaction, and the fields of fire for the Boys rifles and automatic weapons brought back from Greece.

Rankin blushed as he pointed out the woven foliage cover over "the runs", and the camouflaged individual positions that would ensure they would remain invisible to the German aircraft. "This is the Rabbit Run, sir," Rankin had said, showing them a passage concealed behind the undergrowth and scrub growing along the edge of one terrace. "We can traverse a good distance behind cover" – he pointed out places where terraces were intersected by shallow cuts, often marked with a stunted tamarisk or other bushy shrub – "enabling us to get up and down in several places

---

5   Brigadier E. Puttick, born Timaru 26 June 1890, Samoa Expeditionary Force 1914–1915, NZEF 1915–1918, CO 3 Battalion Rifle Brigade Oct 1917–Mar 1918; CO 4 Brigade Jan 1940–Apr 1941; CO NZ Division 29 Apr–27 May 1941.

under cover." The two senior officers nodded sagely, looked impressed, and told the assembled men that it was no joke – invasion was imminent. They were about to make history.

"Damn fine show, Rankin," Hargest said as he was leaving. "Your stoush with the Jerries in Greece. Just what we need. Give the Hun a good drubbing, eh? I see some of your men have Boche weapons. Give him a taste of his own medicine, eh? See to it they get used to good effect, boy," and the two of them were off in Puttick's American-made staff car.

"Thank goodness that's over," said Nicholson, standing beside Rankin as the car disappeared down the dusty track.

"Pity our company commander didn't come with them. As far as Gentleman Jim's concerned, we might well be part of 22 Battalion," said Rankin.

"Perish the thought," said Nicholson doubtfully. "He seemed to know who we are."

"Well, let's hope it all works." Rankin stared into the dust trail left by the departing staff car. "He'll be a hell of a long way away when the fun starts."

Nicholson looked at him sharply. "Back to work, I think," he said.

———

"GENTLEMEN, I HAVE called this briefing to record the debt of gratitude we all owe to Colonel Falconer, who went to 10 Composite Brigade yesterday. Colonel Falconer has been the guiding light of this battalion since it formed in Burnham nearly eighteen months ago, and we are all grateful to him for the first-class foundation laid in that time."

The battalion's acting colonel, Major Leckie,[6] stood at the front of the classroom. An angular man with cropped dark hair, he stood before a large plain sheet hanging over the blackboard. The acting battalion Intelligence Officer, Lieutenant Davin, stood to his right, and the Brigade Major, representing Brigadier Hargest and 5 Brigade, stood on his left.

Leckie handed over to Davin, a platoon commander in the battalion until "plucked from the milieu for higher service", as Rankin had heard it described. Davin turned back the cover hanging over the large map on the blackboard, revealing the familiar area between the Akrotiri Peninsula and Suda Harbour in the east and Cape Spatha in the west.

"You are familiar with our dispositions, which are largely unchanged from those initially made when the General took command. Since then, there have been minor adjustments. For example, this battalion has provided a platoon to strengthen the flank of 22 Battalion." Davin tapped Rankin's position on the Tavronitis before continuing.

"As you know, our dispositions have been made with a dual threat in mind. Force threat appreciation considers the airborne landings in our area will be concentrated here," tapping Maleme, "the area to the west, and the area known as the Prison Valley, here, in our sector." He ran his pointer down the valley to the south of Galatas towards a town called Alikianou, southwest of the transit camp.

"It is essential that units tasked with acting as a mobile

---

6   Lieutenant Colonel D.F. Leckie, Invercargill schoolteacher, born Dunedin 9.6.1897, Anzac Mounted Division 1916–19, CO 23 Battalion Aug 1940–Mar 1941, May 1941–Jun 1941.

counter-attacking force, which is the Battalion's remit, maintain their ability to move at a moment's notice. The counter-attack role is in addition to the area defence role, designed to repel any seaborne invasion that lands along the coast, here." The tip of his pointer ran along the beach front, from west of Modhion to Pirgos.

Rankin cautiously surveyed the audience on either side of him. Beads of perspiration had broken out on brows and upper lips. It was hot in the room, but judging by the intensity they were applying to Davin's every word and the screwed-up eyes taking in the map, they were desperately trying to reconcile their defence of a fixed position with acting as mobile reserve.

"The overall strategy requires each threat to be countered – and eliminated – before units return to their allotted position ready to meet the next threat." Davin took a sip of water from the glass on the table beside the map.

"We do not know where the blow will fall, but we expect it in division strength. The air component will likely comprise both parachutists and assault troops." Davin stood to one side of the map and swept his hand across the undefended areas. The eyes of everyone in the audience were riveted to the map, each man no doubt pondering how close to his own position the Germans might land, and in what strength.

"The sea landing is expected to bring with it armoured vehicles, artillery, and motor transport, and comprise both German and Italian forces."

The IO looked about and invited questions on the briefing so far. Several of the more senior officers asked questions about liaison, lack of signalling gear, coordination with other units, and whether there was likely to be any improvement in the equipment situation which might permit them to "deal" with armoured fighting vehicles and artillery.

Rankin sensed that Anderson, sitting next to him, was beginning to shuffle in his seat. As each question was asked and Davin gave his response, Anderson's shuffling became more agitated. Getting to his feet, he spoke. "With all due respect to the planners," he started. Rankin felt a number of officers around the room stiffen. "Are we not exaggerating the risk of a seaborne invasion? Is it likely that either the Italian or German navies can mount an invasion against a defended target? Do they have the shipping? Do they dare risk such a force being caught at sea at night by the Royal Navy, which remains the dominant force? Is it not more likely that the seaborne force will be bringing heavy equipment and heavy infantry, but only after they have won the ground to make that possible?"

"I really think, Lieutenant Anderson, that the staff can be relied upon to have considered these matters, and have taken them into account," said Captain Hamilton dismissively.

Davin held his hand up. "Lieutenant Anderson raises a good point, though, sir. The difference between seaborne invasion and seaborne reinforcement."

Boney was clearly not finished. "A seaborne invasion requires specific equipment. Half the senior officers in the Division served in the Great War; some were at Gallipoli. The General was at Gallipoli. One lesson learned from that campaign was the difficulty of landing against defended ground from rowing boats, adapted merchant ships, and cargo lighters. It was for that very reason Mister Churchill ordered the tank landing craft, which assisted us with our evacuation from Greece. Have either the Italians or the Germans got anything that resembles them?"

Davin shook his head. "No idea, Boney."

"You've made your point, Anderson," said Hamilton. "Let's move on, shall we?" He nodded at Davin.

"We expect that the assault from the air will start immediately after heavy strafing and bombing," Davin continued. "The parachute troops will jump into the immediate aftermath of the bombardment while defenders are still disoriented, shocked, possibly injured, the din still ringing in their ears.

"Individual troops landing by parachute may take some time after landing to form their units, gather their equipment, orient themselves and launch their attack. The time they need to regroup once on the ground gives the defence opportunity to destroy them. In addition, intelligence believes gliders will bring in assault troops. These will arrive as a compact unit but should be vulnerable while extracting themselves from their glider. Men must not be over-awed by this novel form of arrival on the battlefield. It is paramount we remain alert and get on attack immediately. Attack is the best form of defence." Davin looked out to the audience.

Rankin stood up. "From our experience at Corinth, the parachutists will jump low to the ground, so there will be little time to hit them before they land," he began. "The man under the parachute will oscillate a couple of times, then steady. There should be enough time to get a well-aimed shot off at him. My advice is to aim at his feet: he falls faster than you think."

Hamilton leapt to his feet, apparently fit to burst. "That would be against the laws of war, Rankin, shooting at a man parachuting from an aeroplane."

A number of the more senior officers echoed, "Hear, hear," from around the room. "Not sporting."

"No, it would not, Captain Hamilton," said Rankin. "An airborne assault by armed forces by parachute is outside the succour afforded by the principle of distress and abandonment, which—" He got no further.

"Don't you presume to lecture me, Rankin, on matters of military law. No one under my command shall fire at men whilst descending to the ground under parachutes. Is that clear?"

There was a muttered chorus of "oh yes they will", and more "hear, hears" from the assembled officers. Immediately, arguments broke out, voices raised.

"Jesus wept," muttered Anderson.

The vein in Hamilton's forehead was throbbing and he was rapidly turning a shade of puce. Major Leckie hastily held up his hands, stepping forward. "Gentlemen, gentlemen, it is good to see vigorous debate, but frankly we are not going to settle this argument here. Operational unit commanders must issue their own orders on this matter. Move along, Lieutenant Davin."

"We expect them to arrive on May seventeenth," said Davin, looking as if he wished he were somewhere else.

The briefing broke up shortly afterward. Three days to go. Shit, thought Rankin. Both he and Anderson avoided Hamilton as they left, Anderson furious and muttering "incompetent wanker" under his breath. Who he was talking about and what incompetence was the cause of his wrath, Rankin had no time to discover as Anderson was then called away.

Riding back to his platoon, Rankin was struck by how well informed they seemed to be about German intentions. Davin had scarpered as soon as the briefing was dismissed, along with the Brigade Major and Leckie; there was no opportunity to ask him. Rankin did not linger, thus avoiding any further confrontation with Hamilton. The last thing he wanted was his independence rescinded.

Was someone making it up? Surely to God the Germans were not so well informed.

He arrived back to find more mail had been delivered.

"The boys are in great spirits, Skipper. Here's your mail," grinned Reilly, handing him a bundle of letters and two parcels.

"Well, I'll be buggered," Rankin said, turning the bundle over in his hands.

"Have a drink, Skipper," said Reilly, handing him a dixie of red wine. "The boys are celebrating. We won the cricket."

"I'm not sure we should be drinking, Reilly. We're on duty," Nicholson said in his severest tone.

"Have a drink, Nick," Rankin said to Nicholson. "Relax. The invasion's not happening until the 17th. It's official."

Nicholson looked at him. "Really. How do they know that?"

"Ours not to reason why, Nick – ours but to do and die."

"Gordon Bennett!" exclaimed Nicholson. "Is that Christmas cake you've got there?"

———

THE PARCELS, SOMEWHAT battered, were liberally stamped and annotated with redirection orders by the Field Post Office. The one from Katherine contained scarf, gloves and warm socks, wrapped around a half bottle of brandy, and a Christmas card with pictures of snow and red-breasted robins among the holly.

Dearest Neil,   *4 October 1940*
Your postcard from England arrived last week. How wonderful

to be looking forward to a winter Christmas now that Hitler's invasion threat seems to have passed. Snow, roast turkey, coloured lights (hidden by the blackout, of course!) carols on street corners. And roast chestnuts! Why don't we ever think of roasting chestnuts here? There must be plenty of the right sort of chestnut trees. Or do small boys turn them all into conkers? I do hope our parcels turn up in time.

It won't feel very Christmassy at home, I think. The second of this war. How many more will there be? God, please, not as many as the last one.

I went to see your mother the other day. She is terrified for you but puts on a brave face. I know she won't eat or sleep properly until you are home. She told me how all the women used to hide behind their curtains, not daring to move, praying the telegram boy would ride past to another house, anywhere but theirs. And the guilt, when the telegram is delivered to the house next door or down the road, to someone you have known all your life. The huge sigh of relief, the guilt, the grief, throwing yourself into baking and cooking for the desperate blank-eyed women and children in the houses where the telegrams went. And the terror goes on and on, without end.

Ever yours,
Katherine

He put the letter down, a lump in his throat. He felt close to her, missing her. But the guilt … He had blanched as he read the letter. Every action had a consequence. They had decided not to get engaged, but did that give him licence? Is that what Dada had been? An available interlude? He knew Katherine would decline any offers she received. Did that make her morally superior? God.

He understood, too, though she hadn't said it, whose "terror without end" was. He read and reread the letter: so typical of her. Cool, dispassionate, logical, but behind the façade a fiery passion and steely backbone. And it was typical of her to put herself in someone else's shoes; he came back to the paragraphs about his mother and stared at what she'd written.

"Jesus Christ, our Elsie's got herself up the duff!" came from further up the hillside.

"She didn't do it by herself, you bloody halfwit!" Happy laughter from all around.

Rankin's hands were trembling, the tears pricking his eyes, as he took the envelope his mother had addressed and included in the parcel with her Christmas cake. Hands shaking, he tore open the seal.

My Dearest Darling Boy,   *1 October 1940*
It seems so long since you left. It is hard to believe you have been away nearly a year, although the days crawl past so slowly. I get your letters and cards, I know you write when you can, but it feels like the link between us is broken. I don't say what I feel when I write. Your letters feel very guarded.

Oh Neil, I so long for those days when we had such a special bond. You were, are, such a good son. I know it is my fault. I couldn't see past my own tragedy and fear. And after all you did, as boy and young man, to shoulder the burden and fill the gap left by your father. I don't know how we would have managed but for the money you brought home every holiday. Your childhood was stolen from you, but you never complained, or ever said it wasn't fair.

Katherine came to see me. I was feeling low when she arrived.

I confess, I was surprised to see her. But glad. I poured out my heart to her, poor girl. Goodness knows what she thinks of me now. But she was very kind, very gentle, very understanding. She ran up a batch of scones and stayed for tea. She had the motor. She knows how stubborn you are, how easily upset you are. You're just like your father in that – he was slow to anger, but once roused it lingered long as a hurt silence. He never raised his voice to me, not once. I'm not counting the later years – he was not himself, as you know.

She said I should write to you, tell you how I feel, tell you how much I have regretted my decision not to come to your passing-out parade and send-off every day of my life since. It's not just your father who was stubborn – you've inherited from both of us. If I could turn back time, I would do it in a flash. Sometimes we only see the mistakes we've made from a distance.

I told her you should have asked her to marry you before you left. She told me why you both decided not to. I can't imagine what strength that took on her part – or yours. It was a strength your father and I did not possess. You know our first baby died before she was born, when he was already away overseas. I blamed myself. When he came home, and then you came along, I was terrified should anything happen to you. I lived on tenterhooks while you were young. I wasn't a relaxed mother, and I know I got worse as your father got sick. I couldn't cope and I'm afraid you came off second best. I believed that all chance for any of us to be happy was finished, because of that damned war. Then I had to watch you doing a man's job, out in all weathers, up all night, rabbiting every holiday because I couldn't provide. That was the most shameful, hurtful thing of all to endure.

But I was wrong – the greatest joy in my life, our lives, was to see you grow into a fine, caring young man of whom your parents, both of them, are justly proud. The world is a wicked place, Neil, but one day, please God, young men like you will make it a better place.

I know you had to go. I see that – in a way I always did – but desperately tried to ignore the inevitable. There have been some terrible stories, families sent white feathers in the post and men in reserved occupations beaten. I know you could never have stayed and watched others go.

I have tossed and turned at night trying to decide what to do for the best with this letter to you from your father. It is supposed to be given to you when you turn twenty-one, next August. You're in England, the newspapers say the threat of German invasion has passed, that our "Battle of Britain boys" can look forward to a more peaceful Christmas. I have decided to send it with your Christmas parcel, before they send you anywhere else.

I don't know what's in it. I remember him writing it. He was lucid, still in the bank flat in Princes St then. The nightmares were getting worse but the disastrous operation to remove the shrapnel from his spine was still in the future. The doctors said he needed to avoid harsh movements. He was in such pain – there seemed no cure for it. The nightmares made him thrash about so; it was so terribly cruel to watch. I suppose it was inevitable that he would end up in a wheelchair.

He thought the world of you. He so *wanted* children. He was dreadfully upset when I wrote to him to say our little girl had died before she was even born. He was so very far away.

I'm sorry Neil, my memories got the better of me. The smudges you see on the page are tears. I put this down before

I ruined it. The newspaper says the last day for posting to the forces overseas is next Tuesday. Whatever's in your father's letter, you have a right to know. I want this parcel to get to you, wherever you might be, for Christmas.

God go with you and keep you safe, my own darling boy.
All my love to you,
Mother

He was unable to move, sitting with her letter on his knees, tears on his cheeks. He had guessed why she had refused to see him off, but every time he tried to talk it had ended in slammed doors and floods of tears. Now she must be terrified it was too late; he hadn't had a choice. No one did; she had known that, deep down.

He turned her letter over in his trembling hands and read it again, then picked up the letter from his father, heart pounding, hands shaking. It was addressed to "Neil Rankin, Esq." He had seldom seen his father's handwriting, but he recognised it instantly when the envelope slipped out of the parcel. Too afraid to open it straight away, he put it to one side and looked at the rest of his mail. Most of it was inconsequential: letters from friends, prospective employers, Christmas cards.

"Bloody hell! They've called old Tosser Martin out of retirement!" a voice called out.

Rankin didn't hear the reply. He was looking at the last letter: the precise, flowing bookkeeper's handwriting on the envelope. But after the letters from his mother and from Katherine, he wasn't in the frame of mind to read it, so he slipped it into his small pack.

"Bloody good cake, Skipper. Make sure you tell Missus Rankin from me," Reilly said peering over the lip of the trench, pouring another wine from the bottle.

———

HE OPENED THE bottle of brandy Katherine had sent and took a mouthful to steady his nerves. It was dark now. Lively conversations drifted across the hillside, a happy babble in the background. He stared at the letter from his father. Finally, with the brandy inside him, he got up enough courage to slip his finger under the flap.

My Dear, Dear Boy,
By the time you read this you will be a young man, twenty-one, making your own way in the world. As hard as it is for me to write this, I feel that my own demise is imminent, and that I will not see you reach that age. I remember when I was twenty-one: not long married, and on-board ship to the War.

The War, Neil, that damnable War. The lives of millions ruined for ever afterwards. Little do you think of that when you are that age: all you can see is the Adventure and the Patriotic Duty. And all that was part of it, but we thought we were indestructible. It came as a terrible shock to realise we were not. So many good men, boys, laid in the hot dry ground of Turkey, or sucked into the deep grey mud of Flanders.

Rankin looked up to the star-studded sky. His father had foreseen that his condition would worsen. Feeling his throat constrict, he fixed his gaze on a bright star, shimmering in the dark heavens. It was a while before he could bring himself to continue.

Choose your friends wisely. Reflect on their character before putting your life in their hands. Know your enemies. Act with conscience and honour in all things – not the poppycock honour that is trotted out when it suits them, but the real honour, which comes from knowing that you have treated that person as you would wish them to treat you. God gave you an intellect to analyse, consider, weigh up and make decisions. Use it.

Let your head rule your heart when you need, but don't dishonour yourself by being a cad. The joy of being one with a good woman cannot be equalled, but you must be true in your intentions toward her. If you are successful in life, you will find that others who are less successful, for whatever reason, may be more easily taken advantage of. Resist. Only a cad acts this way. It is deeply dishonourable.

His heart leapt into his throat. Jesus! Katherine. Dada. God Almighty.

God forbid you are ever faced with taking another man's life. Think carefully before you make your choice. I have lived with guilt these years for taking the life of a Turk at Gallipoli. We were at war, of course. I was a better-than-average shot. We had a spot out in our trench from where we glimpsed their movements. We had never shot at the water boy. We were thirsty as well. We knew what a torment that was. The water boy was a lad – a boy, a civilian possibly, who could only just manage the cart. For all I know, his father owned the well. I was out of sorts: thinking of your mother, re-reading the letter telling me that her, our, baby girl was dead. Not yet born. In my despair I frequently cursed God, I cried, I railed at the unfairness of it all, that your poor mother had to go through all this on her own.

Their water came up generally at the time of day when we were on watch. A chap I did not get on with had needled me, saying that I was too soft, shirking my duty. Though my eyes were blurred with tears this day, I shot the boy. Not cleanly – we could hear him screaming for an hour afterward. That night they brought up a mountain gun and pasted our lines. Shell and canister. Eight men were wounded, and three killed.

The gun was theirs, but it was me who caused their deaths, their injuries, Neil. And it is me who has been punished for it.

The tears were running freely now and he had to put the letter down to wipe his eyes. He could barely see the words for tears when he picked the letter up again.

Not everyone sees things the way you do. After Gallipoli, we were posted to France, of course. I was a company commander by the lead up to Passchendaele. That cursed place. We had done well in attacks beforehand. Patrolling was a constant drain on the nerves while we were in the line. One day, I discovered that a neighbouring company had a ruse. They had a reel of German wire they cut lengths from, to take back with their report on the raid. You had to prove that you had been up to the enemy wire, you see, and shirking was rife in some units. The bastards! Others were doing the work, and getting men killed. They were hiding in No Man's Land, with miraculously few casualties. I had it out with their man, just before the big push. I'll never forget the look in his eyes.

The day of the attack was dreadful. The rain came down in sheets for a week, the mud was terrible, the barrage got ahead of us. The machine guns took a fearful toll. Everyone was all tangled up. I found myself in a shell hole, with this same man! He was cowering, too afraid to move on. I called him out, accused him of his funk, and as I got up to push on, I felt the most colossal thump in my back, which threw me face-down into the mud. I was lucky not to drown. Later more men came up, and we were shelled. To this day I don't know if it was theirs or ours. That's when I was hit in the back again, by shrapnel. I had been shot by that man. I have never told this story, even to your mother. I know I was shot in the back by a British pistol, as the bullet was taken out in hospital in England, and I still have it. The hate in those baleful, colourless eyes is something I will remember as if it were yesterday, as long as I live.

A chill knifed through his heart. He put the letter down, barely able to breathe, numb with shock.

Several times he lit the stub of candle, pulled the blanket over his head, and took the pages from their envelopes, ensuring that the words in his head had come from the right letter. He read on:

I can feel the black dog coming, Neil, and I will finish here before it breaks down the door. Unto thine own self be true, my boy. Do not be defined by your circumstances, but rather define yourself by being the very best you can be, regardless of the circumstances. Act with honour in all things.

Go out into the world, son, knowing that you take the blessings of your Father and Mother with you, even if, as I fear, we cannot both be there together to send you on your way.

He read the letter so many times that he could recite whole

passages of it by heart, but there was one paragraph he had to read and re-read to make sure he hadn't invented it: *I had been shot by that man. I have never told this story, even to your Mother. I know I was shot in the back by a British pistol, as the bullet was taken out in hospital in England, and I still have it.*

A bullet in the back! Base, gutless, treachery! What sort of a man could do such a thing? Someone who could not face the consequences of his actions. Someone who was prepared to commit murder to cover up his own crime.

The enormity of it preyed on him so that he could not sleep. Tossing and turning, he was unable to still the thoughts tumbling in his head. The cowardly, treacherous bastard had left his father lying face-down in the mud, shot in the back, his life a wreck. The airburst that lodged the shrapnel in his spine would have missed him if not for that man with his hate-filled "baleful, colourless eyes". He was to blame for the whole tragedy that had blighted Rankin's family ever since.

The scene played and replayed in his head. His heart pounded in his chest as the rage in him rose, his fists clenching and unclenching with the urge to strike, to take revenge. In the early hours of the morning, after his rage left him feeling spent and limp, it began to dawn on him that he might owe this baseless man something other than revenge for the suffering he had caused.

What if his father had not been lying face down in the mud in that shell hole? What if he had got up and pushed on? Would he have become just one more of the thousands killed that day in the pouring rain? Claimed by the glutinous mire of Passchendaele. One of the tens of thousands simply swallowed by the earth, with no known grave.

Rankin was rocked to his very core, hot tears of rage dry upon his cheeks. He hardly dared to breathe, staring at the star-studded sky above him as he contemplated that he might owe his very existence to this craven coward.

CHAPTER FOUR

To the Edge of the Precipice, 14–19 May 1941

14 May 1941

The air-raid siren's mournful wail echoed up the valley and off the hillside. They could hear the aero engines climbing out above the flat land to the west but could not see the Hurricanes and Gladiators they belonged to for the tall rustling bamboos across the riverbed. Rankin's platoon, a mile up the Tavronitis River from the airfield, tensed, waiting for the coming storm. Morning stand-to was observed with weapons at the ready, expectant faces peering out of their holes in the ground. Rankin looked at his watch; it was just after 0530.

The bark of the Bofors guns heralded the howling shriek of the German fighters roaring in off the sea, guns hammering. Suddenly overhead, spitting fire and death to the unwary, tearing over the riverbed and across the hill behind them, they were followed by the dive-bombers, twin-engine Junkers 88s, pulling out of their dives and hurtling up the river valley, the crump and boom of the bombs landing on the airfield chasing after them. Dust clouds and black smoke rose high into the sky from around the airfield, invisible beyond the flank of Hill 107.

As the aircraft roared overhead, criss-crossing from west of the river in front of them and from beyond the summit of the hill behind them, the ground erupted, dust spurted, stones and dirt flew; bullets, cannon shells and bombs tore up earth and trees, and shredded foliage. The men cowered in their trenches, fingers in their ears, as around them the noise raged. Clods and stone chips rained down, thumping and pattering the ground. The drifting dust and smoke obscured everything, even the bamboo just across the riverbed.

It was over as abruptly as it had started. Silence fell upon them, leaving their ears ringing and eyes watering. Dust and the acrid stink of explosive hung in the air. Heads emerged above ground, eyes wide and darting, faces pale.

"Fuck me," he heard Duggan say, "they could pick the fuckin' grapes from that height."

"Breakfast, boys," called Nicholson. "Get the grub going and a brew on before Herman comes back. We've got a lot to do today."

Rankin looked at his watch and noticed his hand was shaking. It was nearly 0715 – the shrieking and pounding had gone on for nearly two hours. It was the heaviest air raid yet.

————

RANKIN AND NICHOLSON had gone to ground in the platoon's HQ trench. Another German aircraft roared overhead, from the direction of 22 Battalion's HQ on top of the hill behind them before hurtling westwards. A string of crumps sounded above them in its wake.

Nicholson raised his head above the lip of the trench and

pushed his helmet back from his forehead. Silence. "Damned flash Harries."

"How are the billets working out, Nick?" asked Rankin, standing up to stretch his cramped limbs.

"Very popular. Half the platoon billeted every night. Locals are as keen as mustard." He struck a match and lit his pipe.

"I'll bet they are," Rankin said. "Chits redeemed in good British gold."

Nicholson nodded. He took the pipe from his mouth and pointed the stem towards the southern hills. "You know that bell tower, in the village church. You'd get a good view of the country to the west from there, and likely south to the next village as well. If we pushed our flank out a bit, we might be able to stay in visual contact. It would make sense to put Gibson and a spotter up there."

Rankin looked at him. "You don't think we'd be splitting our limited resources too thin? You know, don't dilute your force."

"Could be. Platoon's bigger than we expected," Nicholson said, casting him a meaningful look.

Rankin smiled. "Gibson will get the other rifle with telescopic sights."

"I know. He's likely to do some good with it. We still wouldn't have any idea of what's happening further towards the hills." He exhaled a waft of sweet-smelling blue smoke. "Or up the track to the AMES station behind 21's position."

Rankin pursed his lips. "Worth a thought. The village is Ay Nikolaos, Saint Nicholas, the Christmas saint." He fell silent, suddenly thinking of home. Would any of them see another Christmas? "What's happening up at the Air Ministry station?"

"Weren't allowed anywhere near it. It's guarded by a platoon from 21 Battalion. Must be very important." Nicholson puffed his pipe contentedly.

"Jerry must know all about it," Rankin said. "It'll be obvious from the air. Two dirty great radio aerials and a little cluster of huts. There must be forty or fifty blokes there. Can't have gone unnoticed."

"By the way, Neil," Nicholson went on. "That story about how 21 got overrun in the Pinios Gorge – I ran into an old chum up at the AMES station, a warrant officer who's drawn the short straw of commanding the guard up there. He had a different version. Said they were badly positioned by the Aussies who cut and ran at the first hint of trouble, leaving them to it with the Jerry tanks already in behind them."

Rankin looked at him. "Always two sides to a story, I suppose."

Nicholson nodded through a cloud of smoke. "Everyone seems to agree on one thing, though. The blimmin' tanks turned up where nobody reckoned they could go." He cocked his head, looking at Rankin. "He was one who told his blokes to throw away their Boys rifles. 'Useless as tits on a bull,' were his exact words. Got fed up watching round after round bounce off, 'like fleas off a rhino'."

"I know," replied Rankin. "We brought out two, and the rest of the battalion's only got two between them."

15 May 1941

"How're the phone lines holding up, Mac?" Rankin asked their Scottish signaller. McIntyre was kneeling in the signals trench in the platoon HQ, muttering darkly. He had just replaced the handset.

"The last air raid must have cut the bliddy line to 22 Battalion again, Skipper. I'll be away to find the break an' fix it."

"I'm not surprised, the pasting it's had lately. We're going to need that line to talk to HQ on the top of the hill when the fun starts."

"Och, aye Skipper. Hae nae fear, 'cos Jock is here."

Rankin smiled. "Take Reilly with you. For protection."

"I'm nae a bookie's runner, Skipper. Me little black bag's got tools in it, nae dosh."

"He knows the drill," said Nicholson, nodding towards McIntyre as Reilly leapt up, Tommy gun in hand. "I was looking forward to a brew."

"Off you go, Reilly, I'll put the billy on," Rankin replied.

After McIntyre and Reilly had left the HQ area, Rankin turned to Nicholson. "I've just been along to see our neighbours up by the bridge. They're very pissed off."

"Oh, really? What's the matter with them?" Nicholson searched for the tea among Reilly's stores.

"That bloody RAF camp. Four hundred idle hands milling about, half of them unarmed. No proper job, no interest in being turned into makeshift infantry."

Nicholson stared at him as Rankin added dry twigs to the fire.

"That's not all. Fergusson can't see the next platoon on the airfield side of the camp. The camp splits their position in two."

Nicholson poured a handful of tea leaves into the billy as the water began to boil.

"Did I tell you the other day? Out of the six rifle platoons 22 Battalion has along the western flank of the airfield, four of them are commanded by sergeants."

Nicholson raised his eyebrows above the boiling billy.

"Us subalterns are a dying breed, apparently," Rankin replied. "And what's worse is that the road bridge covers the approach into the middle of the camp. They're not allowed to demolish it. They've laid mines on the road, but are not allowed to fuse them – in case they blow up a bloody donkey or two." Rankin threw up his hands in mock horror.

"I see," said Nicholson.

"Jerry won't be slow to take advantage, Nick," Rankin said, lifting the billy. "Here, give us your mug."

"I'm sure someone's thought of it."

"Oh, and one more thing," Rankin said, pouring his tea. "That Hurricane that crashed on the beach while the boys were down there yesterday. Shot down by one of the airfield's Bofors guns as it was coming in to land, apparently. The RAF pilots are very pissed off with the gunners, it seems."

———

THE AIRFIELD HAD taken the brunt of the morning's strafing and bombing. Columns of black greasy smoke rose from across the flat brown expanse. Rankin had seen from the road as he cycled along that the exposed Bofors positions around the perimeter had taken another fearful pasting. An ambulance, collecting the casualties, set off down the road towards the hospital, bell jangling.

He leaned his bike against the armourer's workshop and went inside. Albert, the warrant officer armourer, was detailing his "erks" to their tasks for the day. Several were clearing fallen wreckage and overturned benches. Sunlight poured in through new lines of holes in the roof and sides of the workshop. The concrete floor was scorched and pitted. Several workbenches and lathes had suffered the effects of a cannon shell hit, overturned and smashed.

Albert Davies, an RAF warrant officer through and through, was a career man whose life was all about providing the means of taking the fight to the enemy.

"'Eaviest raid yet, Mister Rankin," Davies said when he spied Rankin. "Caught a couple of 'Urricanes out on the 'drome. We'll 'ave to 'ave a gander at 'em later, see if there's anything we can salvage."

That explained the columns of greasy black smoke.

"Morning, Albert. Just as well they're not coming today. How's our little project coming along?"

"Bleedin' lucky Jerry 'asn't scuppered them. But look 'ere, we've done the two AT rifles, just finishing one of your .303s, and the other should be done today." Albert led the way to a workbench in a corner and whipped the dust sheet off the two Boys anti-tank rifles standing on the bench.

Rankin surveyed the handiwork of the RAF armourers. The German telescopic sights were fitted neatly to the top left-hand side of the body of the gun, just in front of where the two-position iron sights had been.

"We 'ad to machine in 'oles for the grub screws for the mounting frame," Davies explained as he demonstrated the attachment and release of the telescopic sights. "You can take the telescope sight off, like so, but re-attaching the rear sight might be beyond lads in the field." He pointed to the mounting for the original sight. "No need to take the front sight off; it don't interfere with the view through the scope."

Rankin hefted the nearer rifle into his shoulder, pressed his face against the walnut cheek pad, and looked through the sight. It was too dark to see much, but the fit looked perfect.

Davies coughed discreetly. "They're not quite as you brought them in, Mister Rankin. We changed the business end for some Suda sent over."

Rankin looked up at him.

"The machine shop over at Suda Ordinance Depot's kaput, see. They've been sending jobs to us. The chief fitter told me Middle East Command sent out some early Mark Is to Crete. Suda wanted us to rechamber these for them, to .55, like the later ones. When you told me your idea, I thought I'd swap yours for two of theirs. Save time, everyone's 'appy."

Rankin raised his eyebrows.

"I'm 'opin' you don't mind, Mister Rankin. Yours are now .50 calibre Mark Is, on the later chassis. We re-fitted your own horizontal muzzle brakes."

Rankin looked at him. "All very well, Albert, but what are we going to put in them?"

"See, that's the point, sir. We 'ad a few 'Urricane IIBs in 'ere. Orphans they are, fitted with six .50s instead of twelve .303s. There's an 'eap of .50 Browning machine gun ammo in store. The 'Urricanes were either written off or went back to Gyppo – left the ammo 'ere, see? Some of your blokes are getting the salvaged Brownings, Gawd 'elp 'em," he said, rolling his eyes. "They'll get most of it, but they'll never miss a few 'undred rounds. All sorts: tracer, incendiary, armour-piercing, explosive, and all. It'll muck up the barrel somethin' awful, but you're probably not worried about that."

Rankin stared at him, then broke into a grin. "You're a saint, Albert."

At that moment the quiet hum of activity in the workshop fell silent, and the men all stood to attention. "Oh, gawd," he heard Davies mutter.

"Carry on, you men," one of the newcomers said, making straight for the warrant officer in charge.

Davies and Rankin both came to attention and saluted. The station commander, Group Captain Beamish[7], the station adjutant and a Royal Marine major were making their rounds.

"Morning, Albert," Beamish said. "How have you fared in this morning's raid?"

"No casualties, sir. No substantive damage, a few new 'oles in the roof, sir, as you can see." He gestured towards the beams of light streaming in through the corrugated iron.

The station commander nodded, looking around, instantly taking in the state of the workshop and no doubt noting the demeanour of the men employed in it.

Beamish and the adjutant sauntered over to a group of men standing by their bench. Tall and solidly built, square-jawed and blue eyed, Beamish was a professional airman and former rugby player, He spoke with a warm Irish lilt and, according to Davies, he was greatly admired by his men. Having only just arrived from Middle East Command to oversee the recovery of aircraft from Greece, he radiated suppressed energy. It was clear he would rather be flying than running a station whose purpose appeared to have already evaporated.

"And who is this grubby specimen?" the major asked, looking

---

7 Group Captain G.R. Beamish, born Ireland 29.4.1905, 26 caps for Ireland and toured to Australia and New Zealand with the British Lions rugby team of 1930.

directly at Rankin, but talking to the warrant officer.

"Second Lieutenant Neil Rankin, NZEF, sir," Rankin answered for himself.

"A colonial officer, no less." His gaze took in Rankin from the top of his field service cap to the soles of his boots – stains, dirt, dust and all. His tone and superior twist to the mouth told Rankin he was about as welcome in this man's domain as a dung beetle. Out of the corner of his eye, Rankin saw the adjutant hurriedly consult the papers attached to his clipboard. Beamish was busy talking to some aircraftsmen.

"Your uniform does you no credit, I'm afraid," the major continued. "You wouldn't last long in my unit," he said, pointedly sniffing, as if confronted with a bad smell.

"I'm sorry to hear that, sir," Rankin said. "I expect that living in a dusty hole in the ground and keeping out of sight of the enemy has taken a toll on my dress."

"Cleanliness is next to godliness, Mister Rankin. You colonials would do well to remember it. I hope you train your men better than you turn them out." Rankin noted the sneer in the way he said the word "mister".

"The training syllabus I have set for my people has more important content than polishing my shoes, sir. They'll give a good account of themselves when the time comes."

"Humph. Let's hope they survive the first five minutes. Cleanliness means discipline in my book. A man with pride in himself will stand in the face of the enemy, look like a soldier, and conduct himself like one." The major turned away and walked over to a work bench. "I don't give much for their chances, however, if what I see before me is anything to judge by," he scoffed. Raising the dust cloth on a bench, he looked at the Browning machine gun underneath.

"I could say the same about your gunners, sir. I certainly expect my men will still be capable of giving an account of themselves when the enemy arrives." It was out before he could stop himself.

The major swung back, breathing hard, face incandescent with rage. "You confounded colonial snot! Those gunners are doing the job I put them there to do, defending this airfield from the enemy! Not skulking in some burrow too frightened to show their faces while the enemy flaunts himself up and down the whole damned island! How dare you presume to malign them! Some snot still wet behind the ears who thinks five minutes of action makes him a bloody expert."

"Oh, I have only the greatest admiration for *them*, sir. My concern is they will no longer be effective when the enemy arrives on the ground, in person, face to face. Our orders are not to shoot until that time comes." Rankin was aware of a deathly silence in the workshop. The erks had ceased breathing.

The major's face changed colour several shades. Had he carried a swagger stick, Rankin feared he may have been slashed across the face with it.

"I'm fully aware of your *orders*," he spat. "Wars aren't won by refusing to give fight! No wonder my general refused to saddle us with some jumped-up colonial commander!"

Beamish said gently, "We must move along." The adjutant studiously consulted his papers.

The major took the hint, turned on his heel and stalked off towards the door, back ramrod straight and shoulders set.

Beamish said in a low voice, "We are doing whatever we can to help the army, Albert?"

"Oh, yes, sir, one of their armourer sergeants has been down and we've 'elped convert a number of Brownings for ground use, for airfield defence."

"Very good, Albert. Do whatever you can to help the army, so long as it doesn't interfere with your real job." He nodded to Rankin as he and the adjutant turned to go.

Albert and Rankin saluted and watched them leave. Rankin let his breath out as the door clanged shut behind them.

"The Group Captain's champion, but that major's a bit of a tartar," Albert said. "One of the gunners told me 'e reacted the same way when your brigadier chappy, with the round face, said something similar. Your brigadier wanted to bring the aerodrome and seaward defence guns under command of area defence." Albert shook his head sadly. "'E 'ad a fit when 'e got back 'ere, apparently. 'E only takes orders from General Weston, and 'e's got the pip because 'e was promised command of the 'ole island, before your man Freyberg turned up."

Rankin stared at him, absorbing this piece of news. "That would be Brigadier Hargest," he said absently. He kept his thoughts to himself: there wouldn't be a Bofors crew left standing come the big day. "At least the two six-inch coastal defence guns on the hill have not given away their positions and might still be there when we need them, Albert."

Rankin went to leave, then turned about in mid-stride. "Hey, Albert, have you chaps been getting small arms and basic infantry training? Presumably you will be detailed as part of airfield defence when the Jerries turn up?"

"Ho, ho, Mister Rankin, you do like your little joke. Things might be different in the colonial forces," he chuckled. "Airfield defence is in the purview of the Senior Service, not us Johnny-come-lately RAF types."

Rankin could only stare open-mouthed after him while he went to a locker behind a work bench. "Oh, and Mister Rankin," Albert called, holding up several oiled japarra packages tied with string. "We finished these little souvenirs you wanted."

"Thank you very much, Albert. A scholar and a gentleman, as well as a master craftsman." Albert's reply was drowned by the rising wail of the air-raid siren.

16 May 1941

"So, all in all," Rankin said to Nicholson, "despite your obvious scepticism, I think the test proved the worth of the telescopic sights on our anti-tank rifles. Penetrative power's similar to the .55 bullet, Albert told me."

They were sitting in the command trench following Rankin's return from testing the rifles with their new sights. They flinched as more German aircraft roared overhead accompanied by the usual bangs and crumps from the airfield.

"We got them sighted at three hundred yards. They'll be accurate way beyond that."

"Good-oh." Nicholson took another puff of his pipe, clearly unimpressed. "We had beggar-all armour-piercing for the Boys rifles, anyway. Most of the platoons threw them away in Greece, as a liability."

"So you've said before," sighed Rankin.

Nicholson laughed. "I heard that one platoon's NCOs carried theirs all the way through Greece to the beach, only to find the gunner had chucked away the bolt. He thought they were going to ditch the gun, back in the hills after the first day. Didn't have the gumption to tell the bloke carrying it!"

"I know they're useless against tanks, but what about soft targets?" Rankin continued, undeterred. "They're lethal to two thousand yards, you know. A bullet big enough to cut an elephant in two, even at that range."

Nicholson had just taken a long series of puffs from his pipe when both men had to duck below the lip of the trench as another German fighter roared up the riverbed, leaving the bamboo on the other side rustling in its wake. Expletives and ribald comments rang out across the hillside.

Rankin decided to change the subject. "Albert told me they've cobbled together mounts made of wood, metal and chewing gum and set up Browning machine guns salvaged out of aircraft overlooking the aerodrome. Electric – you need an aeroplane battery to fire them. Blokes from 22 Battalion have got them."

"Sounds pretty Heath Robinson. Rather them than me. I hope they don't end up killing the blokes using them." Nicholson blew a cloud of smoke over the rim of the trench.

"Speaking of fatal," Nicholson went on after some time, as Rankin had not answered. "There's some potential in your motley ring-ins. They're keen, I'll grant you that."

Rankin smiled inwardly; from Nicholson, that meant they would more than hold their own when the time came.

They were silent, heads down, as another German twin-engine fighter roared past, spitting cannon and machine-gun fire across the hillside. "Beggars," Nicholson muttered. "I'm getting sick and tired of them." He wormed his way lower into the dry dirt in the bottom of the hole. "I went over the track from that village with the unpronounceable name to the rear of 21's position and the Air Ministry Experimental Station with the ring-ins, as you said. We tried movement under cover, ambush technique, going to ground if ambushed, crawling, firing positions, et cetera. Some of them had done some of it before. They need a couple of weeks to get a proper hang of it."

"We're out of weeks," Rankin said. "Intelligence says they'll be here tomorrow."

———

"ARE WE FIGHTING a bloody war or what?" Rankin fumed. "According to Creforce, the buggers are coming tomorrow!"

It was late afternoon. The four subalterns were sitting at a table outside the Pirgos café, enjoying the afternoon sunshine. Rankin had told the others of his talk with Fergusson and encounter with the Royal Marines major.

"I say, Neil, steady on." Robertson looked alarmed. "We're all on the same side, you know."

Pyne chuckled. "Are you after another court-martial offence? Going for the trifecta?"

"Aha, very good, Pyne. The follies of our imperial masters," Anderson said, trying to imitate O'Rourke's superior, intellectual air.

Rankin looked at Anderson. Smug bastard, he thought. "Don't you bloody start. Where is William, anyway? Doesn't he know the Hun's expected tomorrow?"

"His Master's Voice hath called him to higher office at Battalion. Planning to thwart the sea invasion," said Robertson.

"Waste of bloody time. The bastards won't come by boat," said Anderson sourly. "The navy will do for them, but no one's listening."

"I asked William what his brief was," Robertson said. "As

far as he knew, it was to look at our dispositions along the coast and carry out an assessment of what force they could resist, for how long, without reinforcements. Right up his street."

"That's not ridiculous." Pyne poured himself another drink.

"Even you, Boney, must concede that we need to have a plan for reinforcing any sector threatened by seaborne landing," Robertson added.

"I would if someone had taken the elementary step of obtaining naval charts of the coast, looking at the profile of the seabed and what shipping they have. And have they?" Anderson drained his glass.

They all looked at him expectantly.

"No, they have not. They would need specialised landing ships. And do the Jerries have any? Not as far as anyone knows. Otherwise, they can only use the ports of Chania and Kisamos Kastelli," he said, waving his hands to east and west. "Chania's ours and the Greeks hold Kastelli. We should blow the bloody quays up."

"That'll set the cat amongst the sponge fishermen," Rankin said facetiously.

"Exactly!" Anderson poured another ouzo and added water. They all watched it go cloudy. "We're in danger of dividing our force against a myth, for Christ's sake." Spitting out the words, he emptied the glass. "We're diluting the effort applied to the real threat, the airfield." Anderson banged his glass down on the table. The others grabbed for their own rattling glasses.

"How do you know all this?" asked Rankin.

"I took the elementary precaution of buying a chart from a bookshop in Chania. Anybody in intelligence could have done the same. Any fool can read a chart. The sea shore along this stretch of coast shelves. Gently." He glared at them. They all looked back blankly.

He sighed. "A loaded caique would ground too far out to sea. Armed infantry would be trying to wade ashore up to their adenoids in water. They would all need to be seven feet tall, for Christ's sake. They'd drown!"

"Ah, but what about high tide, Boney? Float right up to the beach, and bingo," Pyne said smugly.

"We're in the Med, for fuck's sake, Pyney. Have you seen any high tides here? Or bloody low tides, come to that?"

"Have you told anyone all this?" asked Rankin.

"Of course, I bloody have. The Dimwit told me to concentrate on my own job and leave naval intelligence to the experts. A note I wrote to Freyberg's headquarters disappeared into a black hole. I collared Davin about it, who told me the general has every confidence in present arrangements – whatever the fuck that means."

"It means we should be calling you 'Admiral', Boney, that's what," said Robertson. "I'm sure the people in charge know what they're doing."

Anderson turned on him. "For fuck's sake, Nellie. Get your nose out of Dimwit's arse for once, will you? I've just proved they don't have a bloody clue!"

Robertson's face paled. Standing up, he stepped back from his chair, picked up his hat and stalked off.

"Christ, Boney. Ease up on him, will you? I'd better go and pour oil and all that," Pyne said, getting up and hurrying after Robertson.

"He'll get over it," Anderson said, staring after them. "My faith in those in charge is severely diminished, I'm afraid."

"Jesus, Boney. Don't let on to your blokes." Rankin poured the last of the ouzo into their glasses, which they quickly tossed back.

"What do you take me for? A bloody idiot? Even though we're just sitting here with our balls on an anvil, waiting for Thor's hammer."

Rankin shuddered. "Boney, you've known me longer than anyone else here," he said, taking Katherine's brandy bottle out of his pocket. Anderson looked up as Rankin filled their glasses.

"Hello," said Anderson. "What's this about?"

"Christmas present. From Katherine," Rankin said as he extracted an envelope from inside his shirt and handed it to Anderson.

"Shit, Neil, what's this?" Anderson took a sip and turned the envelope over in his hands. "Isn't a letter from the divine Katherine saying she's got it wrong all these years, and really meant to be with me, is it?"

"God, you're an ass. It's a letter from my father."

Anderson stared at him. "Oh. Shit. I see. What do you want me to do with it?"

"I want you to read it."

Anderson looked at him doubtfully, then opened the flap.

"It was meant to be given to me when I turn twenty-one. Mother sent it, I suppose, in case I never get to twenty-one."

Anderson frowned at him, then drew the pages from the envelope. He settled into his chair, glass in hand. Rankin watched him, imagining where he had got to each time his expression changed.

"I'm beginning to like your father. He's talking about me, here when he says *Choose your friends wisely. Reflect on their character before putting your life in their hands. Know your enemies. Act with conscience and honour in all things – not the poppycock honour that is trotted out when it suits them, but the real honour, that comes from knowing that you have treated that person as you would wish them to treat you. God gave you an intellect to analyse, consider, weigh up and make decisions. Use it."*

Anderson looked up. "I see where you get your tendency to be overly dramatic and pontificate your daft bloody philosophies."

"Huh. He's telling me to use my brains. You should take heed."

Anderson went back to the letter. "Ha, more good advice, Neil. *Don't be a cad with the ladies.* He must have known."

Rankin said nothing. Anderson read on, occasionally snorting and chuckling as he read. On the final page, he sat bolt upright, staring at the page.

"For Christ's sake, Neil. I don't mean to be unkind, but was he sane when he wrote this?"

"Yes. It was before his 'black dog finally broke down the door', as he put it, and came for him, before he was confined to a wheelchair and sent to Seacliff."

"Jesus Christ Almighty," breathed Anderson. "He was shot in the back by one of his own men."

"No, Boney. Read it again. It was another officer, whom he'd threatened to expose for faking his patrols into no man's land." Rankin leant over his shoulder and pointed to the text. "See, there, he'd found the reel of German wire they'd cut pieces from to 'prove' they'd been to the other side."

Anderson stared at the letter, then at Rankin. "Surely, you don't think …? He doesn't name him."

"No. He doesn't," Rankin stared back, holding his gaze. "But listen: *The hate in those baleful, colourless eyes is something I will remember as if it were yesterday, as long as I live.*"

"He's got a fine turn of phrase, your father."

"Puts a lot of what's happened in perspective, I must say."

"Neil, you can't be serious. You can't confront him with this. The whole fucking German army's about to fall on our heads."

"I know, I know. But he's had it in for me ever since I joined. Why d'you think he picked me for one of his platoons if he recognised the name? To keep his enemies close?"

"Bloody hell, that's just fanciful, for God's sake. He's not that bright."

"Think about it. He only let slip about me being like my father when I upset him in Thebes. He cursed himself for letting me see that. Then when I suggested he deserted his post, well, it was like a ghost from his past had caught up with him. He was angry, yes, but the reaction was much, much more. There was real hate. In his eyes. 'Baleful and colourless'."

Anderson stared at him, then folded the letter and put it back in the envelope. "We know he was at Passchendaele," he said, turning the envelope over in his hands before giving it back to Rankin.

"He's put me and my platoon in a position we're not likely to survive the first five minutes, Boney. That's why I wanted you to see it. In case something happens."

"You can't be serious," exclaimed Anderson.

"If anything happens to me, at least you know. It explains a lot," Rankin sighed. "Post this card for me, would you please? It's to my mother."

"Shit, you haven't put anything in that about this, have you?" he asked, looking alarmed.

"Of course not. It's just to say her Christmas parcel turned up and we all loved the cake." He was silent for a minute. "It may be too late."

"Jesus, Neil. Fine way to enjoy a final drink, standing on the edge of the precipice." Anderson drained his glass and stood up. "I've got to get back."

Rankin took a small japarra-wrapped package from his pocket and held it out to the other man. "Good luck, Boney. Whatever happens next, I'm sure we'll meet up again somewhere. You know what they say: *aprés moi, le deluge* or some such. Tell Bernard Clutterbuck this is for him, with my compliments."

Anderson turned the little package over in his hand. "I'm sorry I've been such an arsehole all these years, Neil. Good luck." He hung his head. "I mean it. You're my oldest friend. Often the only bugger silly enough to put up with me. Sorry if I've overstepped the mark from time to time."

"For Christ's sake. We're not dead yet!"

"I know. I can't say I am filled with confidence. I'm sure the next few days will go swimmingly. If not swimmingly, certainly with a bang."

THERE WERE TWO more air raids before he got back to his own perimeter on the Tavronitis. Nicholson greeted him with a relieved smile and told him the eggs had been delivered. Gibson and his spotter were the last in, from their OP in the church tower at Vlakheronitissa.

Dusk fell, the German aircraft went home, and the evening became a tranquil haven of peace: quiet, cool, and soft of light.

Rankin called the men together before standing them down for the night. Climbing on top of the parapet of one of the front positions nearest the road, he called for quiet as he surveyed the faces in front of him. Twenty-four of them belonged to men who had been with the platoon since it was formed at Burnham nearly a year and a half before. Six weeks earlier 35 of them, including himself, had arrived in Greece. He smiled inwardly as Smith lit a cigarette and positioned it in the corner of his mouth. Corkhill and Glover stood together, their bond forged at Kokkinopoulos still strong; Reilly, eager as always, wore his usual look of anticipation. Their names, faces and characters were as familiar now to Rankin as if he had known them all his life. And the ring-ins, a mixture of drivers, mechanics, pioneers and labourers. Despite Nicholson's misgivings, they now made up nearly half the manpower of the platoon. If they're all half as effective as Graham, Rankin thought to himself, they'll do alright.

"I don't want to make a speech," he said, to which he heard the inevitable muttered reply, "But you're going to anyway."

"Creforce believes the invasion will start tomorrow. Every one of you needs to be wide awake, listening out and looking out – for the Jerries and for each other. I'm sure you won't mistake him when he arrives." The men looking back responded with muted laughter.

"Remember Corinth. Kill him in the air. If he's alive when he hits the ground, kill him before he untangles himself. Once he's free, he's ten times more lethal."

He looked around the faces in the gloom.

"Ah, Skipper, a written order came round while you were out," one of them said. "We're s'posed to wait until the man hits the ground before opening fire."

Rankin felt his face flare. "Very well. You won't hear me contradict a direct order. But I suggest you use the paper next time you take a shit." A few laughed. "We've been over it a thousand times. Kill him before he kills you. Kill him when he can't kill you. In the air, tangled up on the ground, or hanging upside down in a bloody tree." His temple throbbed. "He will not give you a second chance."

They stared back in silence.

"Remember how it feels to hide in a hole in the ground. Remember the friends we left behind in Greece. When they get here, remember, it's time for payback."

He could see that all eyes were riveted on him as he spoke.

"Before you go off duty this evening, Sergeant Nicholson has an issue of two fresh eggs and some oranges for each of you, and I have some awards."

He fished in his pocket and pulled out the oilcloth packages.

"Smithy," he said, "and Tub." Looking awkward, the two stepped forward and came to attention. After saluting and shaking hands, they each took a proffered packet.

"And one more. Driver Graham, come forward."

Astonished, Graham stood to attention and snapped off something very close to a regulation salute.

Smith and Sutherland unwrapped their packets to each find a brass profile of a Puma eight-wheeled armoured car, about an inch and a half long, with a pin and clip soldered to the back. Inscribed on each were the words "Kokkinopolous, Greece, 17 April 1941".

When Graham opened his, he found the snub-nosed profile of a canvas covered 15-hundredweight Canadian Military Pattern truck, inscribed "Monemvasia, Greece, 29 April 1941". He stared at Rankin, eyes glittering in the fading light.

"For the meritorious use of a truck as an offensive weapon, Graham," Rankin concluded.

17 May 1941

The pounding went on for what seemed like hours. Their hillside was sprayed with bullets and cannon shells as the Luftwaffe ferociously attacked 22 Battalion's position on the crest of the hill above them.

Rankin's gut was in knots, threatening to heave its contents into the bottom of his trench. His head pounded and his temple throbbed. Aircraft roared, whistled and whined overhead on their way to or from the airfield. The sky and the view in all directions was obliterated by drifting dust and smoke; the air stank of high explosive and burning wreckage; the very ground beneath them shuddered and bucked, indeed heaved as if the earth itself was in torment. He cowered at the bottom of the trench, grasping his rifle for dear life, fingers white with the force of the grip, while at the same time clasping it to his body in order to keep the dirt out of it. Time passed infinitely slowly, measured in bangs, rattles and jarring shocks rather than hours or days, slower even than time spent in the dentist's chair.

Dirt and dust rained down and covered everything, got into everything. Inside his shirt, his nostrils, his ears, even inside his boots. How dirt and tiny pebbles could get inside tightly laced boots and gaiters he had no idea. Beyond the trench, clods and stones pattered down amongst the vines and branches, thrown high by whatever was landing on the top of the hill, while near misses whipped leaf and twig and foliage shredded by blast and shrapnel fluttered down like green snow.

Then, silence.

Or had he just gone deaf?

Rankin looked at his watch: 0830. The bombardment had lasted two hours.

Heads started to cautiously appear above ground level. Despite the sound and fury, the only damage was to an enamel bowl. Dropped by someone when the siren up the valley sounded, it now had a hole in it. Although the hillside had been liberally sprayed and peppered, Rankin wondered if the Germans had actually been aiming at anything, or whether their position simply collected overs from the strafing runs against the more clearly defined targets, the airfield itself and the unfortunate occupants of the battalion HQ on top of the hill.

"Jeesus," he said to Nicholson, pointing. "Something's cut the bamboo in half over there." A lengthy stretch of the bamboo lining the opposite riverbank was now a line of shattered, splintered poles pointing skywards. Their feathery tops were gone, and they all stood at different heights. "What the hell did that?"

No multi-coloured parachutes blossomed in the sky, no gliders swooped low, no aircraft engines throbbed in the distance, signalling the approach of transport aircraft in great numbers. Instead, there was silence.

The heads he could see started to turn this way and that, checking they were alive, their mates were alive, and if the sky was empty. No swarm of Jerries were rushing up the road.

"Bugger me," he heard Smith call out. "Herman's late. Must have heard about the reception committee, Skipper. Lost his nerve."

"Stopped for a second plate of sausage, I shouldn't wonder."

"Still got all day," someone called back.

Comments rose across the position. Rankin blew his whistle and called for silence.

"Hear anything, Corky?"

"No sir, nothing."

"Right, we'll get on with the day's work, then, won't we?" he said.

The hillside let out a collective groan.

Around the hillside, men held out their hands, exclaiming, "See? I bloody told you they wouldn't come!" and collected their bets. Those that had bet on the official position, invasion on May 17, muttered bitterly about those in charge and dug into their pockets.

"Fuck those bastards," a voice wailed. "I was saving those eggs and now they're smashed!"

19 May 1941

At dusk Rankin led a five-man patrol along the track through the vineyards past the village of Vlakheronitissa. The first tactical exercise was to see if they could surprise the church bell tower lookout; Rankin was gratified to hear Gibson's voice shout out that he had a man dead in his sights, and if the silly blighter took another step, he'd drill him through the space where his brain ought to be.

Rankin called Gibson and his spotter in and sent them back to the platoon position for dinner. It was hard to maintain vigilance, they all agreed, in the face of continued air attack and without the ability to fight back. "It'll come soon enough," was the constant response. Even the little exercises were wearing thin.

The patrol continued along the track up the valley and over

the saddle into the neighbouring valley and down the dusty hill track until they came to the rear of 21 Battalion's position. Again, the sentry was awake, the challenge was given from the gathering gloom, and answered. They passed through to find 23 Battalion's area.

Rankin made his way to Anderson's billet while the men sought out a mug of tea and some friendly faces.

"What ho, look what the wind's blown in," Anderson said to Pyne, who was sitting on a crate across from him. He turned to Rankin, "What are you up to?"

"Patrol. It's getting harder and harder to keep them motivated," Rankin replied, pushing his helmet to the back of his head and wiping his brow. "They've had a gutsful of sitting around getting bombed and shot at but not allowed to shoot back. Half the blokes don't think it'll happen at all."

"You don't have to tell me, mate," Anderson sighed. "It's getting harder and harder by the day to restrain myself from firing a single shot and dispatching the Dimwit to pastures green. Several times I've seriously contemplated where to shoot him and concluded that a shot to the head would be a waste of a bullet. Fired into vacant space."

"Huh, that's exactly what one of my blokes said about someone else a few hours ago," said Rankin. "What's he done now?"

Pyne's face creased with laughter. "I used to think you two were making it up. I have to confess, I'm not so sure now."

"Nothing," Anderson said morosely in answer to Rankin's question. "That's the problem. There seems to be no urgency about anything. I have had to practise movement along the designated route to the airfield several times with parties of my own platoon, not allowed to take the whole platoon. We're not doing company manoeuvres in case we're spotted from the air. Chances are we'll do it for real in the middle of the night, with all sorts of shit flying, yet there's no urgency to make the men get to know every nook and cranny along the way. We should be doing battalion-strength night exercises, but there doesn't seem to be any appetite there, either."

"How's Nellie?" asked Rankin. "I hope you've calmed him down after your last outburst."

"Oh, he's alright. Poor blighter had to distribute the order that went round forbidding the men to fire at Jerry coming down by parachute," said Pyne, pushing a wayward strand of fringe away from his face. "I kept it to myself."

"So did I," said Anderson. "Bloody imbecilic."

"I told them to use it to wipe their arses," Rankin said. "By the way, how did Bernard like his souvenir of Kokkinopolous?"

"Tickled pink he was. Called it the 'Order of the Fire-spitting Cat'," said Pyne. "He at least can be relied on to do things with a sense of urgency. So can old McKenzie, but there's only so much an adjutant can do."

"Yes. Pity he's not the boss," said Anderson.

"I don't know if you've heard," Pyne said. "The word is that the RAF has admitted defeat. They flew their last aeroplanes off to Egypt today."

"I hope the bloody erks got on a boat and went with them," Rankin muttered.

"I didn't read that in the *Crete News*," Anderson said, picking a copy off the table. "It did have a cracking story about a cricket match. The conditions were not ideal: the outfield was slowed somewhat by a shower of cannon shells, which roughed up the boundary. The Heraklion Hercules were unable to score any fours down the leg side, thus ceding the game to the Chania Crushers."

"Yes, I saw that," replied Rankin. "The only truck belonging to the whole of 5 Brigade delivered our copies this afternoon. The blokes thought it was wonderful."

CHAPTER FIVE

The Hammer of Thor, 20 May 1941

THE LUFTWAFFE'S EARLY morning wake-up call followed its recent pattern: vigorous and noisy, showering them with dirt and hiding the blue sky behind the drifting curtain of dust and smoke. Emerging from the protective earth, the men started their early morning rituals: shaking off the dirt, lighting cigarettes, scooping fallen dirt from the trenches, piddling up against a nearby tree. With breakfast preparations underway, renewed wailing of the distant siren came as an unwelcome surprise.

"Fuck! I haven't made me brew," a voice complained.

"Get under cover and keep an ear out!" shouted Nicholson.

"I'll give five to one; today's the day," called a voice from up the hill.

"I'll swing for him when this raid's over," muttered Nicholson as Gardiner's offer was scorned or accepted by a rowdy chorus of voices.

A bang from the top of the hill behind them was followed by a pair of Junkers 88s, trailing their distinctive whistling roar and thin lines of blue smoke, hurtling out over the dry Tavronitis. Rankin secured the chinstrap of his helmet and peered over the lip of the trench to see that everyone was back under cover. The morning routine had hardly varied lately, and the risk was that the men would become complacent.

The platoon HQ site did not allow observation along the whole length of the platoon's position; the two section corporals on the flanks had practical autonomy over fighting their own area. Rankin went over it all in his head, for the thousandth time. The terraces on the hillside were planted in vines and fruit trees. The grapes were sturdy, shrubby plants on thick trunks three to four feet high and ran the length of the lower terraces, usually two or three rows to each terrace. While they provided good cover, getting over or through them in a hurry was not simple. Visibility was reasonable along the line of the vines, but a man could lurk unseen a few feet away on the other side of the row.

Olives and citrus trees grew in other parts of the terraces, such as around the platoon HQ area. These presented their own problems. Bright light alternated with deep shadow, meaning a man who kept stock still in the shadow could remain invisible to a man in the bright light. Plunging out of the brilliant sunshine into the shadows under the trees left a man half blind in the gloom.

The terraces themselves posed another problem. The height difference (often six feet or more) created large dead areas when looking either up or down to the next terrace, and the rough earthen banks, often overgrown, were difficult to climb. The lower slope of the hillside ended with a narrow flat strip of land before the dry, shingly riverbed that was filled with scrub and low plant cover. The far bank of the river was lined mostly with bamboo and was virtually impenetrable from the platoon's side of the river. Rankin and Nicholson had practised movement and search and concealment in these conditions since they arrived. He prayed to God that it had been sufficient to keep some of them, at least, alive.

"Poor bastards on the hilltop getting it again," Reilly shouted above the noise, dragging Rankin back to the present.

"Just be thankful you're down here and not up there," Rankin replied, hastily withdrawing his head below the rim of the trench and trying to squeeze his body into a ball smaller than his helmet rim.

More aircraft howled past. More whistles, bangs, crumps and rattles followed them. The air filled anew with dust and palls of smoke rose in columns from beyond the hillside, towards the sea.

Rankin's gut felt tied in knots; this was not the usual pattern.

A rattling roar passed just over his head, followed by a shrieking whistle. The ground shook and bucked, earth sprang from the sides of the trench and clods and stones rained down onto his helmet.

A large clod struck him on the shoulder. "Jesus!"

Silence. The hillside was shrouded in its own brown fog.

"Blue? Blue! Where are you?"

The shout was followed by a shriek. "Blue! Blue! Where the fuck are you?"

Rankin scrambled out of the trench and ran to the sound – Trevor Kennelly, one of the ring-ins, knelt at the rim of a hole in the ground, screaming. Rankin peered into the hole, still wreathed in whitish, acrid smoke. Amongst a few tattered scraps of material and battered kit, a single boot with its sole half torn off lay on its side in the dirt at the bottom. The lace was tied, the foot still inside.

He rocked back on his heels. There was hardly a leaf on the

trees for yards around. Tree trunks had been splintered and tossed aside. The trench had taken a direct hit.

Realisation finally dawned on Kennelly. Friends, he and Blue normally shared a trench; but the second raid that morning had caught them off guard and out of position.

"Bugger it!" Rankin swore. Blue was his first air raid casualty, and he could not remember the man's surname. Rankin dragged him, sobbing, to his feet. "Get back under cover," he shouted, propelling Kennelly towards the hole he had come from.

More bangs and crumps sounded from the direction of the airfield. As Rankin bolted for his own trench, a Messerschmitt roared past from the direction of the airfield. He threw himself flat behind a chaotic pile of olive branches and glimpsed the shadowy shark-like shape through the surrounding brown veil.

"Christ, Skipper, what was that all about?" asked Reilly when Rankin tumbled into their trench.

"Bomb. In a trench," he panted.

"Jesus." Reilly shrank back into the dirt at the bottom of the hole.

"Would have been quick, at least," said Rankin, still angry with himself as he scrambled upright. "And get that bloody Tommy gun inside the trench before something smacks it in half."

Reilly flinched and retreated to the end of the pit, dragging the gun by its sling.

It's not his fault you can't remember Blue's name, Rankin thought to himself, shocked by Reilly's reaction. Aloud, he said, "Keep it out of the dirt, son, and make sure the safety's on."

SILENCE AT LAST. He looked at his watch: 0815. Just over two hours. It had seemed an age. Men emerged from their burrows, heads cautiously turning this way and that, eyes darting in every direction. The raid had added to the chaos within their perimeter: uprooted vines, branches ripped from tree trunks and flung across terraces, bomb craters scattered about with raw earth. Foliage was gone from some places, stripped by blast – clearing their view, but also reducing their cover.

The HQ area was a shambles. A second bomb had destroyed or flung away anything not tied down, leaving a gaping crater where a tree had stood. The terrace embankment had given way in several places, spewing rocks, earth and tangled vegetation downhill.

The feeling of shock among the men was palpable. There was none of the usual banter. Rankin surveyed the damage; two bombs had landed on top of them. Had they been aimed or were they unlucky overshoots?

Opaque brown clouds, full of the stink of explosives and burning, drifted past. Cloying and smothering, slowly they began to dissipate, giving glimpses of the clear morning sky.

Rankin cleaned the muck from his nostrils, ears and eyes, shook the small pebbles out of his shirt and brushed the soil from his skin. He then cleaned out his rifle before retrieving his small pack, brushing it down, and checking the precious telescopic sight was undamaged in its case.

The bamboo across the riverbed emerged from the fine brown haze. Everywhere dirt-covered men crawled tentatively from their holes, like animals emerging from a brown hibernation. Rankin heard a runner arrive from his left flank. Lawrence's report, no casualties. No word yet from Johnstone on the right.

His head was ringing. Surely now it should be two or three hours before the next raid. Time to put things back in order and get the men focused.

"Phone to both sections and 22 Battalion out, Skipper. I'll have to go and find the breaks," McIntyre called out. Not surprising, but now they were out of contact with everyone.

Shocked silence slowly gave way to the sounds of men getting themselves together, ready to start the day: urinating on the ground, dry retching, lighting cigarettes, telling nervous jokes.

From higher up the hill, over the subdued chatter, Corkhill yelled: "Skipper, listen! Quiet! Shut up, you blokes!"

Talk stopped mid-sentence. A low, throbbing hum, like a distant swarm of millions of bees, was rising and falling on the air waves.

Nicholson looked at him. Rankin was rooted to the spot, mouth open, straining. The throbbing hum got louder.

Right in front of them, a shadow flitted over the riverbed, a shape swished along beneath the brown veil, first above the bamboo, then low down above the rocks and stones.

"Jesus, some bugger's bought it!"

The throbbing got louder.

Rankin stared at the shape. It flattened out just above the dry riverbed, then hit the gravel and bushes and slithered to a halt in a cloud of dust about 200 yards away.

"Hey, look, here comes another one," a voice called.

Corinth!

"Gliders! Jesus, it's on!" he screamed at the top of his voice. "Fire! Fire! Get them before they get out!" Desperately dragging his whistle out of his shirt pocket, he blew it with all his might.

Pandemonium broke out. Some men who were out of their

126

trenches leapt back into them; others simply raised their rifles where they stood. Others had to race back to their positions. Shots cracked out, first singly, followed by many more, then quickly becoming a sustained fusillade.

An opening in the side of the first glider suddenly appeared, filled by the figure of a man. He disappeared as bullets peppered the glider, kicking up the dust around it. Away to the right a Bren gun chattered.

Another glider skidded along the riverbed downstream towards Fergusson's platoon. It had hardly shuddered to a halt before it was surrounded by dust spurts, and seemed to wilt, like a cut flower, the wing sagging into the stones. He heard the solid boom of a Boys rifle. "That'll shake 'em," Rankin muttered, snapping his own telescopic sight onto Albert's mounting.

More gliders appeared through the haze drifting inland from the airfield, thumping down along the riverbed and slithering into the dry gravel and dust. Those that landed closest to the far side of the river disgorged their loads, figures scrambling and scurrying into the bamboo and brush pursued by dust spurts. Those nearer the occupied bank and hillside were riddled as they landed. When a door did open, a couple of figures would fall out of it and lie still, the glider's fabric fuselage shredded by gunfire.

Rankin, Nicholson, and the two corporals ran among the platoon, shrieking above the noise, focusing the men. The first bullets began to strike from the opposite bank. They needed to cajole the inexperienced back into cover.

As he dashed back to the platoon's command position, something made Rankin look up as he jumped into the trench. A stately procession of aircraft was passing overhead, dark against the blue sky, unheard in the mounting gunfire but seen between the trees and leaves through the drifting haze.

"Jesus Christ Almighty," he breathed. The young Scot, McIntyre, only yards away in the communications trench, was concentrating his rifle fire on the far riverbank. Rankin scrambled to him, bullets whistling and whining over their heads, shook him by the shoulder, pointing, yelling: "Look up! Look up! Parachutes!"

A team from a glider that had landed close to the opposite bank must have managed to get a machine gun into position. Bursts of machine-gun fire ripped through any remaining foliage overhead and thwacked into nearby tree trunks, sparking and whining off the stones in the terrace walls. The planting that had hidden them from the Luftwaffe now hid the parachutes falling from the sky.

Rankin yelled above the din for Tub and Smith to find the gun and clean it out. He had no idea whether they could hear him or not. Probably not. But within seconds .50 calibre rounds boomed out from left and right, both rifles hopefully aimed on the muzzle flash from the Spandau. There was no time to see if they were effective.

The noise drowned out the throb of the Junkers 52 transports passing sedately overhead, flying in groups of three, coming over the crest of the hill on a course parallel to the coast. The planes flew right over the top of them, disgorging their loads in long strings of wavering, oscillating blobs below the blossoming mushrooms, before turning towards the sea.

Rankin blew his whistle again, another long blast, and yelled to look up. Rifles banged and popped, men excitedly pointing and shouting at the parachutes coming down over their heads.

Rankin was out of his trench, oblivious to the risk from the opposite bank, standing in the open in a gap between two trees, giving him a clear view of the sky above, firing at each figure appearing in his sights. Some jumped and thrashed as they fell, others hung still, plummeting towards the ground. Some fired back. He rested the rifle on a broken branch, crouching behind it, focused on a string of parachutes floating into view; most of them were a dirty-white, but others appeared pastel-coloured. Aim and fire, aim and fire, aim and fire, until they disappeared from sight.

"Aim at their feet!" he shrieked, as loud as he could, above the roar of rifle and machine-gun fire.

"Duck shooting season," shouted an excited voice nearby. "Opening day!"

"Better late than never," shouted another happy voice, followed by a gunshot. "Been waiting ever since Greece for this, you bastard!"

Some soldiers scrambled up the hill to stand on the terrace edges in order to get a better shot. They were yelling and shouting, joking, calling out to their friends, firing and firing. Parachutists began hitting the ground all around them, some to crumple into the grass and lie still, others to be clubbed down by a swinging rifle butt before they could get to their feet. Screams, shouts, pandemonium, chaos, death.

"That's another bastard, dead on arrival!" Rankin heard from nearby.

The Luftwaffe might have been disappointed at the results of their bombardment. Far from sapping morale and cowering the defence, the attack had galvanised them. Action instead of lying in a hole; meting it out instead of taking it; the rising bloodlust well fuelled by the long frustration of waiting. It was as if the Germans were descending into the middle of a burning, boiling, crackling cauldron, whose flames licked upwards to consume them.

Just as he was aiming at a figure under a canopy, in the air, less than 100 yards away, there was a crash, a grunt, and what sounded like swearing. A pair of boots crashed through the branches behind him.

"Jesus Christ, a fuckin' parachutist," yelped McIntyre from a few yards away. As the man hit the ground, the canopy collapsed and he landed awkwardly, off balance, falling on his side as the parachute draped itself across the tree.

Trying to drag his helmet back from his eyes, the parachutist let out what could only be a string of oaths aimed at McIntyre.

"What's he saying, Skipper? What's he wantin' me to do?"

"Shoot the bastard!" Rankin shouted. The man struggled with his parachute as the breeze tugged it over the tree, pulling him after it. He had a knife in one hand, and was trying to gather the lines, attached to a ring on his back, with the other. He got himself onto both knees, back towards Rankin.

McIntyre was rooted to the spot.

The knife dropped; he scrabbled in his smock.

Rankin worked the bolt of his rifle, pointed it at the man and pulled the trigger. Nothing happened.

Empty! For the love of Christ!

"Shoot the bastard!" Rankin screamed again, as the man desperately dragged a Luger pistol out of his jacket. He was half off his knees, struggling to his feet, hampered by his harness.

Rankin launched himself at the man's back, driving the muzzle and foresight into his kidneys with all his weight, knocking him sprawling. He went down with an agonised gasp, the pistol sent flying. McIntyre finally came to his senses and pointed his rifle at the German, now writing on the ground, one hand clasping his lower back, howling in pain. Rankin leapt for the pistol and knife. The young Scot was deathly pale but kept the wavering rifle pointed in the man's direction, while keeping his distance.

"Pull the fucking trigger!" Rankin screamed at him, enraged.

McIntyre was still pointing his rifle at the man, immobilised, while Rankin reloaded his rifle with a clip from his web pouch.

"He's unarmed, Skipper," wailed McIntyre.

The man on the ground turned to look at Rankin, who motioned to him to clear himself from his parachute. The German staggered to his feet, pale, bent at the waist, clearly in pain, and began to struggle with the harness. Rankin thought he was stalling and shouted angrily, "Schneller, schneller!" and gave him another solid poke with the rifle. The German protested loudly, gave him an evil look followed by another barrage of angry German.

After what had seemed to take an age, eventually he was free. Rankin used the man's knife to cut a section out of his lines and motioned him to shed his helmet, smock, and boots. Then, forcing him at gunpoint to stand against the tree in which he had landed, Rankin tied the man's arms behind him to a branch. The German continued to protest bitterly , no doubt telling Rankin the niceties of the Geneva convention, until Rankin jammed the barrel of the Luger hard into his neck.

"Shut it, or I'll bloody shut it for you," he hissed.

"Sorry, Skipper," wailed McIntyre, close to tears.

"Pull the bloody trigger next time and we might still be alive tonight."

He looked about. The sky was empty. It had taken far too long.

"They must have all landed," Rankin said to McIntyre. "You come with me."

Gunfire popped and banged all over the hillside. Nothing was coming from across the river: they couldn't fire now, for fear of hitting their own.

"You take the inner lane, Mac," Rankin said, much more gently, pointing towards the earth bank separating the terrace from the one above. "Remember how we practised this? How to look out and how to keep in contact with me?" McIntyre nodded dubiously; Rankin prayed that the rudimentary training the signaller had received would be sufficient.

They edged along the hillside towards the right flank according to their plan, which called for Nicholson to patrol towards the left flank with Reilly while Rankin went right. The sound of shooting was all around them. Any movement among the vines was nerve-racking.

On more than one occasion, a rustling, billowing parachute caused a panicky dive for cover. Away on the flank facing towards Fergusson's platoon, a Bren gun rattled. "Bloxham," Rankin called through the row of vines to McIntyre. "Keep your eyes peeled."

Bodies and parachutes littered the ground among the rows of vines and the scrubby uncultivated slope above and as the terrain offered cover for both sides, movement along the terraces took nerve and time. Making his way along the terrace, Rankin observed parachutes everywhere – draped over trees and scrub, rustling in the light breeze – mostly white but others appeared to be pastel-coloured. Despite these distractions, his greater need was to know how Johnstone's section on the right had fared. The noise coming from that flank and beyond, towards the airfield, continued as an uninterrupted roar. Was Johnstone's section intact or was he battling for his life to hold them off?

Coming to a grove of olive trees, Rankin and McIntyre kept to the shadows as they edged past more German bodies, one still attached to a parachute hung over the scrub growing up the bank near McIntyre. A white canister, about five feet long, marked with coloured bands and some printed words, had come down across the vines. Not far away two khaki-clad bodies lay, one practically toe-to-toe with a dead parachutist. Rankin's heart was hammering in his chest, mouth dry as dust; they needed to push on. There was no time to examine the canister or identify the casualties.

They came to the end of the trees on the uppermost terrace where above them scrub and spiky grass covered the uncultivated slope, which featured a rocky outcrop surrounded by several spiny cacti. As Rankin searched the area of open ground, a rifle shot banged out from a bush some 50 yards away. Up the slope, halfway to the rocky outcrop, a shape emerged from behind the scrub, fired a burst from his Schmeisser, catapulted over something hidden in the tall brown grass and disappeared.

"Ha, ha. Ya missed, Fritzy!" shouted a voice from the bush.

Rankin recognised the voice as belonging to Brian Venables, one of his originals. Another shot banged out from further along the hillside, raising a puff of dust from the German's position. Venables was not alone, it seemed.

Several more shots raised dust and stone chips from around the place where the enemy soldier had disappeared.

"Come on out, Fritzy! We know you're in there!"

A sliver of parachute smock appeared in Rankin's sight. The man must have altered position fractionally to provide better cover from whoever was taunting him further along the hillside. More dust and chips flew as bullets whined and zipped nearby.

Rankin motioned for McIntyre to move back, then climb higher, and try to winkle him out of his cover. More shots rang out, followed by another burst from the Schmeisser. Venables taunted him again.

Rankin moved further to his right. Keeping a small scrub bush between himself and the German, he leopard-crawled five yards up the slope to improve the angle.

A Schmeisser rattled from somewhere above, further up the hill. The ground in front of Rankin's rifle cracked, whined and whistled, and a cloud of dust and dirt flew into the air.

"Jesus!"

McIntyre must have broken cover; the Schmeisser's attention switched to Rankin's right. The man behind the first rock moved again, appeared in Rankin's sight and Rankin pulled his trigger. Another fusillade of gunshots erupted to his left, followed by silence.

"Who the fuck's that?" yelled Venables.

"Rankin," he shouted. "Are you alright, McIntyre?"

"I'm here, Skipper," called back a small voice.

"There's another fucker up the hill!" cried Venables.

"Keep me covered," came a voice from beyond Venables. Rankin saw a figure in a khaki shirt and British helmet rise out of the scrub and run forward. A rifle cracked from somewhere away to their right. There was no response from behind the rocks.

Rankin scrambled to his feet and ran for a tree a few yards higher up the slope. Panting with the exertion, he could see the second German further up the hill, sprawled over a rock. Venables' mate reached the first German and called out, "He's done for."

"So's the other one," Rankin replied, crouching behind his tree and searching the hillside beyond the body through his lens. "Who the hell shot him?" Rankin muttered. It couldn't have been McIntyre.

Their group now numbered four. The fourth man, he saw, was one of the ring-ins, Stephens by name. In the meantime, the volume of gunfire on the hillside had reduced so Rankin put them into a line covering the terraces, and slowly continued towards the platoon's northern flank, from where Bloxham's Bren gun could still be heard, but less frequently.

They had not gone far when McIntyre nervously called out. "Skipper, there's one of the wee plane things standin' on its nose over here." Rankin halted the patrol and cautiously climbed up to the next terrace, where McIntyre was crouched in a shadow, his rifle levelled at a wrecked glider. It appeared to Rankin to have ploughed through the olives on the terrace above, where it had lost its wings, before toppling over the bank down to the level below. It was resting on its nose, its back broken judging by the crumpled and torn fabric covering. Rankin estimated the fuselage to have been 30 feet long or so.

Peering in through the shattered cockpit, he saw a mass of tangled and crushed passengers, looking as if they had been catapulted into the front. Bloody handprints stained the door frame, the door itself lay broken on the ground. A couple of bodies among the olives a few yards away might have been the only ones to get out.

"They may be wantin' their money back, Skipper," McIntyre remarked.

The patrol resumed, but they had not gone more than 50 yards when Venables cried out in surprise from lower down the hillside.

"Hey Skipper, Jacko's here with a couple of Jerry prisoners. He's been hit."

Once again Rankin halted the patrol. Clambering down to Jackson's terrace, he found Jackson sitting with his back to the embankment, pale and sweaty, as Venables held his water bottle up to his mouth. The wounded man grimaced with pain as he greeted Rankin, "Bastards put a bullet through me foot, Skipper," he croaked. Clearly in no mood to brook any nonsense from his prisoners, he held one of their own machine pistols pointing at them. The two parachutists were propped up against an olive tree opposite, badly battered and barely conscious, their breathing coming in rasping gasps.

"At least they came off second best," Jackson added with a crooked grin.

Rankin nodded as he inspected the injured foot. The heel of the boot was shot away, with blood dripping out of it.

"Bastard got me from up there," he said, jerking his thumb toward the terrace above. "Jimmy and Phil clobbered them, then rolled them down here so's I can keep an eye on them." He was panting with the strain of it all. "They went that way," he gasped, gesturing towards the sound of the continuing uproar from beyond the curve of the hill, in the direction of Fergusson's platoon and the airfield. "There's two more of this lot," he grimaced. "I'd kill for a fag."

McIntyre knelt, lighting a cigarette for him, when Venables and Stephens started shouting and pointing to the sky. Rankin looked up. Another stately procession swept over the top of Hill 107, heading west, disgorging parachutes as it went. The planes couldn't have been very high above the top of the hill, their open doors clearly visible.

Trees and vines all along the hillside seemed to come alive, spitting fire at the passing armada. A Spandau chattered, sending a long stream of tracer which clawed its way towards, then into, one of the passing planes. By this time no one needed to be told what to do. They stood in the open and fired into the lines of descending parachutes.

"No, you fuckin' don't!" Jackson swore loudly. Rankin turned in time to see him empty the Schmeisser's magazine into the two wounded paratroopers.

"Bastards thought I wasn't watching 'em," he said grimly.

Rankin shrugged. He hadn't seen them move. They weren't going to now, either. Their smocks were riddled with new holes which leaked blood even as their eyes glazed over.

McIntyre had his rifle braced against the branch of a nearby tree, firing repeatedly into the flock of parachutes drifting serenely overhead. Rankin did the same, methodically aiming at their feet. In seconds it was over; the long train of Junkers 52s ponderously flew on and began their turn out to sea before they were lost to sight. Parachutes continued to drift down across the hillside, out over the riverbed and out of sight beyond the bamboos hiding the unguarded land to the west.

Gunfire rippled all along the hillside. Many of the parachutists that had come down on the higher slopes of Hill 107, above the area occupied by the platoon, but below 22 Battalion's perimeter, would have hidden themselves anywhere they could. Their confusion was easy to visualise; the need to hide obvious but working out where death lurked would not be easy.

"You two stay here with Jacko," Rankin said to Venables and Stephens after the armada had passed. "See what you can do for his foot and get him as comfortable as you can. Keep your eyes skinned, the pair of you. Mac and I need to check on Robbie."

"Yeah, she's all good, Skipper," Venables answered. "Any more of the buggers pop up here, we'll take care of them."

Johnstone's command post was in a trench on a terrace planted with citrus trees. His position, being further along the hillside and slightly off the line the bombers had taken as they overflew 22 Battalion's position above earlier in the day, remained largely as Rankin had previously seen it. And while there were parachutes draped over the orange and mandarin trees, and more bodies, the area had escaped bomb damage.

Rankin found Johnstone near the section command post.

"Jesus, Skipper, am I pleased to see you," he beamed as Rankin approached. "We've been going at it hammer and tongs since the first landing." He grinned from ear to ear. "Boys have given them a fair hiding."

Rankin shook him by the hand, relief flooding through his body. He was suddenly aware of how keyed up he had been.

Johnstone pointed to a glider that had crashed along the slope among the scrub and cacti in the initial landing, about 250 yards away, between their position and that of Fergusson's platoon. "Bloxy got a couple with the Bren early on, as they were getting clear of the glider, and the boys put up some steady rifle fire in their direction," he reported. "We haven't seen them since, Skipper. Parachutists that came down with the first lot out there will have survived, but the boys had the hang of it by the time the second lot came down," he concluded with a weary grin.

"I'll bet they did," Rankin chuckled. "Any casualties?"

"Yeah, a few. Fewer than we might have expected given the experience of some of them." He looked away into the distance and took a drag on his cigarette. "I think it's three killed and another couple wounded. Plus, a handful who are still game to carry on despite being hurt."

Rankin nodded. Certainly better than he feared.

"Many of the Jerries that came down on top of us were done for before they hit the ground, or very soon after," Johnstone said with a meaningful look. He pointed to the open ground towards the airfield with its billowing parachutes "Out there, and between us and 22, it'll be a different story. Plenty of them'll be alive and kicking, ready to make a bloody nuisance of themselves as soon as they sort out their arse from their elbow." He lit a cigarette and took a deep drag. "All the same, Skipper, boys are bloody chuffed. Not too many of this lot'll be doing another Heil Hitler in a hurry," he chuckled.

"You don't normally smoke, Robbie," Rankin said.

"No breakfast, Skipper. Look," he held out his hand, "bloody hand's got the hunger shakes." His hand was shaking like a leaf.

"Too much excitement, Rob," Rankin smiled.

"Yeah, before breakfast, too! It's been bloody hard yakka."

No contact with Fergusson's platoon was possible as they were too far away, across dangerous ground. From the noise that came from that direction, they were heavily engaged. Any view beyond the spur beyond the spur was impossible, obscured by the brown haze. Rankin searched for long minutes through his binoculars for a sight of anything that indicated Fergusson's platoon was still in place. Nothing moved, apart from the softly undulating parachutes. Whether they concealed a living being or a dead body he had no way of telling.

"JOHNSTONE'S HOLDING HIS own, Nick," Rankin reported as he slid into the headquarters trench on his return a good half hour later. Nicholson and Reilly, looking tense, had their weapons ready. Rankin and McIntyre had passed what seemed like dozens of bodies on their way back from Johnstone's flank, strewn through the terraces with more visible on the open hillside above.

"Just as well you called out the password, Skipper," Reilly said. "Sarge got this bugger without even leaving his pit." He jabbed a pair of boots that lay across the sandbag parapet. "Fell right into the trench. Had a bugger of a job heaving the brute out."

"All right, Tim," Nicholson said, sending him off on an errand with McIntyre. He turned to Rankin, "I've been out to Lawrence's section post and his runner has just reported the left flank clear after that last drop. Probing activity now is coming from the direction of the village."

"Casualties?"

"Confused but appears moderate. Jerries have taken a hammering, all dead or run for it. Hardly any prisoners, and reports of thirty-plus killed, but I don't know how reliable that is. There's probably more now with that second drop," Nicholson reported flatly.

"I saw a dozen or so in a wrecked glider, on the way to Johnstone's post. Crashed into the trees by the look of it. Only a couple in any condition to get out of the thing, but they didn't get far."

"You wouldn't catch me in one of those things," Nicholson muttered.

"They should sue their transport operator," Rankin replied with a smile as Reilly reappeared, holding a mug of tea. Firing had reduced to sporadic shots, and an occasional machine-gun burst from across the dry riverbed. Rankin realised he was parched.

As he sipped his tea, another wave of parachutists materialised out of a clear sky above the dirty, drifting cloud. They didn't hear the aircraft trailing their mushrooms behind them, until they were directly overhead, the noise drowned out by the background roar from the airfield. Instantly whistles blew, hoarse shouts went up from parched throats and the hillside again erupted. No orders were necessary, every man knew exactly what to do.

Rankin had barely dragged his rifle out into the open, aiming at the boots of a falling parachutist, when a Junkers aircraft clattered up the stream bed, lower than the others, trailing oily smoke. Half a dozen parachutes emerged in a cluster as the plane banked right and disappeared towards the west.

Rankin swung his rifle towards the blossoming parachutes, about the length of a rugby field away.

The parachutes snapped open mere feet above the riverbank. No sooner had Rankin got his sights on the first than the man jerked to a halt in mid-air.

"Bloody hell," Rankin cried out loud.

Magnified in his sight, the parachutist thrashed the air, caught in the broken bamboo poles. The man's arms and legs flailed, driving his body further onto the broken, razor-sharp ends of the poles, ten feet off the ground. Another, then another followed; Rankin stared in mounting horror. "Jesus Christ Almighty," he gasped, as each succeeding man crashed into the bamboo, jerking to a stop, arms and legs thrashing in the macabre ballet of a demented marionette. Sick to his stomach, Rankin could not tear his eyes away. Mercifully, in seconds the parachutes silently descended over the thrashing figures, shrouding them from view.

He dry-retched, leaning against a tree. "Jesus Christ Almighty," he repeated softly.

He looked back, unable to believe what he had just witnessed. Sure enough, the whole lot had gone into the bamboo, their parachutes strung up among the shattered poles like so much dirty washing.

"Are you alright, Skipper?" This from Reilly, kneeling by his side. "You haven't been hit, have you?"

Rankin dragged his eyes away, shaking his head dumbly. "No, Tim. I'm alright."

The defending troops were well versed in the drill by now; once the drop was complete and the targets in the air were on the ground, the men fanned out along the terraces singly, or in pairs, and hunted them down. For once they had something of the advantage; they knew the lay of the land, they understood how the light played tricks amongst the trees, and they knew how difficult it was to flee through the vines. It was, they also soon discovered, deceptively easy for a parachutist to feign death and shoot or toss a grenade at close range when your back was turned.

The fighting on the ground was brief and brutal. A deadly game of cat and mouse developed among the vines and olives resulting in few prisoners. Many of those hanging from a tree or pitched lifeless on the ground received another bullet for good measure. Numbers of the defenders were now armed with German sub-machine guns and the ubiquitous Lugers. Highly prized as souvenirs, these compact weapons went into assorted pockets, while the Schmeissers slaughtered the parachutists still in the air or strung up among the trees. Those who managed to hit the ground and begin struggling out of their harnesses were shot at in wantonly long bursts, with ammunition easily replenished from the pouches worn by the dead. Any movement at all drew fire and rustling parachutes were no exception. Target identification at close quarters posed difficulties. How many were shot, on both sides, by their own comrades would be known only by God.

Fewer parachutists had come down directly over the platoon position in this drop. Those who survived the landing hurriedly went to ground. They only had to look about them to see what fate had in store if they lingered. They quickly disappeared, leaving behind their canisters of equipment, ammunition and other supplies.

Order of sorts was soon restored and once it appeared that only the dead or disabled remained within their perimeter, Rankin made his way back to the platoon's HQ area. He found it deserted except for McIntyre, who was bent over his telephone exchange.

"Keeping a good lookout, Mac?" Rankin asked.

The Scot leapt upright and lunged for his rifle. "Jesus, Skipper, you scared the be-Jesus oot o' me!"

Rankin laughed, nodding at the telephone pack. "I'll bet that doesn't work."

"Not a single line. All cut." He held up the handpiece, "Bliddy useless."

Rankin jumped into the other end of McIntyre's trench and slumped to the ground. Pushing his helmet back from his forehead, he wiped an arm across his brow. "Well, Mac, we're not going to try and fix it now. Far too bloody dangerous, especially the line to 22 Battalion." He took his helmet off and ran his fingers through his sweat-damp hair. "It'll be crawling with Jerries up to 22's wire. Assuming they're still up there," he added bleakly. His mood had changed since the incident with parachutists impaled in the bamboo. Somehow, that episode had demonstrated the pointlessness of it all, that their apparent success seemed too good to last.

"Like Al Capone and his gangsters," Reilly enthused when he returned to the HQ area, beaming from ear to ear. He now also sported a German sub-machine gun slung round his neck, along with a sort of bandolier that held a dozen magazines for it.

"Look at these, Skipper," he said, dropping half a dozen packets marked 'Esbit' on the ground beside Rankin. "What do you reckon these are?"

Rankin opened the waxed cardboard packet and pulled out a flat metal box the size of a large cigarette tin wrapped in greaseproof paper. He turned it over in his hands and ripped off the paper cover. The two ends broke open at a coarse serration midway along one side. Inside was a waxed paper packet with pictures: fuel tablets. An impression had been stamped into the floor, exactly the size of one of the tablets. "Well, I'll be buggered," Rankin said. "Look at that, it's a cooker. Legs fold down; and these are fuel tablets, see?"

He set it on the ground by the lip of McIntyre's signal trench. "No more fires for a brew up, Tim. You won't miss that."

"Care for coffee, Neil?" asked Nicholson, walking into the platoon HQ area holding a thermos flask. "Hot coffee, packed in Berlin along with a Spandau, spare barrels, ammunition in boxes, food and some medical kit."

Rankin examined the thermos, marvelling that it had been brought with the Germans, landed by parachute. He took the metal cup off the top, opened the flask and poured it into the cup. By a miracle it was still warm, smelled divine and tasted fabulous. It reminded him, with a jolt, of Dada's coffee, a lifetime ago. He leaned back against the side of the trench, sighed, and took another sip.

Soon afterwards Duggan arrived to report that their area was clear. "Look at the gear the buggers have got," he muttered, glancing enviously at the thermos as Rankin refilled his cup. "No wonder they're winning the war."

"Cheer up, Duggie," said Reilly, grinning. "Have a cooker. Stick your dixie on that next time you brew up. Courtesy of Uncle Herman." He threw him a stove in its packet.

"Brew up!" scoffed Duggan. "Brew up! Chance would be a fine thing, with Jerries falling like the leaves in autumn. If you're so pally with Uncle Herman, tell 'im to drop us a load of shovels. Going to fuckin' stink here tomorrow."

"Shit, I hadn't thought of that," said Reilly.

"Trouble with you young blokes, you never bloody think," said Duggan, stumping back towards his position.

CHAPTER SIX

Tavronitis River, 20 May 1941 (Afternoon)

RUNNERS FROM BOTH section leaders had reported their areas clear and the perimeter secure. Safe for the moment, Nicholson and Rankin sat in the communications trench with McIntyre, sharing a tin of bully beef that they washed down with water from a bucket Nicholson had bought a few days earlier. The volume of gunfire nearby had died down, but the steady roar from the airfield continued unabated.

"There are hardly any prisoners, Neil. Battalion needs prisoners." Nicholson's face wore a worried expression. "They stressed the need for Huns to interrogate."

"It's not that bloody easy, Nick. I tied one to a tree up the hill a bit. He's lucky he's only got kidney failure ... isn't he, Mac?"

McIntyre's face flared red under the grime.

"He'll be pissing blood for a week," Rankin said.

"Och, I need to go out and find the breaks in the wire," McIntyre said.

"You'll do no such thing," said Nicholson, glaring at him. "Who knows how many of the blighters there are between us and Battalion?"

"Sarge is right, Mac," said Rankin, who had seen the momentary flash of anger and frustration cross the Scot's face. He turned back to Nicholson. "What patrols have gone out, Nick?"

"As per the plan. Patrols have gone out beyond the perimeter to gauge the situation and hopefully bring back some prisoners," Nicholson replied. "There's been no contact with Gibson, so we don't know how things stand in the village." He nodded towards McIntyre's field telephone. "And, as you know, the phone's dead, so we've had no contact with 22 Battalion HQ."

"Right. We can't contact Fergusson's platoon to the north, either. Johnstone reports Jerries out there, but we don't know how many," Rankin said. "There's too much open country to risk an attempt to link up."

Nicholson nodded; his brow deeply furrowed.

"Our priority is to keep the track towards Khamoudhokhori and the AMES station open," Rankin said, trying to sound more positive than he felt. "I'll take the patrol up there. It would be handy to know what Gibson's seen, though."

"Lawrence's section has sent patrols out that way. We'll know more when they get back. If they can get through to Vlakhy-whatsit, that is. And we have no idea what's going on over there." Nicholson shot a worried look across the river, beyond the line of parachutes snagged on the bamboo.

"Crawling with Jerries, I should think – landed unopposed. And causing trouble over there," Rankin nodded towards the airfield, "judging by the din coming from the aerodrome."

Nicholson nodded glumly. "I suppose so."

Rankin glanced at Nicholson. "C'mon, cheer up, Nick. Johnstone's got the northern perimeter in hand, but we'd need half the platoon to push a patrol out to Fergusson, and we don't have them. Some of the patrols will have been combined due to casualties, so let's focus on our primary objective: keeping the track to 21 Battalion open for a counter-attack when it's needed."

"I suppose so," Nicholson said, still nodding.

"You stay here, Nick – take over till I get back. Get Mac out to fix the lines to section posts when Reilly comes back from doing whatever he can for the wounded with Corky. Reilly can keep him covered, but only let them go if there's someone else here to cover you. Otherwise, they stay put, understood?" Nicholson nodded; McIntyre rolled his eyes.

"I'll take these fine, keen blokes to Khamoudhokhori and see what we can see." Rankin gestured to an engineer named Seddon, waiting under a tree with Glover, both cradling German Schmeissers, and McNulty, a mechanic, with a rifle.

"Where did you say that Hun prisoner was?" Nicholson asked.

Rankin pointed up the slope as he climbed out of the communications trench and hurried off with Glover and the other two.

————

FLUTTERING PARACHUTES RUSTLED in the light breeze. They passed a number of dead parachutists and several khaki humps lying in the grass on the way to the perimeter in Lawrence's southern sector. Mitchell, in his slit trench with his Bren gun and loader on the platoon's flank, made the challenge. He reeled off the patrols that had already passed through their perimeter.

Rankin's heart was pounding and every sense was on high alert as they made their way along the hillside parallel to the road leading to the village of Vlakheronitissa. They had not gone far before they came across more bodies strewn through the plantation. Canisters, still attached to their coloured parachutes, lay broken open, the contents scattered on the ground. It occurred to Rankin that the colour of the parachute probably indicated its contents to the intended recipient: whoever had ransacked these had only been interested in weapons and ammunition and discarded the rest.

A short way further, as they skirted around the southwestern slope of Hill 107, McNulty spotted a glider that had crash-landed on the track that led up the valley towards Khamoudhokhori. Searching with his binoculars, Rankin saw several mounds lying near it, but no sign of movement. Beyond was the village of Vlakheronitissa, which lay on the southern side of the shallow valley. Parachutes draped its whitewashed walls, stone yards and terracotta tiled roofs. More were scattered through the trees and vines across the valley floor. The village, and the surrounding orchards and vineyards, seemed asleep. Any figures he could see were too far away to identify, even through binoculars. Nevertheless, the crackle and pop of gunfire was evidence enough of the deadly game being played out in a scene of the utmost bucolic beauty.

Rounding the foot of the spur, they followed the contour leading towards Khamoudhokhori to the east. Beyond this point, the hillside was terraced, similar to the platoon's position overlooking the Tavronitis. Rankin thanked God again that they had practised movement along the terraces before the landing. It was tedious and difficult, however, and extremely nerve-racking. A patrol with a man on each terrace had proved the most effective, if you had the men. But in reality each man was on his own, communicating by low calls or whistles to the man on the next terrace, above or below.

It was not long before Seddon, on the terrace above Rankin, reported a body. Stripped of his boots and jump smock, the man had been shot several times, but the coup de grâce appeared to have been delivered by something sharp. Presumably whoever had killed him had taken his weapons and kit. Like all the others they had seen in the morning, he was dressed in the blue-grey uniform of the Luftwaffe. Rankin was surprised that he still wore his watch.

Spread out across the terraces, the men found the going painfully slow. It took forever to move forward, keeping to the shadows of every tree they passed, accompanied by the gut-wrenching fear that even now someone had them in their sights.

Rankin was searching the ground ahead from the shadow of a tree, when Seddon, above him to his left, crouching behind a flowering bush near the edge of the terrace whistled a warning. Rankin hurriedly found a spot concealed by scrub and clambered up the five feet or so join him. Within a few moments they spotted three men between two lines of trees dragging something. They looked to be about 50 yards ahead of the New Zealanders and like themselves were using the trees and shade as protective cover.

Rankin signalled Seddon to lie flat and keep a lookout while he crawled further across the terrace to his left. Kneeling behind a gnarled old olive tree, he cautiously brought the rifle to his shoulder. A sudden shout and a commotion from higher up the hill were followed by a gunshot and a burst of automatic fire. The three men to Rankin's front instantly went to ground. Rankin gripped the rifle tight, knuckles white, keeping the lens steady and not moving a muscle. All his years hunting rabbits, mostly at night, had taught him how to stay as still as a corpse and be patient. The quarry would eventually reappear, sometimes to hop past just a few feet away. And there it was! A minute later a pale smudge appeared in the shady gloom. A face, only half visible, like the crescent moon peering through the clouds.

From higher up the hill came more shouting and firing. Rankin shrank himself further into the shadows, steadying the rifle in a crook of the tree. The smudge had moved with the distraction, but now it was back, topped by the flat rim of its helmet, in Rankin's sight. A pair of Schmeissers chattered among the olives in front of him – the man in front's companions, firing blind, Rankin hoped. Bullets whistled through the foliage and thudded harmlessly into the top of the terrace embankment to his left. He fought the urge to move and hide.

He had not seen muzzle flash or movement: surely, they must be the other two with the canister. Had they seen something? Or were they just jumping at shadows, shooting blind at the noises that came from further up the hill? The first man had not moved, the rest of the head still obscured by grass. Was he talking to someone? Rankin strained with the effort of searching and listening, every sense stretched taut as a fence wire with fear.

He squeezed the trigger and in return bullets thudded and thwacked into the trees nearby. Most of the bursts had gone high, through the leaves and twigs above his head. Rankin crawled away through the grass, cautiously coming to his knees behind another tree. He peered around the trunk.

It was a very deadly game; every time he raised his head or looked around a corner, he could come face to face with the enemy.

More shouts and gunshots echoed from up the slope. Glover and McNulty were up there, somewhere. Sustained firing sounded lower down the valley, to the right. Jesus Christ! Who the hell was that?

Rankin crouched motionless in the shadow of a tree and searched the area where the three with the canister had originally gone to ground. It took a huge effort, holding the rifle steady, his hands shaking, hardly daring to breathe, to keep the scene steady in the sight.

Then movement! A leaf on a twig sprang back, a hand and sleeve entered a chink of light filtering down through the trees. Estimating where the torso was from the position of the hand in the lens, Rankin fired and immediately dropped to the ground. There was no answering burst from the Schmeissers.

He crawled back to Seddon, keeping to the dark shadows under the trees, and softly whistled to him to follow. They retreated a short distance, along the terrace away from the men with the canister, before they climbed the bank onto the terrace above. With every nerve shrieking, they crept towards the sound of the earlier gunshots. Seddon, by now ahead, had disappeared between the lines of trees when several more short bursts of automatic fire sounded from above – the next terrace? Glover should be on that terrace: Glover also carried a German weapon. It was impossible to tell who was shooting at who.

A figure suddenly lunged at Rankin from a gap between two nearby trees. Instinct and adrenalin made Rankin point his rifle one-handed and pull the trigger pistol-fashion. The man, hit in the chest, collapsed in a heap, grunting loudly. Rankin leant against a tree, thanking Christ he had one up the spout and the safety off.

A second man, whom Rankin had not seen, limped into the sunlight with one hand up, crying, "*Kamerad, Kamerad*". The fight had gone out of him: his knee was braced with sticks and bandaged to form a makeshift splint, his face ghostly pale. A Schmeisser dangled from its sling around his neck, his other hand gripped the stick he leant on to take the weight off his injured knee. He could not take his eyes off his friend, writhing on the ground.

"Christ, Skipper, where the hell did they come from?" Seddon stepped out from behind a tree a few yards away, and advanced cautiously towards the injured German. "Hande hoch, Fritzy!" he called, motioning with his weapon.

"Jesus, I never saw them," Rankin mumbled, shaking. Keeping his own rifle pointed at the man with the makeshift splint, he knelt down beside the other German, whose breath was rattling in his throat, his lips flecked with blood and froth. "This joker's a goner," Rankin said softly, patting the pockets in the man's smock, and picking up his Luger pistol from beside his hand as his eyes began to glaze over.

Glover's face appeared over the top of the terrace wall. "We've got another one up here, Skipper."

"Dead or alive, Kenny?" Rankin asked.

They heard McNulty before they saw him: "Put it this way, he won't be needing any of the tucker I found in his little bag."

"This one's not going anywhere, either, Skipper," Seddon called out, relieving the injured man of his machine pistol. "We've got more bloody Schmeissers now than we can carry!"

The German with the splinted leg was a big man, over six feet tall. His large head made the cut-off parachute helmet look too small for him, and he appeared to have a powerful build under his jump smock. Mottled green in colour, the smock was a sort of overall comprising full padded jacket and short trousers, worn over the blue Luftwaffe trousers and tunic. The man was sweating profusely, which might have been put down to the heat of the day had he not been as pale as a ghost. They helped him down to the next terrace, to the supply box and the two bodies lying nearby. Blood and brains were sprayed down the back of one of them where the flies were already buzzing. Rankin felt his stomach heave.

"Came prepared, Skipper," whispered McNulty, nodding at the supply canister. "Brought their own bloody coffins with 'em."

"Keep your guard up," Rankin whispered, pointing along the terrace. "You, too, Kenny. There'll be more where this lot came from."

The canister was similar to the others they had seen, a white box about five feet long with a handle at one end and two wheels at the other. "It's a bit short for a coffin," Rankin said, glancing at the two bodies.

The injured man sat down awkwardly, resting his back against a tree and bracing his stiff leg out in front of him. Rankin knelt beside him. "He's in shock, but it seems to me there must be more than just whatever's happened to his knee," Rankin said softly, feeling his pulse.

He offered the man a German water bottle, which he grasped with both hands. He croaked his thanks in a weak, raspy voice. "Vielen dank."

"We can't improve on what his mates have already done for him," Rankin said, eyeing the splinted leg.

"Let's see what they've got in here," said Seddon turning his attention to the canister. He rolled it over and unclipped the clasps. A panel down one length popped open like a hatch, revealing a Spandau machine gun, minus its barrel, clipped into a rack along one side.

Seddon whistled. "Eu-bloody-reka, Look at this!" He rummaged through the boxes and packages nestled neatly between the gun and its spare barrels. "Ammo cans, dressings, grub, some potato mashers – and this, Skipper." He triumphantly held up a thermos flask.

Rankin got up from the wounded German and took the flask. "I'm not sure how long he'll last. Besides, we need to get cracking." Rankin weighed up the chances of the man being able to make a nuisance of himself. "The machine gun's too heavy to carry, it'll slow us down. We'll have to tie this bloke's hands and feet with boot laces and leave him here,"

"I thought Jerries all wore jackboots," said Seddon, the engineer in him still admiring the construction and contents of the box. "No laces."

"That's army," said Glover from a few yards away. "These are air force. Their boots would fall off when the parachutes opened."

"Fuckin' think of everything," muttered Seddon, lighting a cigarette from a pack in the container before throwing the pack to McNulty. "Just look at the way this is put together."

"What happens if he escapes and gets the Spandau out before we get back?" asked Glover. Rankin was sniffing the coffee in the thermos.

McNulty moved closer and lit a cigarette. "We'll have to take him with us," he said through a cloud of smoke.

"We can't do that," said Glover. "There's only four of us as it is. I volunteer you to stay with him, Rory."

"Fuck that," McNulty spat. "I'm not staying here on my own. These terraces give me the shits."

"Tap him on the head, then, Thumbs," Seddon suggested to Glover. "Knock him out cold, tie him up for good measure, and we'll pick him up with the box when we come back."

"That'll do," said Rankin, gulping down his coffee and passing the thermos to Seddon.

From down the hill came a hideous scream, followed by a gunshot.

"Jesus Christ!" exclaimed Seddon. "What the fuck was that? That was no bloody rifle."

"No," said Rankin, looking at Seddon, who handed the coffee onto McNulty. "Nip down there and see who that was. Be bloody careful, eyes peeled."

Glover had pulled the prisoner's boots off, despite his terrified protests and yelps of pain. He used the laces to tie the man's hands behind his back, then propped him up against his tree again.

"Now, Thumbs, give him a wee tap with your rifle butt, and he'll be all tucked up fast asleep until we come back," McNulty said in a voice he might have used to put a child to bed.

Out of the German's sight, Glover picked up his rifle and swung the butt at his head. The brass butt-plate connected with the man's head just above his ear, making him bellow as he went over on his side. Glover's lip quivered.

"Jesus, mate, too soft. He's a big bugger with a tough bloody nut," said McNulty, who then struck at the German, but this time he saw the blow coming and managed to avoid its full force. Shock or no shock, he was yelling blue murder now, lying on his side, struggling to get away, kicking out with his one good stockinged foot.

"For Christ's sake," said Rankin. This was taking far too long. "If you want a job done, do it yourself." He brought his own rifle butt down on the man's head and hit him with a sickening crunch. The man pitched over onto the ground and lay still.

"Oh. Jesus Christ," said Rankin, the colour draining from his face as he saw blood oozing from the man's ear.

Glover's mouth opened and shut, but no sound came out of it. "Shit, Skipper," said McNulty before retching into the grass behind a tree. "Bugger, lost me ciggy," he grumbled, wiping his chin.

Rankin grabbed at the man's wrist and felt for his pulse. There was none.

"Untie him, for Christ's sake. Drag him over there somewhere," said Rankin, spilling water down his chin as he tried to drink from the bottle in his shaking hand.

Seddon came back up the hill. "Skipper – oh, shit. What happened here?"

"I tapped him a tad too hard," said Rankin.

Seddon looked at him and shrugged. "I think I found the other man. Someone else got there first. Poor bugger looked like he'd been shot point-blank with a shotgun and finished off with something that nearly split his skull in two. Gear's already gone."

"You didn't see anyone else?"

"Villagers, skipping away through the vines. Too far away to see if they were carrying his boots and gun."

Rankin stared at him. More gunfire echoed from down in the valley.

––––––––

THEY SPREAD OUT again, taking a terrace each, and moved off through the trees. The pop, bang and rattle of gunfire sounded all along the valley below, but search as he might, Rankin seldom gained more than a fleeting glimpse of anyone moving in the open. He'd taken the right flank, nearest the track and the vineyards beyond leading down to the valley floor. Progress again was painfully slow. Each open space was crossed, heart in mouth, after a hard search. Leaving the shelter of a friendly trunk for the uncertain succour of the next took a huge effort and more than once his heart leapt into his bone-dry mouth, where his tongue seemed twice its usual size. It was the same for all of them. Sudden movements threatened to engulf them all in a fusillade of bullets. More than once, he flung himself down behind trees or rocks, getting up sheepishly looking at a fluttering parachute snagged by a tree. More than once, too, the parachutist was still attached to it, lying in the grass.

"Jesus, Skipper, come and look at this!"

Seddon's voice came from the terrace above, just a decibel below hysteria.

Cautiously, Rankin side-tracked up the slope, taking care to climb the embankment in the cover of tree and shadow. A man sat with his back against an olive tree, beneath the canopy of his parachute, the harness dangling beside him. He was barefoot and bareheaded, boots, smock and weapons gone. One of his legs was splayed out at an impossible angle.

But that was not what had made Seddon call him and then vomit into the grass. The man's belly had been opened, through his shirt, slashed from one side to the other, spilling his guts onto the ground in front of him. The purple coils slithered between his legs; blood and shit covered his trousers and splattered up the tree trunk behind him. The man's head hung on his chest, mouth a rictus of agony and terror, lips drawn across his teeth, hands were frozen into claws, pitiably trying to hold his guts in his belly. The hum of the flies drowned out the gentle swish of the breeze and rustle of the parachute.

Rankin felt his gorge rising, and began to violently retch.

"Jesus Christ Almighty." Rankin wiped his mouth with the back of his hand.

"Jesus. Who in God's name would do that?" whispered Seddon.

"Who? And with what?" Rankin took a mouthful of lukewarm water from his water bottle.

Sweating, shaken, pale and clammy-cold, despite the warmth of the day, the men spread out and moved on, alone with their thoughts.

The words from a school prayer came to Rankin: *Though I walk through the valley of the shadow of death, I fear no evil: for Thou art with me, Thy rod and Thy staff they comfort me.*

"Bloody bullshit," Rankin muttered out loud, forcing himself to step into the light between trees.

———

THE ROWS OF olive trees ended and were replaced by rows of vines, about four feet high. The lowest terrace had by now narrowed and merged into the rising valley floor. The track to the AMES station continued along the hillside 50 yards or so below the bottom terrace. Rankin signalled a halt, about 100 yards from a farmhouse. Typical, square and solid, it had an open-top storey surrounded by a parapet and shaded by bamboo screens. Rankin was on a terrace roughly level with the house's top floor, staring at it through his binoculars.

The shuttered windows, the doors and open roof, gave no hint as to whether the house was occupied. At one end were animal enclosures, formed of stone walls and wooden fences; at the other a walled orchard extended behind the house. A couple of humps lay in the grass between the track and the house. Nothing moved in his lens. It looked as if the owners had vanished when the parachutes started falling.

This was the first of several houses situated close to the track on this side of the valley. Most people lived in the tiny villages scattered along the valley floor. Rankin looked at his watch; they were not yet even halfway to the village of Khamoudhokhori.

Calling softly to the others to move off along their respective terraces, keeping to the cover, Rankin had gone about 30 yards when a sharp crack echoed around the valley.

"Sniper!" he yelled. "Stay down. Crawl back into the olives!" Taking cover behind the nearest tree, he called out their names. There was no answer from McNulty. He called again. Nothing.

Rankin scrambled up to the terrace above McNulty's, keeping out of sight of the house. He could see McNulty lying still between two rows of vines. Seddon crawled up beside Rankin at the verge of the olive trees, where they were soon joined by Glover.

"You two keep lookout, for Christ's sake!" Rankin hissed angrily. The three of them lay prone in the grass, hidden from the house by the bushy lip of the terrace.

"Jesus, Skipper, I'll go down, crawl out and drag him back under cover," said Seddon, laying down his sub-machine gun and unclipping his web gear.

"No!" cried Rankin, grabbing his arm.

Seddon looked at him, horror in his eyes. "We can't just leave him there."

"Skipper, please." Glover looked from Rankin to McNulty and back.

McNulty's body twitched.

"No! For Christ's sake! Seddon, keep your eyes peeled ahead,

Glover, look out behind!" Rankin crawled closer to the edge of the terrace for a better view of the house and raised his binoculars.

"Jesus, mate, we can't just leave him there!" Seddon cried.

"That's exactly what he wants you to do!" Rankin did not take his eyes off the open rooftop.

"Skipper, please," repeated Glover.

"No, Kenny. Wait!"

The longest two minutes of his life ensued, racked by doubt and foreboding. He could feel Glover's anguish and Seddon's anger, even though his eyes were glued to the rooftop.

Another sharp crack echoed around the valley, shivering the leaves just above McNulty's body as a bullet hissed through the vines and thudded into the embankment below them.

"Jesus," cried Seddon in fright.

"Bingo!" Rankin edged further back into cover. "Kenny, come here, keep a sharp lookout on that house through the binoculars. Keep behind cover, for God's sake. Seddon, look out front and rear, shoot anything that moves."

Rankin carefully sighted his rifle on the point he had seen the Mauser's flash and fired. A puff of dust rose from the parapet, but a glint under the rattan roof cover was all he saw. Through the edge of his lens the snout of a Spandau pushed through the shutters of a window below, its bipod legs settling on the windowsill.

"Take cover!" he screamed, curling himself into a ball at the base of the olive tree as the gun roared. A stream of tracer went whining and whistling over their heads, shivering the vines and thrashing the leaves, bouncing and sparking off stones in the terrace embankment. The next burst savaged the trees they were cowering behind, bringing branches, leaves and twigs raining down from the canopy.

"Shit," yelled Seddon. "You dirty bloody bastards!"

The pounding stopped. "Barrel change! Quick, Seddon, leave me a Schmeisser and you scarper back to that box and bring that bloody Spandau back here, with as much ammo as you can carry." He paused for a moment. "Kenny, you go with him. I'll try and do something for Rory."

Their eyes were wide with shock and fear.

"Keep your eyes open!" he called after them.

Rankin sighted on the window again and fired, putting another round into the rooftop terrace before slithering to a different tree.

He had no idea how long Seddon and Glover had been away, but it seemed like hours. Between each series of shots at and from the house, he searched the hillside terraces for movement and changed position himself. With any luck they might think more than just one man was on the hillside. Every now and then, to liven things up and keep him on his toes, the Spandau would nose out of a window and hose the area.

"Pull your bloody heads in," he murmured, after firing a shot into the Spandau's window.

He and the German rifleman continued to trade shots, each vying to score a hit. Each move had to be made with rifle and Schmeisser in case they decided to rush him and every move increased the odds of a bullet in the back. It sapped a lot of energy.

One shot into a downstairs shutter resulted in a particularly savage response from the machine-gunner, who was firing from a window above. The bursts stripped leaves and branches from a nearby olive tree, and a stretch of vine between him and McNulty, who had not moved so he could not tell if McNulty had been hit again, or if he was still alive.

Twice he started to crawl towards McNulty, and twice his

progress was halted by a burst of bullets from the Spandau tearing through the vines, just above ground level.

The physical effort of changing positions, climbing up and down between the terraces, carrying both rifle and Schmeisser, was exhausting him. This, coupled with the mental effort and fear involved, he knew he could not keep it up for long. Leaning back against a tree, panting with exertion, cradling the Schmeisser, eyes darting every way through the orchard behind and vines in front, he was reaching his limit. Another stream of bullets zipped and cracked around him, forcing him to duck. Peering around the trunk, his heart leapt into his mouth as he spotted a shadow flitting between the rows of vines, a mere football field length beyond McNulty's body. Christ!

His tiredness evaporated. Every nerve twanged taut. Had the interloper come from the house or from further up the valley? Was he on his own or did he have company? Was he directed or been attracted by the shooting? As if in answer, another shadow crossed the lane between the vines. Shit! Rankin slithered backward, deeper into the protective shadows.

Another shadow – Jesus! They were heading uphill, trying to outflank him.

"Keep calm," he whispered to himself over his pummelling heart. They could not know exactly where he was. Withdrawing a little further, he used the cover of the trees and shadows to clamber up to the next terrace. From there, he found a blue-grey form crawling along the edge of the row of vines towards McNulty's body. Using the grass between the olives as cover, Rankin worked his way to the left. Raising his head a fraction, he found another grey shape on his own level, crawling towards him. Jesus!

Instinct took over. He slowly pushed the rifle forward, disturbing nothing. He aimed at the centre of the man's head, and, expecting it to be the last thing he ever did, fired.

Bullets thrashed the leaves and trees above. He instantly rolled back to the right, in time to see the man on the terrace below leap to his feet and heave a grenade up onto Rankin's terrace. The grenade exploded with a crack amidst a cloud of debris but well short of its target. The German turned and fled back the way he had come. He made an easy target and dropped like a stone when Rankin fired again.

Once more bullets again sprayed through the trees, thudding into trunks, snapping branches and shredding leaves. Some of the fire came from above. There must be more of the bastards! But where were they?

He saw Seddon first, jinking between the rows and from tree to tree. He dropped the machine gun onto its bipod with a couple of belts of ammunition beside it and flopped into the grass next to Rankin, gasping.

"Jesus, mate, we heard the shooting. Run all the way," he panted. His face was red and streaming sweat, his shirt stained and soaked. "Wasn't sure we'd find you in one piece."

Glover staggered up, carrying two more cans of ammunition and a belt slung bandolier-fashion around his neck. He also had half a dozen grenades stuck in his belt, but was too winded to speak.

Rankin quickly outlined his plan, pointing to where he wanted the gun positioned. Glover would need to load and spot for Seddon as gunner.

"Remember," Rankin whispered hoarsely, "Jerry can't see over the lip of the top terrace from the house. But there's more of them up there. Don't stand up, for Christ's sake."

They nodded and dragged the gun and ammunition back the way they had come so that they could climb up to the top terrace, unseen from the house, and hopefully unseen by whoever was already above them.

Rankin dropped down the five feet or so to the next terrace, then ticked off the minutes.

The Spandau above him fired and was immediately answered from the house, the bullets thrashing through the foliage. A hideous shriek was cut short by the crack of a grenade on the terrace above – smoke and debris flew through the scrub along the terrace edge and a body tumbled down, all flailing arms and legs, landing on Rankin's terrace. Rankin could see nothing of what was happening on the terraces above. But suddenly another man leapt out of the vines about 50 yards in front of him, his flight cut short by Rankin's bullet. In response the machine gun in the house again thrashed the trees and vines on the terrace above.

The man that had tumbled onto Rankin's terrace let out a loud moan, and an anguished cry.

Once again Rankin fired into the window of the house, provoking a retaliatory burst of bullets which cracked into the tree trunk inches above his head and flailed the scrub growing up the bank at the edge of the terrace. In turn, Seddon's gun raked the house with a storm of bullets, shattering a pair of window shutters and collapsing the rattan roof screen, ricochets flying off at all angles and leaving the hose wreathed in plaster dust. Jesus! Rankin curled himself into a ball, knowing the response would come.

The man on the terrace cried out again, this time the cry ended in a scream.

Rankin hastily backed away, deeper into the shadow, out of

sight of the house as the enemy Spandau again raked the terraces. There was only one conclusion possible: they were too strong – it must only be a matter of time before another or all of them were hit. They had failed in their endeavour to get to the objective at the end of the track. And forcing a way around this obstacle in daylight would take firepower they did not have. With time running out, there was no option but to return.

Rankin took one last look at McNulty. His position had not changed, it was impossible to say if he was still alive. Sadly, he called Seddon and Glover back from their position, and away from McNulty. There was nothing they could do for him.

The man on the terrace screamed again, but it was cut short by a single rifle shot from Seddon's terrace.

———

"JESUS, NICK, I'M whacked." Rankin slumped down into the trench, running his hand through his sweat-soaked hair. It was after 1700. "We lost Rory – had to leave him behind."

"Reilly!" shouted Nicholson. "Get over here and get the boss something to eat and a brew."

Rankin glanced up. That was not Nicholson's usual tone of voice.

"You alright, Nick?"

"No, I'm not alright. We've not heard from anyone all day. We could be the last platoon left for all we know. I sent young McIntyre up the hill with Corkhill to see if he could contact anyone from 22 Battalion. They shot at him!" Nicholson's red face looked angry enough to shoot the man himself. "Held his helmet up on his rifle to show he wasn't a Hun, and some clown put a bullet through it," he fumed, breathing heavily.

"Alright Nick, calm down. No need to blow a gasket," Rankin said soothingly.

"We've had no contact with Fergusson or anyone else on our flank. We've heard nothing from Gibson in the village. And Graham and half a dozen of his motley crew have run off."

Rankin stared at him, now understanding the real cause of his anger. "Jesus Christ, surely not."

"I told you what I thought of them in the first place. Nothing but trouble." Nicholson's fists were clenched so tightly around his Tommy gun the knuckles showed white through the grime.

"Good to see you back, Skipper," said Reilly, edging past Nicholson and beaming from ear to ear. He doled out a mug full of water and set it on a German burner. "We've given them a real hiding, eh?" He produced a Luger and a pair of Zeiss binoculars from a leather pouch. "Look what I've got! Belonged to a great brute of a beggar dangling in a tree, all trussed up like a Christmas turkey."

Rankin looked at Nicholson. "See, Nick, success makes them happy. Cheer up."

"Cheer up?" Nicholson exploded. "That's exactly the problem. They're running all over the hillside banging away at everything that moves like it's blimmin' hunting season! They'll end up shooting each other if they carry on. And where are the prisoners the IO wanted to interview? There are none!" He glared at Reilly, who simply shrugged. "They've turned into a rabble!"

"Calm down, Nick. That's a bit harsh. This sort of fighting, there's nothing you can do with 'em. I left you one up the hill. Tied to a tree. Where is he? I haven't seen him."

Nicholson looked at him, then looked away. "Hmm. Neither

have we. He must have scarpered." He turned back to Rankin. "He won't go far without boots."

"Come off it, Nick. There are enough boots out there to shoe an army. And weapons to boot."

Reilly handed him a mug and a slab of oily corned beef on a slice of stale bread. Rankin took it with a dirt- and gore-covered hand.

"Bastards are everywhere, Nick, in front, behind, beside, up the bloody trees! Don't expect prisoners. It's dead or be dead." He looked up at Reilly as he tried wiping his hands on his equally filthy shorts. "God, Tim, can we spare any water so I can wash my hands?"

Reilly scrabbled out of the trench and disappeared towards their water butt.

"Poor Rory," Rankin said to Nicholson when Reilly was out of earshot. "Bloody sniper, in a house on the track. We weren't even halfway to the AMES Station. A Spandau in a window and the sniper on the rooftop. It's as far as we got."

Nicholson looked at him but said nothing.

"The Spandau we found is the only reason we got away." He took a big swig of his tea, and another chunk of bread and beef. He went on in a quiet voice. "We did try to bring a prisoner back, but it didn't work out. But I got these," he said as he dropped a couple of German paybooks on the ground.

THE NOISE OF battle from beyond the spur was like distant breakers crashing onto rocks; a constant cacophony rising and falling on the breeze as the lowering sun glowed orange through the haze and the heat of the day faded. Rankin licked his lips. His tongue was dry and furry, but the bottle was empty, and he had already drunk his allocation. There'd be no water delivery. Who knew how long they might have to make do with what they had? On top of his thirst the dirt in his shirt from this morning's bombing and the sweat of the day had combined to create a series of brown, grubby rivulets down his body. He was glad he could not smell himself.

"Feeling any more optimistic, Nick?" Rankin asked, tongue thick in his mouth. Their sector had been quiet now for an hour or more, apart from the occasional shot from across the riverbed. "I could murder another mug of tea."

"I don't like it, Neil. We have no idea what's going on out there."

"We've pushed our patrols out. We just have to wait for them to come back." He thought for a while. "Nick. I admit, I might have made a mistake about Graham. I certainly didn't expect he'd just bugger off and take half his chums with him."

"Well, on this occasion I am going to say 'I told you so'," Nicholson said. "I make the platoon strength now twenty-eight effectives without Graham and co, down from our reinforced strength of forty-two."

Rankin leaned back on the side of the trench. "Jesus."

"We've used a lot of ammo, too, though most of the boys have picked up a German weapon and foraged some of theirs."

"I suppose," Rankin said quietly, "that seventy-three of theirs for fourteen of ours is not a bad ratio, if that's a meaningful fact. It only includes the definites inside our perimeter; there are a lot more outside. I would say we've accounted for at least a hundred and fifty."

Nicholson's answer was lost as the foliage screen rustled and

McIntyre's face appeared.

"A runner from Corporal Lawrence, Mister Rankin. Patrol coming in with a prisoner."

"Well, well, Nick, your prayers are answered. Who's this, I wonder?"

A moment later Graham's frame appeared behind McIntyre. Squatting beside Rankin's trench, he held up a leather satchel and map case.

"Skipper, I found this," he said, beaming from ear to ear. "Looks fuckin' important."

"Where the devil have you been, Graham?" roared Nicholson.

"Out huntin', Sarge. Er, on patrol, that is. Jerries everywhere. Shit, we didn't half clean a few of the buggers up," he laughed. "I dunno what they were expectin' when they landed here, but they didn't expect the bloody hosing they got, I can tell you that for nothing."

Nicholson opened his mouth, but Rankin held up his hand. "I think the Sergeant is annoyed because you went off without telling him, and he was worried about you," said Rankin. Out of the corner of his eye he saw Nicholson turn puce and swallow hard.

"Er, yeah. Sorry, Sarge. You were busy and our area was done over, but there were plenty of the buggers left and we wanted to get our share."

"So you've brought a live one back with you, Graham?" Rankin asked before Nicholson could get a word in.

"Yeah – more or less. Jerry officer. He's a bit shot up. Had these," he said, holding out the satchel and map case for Rankin to take.

"Looks impressive, I must say." Rankin's tiredness fell away as he opened the satchel. "You might have to revise your ratio of losses, Nick. And this could keep the IO busy for quite some time."

"Maps, papers, shit like that," said Graham. "The joker I took prisoner was with another Jerry officer, but he was a goner."

"Was he now?" Rankin said.

"Yeah, didn't get his bloody hands above his head quick enough," he chuckled. "Mind you, may not 'ave been 'is fault: 'e was pretty bashed up. By the state of 'im, 'e came down arse over tit through the fuckin' tree 'e was sittin' under."

Rankin caught Nicholson's grimace as he leafed through the contents of the satchel. It appeared quite high-level, a lot of the German was beyond him. The general thrust of the papers he could have interpreted with time, but the map, showing circled landing zones, arrowed objectives, and what looked like estimated opposition positions and strengths, was unmistakable, as was the timetable for taking them.

"Jesus Christ Almighty! They haven't half set themselves a cracking pace," he muttered.

"What's that, Skipper?" asked Graham.

"Let's have a look at this Jerry of yours." Rankin looked hard at Graham. "Whatever happens, don't let on that I know a few words of German."

The man was propped up against a tree, guarded by one of Graham's companions. He appeared agitated, muttering when Rankin introduced himself. He had been shot in the thigh and the arm and judging by his clothes had lost a lot of blood. His dark hair was slick with sweat, his face the colour of porridge. It was a wonder Graham had been able to get him this far.

"What sort of insignia did the chap carrying the satchel have, Grazer?" Rankin asked quietly, pointing to his collar.

"Insignia?"

"Rank badges."

"Er, gold wings. Three of them, I think, on each side."

Rankin pursed his lips in thought. The man leaning against the tree did not take his eyes off him.

"Good afternoon, Herr Hauptman," Rankin said in English. "We will try to do what we can for your injuries – but, as you may imagine, we do not have much medical equipment available." Rankin waved the satchel in front of him. "While we're waiting for the medic, you can tell me what this means."

The German slumped back against the tree, closed his eyes, and said nothing.

Rankin took the papers out and pretended to study them for the first time. There was no point hiding the fact he knew what the map signified; a schoolboy could have worked it out. He pursed his lips and whistled theatrically.

The German officer squinted at him, struggling to sit up.

"Who was your commander? What unit did he command? Where are you on this map?" Rankin asked him.

The officer examined Rankin intently through eyes hooded by pain. Rankin felt him trying to penetrate Rankin's mind, to know what Rankin knew. There were other emotions there, too. Anger, frustration and loathing. For whom? The officer who had brought this with him or Rankin? The man showed no reaction to the question, betraying no hint as to whether or not he understood English.

"Ich habe diese arrogante Scheisse erzahit," he muttered to himself. "*I told that arrogant shit*," Rankin translated to himself. Well, well.

"We need to get the satchel to Battalion as soon as we can,"

Rankin whispered to Graham. Graham nodded, drawing hard on a cigarette.

"I don't think he liked his superior," said Rankin to Nicholson, back at the HQ trench. "He called him an arrogant shit and muttered that he'd told him something – that he couldn't bring that stuff with him, would be my guess. He's bloody angry."

"The lot of a good adjutant," said Nicholson, "trying to control a wilful superior."

Rankin stared at him. Nicholson's face was expressionless.

"We need to get this stuff back to Battalion," Rankin said, dumping the satchel on the lip of the trench. He slumped to the ground. "Jesus, I'm knackered."

"Well, you sit still for ten minutes. Reilly will get you a brew, and I'll find someone to take care of it," said Nicholson.

———

DUSK DEEPENED INTO early evening, and Rankin fell into a fitful sleep. The firing died down as darkness fell. The patrols they had sent out earlier reported in, most of them cock-a-hoop, emboldened by success. Bravado for some was tempered heavily by losses: they spoke darkly in hushed tones of revenge exacted. Patrolling in the afternoon had cost the platoon dearly: four killed and one seriously injured.

"And d'you know what, Skipper?" asked Blake, returning incredulous from a patrol. "We saw the darnedest thing – some old Greek duffer, draped in a Nazi flag and waving a great curved sword even though he was staggering under a load of stuff. Schmeissers, ammunition, boots, clothes, you name it. Like a bloody pirate, he was. Most of the village was out there, as far as we could see. It was just like race day. There're dead Jerries all over the place, and they're busy stripping everything off them. Some of the poor coots looked like they'd been hacked to death before they could get out of their bloody parachutes."

Rankin looked at him. A scimitar? Could that be what had disembowelled the man under the tree? From Blake's description, it could just as likely have been a spade.

The last of them reported in darkness and confirmed that the local villages must now be awash with German weapons. Most of his own men had souvenired a Luger, along with watches, wallets, money, binoculars, sunglasses, helmets, smocks, knives, and the little one-man cookers. Some of them came back laden, looking like "bloody gypsy tinkers" according to Nicholson.

More than half of them now carried German weapons and had foraged stocks of ammunition for them so that the platoon now boasted three Spandau machine guns in addition to its two Brens. Spirits were high with the day's work. Casualties might have been heavy, but they reckoned the damage inflicted was far higher. Done in, but generally positive, the platoon on the Tavronitis exuded confidence for whatever tomorrow would bring. After reporting, they collapsed into their trenches, or onto the ground behind a tree, and instantly fell asleep.

"Jesus, Nick," Rankin said, his mood lightening as each patrol reported in, barely able to contain himself. "We've given the buggers a real black eye, I'd say. Maybe a bloody nose even."

Nicholson looked at him in the gathering gloom. "Don't forget, we haven't heard a jot from Fergusson and co or 22 Battalion up the hill. Jerry's in the RAF camp, Johnstone thinks, and possibly on the airfield. And don't forget he's gathering strength out there," he said, pointing across the Tavronitis. "And to cap it off, the patrol I sent with Graham's satchel came back, saying there were too many Huns to risk it."

"Yes, yes, those areas you mentioned were always going to be problematic. Now, though, the plan swings into action. 23 Battalion comes forward down our valley and uses this position as a jumping-off point. Half the battalion clear the opposite bank and go north to the bridge and the RAF camp," he said pointing towards the airfield. "The other half strike south past Vlakheronitissa. The rest of 5 Brigade comes forward along the coast and through the airfield to join up with 23 and round up the buggers over the river," Rankin said, clapping his hands together as if disposing of something with a bad smell. "Bob's your uncle! A first-class kick in the goolies for Uncle Adolf." Rankin chuckled childishly in the gloom.

Nicholson sat in silence for a long while, puffing his pipe. "It all seems too easy, somehow."

CHAPTER SEVEN

The Shield Falls, 21 May 1941

RANKIN WAS FAR away, oblivious in sleep. The world was dark and peaceful, smelling of the coal range baking bread in his mother's kitchen. For the moment the trials of the day had been shut away in another room. From away in the distance some pest was calling to him. Grumbling, he turned over, but the pestering continued. Someone was shaking his shoulder.

"Neil, Neil, wake up! Sergeant Norton's sent a runner."

Rankin was slow to respond. Nicholson's voice and dark outline under the night sky swam wearily into focus. Who the hell was Norton?

Beside Nicholson he could just make out another figure, who coughed nervously. "Mister Rankin, boss, sir," the unknown man cleared his throat again and in the gloom Rankin could just see him transferring his helmet from one hand to the other. "The sarge sent me to tell you. Battalion's gone."

Rankin sat bolt upright. Norton was Fergusson's sergeant, he remembered. "What? Gone? Gone where, for Christ's sake?" That didn't make sense. "Why has the sergeant sent you? Where's Fergusson?"

"He bought it, boss, soon after the first buggers landed. Sarge has been in charge all day."

The news hit Rankin in the stomach. Niall, the genial giant, struck down. "Gone? Gone where? When did this happen?"

"The Sarge doesn't know, boss – only that they've gone. He's getting our blokes ready to leave and sent us on ahead. To warn you. So's not to get shot."

Rankin blinked and stared at the man, then at Nicholson, their teeth and eyes gleaming in the dark. He felt a familiar great pit opening up inside him. "That can't be right! How does he know they've gone? They can't have gone! Why've they gone?" The last question came out as a savage hiss.

"Sarge sent a patrol up to the wire. Came back and said the whole place is empty."

The man sounded as if he was shaking.

"Jesus Christ All-fucking-mighty," Rankin whispered hoarsely. "Nick, warn the section leaders to be ready to move – every man to take weapons and ammo, water, as much food as they have, carry the wounded, and leave whatever they can't carry. We need to be well clear by daylight if it's true."

The shadow that was Nicholson nodded. "What are you going to do?"

"I'm going to look for myself. I can't believe it – no offence to Tom." He nodded in the direction of Norton's messenger. "I need a Schmeisser, a couple of stick grenades, and a Very pistol. I want a couple of those parachutists' smocks, too. If I can't get back, I'll fire a rocket, and you scarper."

"You're not going on your own," Nicholson's hoarse whisper was laced with panic.

At that point, Graham pushed around Reilly. The platoon's

command post was becoming crowded.

"Get a weapon, Graham. Plenty of ammo. Don't ask questions and be back here in one minute flat."

He was as good as he was bid. They each pulled on a German parachute smock and prepared to set off. McIntyre, who had overheard the whole exchange, gave Rankin a German parachute knife.

"Here, sir, in case you need it."

Rankin looked at it. He had never stuck a knife into another human being and did not want to start now. But he took it and slipped the knife into a pocket.

They hurried up the hill, stopping and listening every few yards. The wire that surrounded the 22 Battalion HQ position was high above their own. How could Tom Norton have got something so terribly wrong? It had to be wrong! This was the key position to the whole sector defence. Why would an old warhorse like Les Andrew abandon it when they had given Jerry such a bloody hiding?

Graham knew enough to keep a lookout, listen hard, and stay silent. Rankin puzzled, debated and argued with himself as they climbed. None of it made sense.

"We're at the first wire," Graham hissed, intruding on Rankin's raging argument with himself. For the first time, Rankin looked around, aware of how far they'd come. The hill with its grassy slopes, rocky outcrops and occasional cacti was ghostly in the half-light. There was no moon, and the stars were partially obscured by the drifting clouds of stinking smoke. A sporadic pop and rattle broke the silence, and every now and again a flash of light silhouetted the outline of the hillside separating them from the airfield.

"Shit," he whispered as they crossed the multi-wire fence making it twang. They stopped, listening. Nothing, except the soft breeze in the leaves and grasses.

They arrived at the next barrier, and Graham swore as he tripped over a body lying in the grass in front of it.

"Fuck!" he swore under his breath. "Mongrel bloody Jerry."

Both crouched down and searched the hillside, looking for movement, listening for noise. Nothing moved, the only sound the gentle whisper of the breeze.

"Grab an arm," Rankin whispered, nodding to the body.

"What're you going to do?" hissed Graham.

"Grab the other," Rankin said. Together they heaved the dead man upright, then pitched him across the coils of barbed wire. He fell across the wire with a thud and a springy metallic rustling.

"Jeez, ta, Fritzy," Graham muttered, placing one dirty boot onto the man's back. Rankin clambered over the body after Graham, keeping clear of the razor-sharp barbs.

They followed the last wire to the open entrance way, covered by a gun pit. No one challenged; the slit trench was empty. In mounting panic Rankin almost ran to the crown of the hill, the heart of 22 Battalion's position. In the dim light it resembled the craters of the moon. Uprooted trees, smashed and abandoned equipment and dead bodies – some horribly mangled, others looking to be quietly asleep – the evidence of the intensity of the bombardment was everywhere. After a few minutes, rushing from one abandoned post to the next, he was convinced: they were the only living souls on the hilltop.

He stopped and stared at the devastated and abandoned hilltop. "For fuck's sake," he muttered. It was true: the most important position on the whole island of Crete had been abandoned. The dead Germans scattered over the hilltop appeared to have been killed as they landed, many still attached to their parachutes; the New Zealanders either blown apart in the bombing or shot in the battle that followed. But the fact that the German bodies were there at all showed a spirited defence had been put up when they dropped from the sky.

Beyond the summit occasional flashes lit the sky, like summer lightning. Yellow, white, red, some flashes sharp, a sudden blaze of light then dark, others slow to fade, lingering in the distant night. Rankin could barely comprehend what he had seen. There was no explanation.

They slowly retraced their steps.

Grahan made his way across the wire again, using the dead German's back as a bridge. Rankin followed, also stepping onto the dead man – and slipped. A barb gashed his arm as he put his hand out to break his fall, causing the wire to make a loud tinny rattle.

"Fuck!" he swore, loudly.

Graham, who was leading, hastily went to ground and looked back, eyes shining brightly in the night light.

"Fuck," Rankin repeated, hissing under his breath, as he extracted his arm from the barbed wire. He felt in his pocket for something to put over the wound. Clambering to his feet, he again lost his balance and fell heavily across the German's body.

A combination of rage, frustration, disappointment and revulsion welled up inside him, bursting like a dam under strain as his fingers closed around the handle of McIntyre's knife.

"Bastard, bastard, bastard, fucking bastard!" he cried, the unsheathed blade rising and falling, plunging into the inert body, steel grating on bone and metal.

Graham dragged him off the body. "Christ, man, get a fuckin' grip of yourself."

Rankin stared at the blade in his hand. He hurled it away to land with a metallic clatter.

Shaking, he scrambled to his feet, catching the look on Graham's face in the starlight.

"We're stuffed," Rankin muttered. "Don't you understand? Not by the bloody Jerries. By our own fucking side."

A bit further down the hill Graham plucked at his shoulder, whispering, "It can't be that bad, Skipper. Why don't you put the platoon up there, occupy the position, while someone goes for help?"

"I thought of that when I realised the place was unoccupied." Rankin's murmur had a hoarse edge to it. "But Jerry will be up here in a jiffy, as soon as he realises it's empty. They must have patrols on this hillside. Thirty have no show of doing what a couple of hundred reckoned they couldn't." Rankin took a swig from Reilly's water bottle. The clean, cool water made no impression on the bitter taste of bile in his mouth.

"It might be worth givin' it a shot," said Graham, pausing to take a long pull from his own bottle, before picking up his Schmeisser and turning downhill. Rankin stared after him.

Perhaps, he thought. *Perhaps.*

"WHAT WAS LEFT of Tom's platoon passed through twenty minutes ago, Neil. There's nothing between us and the camp," Nicholson reported on his return to the platoon HQ. "They were the last. Sounds like the platoons down there have had a real mauling."

Rankin pondered the news. Any thought of putting the combined platoons onto the hilltop had evaporated. Norton wasn't under his command, but he might have consented with a good enough argument. Had his own stubbornness, his unwillingness to believe the unbelievable, his need to see for himself, cost them the opportunity of joining forces and holding the crown of the hill? They might have been able to send for help along the top of Vineyard Ridge, the high ground between Hill 107 and 23 Battalion. He had no doubt the Germans even now were scrambling for the upper slopes, unable to believe their luck. The key to the whole sector, theirs for the taking.

Rankin nodded vacantly. He was numb, the pit of his stomach a great, dark, empty void.

"We need to get going, Neil," Nicholson prompted gently. "Boys are ready, waiting for the order."

Rankin stared at him. "I'll get Corkhill to put a dressing on that," Nicholson added, looking at the stream of blood on Rankin's arm.

"Yes, I suppose so. I'll bet they're complaining like buggery," he sighed. "We beat the bastards," he muttered as Corkhill tied off the field dressing.

Nicholson relayed the order to the waiting section leaders. Muttered groans, whispered complaints and the clink and creak of equipment being shouldered were the only sounds from the platoon in the dark. Silently, they moved off in two extended files.

Two two-man patrols scouted the valley above and below the track leading towards the AMES, and the little saddle that would take them into the area around Dhaskaliana where 23 Battalion was based. *Were they still there?* fretted Rankin. What had caused 22 Battalion to up stakes and abandon its position?

They had seemed to be holding their own. What had happened to force them off Hill 107?

————

A PATROL RETURNED to the column from the direction of Vlakheronitissa, reporting that they had heard German spoken and the noise of men moving through the vineyards across the valley. And snoring! Not everyone in the Valley of Death was dead. Rankin felt a pang of guilt for Gibson and his spotter. They had been out of contact all day; a risk Gibson relished when he took on his lone observer role.

It was nearly 0100 hours when Rankin heard the 21 Battalion picket challenge the leading patrol out in front on the lower slopes of Vineyard Ridge, and he went forward to report. They had skirted the little village of Khamoudhokhori and were making their way down the track parallel to the Sfakoriako River.

The pickets warned that there could still be German parachutists in their area and further down the track to 23 Battalion. "Most of the buggers who came down here won't be worrying about you, though," he was told.

————

IT WAS AFTER 0200 when Rankin reported to Battalion HQ. The place was in an uproar, abuzz with excitement. People rushed in and out of the rooms, some carrying pieces of paper, others empty-handed. No one had time for him. The question on everyone's lips was whether B Company had yet got through to the airfield and linked up with 22 Battalion.

"Linked up with 22 Battalion?" Rankin mumbled to himself. How could they link up with 22 Battalion?

Rankin found the Intelligence Sergeant's cubbyhole. The man looked harassed, trying to juggle several conversations at once as various messengers vied for his attention. The office stank of cigarette smoke and the single lantern in a corner was almost lost in the haze. "Where's Davin?" Rankin demanded, trying to get the man's attention. If anyone should know anything, he should.

"Sergeant," Rankin repeated loudly, "do you know what's going on? Why, in God's name, has 22 Battalion abandoned Hill 107? I heard over there B Company's gone to link up. Is there anyone still on the airfield? And where's Lieutenant Davin?"

The man appeared not to have heard him, calling out something to someone at a telephone.

Rankin grabbed him by the arm, spun him around, and repeated his question.

"Mister Rankin, sir, oh, hallo, sir. Mister Rankin?" A frown crossed his face. "What are you doing here?"

"We're here because 22 Battalion have cleared out from Hill 107! Without them up there, I'd be dead by midnight."

The sergeant stared at him. "Who's on top of the hill, then?" he asked, turning to the map on the wall behind him.

Rankin pushed past him and stabbed his finger on the big blue circle marked "22Bn A Coy" with its flag denoting Battalion HQ on the airfield side of the hilltop position.

"No one, Sergeant, that's what I'm trying to tell you. There's no bugger up there as of four hours or so ago. Where's Mister Davin?" Rankin saw expressions of comprehension, confusion and dismay follow each other across the man's face.

Rankin rushed on, floodgates open. "They up and left, never

told us, never told their own platoons next to us on the south side of the bridge." He viciously stabbed at the map again. "The whole position's wide open. If Jerry's already got onto it, we're fucked."

The sergeant was gaping at him, as if at some sort of lunatic escaped from an asylum.

"And one of our patrols captured this earlier today. You don't have to be a Rhodes Scholar to work out the meaning of the map that's in there. Its former owner is with our wounded." He dropped the German satchel and map case on the table, the golden Luftwaffe eagle stamped on the flap gleaming dully in the low light.

Rankin looked at the man, who was still open-mouthed, looking as if everything he had said had gone over his head. "And speaking of Rhodes Scholars, where the bloody hell is Davin?" Rankin shouted at him.

The sergeant managed to stammer, "Mister Davin was wounded, sir – head wound – in the drop today. He's been evacuated to the Regimental Aid Post."

Rankin took a step back in shock. He was about to open his mouth to apologise when a commotion broke out in the corridor behind them, stilling the hubbub in the headquarters as if a tap had been turned off.

They both turned their heads to stare as the measured tones of Colonel Leckie, 23 Battalion's commanding officer, fell into the silence like a stone into a pond: "Why, Colonel Andrew, this is a surprise."

"HAVE YOUR CHAPS had anything to eat all day?" The kindly, avuncular face of 23 Battalion's supply officer peered down into Rankin's tired eyes.

"Not much. Most of us missed breakfast, sir," he replied, struggling to his feet. Rankin had been sitting in a corridor for what seemed like hours waiting to see someone to make his report.

"Sit down, sit down, dear boy. Let's see if we can't get something organised for them, then," said the older man, who Rankin had always found somewhat shy and retiring, but always sympathetic and quite effective in his position.

Rankin took him outside and showed him where the men were sitting and smoking. A number had already lain down and fallen asleep. Nicholson jumped up to salute the other officer.

"We may be able to get something hot for your men," repeated the supply officer, before hurrying off to where the cooks had set up their cut-down drums and tins.

Nicholson arched his eyebrows at Rankin.

"Bloody chaos," he replied. "I overheard something about our B Company being sent to link up with 22 Battalion on the airfield. Sounds like they're still there or still getting there. Les Andrew just arrived, which took everyone by surprise. I don't think any of our blokes knew they'd abandoned Hill 107 either."

Nicholson nodded and turned his head away for a moment. "We can draw some ammunition, but half the men have got German weapons. It'll be limited use."

"Get as much of anything you can. I have a feeling we'll be needing everything we can carry," said Rankin. "I need to finish my report to Battalion. I only got halfway through it before."

Back inside, the uproar had redoubled. A couple of telephone operators talking into their hand pieces and the Intelligence

Sergeant interviewing a 22 Battalion officer filled one small room. The senior officers huddled in conference around a map in another. Runners with messages and people shouting queries, instructions and reports seemed to occupy every space.

Rankin approached the sergeant, who was taking notes as a dirt- and sweat-stained captain from 22 Battalion recounted his story. Rankin was struck by the officer's brittle demeanour and haggard eyes.

"We had no contact from C and D Companies or anyone else after the first German air attacks," the captain said in a distant voice, reliving the experience. "We've never had such bombing and strafing. A head above the trench would draw another bomb or fighter. It was almost impossible to get casualties to the clearing station."

The man raised his mug, hands shaking so much he was barely able to get it to his mouth. "The men gave a good account of themselves when the parachutists rained down on top of us. Dead everywhere. Once they came down the bombing and strafing mercifully stopped."

He took another sip, tea dribbling down his chin, and sat for a moment, staring at his cup. "We still had no word from anyone else. Colonel Andrew has been firing the 'assistance needed' flares all afternoon. Runners sent to contact C and D Companies couldn't get through or never came back. We couldn't see the airfield at all. Dust and smoke, you see."

He paused to light a cigarette. The sergeant lit the match for him as he was unable to hold it steady.

"The counter-attack with the two tanks failed. The ammunition for one of them, it turned out, didn't fit the gun." He drew heavily on the cigarette, then raised his head to face the sergeant. "For

God's sake! Did we have to wait until today to find that out?"

The man's face muscles jerked in little spasms, the corners of his eyes twitched uncontrollably, and occasionally he lost the thread of what he was saying. Waxy, pale, a half-corpse, his eyes glittered on the surface, but inside were dull.

God, thought Rankin, do we all look like that?

"Thank you, Captain Burns, you've been most helpful," said the sergeant. "Go and see if you can get something to eat."

The captain pushed past Rankin, eyes downcast, holding his helmet in his hand.

"He's on the verge of a crack-up," Rankin said to Robertson, who had just come in. "Poor bugger."

"Yes, poor bugger indeed. It's been a trying day for all of us. You don't look so flash yourself." Robertson eyes darted anxiously all about him, starting to turn away. "What can I do for you, Neil? I need to deliver these casualty figures."

"Casualty figures?" Rankin grabbed him by the sleeve and swung him around. "We need to organise a counter-attack, Nellie, we need to get back on top of that hill. It's the key to the whole bloody island."

"Hey, steady on, Neil. I'm just a platoon commander, same as you."

They were interrupted by the arrival of Lieutenant Colonel Allen[8] and several other officers from 21 Battalion. Allen and another officer went into the room with Leckie and Andrew. The door shut behind them.

---

8   Lieutenant Colonel J.M. Allen, born England 3 Aug 1901, farmer and MP (Hauraki) 1938–41, CO 21 Battalion 17 May 1941–28 November 1941, killed in action 28 November 1941.

"There you go, Neil," Robertson said, pulling free. "Brass have arrived to make the decision. Battalion commanders' conference."

"What about Hargest? Surely he's issued orders to retake the hill?"

"I'm not sure he's aware of the withdrawal yet." Robertson looked solicitous. "You can rest assured, Neil, that we all recognise the gravity of the situation."

Rankin stared at him, open-mouthed. "Not aware? You mean the withdrawal happened without Hargest's say-so, Nellie?"

"Here, hang on a minute. I don't know. I'm only a small cog in a big wheel," Robertson answered testily.

Rankin grabbed him by his shirt front, his face only inches from Robertson's. "Freyberg's orders are to retake lost ground with all due dispatch, Nellie. Our mobile defence role. The airfield and those heights are the key to the whole bloody island!"

Robertson angrily pulled free and stepped back a pace. "I'm aware of that, Neil. I'm also mindful of the requirement to defend the beaches against invasion."

"But the Germans won't 'invade' by sea. Not until they've secured a harbour. We hold Chania, and Kastelli out west is tiny," Rankin pleaded.

"You shouldn't pay too much attention to Boney Anderson," Robertson said, rising to his full height, "We have our orders, Neil."

"Boney's right! I've seen his chart. We need to strike now, hit him hard. Hill 107 overlooks Vineyard Ridge as well, Nellie. The 21st won't be able to stay there. Counter-attack with everything you've got – the exercise, Nellie. At Burnham. Knock them off balance! Remember?"

A captain poked his head around the door frame. "Lieutenant Robertson, you're needed."

"Sorry, Neil, got to go." Looking relieved, Robertson hurried out, leaving Rankin staring after him.

———

SEVERAL HOURS LATER, D Company HQ was in equal uproar, if on a smaller scale. Rankin's platoon had made its way to company headquarters, a building in the scattering of houses that was the village of Dhaskaliana. D Company's position was to the east of a little church with a low tower, anchored on the intersection of a watercourse and the irrigation canal. Headquarters Company was to the west of them, on the other side of the church, covering the road from Khamoudhokhori to the coast road.

"Mister Rankin? Why, look, our very own Jerry."

"Hello, Bernard. God, what a day!" Rankin looked at him, then down at the German overall he was wearing over his own filthy, stained uniform. He sat down on a box, shoulders slumped, and pushed his helmet back from his forehead. "What are you up to, this late at night?"

"I could ask you the same thing. Tallying their casualties. Hard to believe these bloody numbers, frankly." Counting casualties for both sides had proved difficult – not because of the lack of numbers he had received, but because Bernard Clutterbuck thought they sounded far too optimistic.

Captain McKenzie appeared outside the door of the little room which was Clutterbuck's domain. "Evening, Adjutant," Clutterbuck said, looking past Rankin's shoulder.

"Cripes, young man, you look like the weight of the world's

fallen on your shoulders," McKenzie said to Rankin. "What're you doing here? What happened to the joys of the leafy, limpid Tavronitis?"

Rankin sighed and retold his story. McKenzie and Clutterbuck listened silently, occasionally looking at each other.

"There must have been three hundred dead in the valley," Rankin concluded, head drooping.

"Same around here. Even Captain McKenzie shot two without getting up from his desk, hardly took his eyes off his ammunition returns," said Clutterbuck, shaking his head.

"You do exaggerate, Bernard. But yes, even I added to the grand tally, as did Captain Hamilton."

At that point O'Rourke burst in, his normally immaculate grooming uncommonly dishevelled.

"Oh, hello, Neil. Neil! What the hell are you doing here?"

Rankin looked up, too tired to repeat the whole story.

"I've got bad news," said O'Rourke. "22 Battalion is coming back from the airfield. B Company's falling back with them."

Rankin and Clutterbuck looked at each other.

McKenzie's shoulders sagged, his voice a whisper: "Oh no! By the great Christ."

———

DAWN WAS BREAKING. Rankin had just finished supervising the return of his platoon to their previous positions, which had been vacated (with a lot of grumbling) by the units that had taken extended positions in their absence. He was tired to exhaustion. Reilly had heated a basin of water for him using one of the German fuel tablets, and Rankin was lathering his face for a shave, hoping it might compensate for lack of sleep.

The news of 22 Battalion's withdrawal had gone through the New Zealand positions like wildfire. Arguments broke out; some simply did not believe it. The German casualties reported by every unit were crippling. It got around that B Company had got up to 22's perimeter, although only by dint of liberal use of bayonet and grenade. They had been just in time to meet 22's platoons creeping off the airfield, coming the other way, many with their boots strung around their necks to avoid waking the enemy snoring soundly nearby.

He heard Anderson's voice enquiring where he was from the doorway of the house they occupied. "Morning, Neil. I heard you were back." Anderson extended his hand. Rankin wiped his, and they shook.

"So, tell me all about it. Independent command and all that."

Rankin started scraping the razor down his face. "Get a cup of coffee, Reilly, or a brew, for Mister Anderson and me."

Anderson leant nonchalantly against the doorpost, examining his fingernails.

"Everything went swimmingly," Rankin replied, going back to his shaving mirror. "Until we found out our top cover had disappeared."

"So I gather. If the stories can be believed, there are thousands of dead Jerry parachutists, and more from their gliders. Yet, we seem to be the ones on the run. Something doesn't add up."

"Morning stand-to in fifteen minutes!" The call came from out in the street.

"Oh God," grumbled Anderson. "Here we go again."

Rankin stared at Anderson, suddenly angry, razor in mid-stroke. "We expected you buggers at nightfall. What happened?"

"We expected the call all afternoon. Hardly any Luftwaffe, with their blokes scattered everywhere. We'd mopped up pretty much by early afternoon. I happen to know the Boss got through to Brigade and told them so. The order never came. We're still waiting."

Rankin stared at him, mouth agape, cold fury welling up inside. "You mean to tell me, Hargest knew 23 was available, and he let Andrew withdraw?" He felt tears of frustration and rage spring into his eyes. "For fuck's sake, Boney, they needed to get people on the top of that hill – *any* people. Fucking catering corps would do! They needed to reinforce the airfield with whatever was available! What about immediate counter-attack?"

"Couldn't agree more, old boy. I don't think 21 was under much pressure either once they'd cleaned up their own area."

Rankin strode over to Anderson, still leaning against his doorpost. Rankin jabbed him in the chest. "Counter-attack, Boney, hit them with every last man we can muster!" A dollop of shaving soap appeared on Anderson's shirt, causing him to step back hastily in order to avoid the next jab.

"Two battalions could make a hell of a mess of them, but we need to do it now! We're handing it to them on a bloody plate!" Hot tears trickled over the rims of his eyes, and down the freshly shaved skin of his face.

"Jesus, Neil, take it easy! You'll blow a fuse if you're not careful."

"We had them on the ropes!" Rankin fell silent, impotent, staring wide-eyed at Anderson as more tears spilled down his face. "All those dead blokes ..." It was barely a whisper.

Anderson put his hands on Rankin's shoulders. "Calm down, Neil. Don't say I didn't warn you. When they come to write this one up, it won't be the ordinary blokes or you and me who get the blame." He paused, dropped his hands to his sides, and smiled wistfully. "Poor old Leggat,[9] legging it the five miles to Hargest's HQ and back all night. Why wasn't Hargest here for fuck's sake? Where he's needed." He shrugged, then wagged his finger at Rankin. "You're always telling me to keep my trap shut. Take your own advice! And keep your bloody head down. The Luftwaffe will be making up for lost time today." He held out his handkerchief. Rankin wiped the tears mingled with lather from his face, then loudly blew his nose.

———————

RANKIN LOOKED AT his watch: just after 0700. He sighed. His rounds of the platoon's positions had shown the troops were dog-tired but ready for another crack at them. Today must be the day, he thought to himself. His stomach was tied in knots. This had to be the day for the full-blown counter-attack to retake the airfield.

The familiar buzz of a lone Fieseler Storch came and went as it meandered its way above the battle ground. It flew above Dhaskaliana, then over the village of Pirgos, Hill 107, disappeared for some time in the direction of the airfield, then reappeared again, flying along the beach from the west. No one, anywhere, moved a muscle. The order not to shoot at "Egbert" was so ingrained no one needed to be told.

Nicholson had looked questioningly at Rankin as the aircraft wandered over Dhaskaliana and 23 Battalion, easily heard inside

---

9   Major (later Lieutenant Colonel) J. Leggat, Christchurch. Born Glasgow 19 December 1900, head Christchurch Boys' High School, 2 IC 22 Battalion.

the house used as the platoon's command post. He was clearly aching to give someone the order to put a burst of machine-gun fire into it. It was certainly low enough.

"Orders," sighed Rankin, staring at the wall. "No one wants the shit bombed out of them just because you can shoot that bloody pest down."

"I know all that. You're the last one to follow orders when they're pointless," Nicholson retorted.

"Maybe they're not pointless," he said going to the window and staring wistfully at the whitewashed houses with the terra-cotta roof tiles that made up the little town. "No one wants the shit bombed out of them."

"I understand that. They know where we are, because they're right there!" Nicholson fumed, raising his voice as he pointed. "Who knows who's in that damned plane. It could be their general for all we know."

"Yes, well, one little Storch more or less probably isn't going to make much difference either way."

"That's not like you, Lieutenant. Their little swastika flags'll be all over the heights," Nicholson continued. "It'll be plain as a dog's bollocks who's where, from up there!"

Rankin stared at him in surprise.

They heard the phone ring downstairs, and McIntyre pick it up. "Aye. Aye. Aye, sir. Right away, sir."

Rankin and Nicholson went downstairs to join him in the cubbyhole that served as the signals room.

"Battalion HQ has come under fire from the high ground behind them, sir. Asking if our platoon can be spared as reserve to support the HQ Company platoons going to get rid of them. Can we move to the junction of the Kondomari road and secure the road and houses?"

"I'll do this," said Nicholson, angrily picking up his Tommy gun, "Call Johnstone. I need to kill somebody. You stay here. Keep your head down and the rest of them in check."

Rankin didn't argue. He heard Nicholson hurry out and send a runner for Johnstone. Rankin was still thinking about what he had said when he heard the section assemble, receive their instructions and their boots crunch off down the roadway.

What if their bloody general had been in that plane?

———

HE WAS DOZING, secure in the knowledge the pickets were keeping a lookout, when he heard what sounded like a Junkers 52 clatter overhead, low down, going in the direction of the airfield. Shit!

Rankin was down the stairs of their commandeered house and up into the adjacent church tower before he knew what he was going to do. There he found Gardiner, behind a Spandau, and Kenny Glover, both searching the surrounding countryside through pairs of German glasses. The tiny tower was only just big enough for the three of them.

The aircraft had disappeared behind the rooftops of Pirgos, 600 yards away.

"What sort of aeroplane was that, Wilf?"

"A Jerry one."

"I know that, Gardiner, for Christ's sake! Bomber, fighter, or transport?"

"Ju 52, Skipper," said Glover. "Looks like it was heading for the airfield."

A bang echoed off the hillsides from near at hand. Away in the distance, from the direction of the airfield, smoke rose into the air, followed by a far-off crash rumbling off the hills. The bang was quickly followed by another, the unmistakeable sound of an artillery piece. A fusillade of machine-gun and rifle fire followed, echoing around the hills. Smoke and dust rose in a black-brown cloud above the rooftops. Noise piled upon noise, until it was impossible to say where each element came from.

"Well," said Rankin, between the booms of the field gun, wherever it was. "Next transport you see heading in that direction, Gardiner, give it a belt of your best. It seems the prohibition against shooting at aeroplanes, and anything else that's clearly German, has been lifted."

A flight of Messerschmitts hurtled across their front, spitting cannon and machine gun fire. Out of sight, above the church belfry, they heard the shriek of a Stuka siren winding up to its terrifying crescendo, followed by another and another. The sky was suddenly full of aircraft, whistling bombs, shrieking dive sirens, roaring engines, the crump of explosions, dust, chattering machine guns and the deeper *thump-thump-thump* of cannon. A pall spread across the little town, enveloping everything in its silent brown shroud.

The three of them cowered on the floor of the tower, covering their faces with their hands, trying to shrink into the puny protection of their steel helmets, praying against all the odds and evidence that the whole of the Luftwaffe was not aiming at this one tiny church. It seemed the centre of a terrifying maelstrom of noise and destruction. Something whacked into the side of the tower with a fearful crack, sending a shudder through the stonework and setting the bells tinkling; chips and splinters whizzed and whined through the openings, clattering onto the floor and into the old timber framing in sizzling, hissing, smoking shards.

"Jesus Christ!" screamed Gardiner, scrabbling away from a hissing metal splinter the length of his forefinger, glowing red hot on the stone floor. "The bastards are trying to kill us!"

"You catch on fast, Gardiner," muttered Glover between bangs and cracks.

Half an hour later, silence descended through the dust cloud. Weary soldiers raised their heads, looked about, marvelled at the fact they were still alive and intact, and reached for their cigarettes and Esbits to brew a mug of tea.

NICHOLSON REPORTED BACK to the platoon HQ late in the morning. The operation, interrupted by the air raid, had dislodged a platoon-sized enemy force which had been foolhardy enough to disclose their presence by firing on the battalion's headquarters area from a high point to the rear when the artillery barrage started. A couple of platoons had hunted them down through the low scrub and olives. The best part, Nicholson reported, was that a low-flying German fighter had strafed the hillside viciously, landing twice as many shells among the Huns.

"Caused a lot of angry swearing," Nicholson said, laughing. "They chucked it in shortly after that. That'll teach 'em!"

They had taken half a dozen of the Germans as prisoners, Nicholson told him.

"Well, that'll satisfy the IO's thirst for prisoners," Rankin replied without enthusiasm. "Any word of the counter-attack?"

Nicholson shook his head.

Rankin rolled his eyes. "We had a bit of excitement here, and there's been plenty of shooting at Jerry, but otherwise things are as you left us."

A short while after Nicholson's return, a Ju 52 swooped in from the sea and dropped down towards the beach east of Dhaskaliana. By the time Rankin had run up to the observation post in the tower, the plane had disappeared from sight. Judging by the noise and the column of smoke rising above the broken ground in that direction, someone else had already dealt with it.

"I took notice of what you said earlier, Nick," Rankin said, after returning from the church. Nicholson tore his attention away from his sandwich and mug of tea and wearily raised his head.

"I had another look at our dispositions. Assuming we're going to take part in a counter-attack after dark, I've done a bit of repositioning to make it easier to strike down the water course or along the roadway under covering fire from here."

Nicholson nodded as Rankin pointed out the various positions and features. The road down the slope from Khamoudhokori and the AMES station behind them to the coast road in front of them was lined on both sides with waist-high stone walls. The stream that drained the saddle area in which they were based had gouged a wadi deep enough to provide covered access to the coastal road. The irrigation canal that crossed the hillside to their front formed a natural obstacle deep and wide enough to slow an infantry advance.

The village itself, being elevated, gave them a good view out over the surrounding country, across the fields of wheat and corn, and encompassed a stretch of the coast road. Beyond the road, broken ground led to the beach itself, and beyond that the beautiful turquoise sea. Everywhere the land was studded with trees, stands of bamboo, and groves of fruit trees and olives.

Everything in sight was littered with the bodies of the dead and their softly billowing silken shrouds.

MOST MEN DID not venture far from their ready positions, for fear of attracting the attention of the ever-present Luftwaffe. Dive-bombers shrieked down on the villages of Pirgos and Maleme in the middle of the afternoon. Rankin watched as the buildings disappeared behind a cloud of thick brown dust and dirty black smoke, shot through with flashes and flames. Half a mile or so away, every concussion brought down a shower of plaster dust from the walls and floor above in the platoon's house, until everyone's face and eyebrows were chalk-white, mouths gritty and dry, noses blocked. He thought sadly of the little square, the plane trees and fountain, the friendly taverna, and the inn-keeper's daughter with the rope of thick black hair.

Fountains of dust and smoke rose as each screaming aircraft pulled out of its dive before careening away above their heads and out to sea. No one fired a shot, not wanting to bring attention upon himself; someone else getting a pasting was someone else's problem. Even if they were civilians. Everyone had enough problems of their own without asking for more.

The tempo of the strafing kept rising. Bombs fell, splinters, bullets and cannon shells whined and whistled in what seemed a continuous roar, a thunderstorm where the lightning and thunder flashed and banged without ceasing. Buildings shook, the earth itself heaving in protest. The sun disappeared behind a brown cloud, turning a doleful red. Underneath the bombardment, heads reeled, and senses were numbed.

Suddenly the cacophony ceased, as if a spigot had been turned off. The deafening silence was disorienting in its abruptness. Soon, heads were cautiously raised and eyes peered out of haggard dust-covered faces. The soldiers had become used to the fact that trouble often soon followed such a "softening-up" air attack. Men nervously checked their mates, looked up, looked out, looked sideways and behind, squinting into the cloud of dust and smoke, trying to fathom what Jerry had up his bloody sleeve this time.

Rankin had his glasses to his eyes, the range of his vision gradually increasing as if a thin, gauzy veil was gradually lifting. The houses of the village of Pirgos had largely been turned into rubble, those walls still standing stared out with eyeless sockets for windows and gaping smoking pits where the roofs once were. Flames leapt and guttered amongst the ruins, wreathing the town in smoke. Gradually, the onshore breeze cleared the pall and the coast road came into view.

Shapes were moving in the thinning haze, indistinct, but the crouching run could only mean one thing. Jesus Christ Almighty!

Rankin blew his whistle. "Jerries! Range 600 yards, making for the crossroads! Rapid fire!"

The words were not out of his mouth before machine guns and rifles opened up all about him. The roar was deafening. Shapes fell, but they still came on. The Spandau in the church tower next to them, a Bren gun to the right, rifles firing steady, measured, aimed shots, the boom of a Boys rifle – the whole Battalion front came alive with gunfire.

The New Zealand front overlooked the coastal road that the Germans were making for. The defenders' elevated positions in bombed houses and slit trenches gave them for once an advantage. A frontal assault against a defended position! With the Luftwaffe's bombs and shrieking Stukas still ringing in their ears, they responded with grim satisfaction.

Spandaus looted from supply canisters sent streams of tracer arcing over the ripening crops, dropping into the shapes visible in Pirgos' rubble-choked streets and advancing along the coastal road. Streams came the back the other way, from the rubble of Pirgos, crossing in mid-air, pitting buildings, sending stone chips flying, splintering shutters and doors, mangling flesh and bone.

But the Germans kept coming. They ran into a zone where the grass danced to the tune of the falling bullets. Each push left a new high-water line of humps in the open, like so much flotsam borne inland by the flood tide.

No one noticed the stately procession of Junkers 52s passing overhead until the parachutes started falling into the fields in front of them. Defenders leapt from their cover, into the open, safe from return fire as men and their supply canisters descended into the deadly green fields between Dhaskaliana and the coast. Many of those who dropped amidst the unripe wheat were scythed down as they hit the ground by the troops on the slope above them.

There was no holding the New Zealanders back. Safe for the moment from return fire, transport aircraft flying sedately up the coastal strip at 300 feet made for a very tempting target. Every vantage point within the defence perimeter spouted machine gun fire, often from captured German guns hurling streams of tracer sparkling across aircraft wings and engines, into doors and windows. Several aircraft caught fire and turned away, out to sea, one leaving a string of pale smoke trails from the plummeting, burning parachutes it spawned. Another stopped dead in mid-air over Pirgos, to burst asunder, shedding wings, engines, tail and debris from the midst of a ball of black smoke.

Once the Luftwaffe had gone, unable to strafe or bomb for fear of hitting their own on the ground, the battered and cooped-up soldiers were free to roam and hunt. Parties struck out down the wadi and along the road, between the protective stone walls, towards the coastal road. Some had to be ordered to stay put, focused on the rubble of Pirgos, to counter the push coming from that direction. The Germans coming from there had not yet reached the perimeter wire or the road junction, even with the distraction provided by the airborne flotilla overhead.

By the time Rankin was satisfied with his defensive positions, the only person left to accompany him was McIntyre. His telephones were dead, the lines cut again by the bombing.

"Come with me, Mac. We'll get you a nice fresh Jerry." Rankin tried for a Scottish accent.

McIntyre grimaced, muttered something about "gallows humour", but picked up his rifle and followed him out into the street.

The dry watercourse they took gave cover from the more open ground on the slopes of the hillside. It led down to the cultivated fields at the foot of the slope, nearer the coastal road. Even before they reached their own perimeter they came across bodies and parachutes strewn through the wadi. The sound of firing was little guide to where the threats might come from, since it came from all directions beyond the gully itself, making it impossible to tell who was shooting at who. Sticking one's head up above its lip would just invite someone, friend or foe, to put a bullet through it. It was time-consuming, working their way downhill along the rock-jumbled watercourse, cautiously clearing each obstacle and ensuring that the dead were indeed dead. Each rustling, billowing parachute was a cloud of silk which could conceal any number of the enemy.

Near the bottom of the gully, they came to a rock partially covered by yet another dirty-white parachute. McIntyre advanced cautiously, ready to expose the rock behind the rustling fabric. Without warning, a figure leapt out from behind an earthfall a pace or two away on the other side of the gully. Grabbing the unsuspecting McIntyre's rifle by the muzzle, the man swung him violently into the boulder, tearing McIntyre's rifle from his grip. The hapless Scot ricocheted off the boulder and went sprawling in the dust.

Rankin, behind McIntyre, managed to bring his own rifle to bear before the parachutist did the same, and fired from the hip. The man grunted loudly and collapsed. Meanwhile, McIntyre was yelling blue murder.

Breathing hard and shaking with fright, Rankin managed to croak, "Jesus, Mac, they do seem to have a thing for you!"

The parachutist writhed and whimpered among the gravel and weeds, gut-shot, clutching at his abdomen. "You're bloody lucky he seems to have lost his Schmeisser," Rankin said, cautiously peering around the next corner.

McIntyre, white as a sheet, retrieved his rifle.

"Get his knife," Rankin said, searching the landscape. "I owe Reilly one."

McIntyre grimaced, slung his rifle and reached for the man's belt and sheath. The man clutched at McIntyre's arm, piteously crying and gasping, calling out something neither he nor Rankin understood. Eventually, McIntyre pulled the knife free along with his water bottle.

"Splash some water over his face," suggested Rankin, still concentrating on the ground ahead, "and let's get going."

McIntyre left the bottle beside the man's grasping hands.

"Good work, Mac. We might make a proper soldier out of you yet."

Crawling out of the wadi, the two made for a clump of trees visible through a field of waist-high green wheat. After about 30 yards, over which Rankin risked raising his head now and again, he spotted a group of three men, about 50 yards away, crouching over something on the ground.

He tapped McIntyre on the shoulder. "Over there," he said, indicating the direction through the wheat. "You take the one on the left, I'll take the right. Keep your rifle below the wheat."

McIntyre raised the barrel of his rifle between the stalks and brought it to his shoulder. "OK," Rankin whispered, straining to keep his weapon steady, fixing his aim. "On my count of three," he murmured.

As soon as they fired, the Germans disappeared from view.

In the corner of Rankin's eye, a shadow flitted by a solitary tree out to their left. McIntyre saw it, too and reloaded and fired. The shadow disappeared.

"Jesus! Get down!" Rankin cried, dragging McIntyre to the ground.

A bullet whistled through the stalks a few feet above their heads. The pair continued to hug the earth and crawled away as from somewhere out to their right came a burst of machine-pistol fire.

As the wheat around them rustled gently in the balmy morning breeze, Rankin imagined meeting an unseen enemy on hands and knees, face to face between the stalks. Heart thumping, he raised his head to peep through the wheat. A figure wearing a parachutist's helmet reared up out of the crop some yards away; he had hardly got to his feet before a Schmeisser rattled and he collapsed and disappeared. Jesus!

A head raised itself briefly above the wheat. McGeorge! No more than 10 yards away, he had been unseen and unheard. Rankin whistled to him, a call he hoped he would recognise. "We're over here, Skipper!"

McGeorge was with Blake. They were both very pleased to see friendly faces. "Crawling around in a bloody wheat field, fuck, you never know who you'll run into," McGeorge muttered, wiping the sweat from his face.

"I don't think those buggers will give much more trouble, Skipper," Blake said softly, jerking his thumb in the direction of the three Rankin and McIntyre had first seen.

"Jesus, I could do with a fag," McGeorge sighed with feeling. "Bloody hard on yer nerves, this."

They crawled to inspect the group of Germans near the tree. One was lying on the ground, dead, shot through the head; presumably the one Rankin had shot. Another lay on his back, whimpering and deathly pale. His tattered and blood-soaked Luftwaffe-blue trouser legs had been cut away and bandaged with field dressings, possibly by the men Rankin and McIntyre had seen crouching over him earlier. "This one won't go anywhere in a hurry," muttered Blake, moving the machine-pistol lying on the ground and its spare magazines out of the injured man's reach.

A trail of crushed wheat stalks leading away from the trampled circle indicated the direction the other two may have taken. "Shit!" Rankin swore. "Mac, one of these is yours, I think," he pointed to blood spatters on the ground and crushed stalks. "You and Blakey, see where this leads, will you? Take this bloke's Schmeisser." He indicated the automatic that Blake had just pushed to one side.

McGeorge found the German's cigarettes and lit one, putting it between his lips and pocketing the pack. "He's not gonna need them where he's going," he said in response to Rankin's raised eyebrows.

A few minutes later the other two returned to report that while they had found more spots and splashes of blood on the ground and stalks, the birds had flown. "Good shot, Mac, looks like you winged him. He'll have something to remember you by," Rankin smiled. McIntyre muttered something inaudible in response.

The wounded German hardly seemed to be aware of their presence. They left him with his water bottle and pressed on towards the coast road, taking weapons and the dead German's water. Covering each other as they moved forward, creeping through the wheat, they soon winkled another parachutist out of a clump of scrub. The man had made the mistake of calling out to them when he heard the wheat rustling and was answered by a burst from the Schmeisser. He was armed only with a pistol, which Rankin gave to McIntyre. Eventually, to the relief of all four, they spotted through the standing wheat the protective stone wall which ran alongside the coast road.

German troops plainly occupied the broken ground and fields on the other side of the road, between the road and the beach. Gunfire came from the seaward side of the road. Most of it went high, above the roadside walls, for fear of hitting the parachutists who were struggling against the odds amongst the orchards, vines and wheatfield on the lower slopes of the inland hills. The New Zealanders left in the fixed positions in the village, higher up the slope, kept up a steady fire aimed at the Germans on the seaward side of the road.

Creeping up to the wall, staying well below the line of sight of the enemy on the other side, Rankin and the others took shelter against the comforting, sun-warmed stones.

"Pooh," said McGeorge. "Yesterday's lot are beginning to pong."

"Yeah, you can hear the flies buzzing from ten feet away. You wouldn't want to step on one, Jock," Blake laughed at McIntyre. "He'd burst like a ripe tomato, and you'd never get the stink off your boots."

McIntyre shuddered and pulled a face. The seaside town of Dunoon had not really prepared him for eventualities of this sort.

"I bet that farmer's going to be pretty pissed off," McGeorge said, nodding in the direction they had just come. "His wheat field's fair trampled…" He got no further, covering his head with his hands as a burst from a machine gun raked the top of the wall at their backs, sending chips and splinters raining down on them.

"Joker wants his ciggies back, mate" Blake quipped, elbowing McGeorge in the ribs.

"Fuck off, Blakey," McGeorge replied, curling up and making himself as small as he could.

"Just as well there's a nice wee stone wall on the other side of the road, too, Skipper," McIntyre said. "We're safe and sound here."

"For the moment. It wouldn't take much to chuck a few grenades over to our side," Rankin replied. He was sitting with his back to the wall, taking a mouthful of water. "No chance of going any further towards the beach."

Just then a stream of tracer whistled overhead from the village towards the beach.

"Jesus Christ, Skipper! I hope the blokes you left behind don't drop shorts," cried McGeorge.

"Better put your dancin' shoes on, Sid, old son," laughed Blake.

They rested for a few minutes more before turning towards Pirgos village and advancing towards the junction. Progress was slow, the men crouching below the level of the roadside wall and carefully searching the field ahead, to the side and behind, for parachutists before moving on.

As they pressed on, they met more of their own men who had come through the planted fields to reach a dead end at the stone wall. They also passed a number of khaki-clad bodies, some of whom looked to have been killed by the Germans across the road judging by the positions and head-shot wounds.

They came to a halt about a hundred yards from the junction of the road coming down the hill from Khamoudhokhori to the coastal road. Resting with his back to the wall, Rankin watched the others enjoying a drink and a smoke as he pondered his options. Gunfire rattled and cracked continuously, background noise now rather than a roar. It was impossible to make sense of what he heard, since the noise seemed to come from every point of the compass.

A few minutes later Nicholson, cradling his Tommy gun, and Johnstone with half his section, crawled out of the orchard flanking the road at this point. "Crikey," Nicholson said, wiping his brow. "It's blimmin' hot work out there."

Rankin nodded. "Any luck?"

"Singles and pairs mostly. Plenty never got loose of their parachutes." He took a gulp of water from his bottle. "It'd be blimmin' easy to get shot by your own up there," he said, nodding back the way they had come. "If they don't get you, the blighters across the road will."

"Yes, I was just thinking about what to do next. Try and cross the road here and risk getting shot or retrace our steps and see if we can't force a crossing further down the beach."

Nicholson's reply was drowned by a muffled bang followed by a cloud of white smoke that billowed above the trees between them and the road junction. Several more thumps followed, each producing a spurt of white smoke hiding the view behind an acrid fog, which then drifted inland on the gentle sea breeze.

"Smoke! Take cover!" Nicholson had the words out before Rankin.

"Keep a good lookout," Rankin shouted unnecessarily. Every man among them scrambled around to crouch behind the wall, straining their eyes into the gloom. The shooting from across the road had stopped.

"The buggers are up to something," Nicholson shouted.

Cautiously, they raised their heads above the top of the wall to peer into the fog. An aircraft turned in from the sea to the east of them, beyond the smoke, and dropped down towards the beach about a quarter mile distant.

"That one must have caught a packet," mumbled Blake, as the aircraft descended to the level of the treetops.

"Doesn't look damaged to me," McGeorge drawled, squinting through his cigarette smoke. They watched as the Ju 52, seen fleetingly through the trees and scrub, landed on the beach. It slewed to a halt, and the door opened.

"What the fuck?"

"Jesus Christ! Hit the bloody thing, Bloxy!" Johnstone shouted. "There's Jerries jumping out!"

Bloxham hoisted the Bren gun onto the top of the wall and fired as the first figures emerged from the doorway of the plane. Rifles along the length of the wall cracked and banged as Bloxham fired another burst. Rankin got the cockpit window into his sights, lowered fractionally, and fired, reloaded and fired again.

Bullets ricocheted and whined off the protective stones, sending chips flying. Nearby, a man grunted and fell backwards, the back of his head gone. Despite the German fire coming from the beach side of the road, the next aircraft to land also ran into a fusillade of rifle and machine gun fire as it crash-landed on the beach, slithering to a halt in the sand.

Beyond the broken ground on the seaward side of the road, a mortar bomb exploded, throwing up a gout of sand. Another fell within a yard or two of the first plane, breaking its back and spewing its contents over the beach, before catching fire, raising a plume of greasy black smoke. There was no time to question where the mortar bombs had come from, as another aircraft, unheard in the general racket, ran into the second, shredding its tail in a shower of sparks and twisting it violently around towards the sea. Rankin shifted his sight to the cockpit windows of the new arrival.

The fire from the German side of the beach slackened as bombs continued to explode. More aircraft could be seen queuing up out to sea, but on the beach, each new arrival was met with a hail of gunfire and mortar bombs. Soon, columns of greasy black smoke rose into the air all along the beach and drifted inland on the peaceful, gentle breeze.

Enemy aircraft were now landing far to their right, down the beach to the east, out of sight behind the trees. The gunfire from the Germans in the rough ground beyond the road picked up again. Shots pinged and whined off the wall but were met with a savage response from the New Zealanders, whose numbers had grown as more arrived through the crops and orchards. The aircraft on the beach might appear wrecked but judging by the increasing volume of gunfire coming from the beach, at least some troops had got out and added their weight to those who had parachuted in before them.

"Skipper!" A frantic call from his left.

Jesus, the smoke!

The smoke covering the road had thinned, but the ruined houses of Pirgos remained mostly concealed. However, shadowy movement was visible beneath the thinning veil in that direction: pairs of feet, running, stumbling, bare legs and shorts, slowly morphed into a mob of RAF ground crew, shambling along with their hands above their heads. Wreathed in the swirling mist, a Bofors 40mm anti-aircraft gun on its four-wheeled carriage followed, pulled and pushed along by more ground crew. Rankin was close enough to see the abject terror on their faces; blue-grey figures behind them drove them on.

"Jesus," Rankin gasped. "The bastards! Look left, look left!" he shouted, swinging his rifle to the new threat. Bloxham had the magazine off the Bren, his loader slapping on a fresh one.

He glanced at Nicholson whose face was a picture of fury.

Rankin pulled his whistle from his breast pocket, took a deep breath and looked at Nicholson a few yards away, crouching behind the wall, cradling his Tommy gun. Nicholson understood and nodded. The nearest men in the crowd running along the road could only be 30 yards away.

Rankin blew a single blast on his whistle, as loud as he could, and both of them leapt to their feet, shouting. "Get down! Get down! British, get down!"

The roadside wall erupted in gunfire. Bloxham's Bren gun stuttered, bullets sparking and ricocheting off the Bofors gun. Some must have hit its magazine, as Rankin's eye captured an image of 40mm rounds flying, the brass cases glinting in the sunlight as they scattered. A number of the British hostages hit the ground as soon as the whistle sounded, but not enough. Those too slow to react, and the Germans behind them, were engulfed in a storm of bullets, throwing up a welter of dust and ricochets. Rankin searched for someone responsible, the man in charge. Dead and wounded littered the road around the gun. It could have been any or none of them.

The shooting coming from the seaward side had either slackened, for fear of hitting the Germans on the road, or was forgotten in the general chaos.

Kiwi soldiers ran along their side of the wall, some vaulting over it to run up the road, yelling and beckoning the British survivors to make a run for it, screaming at the tops of their voices, heedless of the Germans on the beach and behind the hostages. Some airmen did run for it, launching themselves at the wall, running down the drainage ditch, making for any cover, beside themselves with terror. In their confusion, a number went across the wall on the German side of the road. Some of them never made it anywhere, slumping into the ditch or collapsing onto or against the wall, caught in the ferocious crossfire coming from both sides of the road.

Nicholson was on his feet, firing up the road, shouting with rage, face contorted in fury. His gun fell silent only when the 50-round drum magazine ran out of ammunition.

CHAPTER EIGHT

Day Three, The Sword Strikes, 21–22 May 1941

RANKIN SLUMPED DOWN onto the debris-strewn floor, pushing his helmet off his forehead, gazing at the forlorn surroundings with rising misgivings. The earlier bombing had filled the house they were using as platoon HQ with plaster and dirt. A near-miss outside had blown in most of the remaining windows and knocked many of the roof tiles off the side facing the street. Time was passing so slowly that he held his watch to his ear to make sure it was still ticking. It was already after 2000. Surely a warning message to move at a moment's notice was due. He called out to McIntyre in the adjacent room.

"Nothing received by phone or runner, Skipper, just like the last time you asked me."

"Are you sure your line's intact?" Rankin asked testily.

"Aye, Lieutenant, since we fixed it earlier." McIntyre's voice had a distinct edge to it.

"Have a brew, Skipper, and a sandwich," offered Reilly from the corridor. "Take your mind off things."

Rankin leaned back against the wall, closed his eyes, and took a deep breath. A sandwich. The smell of warmth in the kitchen, coal smoke and hot metal from the range in the alcove. "Grated cheese, egg and onion, mixed with Mother's salad dressing, on fresh white bread," he mumbled.

"Ha, ha. Coming right up, Skipper. That'll be a bully on stale bread, then. Like the last one."

A while later Nicholson came in. As he sat down, he took off his helmet and wiped his brow with a dirty hand. "Blimmin' heck," he said. "Jerry's still at it, probing away all along the front." The pop and rattle of gunfire outside testified to the truth of what he said. "After this afternoon, though, the boys are in good heart. Think they've already won the war, to hear some of them talk."

Rankin sighed. "Well, if they believe it, it could happen."

Nicholson took a swig of the tea Reilly passed to him and tore a hunk off his sandwich with his teeth. "How can they take those losses? Only a handful of them can have survived that last jump." He shook his head. "And all those wrecked aeroplanes."

"We clobbered them good and proper, eh Sarge?" Reilly called enthusiastically from his cubbyhole.

"The Germans are prepared to commit everything to win the objective," Rankin said. "Unlike us." He slowly chewed his sandwich and helped it down with a mouthful of tea. "It's not like you to let your optimism run away with you, Nick."

"And it's not like you to be morose and pessimistic," Nicholson retorted. "We've dealt them a hiding. I'm sure the powers that be know what they're doing."

"Yes, we might've given Jerry a bloody nose for now." Rankin looked at his watch again. "No word yet about a counterattack," he sighed. "The longer it's delayed, the lower its chance of success."

—————

NOISES OUT IN the street followed by boots clumping across the floor wakened Rankin from his fitful doze. Looking at his watch, he saw it was a few minutes after midnight. It took a moment to orient himself – the same dismal scene dimly lit by a heavily shrouded hurricane lantern – before he saw the spare frame of CSM Clutterbuck filling the doorway. "Company officers' conference and briefing at 0030, Mister Rankin, if you please."

"Well, well, Bernard, that's capital news. I was about to write a letter to Mister Churchill to ask him to put a sense of urgency into our brigadier and tell him to rattle his dags a bit."

The smile died on Clutterbuck's face. "I suggest you keep your thoughts to yourself, Mister Rankin," he said. "Everyone's feeling the strain. Some more than others, if you take my meaning."

Nicholson watched Clutterbuck go out and turned angrily to Rankin: "I should have thought one pending court martial was sufficient." He stuck his nose in the air. "I have a patrol to organise," he said, turning on his heel and left Rankin staring after him.

Anderson walked in from the next-door platoon just as Nicholson stamped out the door into the street. "Goodness," Anderson said to Rankin, "I just saw Mister Dependable come storming out of here with a face like thunder. What can you possibly have done to piss him off?"

"He'll get over it. I simply remarked to Bernard that I thought we should have got cracking much earlier."

"Hah. I'll bet you did."

"I might have mentioned getting Churchill to gee up our boss. My sergeant seemed to think I was courting another summons, rather than talking plain bloody common sense."

Anderson whistled. "Jesus Christ. Anyone overhear you? The walls have ears, you know."

They hurried into the street and up the road to join the other company officers in the garden of the house that served as company headquarters. Even here, visible in the starlight, a freshly dug patch of earth in the garden topped with a stick and German helmet testified to the death of a parachutist, whose means of arrival was still draped over a cactus.

"Oooh, dear, I bet that brought tears to his eyes," said Pyne, pointing to the cactus.

"Shoot zat man, sumvun hass spiked me in ze ass," said Anderson.

"I sink zat sumvun already shot him in ze ass, Herr Bones," said O'Rourke, giggling. "Bury me in ze garden, Maude. In ze bed of roses."

"Oh, for God's sake," said Robertson, puffing up from some errand, cutting the others' laughter short. "Can't you lot ever be serious?"

"It is uncommonly good and something of a rarity to still be alive, Nellie," said Anderson, "for however much longer the fates may deign. We've got the buggers on the run. The Navy'll pulverise their landing fleet, the whole of Creforce will come galloping down the road and push the blighters off the airfield, and we'll be home by Christmas." Anderson flourished his hand and grandly bowed in his best imitation of Sir Francis Drake. "DSCs all round, eternally grateful country, land fit for heroes and all that, girls clamouring to fall all over you ... Sounds alright to me."

"Bloody idiots," fumed Robertson, pushing past them.

"Goodness. Who's rattled his cage?" O'Rourke said. "What

about you, Neil? I notice you haven't joined the scintillating conversation."

"Trouble with you varsity types," said Pyne, looking at his watch, "you use words no other bugger understands."

"Hah, I tried being optimistic and humorous with the CSM and my sergeant earlier. Fell flat as a pancake," Rankin replied.

A grumpy-sounding voice with a Scottish accent called from the doorway. "You lot, get inside. Even if subalterns are in short supply right now, you're not indispensable, you know."

"Good to see you too, Captain McKenzie," Anderson replied as they filed in.

The room was tiny and airless as the blankets over the windows kept the air out as much as the light in. Hamilton had propped up a door to use as a blackboard of sorts. A diagram of their position was chalked on it, with various lines, circles and symbols marked. The junior officers, headquarters staff, and Captain Hamilton filled the room.

Rankin was shocked at Hamilton's appearance; hunched, the corner of his mouth continually twitching. His skin looked pale and frail, like old parchment. It was hard for him not to feel a little pity, mixed with his dislike. The man was clearly in a funk. Could this really be the man his father had alluded to?

"Gentlemen, I'll make this brief," Hamilton began without any introduction. His voice lacked its previous timbre, sounding almost meek. "You all have jobs to do. I have been at Battalion, receiving orders, outlining our part in tonight's operation."

A shiver of nervous excitement went through the room.

"Firstly, the battalion position. As you know, the Germans attacked in strength this afternoon, co-ordinating their efforts with another parachute drop and a landing by aeroplane. The battalion was forced to give ground on the slopes above Pirgos. We have lost a couple of machine-gun positions and an observation post."

The room was now very still.

"We have no direct observation of the aerodrome, but the battery of 75s hidden in the hills above us has been firing onto it all afternoon. Aircraft movements that were observed were initially thought to be an evacuation ..."

A chorus of ironic laughter and unprintable comments cut him off mid-sentence.

Hamilton held his hand up as Anderson's voice could be heard saying, "... living in fantasy land indulging in wishful bloody thinking."

"Silence!" roared McKenzie.

"But it is now suspected that the enemy has succeeded in landing reinforcements and supplies on the aerodrome. Perhaps also to the west of it," intoned Hamilton, in a curiously flat voice. "Interrogation of escaped RAF personnel, disgracefully used as hostages and forced labour, indicates that activity on the aerodrome has been frantic, with troops and supplies deplaning and being immediately thrown into battle. The aircraft are reloaded with wounded, engines running, and return to Greece. They have suffered heavy casualties, in men and machines."

Hamilton looked up. The baggy pouches and sagging eyelids screamed fatigue. "The enemy ground attack on us from the village of Pirgos was otherwise a failure, with no significant penetrations. Battalion estimate they have suffered two hundred casualties along our front." The audience nodded their heads and chorused agreement: they had all seen them for themselves, bodies draped over the scanty wire out to the front or piled in drifts against walls and filling ditches.

"Similarly, the landings by parachute and aeroplane in our area have met with disaster for the Germans: heavy casualties, and no positions taken." Again, muted applause and nodding heads.

"Our own casualties have been mercifully light." He looked around as the audience nodded agreement. "Brigadier Hargest has asked Colonel Leckie to pass on his sincerest congratulations on the results achieved to date. In his words, the performance of our forces has been exemplary."

"How the fuck would he know?" Anderson muttered. Rankin jabbed him in the ribs.

Hamilton glared at them, paused and took a sip of water. He looks as if he's seen a ghost, Rankin thought.

"Brigade reports a similar position all along the coastal strip. Heavy casualties among the parachute and air-landed troops, and our own casualties are light to moderate." A cheer went up. Now for the coup de grâce!

"Tonight's operation." A thrill of excitement and dread coursed through Rankin. The whole room was motionless, not daring to breathe.

"The 20th and 28th Battalions will attack along the coast road, here," the pointer tapped. "Twenty-eight will advance on the left of the road," he tapped the area south of the road, "and the 20th will advance on the right." He moved his pointer north of the coast road, to the ground between road and sea.

Hamilton turned from his map to face the room. Tension in the room reached a fever pitch as the audience eagerly waited for their part, their order to break out to the west. Would it be the high ground, Hill 107, the key to it all? Or would they be required to fight their way through Pirgos to the airfield itself? Hamilton went on, a tremor passing across the left side of his face.

"Attacking battalions will be forming up on both sides of the road in Platanias about now. Twenty Battalion will be relieved by an Australian battalion coming from further east, and then come forward in their transport. Once the relief is completed, the advance should commence from the start line at the Platanias bridge around 0100 with a troop of tanks leading."

He looked around them, seeming to drag the moment out. *Yes, yes,* they were all screaming inwardly, *but what about us?*

"Our job," he said, the tension in the room electric, "is to keep the area clear for 28 Battalion and mop up after them once they've passed through. Once they have cleared the slopes, they are to link up with 20 on Point 107."

The audience in the room exhaled as one: "Is that it?" stammered O'Rourke. "Sir? Our part? Mopping up?"

A flash of anger passed over Hamilton's face. "You have an objection, Mister O'Rourke?"

O'Rourke stood tall, and palmed the hair back from his forehead. "The 20th is on the very eastern edge of Division's area, sir: it has to come forward five miles just to get to the start line. What happens if the Aussie battalion is held up for any reason? If they don't get cracking by 0100 hours, it'll be well and truly daylight before they're anywhere near the airfield."

"And another thing, sir," said Anderson, hardly waiting for O'Rourke to finish. Hamilton wearily swung around to meet his gaze. "Why does the 20th need to wait for relief? We know exactly where the Jerries are. They're on our front bloody doorstep."

"Yes, sir, and judging by the fire coming from across the coastal road this afternoon," said Rankin, trying to keep his voice level, "20 Battalion may have a hard fight even to get this far.

Then there's Pirgos. Piles of rubble, chock-full of Jerries, perfect defensive position."

Hamilton held his hands up. "Thank you to all the armchair generals among us, but that is the plan sent down from Brigade by Brigadier Hargest. We have our part: to assist the 28th in particular and mop up once they've passed through."

He looked around, defying further comment. "Battalion has issued instructions to re-take the ground lost this afternoon, and to regularise our line. We must make sure our area is clear before the Maoris come through. All companies are to have clear line of sight to the Khamoudhokhori-Pirgos road, so that any movement on the road or between us and the road can be seen and immediately countered."

The briefing continued with the details of who was to go where, jumping-off times, and the injunction to stop once they could interdict the road and the line was straight. Rankin listened with only half an ear. Inside he was seething.

"Sir," Anderson said when Hamilton called for final questions. Rankin stamped on his foot, but Anderson forged on. "It'll take more than just two battalions to push Jerry off the airfield. Then one of those battalions has to re-take Point 107 above it. The Germans aren't just going to give it up when we ask them, even if we did. We absolutely must regain the airfield before dawn, to stop them landing more reinforcements. Otherwise, we're sunk."

Hamilton brought his pointer down onto his table with such a crack that a cloud of dust swirled up into the dim light. He rose onto the balls of his feet. "That's enough! I will not tolerate treasonous remarks from my officers, *Second* Lieutenant Anderson. Recognition signals will be by Verey pistol flares; the signals are jotted on the note the CSM will give you on your way out, along with the challenge and password. This conference is ended. Dismissed," he shouted. The tremor in his face threatened to close his left eye altogether as he stood, stooped and leaning on his knuckles on the table, breathing hard.

Outside, McKenzie told them they could pick up some ammunition that had come up earlier by carrier with an officer from brigade. "Do the job, boys, and don't let me hear you making statements like that again, Mister Anderson. It's not always possible to divine the reasons for the orders you're given," he said, holding Anderson's gaze. "And good luck, boys."

TOGETHER, RANKIN AND Anderson started back towards their platoon positions. As they left the company headquarters, a flash silhouetted the mass of high ground away to the west. Several seconds later a rolling noise, like distant thunder, carried to them on the quiet sigh of the breeze. They stopped, stood stock-still, eyes and ears straining.

There it was again! Flashes silhouetted the hills to the northwest. A soft rumble, carried by the breeze, barely audible – starting as distinct thumps, then merging, becoming continuous.

They ran to a vantage point with a better view across the sea to where it met the star-studded sky. A white finger briefly probed the sky. Sharp white and red flashes lit the far horizon, now suffused with a low orange glow.

"The Navy," breathed Anderson. They both had their binoculars to their eyes. Another bright flash and dull glow lit up the skyline. The land to the west was silhouetted by an orange glow, coming from the sea far beyond the hills. The glow was punctuated by bright flashes. Beyond the closer rattle of a machine gun and *pop-pop* of a rifle somewhere, thunder rolled around the seaward horizon.

"The Navy," Anderson repeated, in awe. "Giving them a bloody hiding!"

Another series of flashes was followed by a bright red-orange glow, which lasted several seconds. The breeze whispered the sound of their thunder seconds later.

"Thank God! I *knew* they'd scupper their bloody invasion!"

Rankin stared at him; it sounded as if he had begun to doubt it himself.

The orange glow behind the horizon was brighter now, shot through with flashes and flares.

"Look at it, Neil! Blasting their bloody landing fleet. The seaborne threat is being snuffed out in front of us! We need to be moving now. And with more than two battalions."

They gazed out to sea, binoculars glued to their eyes.

"*Summer lightning among the mountain peaks,*
Quiet, the distant rolling thunder speaks,
Of home and places far away; and of our fates
Decided, on this mournful day."

Anderson turned to him. "Jesus, Neil, where does that come from?"

"Duffer Watson's English exercise, years ago. Seemed appropriate, somehow."

"Old Duffer, Christ." Anderson shook his head. "Haven't thought of him in years. Mournful day. Shit. You've hit the nail on the head, there, alright."

Anderson seemed to have deflated like a pricked balloon.

He carried on, quietly, almost to himself. "William was talking to someone who had to carry a message to Brigade last night; had to rouse Hargest from his bed. Pyjamas and all. Objected to being woken." He sighed. "Objected to being bloody woken. Can you believe it? The man responsible for the key to the whole island. Apparently, the last time Andrew reached him on the radio and warned him he might have to withdraw, his reaction was, 'Oh, well, if you must, you must'." His voice trailed away, staring out to sea, face morose in the pale light, head shaking. "If you must, you must … For fuck's sake."

Rankin stared at him. "You shouldn't believe everything you hear, Boney. Remember the German paratroopers landing in British battledress?"

"He's five miles away, Neil. Can he even see this?" Another bright flash noiselessly lit the horizon. "Bloody invasion. Not a single Jerry will make it ashore. Not alive, at any rate. But the mere threat of it has done its job."

They turned back to the distant, grumbling, glowing skyline.

Rankin lowered his glasses. "20 Battalion is ten miles away. We should attack and they should take our positions or follow on when they can get here. They should be mopping up after us!" He kicked a rock on the ground. "It's all arse about face."

"It is indeed. Muddled thinking, fear of committing what's needed … Fighting the wrong war. Complete failure to understand the strategic importance of that bloody airfield."

Rankin's hands dropped to his sides. "Anyway, the boys are cock-a-hoop. They'll get another crack at them."

"Yeah," Anderson muttered. "Let's hope they're still cock-a-hoop this time tomorrow."

They shook hands and parted.

———

WHEN HE GOT back to the platoon, Nicholson told him Lawrence was out with half a dozen on patrol. Attempted infiltrations had continued; there had been occasional flare-ups across the company position.

"We have orders, Nick," he said, dragging out his map. "The counter-attack is being mounted by the Maoris, down our side of the coast road, here, and 20 Battalion between road and sea. They need to come from the Kladiso up to Platanias, then kick off together from the bridge."

Nicholson raised his head, open-mouthed. "From the Kladiso? To Platanias? That's five miles away, at least."

"Yes. Five miles before they even get going. And they have to wait for some Aussies to relieve them before they start."

"I see," said Nicholson, after a long pause.

Rankin could see Nicholson was struggling to keep his face from revealing what he really thought. "Let's hope they're here before daylight, Nick."

"God help us all if they're not."

From the entrance to the house came the sounds of raised voices, boots scraping the floor and a pained cry.

"Hey, Skipper," shouted Lawrence from the doorway. "Come and see what we've got!"

Lawrence was standing in the little room that accommodated Reilly and McIntyre, a grin from ear to ear. His Schmeisser was pointed in the direction of a young German, slumped in agony against the far wall.

"Buggers were in a wrecked house, not far from the perimeter, with a machine gun. On the far side of a wee wadi. Weren't expecting company or the grenade that went in through their window."

Nicholson arrived in the doorway, brandishing his map. "Here, show me."

Rankin looked at the prisoner as Lawrence pointed to the place on Nicholson's map. There was something about the German, but Rankin could not place it. He looked terrified, pale as a ghost, skin as taut and grey as parchment, clothes stained with sweat and blood, holding his right arm in his left hand. Blood seeped through his fingers and dripped onto the floor.

"*Wie ist deine Name?*" Rankin asked in his most solicitous tone. Rankin looked up at Nicholson. "We need to put a dressing on his arm, quickly."

The man looked from Rankin to Nicholson and back. He looked to be in his early twenties, blond hair, blue eyes. "Well done, Lawrence, a poster boy for the Aryan master race," said Rankin, "even if he does look a bit the worse for wear."

Rankin turned back to the young German, nodding to his injured arm. "*Wir muessen dich am Arm verbinden.*"

The young man blinked, his face a mask of pain and fear.

"*Tut es weh?*" Of course, it bloody hurts, Rankin thought to himself. He's bound to want a fag. "*Moechtest du eine Zigarette?*"

"*Ja, bitte.*"

"Flick me a fag, someone, will you?"

"*Wir sind alle aus Neuseeland,*" Rankin said, putting a cigarette between his lips, and lighting it for him. The German soldier looked none too reassured, glancing fearfully around the room. Rankin smiled. "*Wo kommst du her?*"

"*Oesterreich,*" came the barely audible reply. Pringle arrived, with a field first-aid kit. "Good on you, Alec," said Rankin. "Patch him up, will you? At least to get him to the RAP."

"*Wie est deine Name?*" Rankin repeated, holding the cigarette for him while he breathed in a lungful of smoke.

"*Albrecht.*"

"*Guter Typ.*" Good lad. "Now I know what to call you," Rankin continued, as Pringle cut away the sleeve of his tunic and got to work on his wound. The bullet had torn a large exit wound and made a terrible mess of the muscle. His tunic and trousers bore witness to how much blood he had lost. He seemed close to passing out, breath rasping with pain.

"So, Albrecht," Rankin went on conversationally in German, "how do you like life in the army?"

The hoarsely whispered answer surprised Rankin. Albrecht was Austrian, enjoying good food, fresh air and plenty of exercise in the Tyrol. That was it! He was not wearing a paratrooper's uniform. Christ! He's German army, not Luftwaffe! Mountain troops!

"A shame you were captured as soon as you arrived on Crete," Rankin said sympathetically, as the next shallow breath puffed smoke into the air.

The answer, interrupted by a fit of pain-racked coughing, was given in a tone that conveyed anger as well as agony. Rankin translated in his head as the man gasped out the words: "We were told you English were kaput. It came as a terrible shock when the plane crash-landed, and we had to run for our lives, straight into action, bullets and bombs landing as we ran." Not everything's going according to their plan, either.

"We're not English, Albrecht. We're from New Zealand," Rankin said sympathetically.

"*Mein Gott! Kannibalen!*" Albrecht shrank back in panic, eyes wide with fear just as Pringle sprinkled Greek brandy around his wound to try to clean it. Albrecht let out a piercing shriek, appearing close to a faint.

"Sorry, mate, brandy's cleaner than the water round here," Pringle said.

"*Brandy, hier ist sauberer als Wasser,*" Rankin translated helpfully. He added that not everyone from New Zealand was a cannibal, and he shouldn't believe everything Herr Goebbels told them. Pale and subdued, Albrecht nodded hesitantly, looking fearfully from Pringle to Rankin. He tapped his breast pocket as he finished the cigarette.

"*Bitte, gib mir meine Pillen.*"

Rankin felt in his pocket and extracted a small vial. He held it to the pale light of the lamp. "*Pervitin*" the label said. "*12 Tabletten 0.003 g.*" Underneath was written "*Wachhaltemittel.*" To keep awake, and a word he'd never seen before: "*Methamphetamin.*"

"What do you call these?" Rankin asked.

"*Piloten salz. Panzerschokolade. Glueckspillen.*" Pilot salts. Panzer chocolate. Happy pills. Jesus Christ! Benzedrine!

"*Also, in welcher Einheit bist du in Albrecht?*" What unit are you in, Albrecht?

"*Einhundertstes Gebirgsregiment.*" It was out before he realised: the 100th Mountain Regiment. Panic crossed his face. He lapsed into a world of pain and shame. Rankin patted him on the shoulder, pocketing the pills as Pringle finished tying off his dressing.

"Well done, Alec. Now, see if you can get him to the RAP." Pringle and another man picked Albrecht up from the floor, eliciting another scream from him as his arm was moved. They got him upright and carried him out.

Rankin turned to McIntyre. "Phone Battalion and get me the Intelligence Sergeant." Somehow the signals staff had managed to repair the damage caused by the morning's bombing.

Rankin paced the tiny room while McIntyre contacted Battalion.

"What was all that about cannibals?" McIntyre asked as he waited on the line.

"Goebbels' propaganda, said a bunch of godless native cannibals had descended on Athens when we got there," he laughed, turning the little pill bottle over in his hands. "Joke was on him, though. The Maoris are the most God-fearing soldiers in the entire empire. The boys pissed themselves laughing."

"What's in that?" asked McIntyre, nodding to the bottle.

"Benzedrine, I think. Keeps you awake."

"Och, aye, that could come in bliddy handy. Can't see us gettin' much sleep this night." He sighed, and held the telephone away from his ear.

They could not find the sergeant, but his corporal came on the line. "Tell them we have a prisoner from One Hundred Mountain Regiment, Corporal; that's regular German army, not Luftwaffe parachute troops. They must have brought them in by air today." As an afterthought, he added, "We need to get onto that airfield. Now."

The man on the other end replied that he got the message and would pass it along as soon as he could.

THE LIGHT OF a distant flare enabled him to check his watch: just after 0230. Rankin was lying in a shallow depression, towards the Khamoudhokhori-Pirgos road. The night was star-lit without a moon: it was no coincidence the Germans had chosen this period to land.

Rankin was with Johnstone's section, half the platoon, as part of the effort to straighten the battalion's front. The object was to intercept German patrols probing from Pirgos and neutralise positions that might interfere with the Maoris' advance later. D Company's platoons were on the northerly (coastward) flank of 23 Battalion's thrust to recapture the ground lost earlier in the day.

The night was alive with gunfire. Parachute flares burst in a sudden, wobbling glare and streams of coloured tracer hosed out over the countryside.

"Keep your eyes peeled," Johnstone hissed, straining to see in the dark. "We don't want to get shot by our own blokes!"

Rankin felt alert, wide awake, feeling as if he could see in the dark, able to hear the faintest whisper a mile away. The stars shone brightly, features in the landscape sharply defined by the patches of deep black, shadow they cast. A burst of machine-gun fire sent a graceful parabola of brightly glowing beads across the hillside. Since taking the German's Pervitin tablet, his fear had evaporated, his senses becoming razor sharp. He gazed at the spectacle in wonder.

On they crept, up the slope and through the scattered trees. Surely it could only be one or two hundred yards to the ridge they were making for. There were a couple of houses here, somewhere, hidden in the dark landscape.

Off to the left he heard a muttered oath, a startled shout, guttural swearing, followed by a gunshot. More swearing, shouting, a burst from an automatic weapon, followed by the flash and muffled thump of a grenade.

Rankin threw himself flat, blinking, as stars and sparks floated across his retinas. Guided by blind panic, he crawled towards a canebrake, momentarily illuminated in the glare. Winking, roaring fire erupted out of the base of the bamboo. Suddenly the air was full of tracer, hissing, angry, multi-coloured bees flying away into the night, sparking up from rocks, thwacking into tree trunks; at least he wasn't blind, some small portion of his brain told him. A scream. Whose? Shouted instructions followed, were they warnings? Another scream and more flashes, the dull cracking thump of grenades exploding, all he could see were lights. A shadowy figure caught in the fleeting glare.

The Spandau machine gun was firing in his ear, deafening him, filling the air with zinging tracer. Another grenade, only feet away, filled the air with hissing red-hot fragments that flailed the bamboo about him.

A flame – *Jesus, we've set fire to the bamboo!* Another explosion. The Spandau stopped chattering; the air was suddenly rent by a bloodcurdling shriek. Then silence.

Rankin was on the ground, head in the grass. Somehow the bamboo was now behind him, on fire, dangerously silhouetting everything around. How had he got here? He remembered only a frantic scramble through grass and dry undergrowth, a figure lunging towards him and suddenly disappearing, another grenade filling the air with hissing fragments and bullets whistling and cracking through the impenetrable bamboo just above his head. The canebrake somehow had yielded to his panicked rush, then he was here, on the ground.

Crackling flames licked up from the dry leaf litter on the ground under the bamboo, emitting dense, pungent smoke, swallowing the stars in the night.

"Bloody good work, Skipper, finding that gap, and clearing the way," Johnstone said, patting his shoulder as he dropped down onto the ground beside him. Rankin was shocked to see a man in German uniform, face down, arms outstretched, just in front of him. He started to stand up.

Out of the blackness, from what seemed like only feet away, rasped a familiar voice: "Gedown, you fuckers!" Jesus! Graham – where the hell had he come from?

Tracer cracked over their heads, coming from somewhere beyond the trees, towards the ridge. Rankin and Johnstone threw themselves flat. Rankin crawled behind the dead German, putting the corpse between him and the distant Spandau.

"For fuck's sake, you'll get us all killed!"

"Christ, Graham," hissed Johnstone. "You can't swear at the officer like that."

"I'll fuckin' swear at any bastard that's gonna to get me killed! We need to take out that Spandau!"

"Yes, we do, Graham," said Rankin. "Where the hell did you come from?"

Graham was flat on the ground a few feet beyond the German, fitfully illuminated by the guttering flames in the bamboo. Rankin involuntarily ducked as another stream of tracer hissed overhead from beyond the trees. From the sound of the firing, it was still some way ahead. "Firing on fixed lines," Rankin said absently.

Without answering, Graham crawled back into the burning bamboo, quickly returning dragging a Spandau. "Here," he said to Johnstone. "The ammo's still in there, under another dead bastard. Get a move on before the ammo goes up when that fire cooks him good and bloody proper. We should be able to liven up their night a bit." He jabbed a finger toward the source of the firing beyond the trees. "Hollis and me will sneak up there for a gander."

Graham disappeared through the grass without a backward glance, leaving Rankin and Johnstone looking at each other.

"Jesus, who wound him up?"

"Colourful character," Rankin answered, suppressing a giggle. "Results-focused." He searched the darkness where Graham had vanished and slithered forward to a tree beyond the circle of light surrounding the burning bamboos.

A few minutes later, Rankin was nestled in a thicket of bushes, searching the terrain ahead, where Johnstone joined him. "Five of them for one of ours," he whispered.

Rankin asked who the casualty was, still scouring the ground leading to the ridge.

"Stephens copped one. Buggered his leg, I'd say. In shock at the mo', but it'll hurt like fuck when he comes out of it. He needs to get to the aid post. We've got their gear, including this coffee," he said, holding out an aluminium coffee pot. "No prisoners, though."

Rankin shrugged. "Oh dear. Sarge won't be pleased." He took the coffee, drawing in the rich smell before taking a sip.

"Coffee pot was on the stove when its owner got the chop," Johnstone answered Rankin's unspoken question. "The boys smelt smokes and coffee before they stumbled over them."

"Good work. Smell of smoke carries for miles on a night like this." He drank deeply and sighed. "Delicious. Can we spare anyone to take Stephens back?"

"In hand. Here's a couple of grenades for you."

Rankin nodded as he drained the dregs from the pot, spitting out a few grounds before tucking the wooden handles of the

German "potato masher" grenades into his belt.

A low whistle sounded from beyond their tree and Graham crawled through the grass to report. Apparently, a number of Jerries occupied a two-storeyed house on the top of the ridge, with a machine gun in a top-floor window that let loose every now and again.

Half an hour later, Rankin surveyed the house through his binoculars from a spot just south of it, on the rising slope that led to Vineyard Ridge. The half-light didn't allow for precise identification, but the window with the Spandau was obvious: it was the only one with open shutters. From there the enemy would have quite a view. More bursts had gone over their heads as they crawled up. Firing in a fixed pattern the intermittent streams of tracer led them straight to the house. Why they hadn't posted concealed pickets to prevent someone following the stream to its source, Rankin could not fathom.

The large white villa was set on a little knoll, from where it would have a commanding view of its surroundings. The walled farmyard on one side was going to be a bugger to get into, according to Graham. The westerly side, facing towards the road, was surrounded by a large, thick hedge. In his mind's eye, Rankin saw evening cocktail parties on a spacious lawn, private behind its surrounding leafy screen. As the sun sank towards the west, filling the garden with soft, golden light and the scent of oleander and jasmine, the buzz of sophisticated conversation was accompanied by a string quartet and the convivial clink of glasses.

"We should hit the bastards from the sides," Johnstone whispered, "where there are fewer windows."

Rankin was jolted back to the dark present. "That front garden might allow someone to get within effective grenade range of the windows," he said. "Cause the occupants enough consternation to send them running out the back." He looked at his watch. In the dim light, the luminous dial told him it was now 0330.

Where were the Maoris? What would happen if they never got there? he fretted. They'd be sunk if they were still out in the open at daylight.

The captured Spandau and a crew of two were left behind a tree to keep an eye on the house, discourage the gun crew upstairs, and "plaster the bloody thing if they spot us". The rest of the force was split, to storm the house from each side.

It seemed to take a lifetime, creeping through orchard trees, praying not to snap a twig, then a field of young wheat. Any minute he expected someone to step on a sleeping man or stumble over a dead body and make a noise to wake the dead. An alert sentry might see the rippling wheat, shoot first and ask questions later. Every shiver of wind through the wheat, every rustling leaf on a tree jangled the nerves. Rankin fought the mad temptation to shout and scream, just to break the unbearable tension.

The pale outline of the house finally loomed squat in front of him.

A faint clink and a kiwi birdcall down the hill indicated both halves of the patrol had got to the objective. So far so good.

They squatted down at the edge of the wheat field, only a few yards from the house. "The blokes inside seem to be on their own, then," he whispered to Graham, whom he'd promised Johnstone he would keep under control. "Listen, you can hear the buggers snoring."

"Not for fuckin' long," muttered Graham, cradling his machine pistol.

Somewhere back the way they'd come, flares went up, casting eerie shadows.

"Fuck!" The patrol flattened itself in the grass, motionless.

Tracer hosed up into the sky in coloured streams.

"Jesus Christ," said Graham in a disgusted tone. "Ammo's no bloody object to this lot. Do they think we're fuckin' angels?"

Rankin's muffled laughter was cut short. The unseen gun in the house joined in, firing in long bursts. They could not see the window or the gun in it from the side of the house, but streams of coloured balls arced gracefully away into the distance. The noise of the Spandau would deafen every man inside.

Rankin pulled his whistle from his pocket. The light of the parachute flares was dimmer, the moving shadows disconcerting. He blew a loud, piercing blast. "Quick, get round the back. Hit anything that comes out!"

Grenades went over the hedge, thrown towards the windows. A burst of automatic fire came whistling and slashing through the hedge from the garden.

The gun Rankin had left to cover them fired, sending angry bees bouncing and zinging off the building, shattering roof tiles, shutters and stonework, tracer flying away at crazy angles – they were aiming high, as instructed, so as not to hit them.

Rankin ran, half-crouching, towards the gate in the wall where the back door must be. Several men body-rolled over the chest-high wall and disappeared into the darkness beyond. The Spandau in the window overlooking the rear garden roared into life again, the muzzle flash silhouetting it in the window and lighting up the room. A German machine pistol rattled. A shutter was wrenched open at a ground-floor window, grenades hurled through, shattering the glass. Shouts and screams from inside, cut short by flashes lighting the room, blasting debris out into the night.

An eerie green light filled the top storey of the house.

"What the fuck …?"

Grenades thumped from the front of the house, facing the road. Rankin had reached the wall. A crack of light suddenly spilled through the doorway. "Christ, they're coming out!" Resting his Schmeisser on the wall, he pulled a grenade from his belt, ripped off the cap, and lobbed it at the door.

As the door burst fully open, a silhouette appeared, crumpled, and another came behind him. The grenade went off, showering the wall Rankin cowered behind with dirt. A man screamed, an animal scream. Guns fired, more grenades exploded, the air was a bedlam of gunfire, grenades thumping, whistling, hissing, red-hot fragments, screaming men and animals, smoke, flashes, chaos, shutters disintegrating, tracer flying, everywhere the air full of murderous, flying, blinding splinters.

His brain registered images like a series of movie stills: flashes momentarily illuminated trees and a running figure in mid-stride, a rearing donkey maddened by fear, a flash in a downstairs window.

Somehow the sound was out of sync with the stills, as if the motion-picture projector had broken; shooting, grenades, the wounded-animal screaming, seemed to be running to a different picture. The shutters of an upstairs window burst violently outwards. Rankin raised the barrel of his Schmeisser and pulled the trigger. He had no idea if the gun fired, his brain only registered a flash silhouetting a body hurled through a gap in a cloud of fragments.

The whole house was wreathed in fire and smoke. Men ran

inside, their long bayonets glinting in the glare. Several figures leaped out through a window, immediately cut down. Shrieks and screams rent the air, inside the house and out.

As quickly as it had started, it was over. Several solitary gun-shots burst into the sudden silence, reverberating around the hillside.

A figure brandishing a pistol and wearing a British helmet ran up to him. Rankin's night vision had gone in the assault's flames, taking all detail with it.

"Who the hell are you?" asked a voice that sounded as if it were used to being obeyed.

"I could ask the same of you," retorted Rankin indignantly. "This was my house."

"That's no way to speak to your superior officer, young fulla. You must be Rankin. I picked up the rear-guard you left back there," he said, jerking his thumb over his shoulder.

"I see, sir," Rankin stammered. "And you are?"

"Rangi Royal,[10] Captain Rangi Royal, B Company, 28 Battalion."

Rankin gazed at the man. "Thank Christ," he said, putting out his hand to shake. "You've got here at last."

ROYAL, RANKIN SAW, was a powerfully built man; big framed, with a large head, making it seem a long way between jaw and

---

10 Captain (later Major) R. Royal, MC and bar, born Muhunoa, Ohau, 23 Aug 1896, served with NZ Maori (Pioneer) Bn World War I, commanding officer B Company, 28 (Maori) Battalion.

high, sloping forehead. His eyes were kindly, lively, and deeply penetrating, but for Rankin the most memorable feature about him was his aura. It radiated authority, competence, decisiveness, the steel of a disciplinarian leavened with compassion. It was clear the way his men approached and spoke to him that he was hugely admired and respected, and greatly loved.

He turned back to Rankin. "Well, Mister Rankin, what exactly were your orders?"

"To clear our operational area and await your arrival. Then to fall in behind and mop up after you'd passed through."

"So, you took it on yourself to push on out here, without orders, and risk a confrontation between your platoon and my company."

Rankin felt his stomach heave and sink towards his feet.

"Yes, sir – well, no, sir. I considered this the edge of our operational area. Our orders were to assist you by ensuring our area was clear, then mop up after you."

"And you didn't think that you needed to wait for us in order to mop up after us? You didn't think that cleaning up after some Maoris was good enough work for you, Lieutenant?"

Rankin's face flared hotly in the dark. "No, sir. I mean, that was not it at all, sir. Our battalion was to re-establish the line on the territory we lost earlier today. If we didn't keep the line between companies continuous, the Germans could exploit the gap, sir, and get behind the companies out in front. Our orders were also to keep the area clear for you. We needed to establish a line from which you can advance. The ridge makes a good line – from which we can follow."

Royal laughed. "Good answer. Where are you from?"

"Otago, sir, Central – and latterly Dunedin."

"Good people from there, Rankin. Some of my wife's people come from down there."

At that point, one of Royal's lieutenants came up and saluted him. The interview was over. Rankin thought he'd passed but wasn't sure and so he turned his attention to clearing out the house they had just overrun.

As he entered the building, the words "charnel house" sprang to mind. The occupants had absorbed the blast and splinters of the exploding grenades. The rooms stank of explosive, blood, and shit.

Johnstone found him upstairs, inspecting the Spandau on its carriage-like mounting. "Weapons, ammo and usable gear collected, Skipper."

"Good work, Robbie. How did we get on, do you reckon?"

Johnstone ran his hand through his hair and lit a cigarette. "Hard to say for sure but looks like twelve or thirteen in the house and rear enclosure, and a couple more out in the front garden, behind the hedge. There's a few still alive, in a bad way mostly. We've done what we can for them."

Rankin nodded as Johnstone dragged the smoke down into his lungs. "We found these in the medical bag," he said, holding out his hand to display half a dozen vials of Pervitin. "Dunno what they're for."

"They keep you awake," Rankin said.

"That could come in handy," Johnstone replied, letting go a cloud of cigarette smoke.

Rankin weighed them in his hand. "Keep half and give the other half to Mo when you see him. They're for any blokes who're at the end of their tether but only give them one. Changing the subject, Rob, there was a weird green light, just before everything kicked off. What the hell was that?"

"Officer's flare pistol. Oaksy, one of the blokes we left behind with the Spandau, said they bowled up and went to ground. Then they got orders sorted about who was going where." He dropped the cigarette stub on the floor and ground it out under his boot. "The men spread out along the line they were to advance on and fixed bayonets. The officer just ups and fires a flare straight in through the top window. Sure got things going with a bang."

"What would have happened if we hadn't been out back?"

"His plan, from what Jimmy told me, was to swamp the place, with blokes running up both sides, going over the walls and taking them on." He picked his rifle up and slung it on his shoulder. "Hardly a word from any of them."

"Jesus Christ," said Rankin. "Looks like we've fallen in with the right lot, then."

While Royal's men stopped for a breather in the garden, under the cover of the walls and hedges. Rankin was summoned to a brief conference between the captain and his platoon commanders. They would have to pull back to wait for the rest of the battalion to catch up; somehow, they had got themselves well out in front. Once the rest of them caught up, the advance would be resumed – in full strength. The company quietly packed up with hardly a word spoken, and moved out, back the way they had come. Rankin felt the disappointment weigh heavy. This wasn't what he had hoped for.

He sent two men to guide the Maoris back over the route they had just covered and to make sure there were no friendly-on-friendly clashes. The rest of the patrol were to stay put, occupy the positions taken. They had reached the intended line of 23 Battalion's area. The two guides going back with Royal were to give Nicholson orders to be ready to move once the rest of the Maoris showed up, then to fall in behind them and come up towards the big house near the Pirgos road.

There was nothing for it but to settle down and wait. Rankin looked at his watch. It was nearly 0500. The eastern horizon would lighten in less than half an hour. The dread feeling in his guts told him they were already too late.

CHAPTER NINE

High Tide, 22 May 1941

RANKIN WAS TOO keyed up to relax. Nerves jangling, he could barely sit still. Was it fear? Or the nagging feeling that it was already too late, and Anderson was right? *It was already nearly six o'clock, for Christ's sake!* Or was it the Jerry Pervitin tablet he had taken? He had no idea what would happen when the effect wore off. Surely it couldn't be any worse than Benzedrine. What he did know was that his head ached and his stomach was in knots. And the Luftwaffe would be back in an hour, ranging freely, making movement all but impossible.

The Germans' kit had yielded emergency rations of which chocolate squares were by far the most popular, but the chewy tinned sausage ran a close second. Rankin's men had also found water which had miraculously survived the carnage. His own breakfast of chocolate went down alright, and he even managed to chew some sausage until it was a dry ball that he could wash down with some difficulty. But the hard-tack biscuit was nigh-on impossible; it dried out his mouth like blotting paper, making it impossible to swallow. A whole bucket of water wouldn't have been enough.

German recognition flags and signal panels were spread out on the ground, hopefully to keep the marauding Luftwaffe away, at least long enough to allow the Maoris to pass through.

As it grew lighter, he searched the ground in all directions from the top floor of the captured house. Away beyond Pirgos, towards the airfield, he saw occasional grey figures moving through trees and vineyards. Downhill, along the length of irrigation canal which ran from the Sfakoriako River (a grandiose title for a water course with bugger-all water in it, he said to Johnstone), nothing moved. In Pirgos itself, an occasional figure fleetingly appeared and vanished. A pall of smoke hung lazily over the whole scene, so different to how it had all looked a few days ago.

Looking east, over the ground to Dhaskaliana and the Battalion's reserve area, he could see the little church tower and the road from the town to the coast road. There seemed to be something on the road at the junction that hadn't been there before, but he could not make it out for sure. It looked as if it could be a carrier hidden in a bamboo grove.

The first glimmer of day had grown into a subdued pre-dawn half-light when the first sounds of battle carried up to them. The tempo quickened, seeming to increase in urgency with the coming day. Haze thickened to brown clouds rising from the coastal strip to the east. The counter-attack!

Late as it was in the scheme of things, the distant noise of approaching battle sent a thrill through him. Could success still be theirs?

Without warning, a gout of smoke and dust erupted between the house and the road, followed by a loud bang and the patter of falling debris. It was quickly followed by another, closer this time, then another.

"Mortars! Jesus! Get out! Get out! Take cover!" The watch on the upper floor ran for the stairs and bolted into the garden. Downstairs was a scene of panic; people seeking shelter under doorways and solid furniture – or outside, leaving the German wounded to take their chances. The next round landed by the garden wall, blowing stonework into the air. The soldier who had been sheltering beside the wall was heaved bodily aside by the blast, and seconds later the screaming began.

Shouting, more screaming, confusion, and yet another unheralded bang. The bomb burst on one of the front corners of the house, bringing down an avalanche of masonry and roof tiles. Figures, shadowy in the dust and pungent smoke, cowered in the garden and beside the wall. The next bomb hit the house and burst on the roof, caving in the centre, sending terracotta roof tiles cascading into the upper floor and garden with a shattering crash.

"Fuck, Skipper, the bastards have got our range! We'll have to get out of here." Johnstone crawled up beside him so that both were pressed hard against the garden wall, trying to shrink into the gaps between the stones.

"The buggers must have an OP on the high ground up there …" The sentence was never finished; another mortar bomb landed beside the house, blowing in part of the outside wall.

More bombs came down beyond the rear of the house, then out to the side, and gradually they moved away. Little by little, it became someone else's problem. A drifting haze enveloped the house and its field nearby, accompanied by sobbing and shrill screams.

"Perhaps they're just probing, area denial, not targeting us in particular." Johnstone exhaled as if he had been holding his breath all this time, his words punctuated by the now-distant thumps of falling bombs.

Rankin stared at him and shrugged, jerking his thumb over his shoulder at the ground floor room full of German wounded. "Perhaps they didn't like the recognition panels these buggers brought with them."

Sobbing and moaning from the wounded, and numbed silence from everyone else. A tourniquet was applied to Nathan Crawford's leg; he had been the man who had been sheltering behind the wall. Their medical kit, combined with what the Germans had brought, was enough to dress his seriously wounded leg. Rankin called for two volunteers to strap him down and carry him back to the RAP on a door that had been wrenched off its hinges for the purpose. Another man had been hit by splinters but refused to leave.

The temptation to shoot the German wounded surged through Rankin's mind, but he dismissed it. Apart from anything else, why put them out of their misery? Let them share the terror of being bombed by their own bloody side. Some of them had suffered further injuries caused by falling tiles and masonry. Remarkably, they bore their wounds stoically.

The top floor of the house was filled with debris, broken beams and roof tiles. One corner had collapsed, and half the roof was gone, leaving the floor open to the sky. The captured Spandau, on its heavy mounting, was covered in rubble and it would take some work to determine if it was still serviceable. The view over the 23 Battalion area and down the coast was obscured by smoky haze. By this time the falling bombs had moved some distance up the hill to annoy someone else.

He looked at his watch. Well after six. "Where the fuck are

they?" he fumed to himself. If they're not here soon, we'll all be pinned down where we sit, recognition panels or no recognition panels. He went back downstairs to find several men digging scrapes under cover of the stone wall with tools they'd found in the house. The mortar bombs could be heard falling in the distance. The haze was beginning to thin.

"Hey, Skipper, looks like we've got company," shouted Hills, relaying the message from the lookout in the upstairs window.

———

THE MAORIS HAD passed through: implacable, determined-looking men. They had moved up to the house and paused along the ridgeline while Royal spoke to Rankin. Nicholson and the rest of the platoon, "mopping up", followed them shortly afterwards.

Nicholson, looking tired and strained, handed Rankin a scrap of paper. "Orders, Neil. We came up behind the Maoris as ordered; no enemy contact."

"*Platoons will follow B/28 extended company order 200yds. Hamilton, OC D/23.*"

"We're to follow on at two hundred yards' distance," Rankin said. "Captain Royal told me B Company is advancing on a front of three hundred yards, using the canal down there," he pointed downhill to the irrigation canal, "as axis and this ridge as start line. We're to follow two hundred yards back, and deal with anything they leave behind."

Nicholson nodded, concentrating on Rankin's words. "Their A and D Companies should be coming up this side of the Coast Road. Some will be this side of the canal, the rest downhill towards Pirgos. 20 Battalion should be advancing along the seaward side of the Coast Road."

Nicholson looked relieved. "Yes, that's what I understood. We are to move up behind them."

"I doubt it will be a doddle, Nick."

Nicholson flinched, then became impassive. "Mister Anderson's platoon is on our left, Mister Pyne's platoon to the right. The other two platoons are in reserve. A couple of tanks waddled up the coast road, just before we kicked off. Don't know where they are now."

Rankin pursed his lips, setting the dispositions in his mind. "We'll spread your section left, up to Boney's flank, and mine right, down to Pyne's. Ready to advance in two minutes. I need to see Tub and Smithy before we go."

Nicholson picked up the Tommy gun. Almost as an after-thought, he added, "Reilly's brought your rifle with him. I thought you might need it."

———

BY THE SOUND of things and judging by the dust and smoke rising ahead of the platoon, the mortar bombs were now dropping on the Maoris. Rankin breathed hard, gut knotted in a solid ball as he looked along the platoon spread out along its line of advance, the ridge. He blew his whistle. It was just after 0645.

They had not gone much more than 50 yards beyond the start line, into a grassy field scattered with trees, before they began to attract enemy fire. Lines of tracer arched overhead and whistled among the trees. The sun, in the Germans' eyes as it rose behind the advancing New Zealanders, had been up for half an hour. The haze drifting inland from Pirgos obscured the trees, orchards, and crop fields, which passed in and out of view. They pushed on into the fog. Soon they came to the first of the Maoris' casualties, lying not far from the opposition they had dealt with.

Machine-gun fire whistled over their heads, coming from their front and, worryingly, from the higher ground to their left. Glancing uphill as he jigged between the trees, Rankin saw two men fall. The main body resolutely pushed on. *Jesus! This is some mopping up!* The coastal road, about 300 yards downslope to their right, was only visible in glimpses, making it impossible to see what was happening down there.

They advanced down the gentle slope towards the Khamoudhokhori road, but the fire coming uphill from Pirgos village was becoming vicious. Movement forward now could only be attempted from positions that were concealed from the village: anything else provoked a storm of machine-gun fire. Shooting was still coming from the hillside above them, on their left, between them and the summit of Hill 107. The route taken by the Maori Battalion before them was marked by khaki and grey-green coloured humps in the dry grass.

A machine-gun nest ahead and to Rankin's left pinned them down. Out of the corner of his eye, he glimpsed figures towards his flank suddenly rush it with grenades and small arms. It fell silent. They got up and pushed on, soon coming across more German and Maori dead and wounded, some practically touching each other. Another sharp engagement with a group behind a wall was decided when Rankin worked Cameron and his captured Spandau into position. A barrage of tracer persuaded the remainder of the enemy to bolt, pursued by grenades and rifle fire as they fled. And even though several more ended up sprawled across the little patch of hillside before the last disappeared into the bamboo, it had cost another man in khaki.

Pausing behind a rock, Rankin wiped his brow. He was dripping with sweat and numb with fear. A glance at his watch told him it was taking far too long. When a German fighter whistled overhead he threw himself flat. It hadn't fired, but every man who heard it above the appalling racket instinctively went to ground. Rankin watched it go and wearily got back on his feet. Presumably it could not tell friend from foe.

Mopping up involved winkling groups of German soldiers out of cover with grenades and savage little charges. None surrendered. The troops believed some of them had played possum when the Maoris went through and were trying the same trick again as the next wave passed. Routinely, bodies were shot or bayonetted to make sure they were not a threat. Any man who broke cover and ran invited a hail of shot. Even so, the effort cost more New Zealand wounded.

The mortar and machine-gun fire became intense. Crawling over the brow of the next rise, from behind the cover of an old olive tree, he saw the reason. They had caught up with the rear of 28 Battalion's advance. At times, the haze drifting across the hillside reduced the visibility to barely 20 yards. Pushing on through a gully, they climbed the next slope; every step talen involved a conscious effort, especially when they were forced to sprint wildly from tree to tree, rock to rock. *That bloody village,* Rankin thought bitterly, as another burst of machine-gun fire swept up the gully from Pirgos on their right, kicking up the dirt and whining off the rocks.

Amazed at not being hit, breath heaving and rasping in his dust-dry throat, he scrambled to the top of the rise and flung himself down beside a Maori rifleman. The ground in front pinged and thwacked as the rounds spurted into the dirt and shook the leaves from the trees. Down to his right, a mortar bomb blew a gout of dirt and stones into the air.

"Where's Captain Royal or your platoon commander?" Rankin yelled, to make himself heard.

The soldier looked at him as if he was mad. "Dunno," he shrugged. "Over the next ridge I s'pose. Some bugger up there's got a Spandau, working over this bit o' dirt." Another burst raked across the open ground in front.

"Christ!" Rankin recoiled from the bullet strikes. "There's bloody machine-gun fire coming from left and right!"

"Bloody oath, boss. Pinned us down. Most of the fullas went through before. Hit two of our blokes, so we stopped here." He jerked his head towards the front. Rankin squinted, and now saw that two of the hummocks down the slope were bodies. One of the "we" was indicated by a pair of boots protruding from behind another group of rocks nearby.

"Fire at where you think he is," said Rankin. "Keep him busy, and we'll try to get someone above him."

Rankin slid back down the rise and crawled off to find Nicholson and Reilly. The rifle fire coming from the ridge top would hopefully distract the gunner. Reilly eagerly took a message up the gully to Anderson's platoon on the left flank.

By now it appeared to Rankin that most of the "mopping up" platoon had crept up to the ridge and interspersed themselves amongst the Maoris already there.

Without warning, a line of men hidden along the low ridge uphill to their left rose out of the rocks and from behind the trees and hared across the next shallow gully through the olive trees. The Maoris let out a cry, leaped to their feet and pelted down into the gully. Had the fire from the left slackened? Rankin and the others jumped up and went after them.

Rankin was dimly aware of figures running and hurdling obstacles on either side of him amidst the swirling haze. Bullets whistled and whined through the air. To the right another mortar bomb landed with a crump, adding to the fog. Terrified, he crossed the beaten ground, expecting a mighty thump to strike him down. It seemed an age till he collapsed, sweating and panting, among some rocks under a tree near the crest of the next ridge.

Gasping for breath, he glanced at his watch. Jesus! Just after 0700 His parched throat rasped with grit; he had nothing in his mouth to swallow. His gut remained in a hard knot, but despite his heaving chest and gasping breath, he could see with astonishing clarity. Even through the fog he sensed the presence of the enemy. He had the weirdest feeling of watching himself on the battlefield, from somewhere else.

The noise, however, was another matter. It was indescribable. The God-awful noise went straight into his brain. Clattering machine guns, thumping mortar bombs, yelling and screaming men all beat upon his eardrums and cerebrum, diminishing mental capacity. There was no escape or relief, the assault made action and thought a supreme effort.

This rise they were on pitched into a deeper gully, more of a ravine, with a dry water course at the bottom covered with broken scrub and boulders. The western side of the ravine was lower than the eastern side they had just traversed, giving a commanding view out to sea and over the mouth of the Tavronitis. At the bottom of the gully lay the village of Pirgos, visible though the drifting haze. Just beyond lay the grand prize: the airfield. As Rankin lay beside his rock, panting to get his breath back, he saw the unmistakeable silhouette of a Junkers 52 turn right over the beach and line up to land on the field.

"You bastards!" he cried, dragging his glasses from their case.

The Maori soldier beside him, who had shouted into his ear that his name was Frank Heke, cupped his hand to Rankin's ear and shouted, "We shoulda been here yesterday, eh boss?"

Rankin nodded. "Yes, we should have."

"We came up the bloody road to help out those 22 Battalion blokes on the first night. We got onto the aerodrome, but the fuckin' Jerries were there already," Heke shouted into his cupped hand.

Rankin gaped at him, stomach turning to ice-water. "On the first night?"

Frank nodded. "Coulda booted the bastards out if we'd had a few more blokes."

Rankin shook his head in disbelief.

"God's truth. Jacko tossed a grenade in a weapon pit, killed three of them. One of the poor buggers was still pulling on his strides!" He laughed at the memory. "Sure gave them the hurry-up!"

Rankin stared at him, open-mouthed. Why had they not been sent with them? Why had Hargest not been here to see for himself? It was all too late now. Rankin patted him on the shoulder and scrabbled back through the gully to find Nicholson, Tub and Smithy.

———

SMITH HAULED HIS heavy Boys rifle into position. "Fuckin' thing weighs a ton," he grumped.

"So does its ammo, so don't give me that bloody sob-story," muttered Duggan. The roaring noise continued, undiminished.

"Shut up, the pair of you," Rankin shouted over the row. "I've brought you, Reilly, to keep a lookout behind. Use the Schmeisser, Tim. Anything that moves – so long as it's Jerry." Reilly gave him an evil look.

"You, Smithy, engage the target. Duggan, you spot for him and fill his magazines." Rankin turned back to Smith. "Smithy, look, from here you can see the aerodrome. I reckon it's eighteen hundred yards: a mile. Spot with the tracer rounds. Anything that takes your fancy. Make as much mess as you can."

He left them arguing about the telescopic sights and slid from rock to rock down the gully to where Sutherland was prone behind his rifle and Nicholson was shouting into his ear.

Another German aeroplane roared overhead. Again, it held its fire.

"Shoot at anything that looks Jerry," Nicholson was shouting. The position was in some boulders, looking down the dry gully, through the haze, into the streets of Pirgos. Judging by the noise and smoke, Pirgos was enduring a major battle. Shadowy figures could be seen darting between buildings through the drifting fog.

"How can I tell they're bloody Jerries from this distance, through all that dust and shit?" asked Sutherland.

"You know, they've got square fuckin' heads," cried Pringle.

"If they're going from right to left, they're ours," said Nicholson, shooting Pringle a withering look. "If they're going the other way, shoot the beggars," he growled.

"What happens if they're going that way because they're running away, Sarge?"

"Shoot them anyway!" shouted Nicholson.

Sutherland fired his first round.

Rankin and Nicholson moved back to their positions at the top of the ridge, Through the drifting fog, grey shapes could be seen moving ominously between the trees. The noise was still mind-numbing.

Nicholson would remain where he was, they agreed, as "HQ" and rallying point if things went wrong.

Rankin crawled into a group of rocks beside Blake. "Fuck me, Skipper, there's a bloody Spandau behind every tree!" It was true. Rankin found targets among the German infantry: sheltered between rocks and trees, advancing grey shadows moved up between the trees, several carrying flags or banners – a splash of colour among the grey-green olives and dusty rocks. A mortar round landed amongst the rocks a few yards away, showering them with rocks. Hot fragments sizzled and smoked amongst the dry grass and rocks.

A bomb dropped in front, and another came down on the reverse slope behind them. More dropped along the slope and crest of the ridge.

"Fall back, take cover!" The voice was stentorian, miraculously heard over the din of the battle, following several short blasts on a whistle. The Maori soldiers glanced at the blokes next to them, Pakeha or Maori, silently confirming the next man had got the message. They slithered back down the slope, then rose and ran for their lives through the gully and up the other side.

Another whistle blast sounded, causing the troops to drop to the ground among the trees and rocks. Mortar bombs fell all along the ridge they had just vacated, exploding in gouts of flame and clouds of dirt and smoke. Rocks and shrapnel flew into the gully and into the trees as men cowered behind whatever cover they had found, however illusory.

The whistle blew again. "Fix bayonets!"

The Maoris rose, as if in a Great War newsreel, grounding their rifles on their butts. Steel glinted in the morning sun as the bayonets arced from scabbard to muzzle and clicked into place. Jesus Christ Almighty, thought Rankin. This can't be happening! Heart racing, gut still taut, he saw the grounded weapons, tipped now with eighteen inches of best Sheffield steel, standing as tall as the man holding it. Loathing, fear and nervous excitement coursed through him in equal measures.

Mortar bombs rocked the ridge line, bursting all along the top of the ridge, with a few overs dropping into the gully. The resulting fog blotted out all sight of the ridge and everything beyond. The bombs stopped falling, the ridge suddenly quiescent in its shroud.

The whistle blew again. Yelling war cries at the top of their voices, the line of khaki-clad men surged forward, down through the gully and back up the slope they had previously occupied, polished steel glinting in the bright light.

Out of nowhere the words of Wilfred Owen's Spring Offensive came to Rankin's mind, last read in Duffer Watson's English class at school, a ghastly portent of what must surely follow:

So, soon they topped the hill, and raced together
Over an open stretch of herb and heather
Exposed. And instantly the whole sky burned
With fury against them; earth set sudden cups
In thousands for their blood; and the green slope
Chasmed and deepened sheer to infinite space.

The Maoris' yelling was infectious. The others, including those whose job was to merely mop up after them, rose to their feet, bayonets fixed, and plunged forward into the brown cloud hard on the heels of the Maoris rushing up the slope.

Another phrase from his boyhood reading popped into Rankin's head: *the clash of armies*. The epic sound of swordsman rushing into a shield wall, of armoured knights crashing headlong into their opponents with levelled lance; here it was, but different. The clash was audible as they met the oncoming Germans at the top of the ridge. A rasping grunt in the sound vacuum left by the suddenly absent mortar bombs, like two packs of heavyweight forwards colliding head-on in a scrum. Screams and shouts filled the void from within the cloud.

Rankin scrabbled up the slope, his face level with the empty scabbard and water bottle of the Maori soldier running up in front of him. The soldier could have been a model from the bayonet fighting manual: forearm stiff, the wicked steel tip held at head height to his front, charging into the unknowing dust.

They were soon swallowed by the silent, dirty cloud, laced with the sour stink of high explosive, drifting across the crest of the slope. A shadow loomed out of the gloom. The Maori soldier's forearm dropped; he turned the point enough to meet the oncoming man at chest height. Rankin was so close he could see expressions of disbelief, rage and sheer terror follow each other across the German's face, visible clearly as the eighteen inches of steel disappeared upwards into his chest.

The German's knees buckled, gave way, as 15 stone of Maori warrior running at full charge impaled him on his bayonet. Arms flung wide, rifle flying from one hand and a stick grenade from the other, he was lifted bodily off his feet and driven backwards. Rankin heard a rasping, hissing grunt and a stifled, gurgling gasp as the bayonet went in up to its hilt, then a metallic clang as the

German's helmeted head hit a rock on the ground behind. Blood and froth gushed from the man's gaping mouth.

The Maori soldier stumbled, off balance at the other man's collapse, sidestepping awkwardly to avoid stamping on him, hands firmly gripping the butt of the rifle to keep his footing as he lurched over the top of the body. The rifle's muzzle and bayonet's hilt, stopped hard against the breastbone, now acted as a fulcrum, dragging the tip of the blade through the man's upper chest with the full weight of the man wielding it. Appalled, but unable to drag his attention away, Rankin almost felt the popping and cracking ribs, heard the sound of steel scraping against bone. The Maori soldier steadied, halting himself beyond the man's head as bright red blood vomited from the prone man's mouth.

Another shadow loomed in front of them. Angered at this unwanted intrusion into his very private theatre of death, Rankin raised the rifle and shot at it, single-handed, holding the heavy rifle tipped with steel in one hand as if it were a pistol.

The Maori soldier turned, tightened his grasp on the wooded stock, and hauled the bayonet out of the still-living body of his enemy. The Maori's eyes met Rankin's: shock, disgust, guilt, fear, horror, all were clearly written on his face. But there was also triumph, elation, lust. The craving to kill again. Hastily wiping the blade on the dying man's sleeve, he was gone into the dispersing brown mist. Rankin ran on, the rattling, gurgling, rasping gasps behind him loud in his ears.

All around, the wounded groaned and screamed as the charge surged over the crest and down the slope on the other side. Whistles blew among the trees below in an effort to regain control of the hard-charging troops. Oblivious to orders and fired with the thirst to kill, the soldiers continued down the slope, their terrorised enemy fleeing before them as fast as they could go. In the distance, beyond the fog, the clamour of battle surged on.

Rankin got his sights onto a couple of grey shadows bolting away between the trees, but he could not bring himself to shoot. Unexpectedly alone, he felt the heated rushing of his blood suddenly chill, like the passing crisis of an acute fever. Empty, washed out, bereft and cold, he felt hollow, betrayed, and close to tears.

He sat down in the dust behind a rock, some distance beyond the crest of the ridge. The field seemed miraculously silent. The passing tornado had picked up its living victims and flung them aside like broken dolls, shattered and crumpled. He'd just seen a man gutted, like a fish on a riverbank, by the most primitive weapon they possessed, as old as warfare itself – a blade on a pole. Terror worked: those Germans lucky enough to see what was coming at them before they ran straight into it had turned tail and fled for their lives, scattering their kit and coloured flags. They would not soon forget what they had seen and heard.

At the foot of the hillside, the dust drifted across the coastal plain to the edge of the airfield. Several columns of dark black smoke rose into the clear morning sky from the airfield itself, their tops dissipating into the bright, pristine blue, smudged into brown-black stains as they drifted slowly inland. From the smoke clouds, Rankin reasoned that 20 Battalion must have reached nearly to the edge of the airfield.

As he watched, another Junkers 52 turned in from the sea, and descended towards the airfield. They hadn't stopped flying in aircraft – even though the airfield itself was under attack.

"You bastards!" he cried. He was consumed by fury, a rage greater than he had ever felt. The inadequacy of the counter-attack was laid bare – they had not even suspended flying operations. The arrogance! Where were those bloody six-inch coastal defence guns? They should be blasting the airfield and everything on it! Why did no one follow the plan? Good men were being killed, trying to retake what should never have been given up. He pounded the ground with his fists, crying, impotent with rage.

The realisation hit him like a kick in the guts. Once the officers had regained control of their men, they would push the Maoris back up here. The Jerries would then mortar and machine-gun them all off this bloody ridge. They've got reinforcements and resupply: we don't. Anderson was right! Bugger him! They'd had one chance to push the Germans off the airfield and that was on the first night.

He roundly cursed Hargest, pounding his fist in the dirt. How the hell could he run the battle from five miles away? Too little, too late. Why had he not come to see for himself?

———

STILL EMPTY OF feeling, he made his way slowly back to where he had left Nicholson in the shallow wadi. He slumped to the ground, propped the rifle against the side of the gully and leant back against a rock, pushing his helmet back from his brow. Nicholson looked at him, concern showing on his face.

"Are you alright, Neil? Have you been hurt?"

Rankin shook his head. He felt his eyes pricking. His body felt cold and clammy, heavy; he had no energy.

"Are you alright?" Nicholson repeated, alarm in his voice.

Rankin heard a tiny voice that he barely recognised as his own, say, "I want to go home."

"What did you say, Neil? Are you alright?" Nicholson's voice sounded close to panic.

"I want to go home." Rankin felt a tear roll down his cheek.

"We all want to go home," said Nicholson.

More tears ran down his face. He could not have explained why as he felt nothing inside.

Nicholson turned to him, put his arm round his shoulder. He held his water bottle up to Rankin's lips. "Here, have you had anything to drink? Drink this."

"I want to go home."

"Yes, Neil, we all want to go home, but we've got a job to do first." He tipped the bottle into his mouth.

"I know that, Nick. I want to go home as *me*." He drew a shuddering breath. "Me, who I am. But I won't. None of us will. I'm not *me* anymore." More tears ran down his face, leaving tracks in their wake. "I'll never be me again," he whispered. "I've seen it, Nick. I've seen all of us." More tears bubbled up out of his eyes and rolled down his face.

"What do you mean? You're not making any sense. What have you seen?" Nicholson cried, voice rising in alarm. He lifted the water bottle and shook it. It was empty. He hurled it to the ground.

Gardiner ran up and started to say something to Rankin.

"Fuck off, Gardiner, will you!" roared Nicholson. "Go and rob some more corpses!"

Gardiner took a step back, dumped what he'd presumably come to deliver, and hastily disappeared.

"I've seen what's in us. The Beast. Inside all of us. The animals we are."

"Perhaps you'd better have a chat with the padre, Neil."

Nicholson reached for Rankin's bottle and unclasped it.

"That's just it. He's peddling a dream. There is no God. We're on our own." He was staring at his boots, drawing a shuddering breath. "We can't blame it all on someone else. Every German belt has 'God is with us' stamped on the buckle. He can't be on both sides, can he? It's us, just us. It's what we are."

Nicholson grabbed his shoulders and shook him. "You listen to me, Neil Rankin! Get a hold of yourself. The men depend on you, for Christ's sake. You don't have the luxury of suddenly wondering why you're here. You are here. We're all here. You act like the first-class officer I've watched you become. I've not seen any other platoon commander I would place more faith in. The men are the same. You've earned their respect and their trust. Now act like it!"

Rankin did not see the slap coming, but the jolt shook him to his core.

He looked up at Nicholson, wondering what had just happened.

Nicholson handed him a bar of chocolate. "Here, eat this. You've exhausted yourself. And wash your face with the rest of that water. You don't want the men to see you like this."

Rankin stared at the chocolate in his hand. Cadbury's milk chocolate, made in England.

"Where did this come from? We haven't had this since Greece."

"Gardiner. Looted from dead Germans' packs, no doubt."

Rankin sat gazing at the chocolate, mesmerised. The wrapper was still intact, he was afraid to open it in case it vanished. He lifted his eyes to meet Nicholson's. "Jesus Christ. Says it all, doesn't it?"

PART TWO

TEN DAYS IN MAY

CHAPTER TEN

Dhaskaliana, 22-23 May 1941

TOO LITTLE, TOO late – precisely as Boney Anderson had predicted.

Rankin and Nicholson cowered in the bottom of the wadi, pressing themselves into the rocks and dirt that lined the side of the gully. In the sky above, the wail of a diving Stuka turned into a shriek, setting nerves jangling and bodies quivering. The bomb hit the hillside just beyond the wadi's lip, cascading dirt and stones on top of them. Rankin's teeth chattered; his body shook with fear. They would be killed if they stayed here.

"We'll be blasted out of here any minute," Rankin cried, pulling the brim of his helmet lower over his eyes, trying to tuck his limbs within its illusory protective sphere.

Two eyes opened beneath Nicholson's dust-encrusted eyebrows; he pushed his hessian-covered helmet back from his forehead and shook himself, appraising Rankin. "It'll take more than a bath to get rid of this lot."

Rankin squirmed as more dirt and pebbles trickled down his neck. He knew that look, knew what Nicholson was thinking: *He's a flake. He's cracked up.*

Just then a runner from Company scrambled into the wadi

and crawled across the rocks towards them. Rankin recognised him as Hamilton's corporal clerk.

The corporal tucked himself into a foetal position between a couple of rocks. His chest was heaving, and sweat had formed muddy streaks in the dust on his face. "Jesus, you're a hard man to find," he gasped, fearfully glancing up to the sky as the next Stuka's siren wound up at the beginning of its dive.

"Nothing's landed in this gully, so far." Rankin forced himself to raise his eyes heavenward as the Stuka's scream ratcheted up another notch. He had to appear normal, although he was shaking like a baby.

"No typewriter today?" he quipped, hoping it sounded casual. The corporal plugged his ears with his fingers and shrank further into the rocks until the bomb landed at which point the ground shook, the wall of the wadi began spouting rivulets of pebbles and soil, and rocks and dirt rained out of the angry black cloud thrown up by the explosion. Wordlessly, hands shaking, the corporal took a dirt-brown, sweat-stained piece of paper out of his breast pocket and handed it to Rankin.

Rankin held the paper in both hands to stop them trembling and quickly read the scribbled order. Wiping the muck off the face of his watch, he noted the time – nearly 1430. It was a miracle they had held out this long. "Orders, Nick. To pull back." He held the grubby order out to Nicholson to read, not trusting his voice.

"Back to the positions we held yesterday," Nicholson mouthed the words as the next Stuka's wail built itself to its crescendo. He exhaled, looking relieved.

Rankin ventured a wintry smile, grimacing as the bomb landed somewhere beyond the gully. "Not a minute too bloody soon."

————————

HARRIED BY THE Luftwaffe all the way back to the positions they occupied the previous day, it had been a miracle that no one from the platoon was killed or even seriously wounded. Rankin's panic had subsided with each dash to safety between strafing Luftwaffe fighters with their streams of machine gun bullets and cannon shells. The house they used as platoon HQ in the village of Dhaskaliana seemed like a haven of peace and normality.

Any reprieve perceived by Rankin, however, soon turned out to be an illusion.

"Mac, run up to Company, quick as you can!" Rankin had just returned to the house from his rounds of the platoon's positions and had to shout to his Scottish signaller to make himself heard above the racket outside. "Tell them an attack's developing on the crossroads. The boys are having a bugger of a job holding them off," he added.

McIntyre called, "Aye, sir," as he scampered for the door, stuffing his souvenired Luger into his belt and picking up his rifle on the way.

Rankin marvelled at his continued enthusiasm.

Bullets whined and cracked against the crumbling stonework of the house on the side facing towards Pirgos and the Germans. An enemy infantry assault was under way. It had started as probing attacks soon after the platoon had scuttled back into their fixed positions. The enemy had quickly followed up when they perceived the battalions were withdrawing. Pressure built steadily as the afternoon wore into evening, and by late afternoon they were probing in strength. By evening, a full-scale assault was underway, intent on taking the crossroads and overrunning

23 Battalion's forward positions.

Nicholson dashed in from the street, out of breath. "Cameron's out of ammo," he gasped. "Our last Spandau. Everyone's low. Need ammunition." He leaned against the doorpost, panting, and mopped his brow with a filthy handkerchief. His face was grey with exhaustion and lined with anxiety.

"Shit," said Rankin. "I've sent Mac up to Company to ask for a bit of help."

At that moment a mortar bomb landed nearby, shaking dust from between the floorboards above and showering them with chunks of plaster from the walls. "We're going to have to find ourselves a new home if this keeps up," Nicholson said, wiping the fine white dust from his face.

———

THE TINY VILLAGE of Dhaskaliana stank. The German attack the previous day had left bodies lying in drifts, and the numbers of dead had increased appreciably as a result of the last parachute drop. Not all the bodies lying out in the fields and gullies to their front were German; the dead of both sides were intermingled and, in some cases, intertwined, testament to the closeness of the fighting. The soft breeze from the sea carried the foetid, sickly sweet smell of death mixed with the burning, acid smell of explosives inland. Yesterday's corpses, piled up around the crossroads, having lain all day in the sun, were starting to bloat. Today's attacking Germans found no cover in the open and were forced to take cover behind them. Repeatedly hit, the bodies of the dead quivered and jumped and spilled their noxious contents.

It was nearly dusk. Some of the forward positions were in

real danger. Mortar bombs landed with a bright flash and dull thump, spouting dirt and rocks. The forward positions could not move without getting their heads blown off. Even a slit trench was not proof against a direct hit. The Germans pressed hard behind their covering fire.

For the second time that day, as one man the Maoris rose out of the rough ground they now occupied between 23 and 21 Battalions and came down the hill in full cry, across 23 Battalion's front, bayonets fixed. The hard-pressed 23 Battalion soldiers, not to be outdone, leapt out of their rat holes and rushed to join them, fixing their bayonets as they ran.

Once again, German soldiers were confronted by these apparitions seeming to rear up out of the very earth itself, screaming like banshees and coming at them wielding their ferocious steel blades. German infantry doctrine, training and the men's experience to date had never anticipated the possibility that the New Zealanders, outgunned and under intense fire, would not simply run for it, or be cowed into surrendering to the all-conquering Wehrmacht. They certainly had not contemplated the beaten rising from the ground and launching themselves at the attackers. Such contrarian behaviour threw the Germans completely off balance.

The charge was brief but brutal. Rising from their slit trenches or emerging from bomb-shattered buildings, without orders, the New Zealand infantry charged across the open ground straight at the enemy. Those who had already experienced a Maori bayonet charge that morning did not linger. They turned and fled, leaving the new arrivals to suffer the consequence of their inexperience on their own.

Blood lust, borne of the bitter taste of frustration and anger, was in the air. Rifle butts rose and fell as the two sides clashed.

The long bayonets and the New Zealanders wielding them took another fearful toll.

The opposition ran for their lives, terrorised and terrified, shedding weapons and equipment as they went, leaving their dead still and silent, and their wounded writhing and screaming in their wake.

The bombs stopped falling, the machine guns fell silent. Their crews were overrun, stabbed, slashed, and bludgeoned. Grenades proved fearfully effective against mortar and Spandau crews alike; shrapnel-riddled and concussed, the survivors were unable to escape the slashing, stabbing steel and bashing rifle butts that seemingly emerged from the explosions themselves.

After dark had fallen, once the defenders were back in their positions, the mood in their lines was like that in the victors' changing shed after a football match: high spirits, action replays, boasting, the occasional silence brought on by mention of someone who had "copped it". The adrenaline-fuelled high, mixed with the relief from the perpetual bombardment and machine-gunning, fed the illusion they could do anything.

Orders had gone around that no fires were to be lit that evening. However, the paltry ration delivery they received with an issue of ammunition that had been brought up by a truck after dark meant a few at least managed to heat something to eat on their Esbit cookers.

Rankin oversaw the deliveries while Nicholson and Reilly refilled their Thompson magazines. He knew, from the furtive comings and goings under the cover of darkness, that those with the stomach for it were venturing back out into the field to augment their own supplies, and, perhaps, add to their stock of tradeable goods.

After telling Nicholson that he would do the rounds in the early dark with Reilly, to give Nicholson a chance to eat something and get an hour's sleep, Rankin and Reilly called into a section post below the village, There, in the ruins of an isolated building, they encountered a group sitting around a hooded candle, carefully covered to limit its little pool of light to the earthen floor. Reilly waited outside as Rankin entered. Hills, kneeling on the floor, swiftly moved his hand as if to conceal something.

"What have you got there, Hillsy?" Rankin asked.

Even in the feeble glow of the candle he could see Hills's face colour. "Nothing, sir."

"Come on, Hillsy, don't bullshit me, I saw you cover something up. What is it?"

Hills reluctantly withdrew his hand. Underneath was a small pink and blue box.

"Pervitin," said Rankin, turning it over in his hand. The box was different to the vials he'd seen; this one looked like it might have been bought in a chemist's shop.

"Do you know what it's for?"

"Keeps you awake and makes you more alert," Hills answered quietly.

Rankin nodded. "Where'd you get it?"

Hills shuffled on his knees, looking at the others.

"I'm not angry. I just want to know."

"Wilf, Skipper," one of them volunteered. "He's got a few boxes. Cost a few bob."

"Has he, by God?" answered Rankin. "Make sure you only take them when you need to, like if we have to bugger off from here in the middle of the night. One at a time, no more than two a day. Might make you feel a bit less hungry, too. The Jerries

TEN DAYS IN MAY

apparently dish them out to their blokes. There must be thousands of them out there. You can pick them up, you know. For nothing."

They all looked sheepishly at each other as he turned to leave their post. "Don't forget to keep a bloody good lookout. Someone needs to stay awake!"

"Jesus Christ Almighty," he muttered as he rejoined Reilly, ready to continue his rounds to the next section.

"What did you say, Skipper?" Reilly asked.

"Nothing, Tim. The boys feel we gave them a whacking and can hold the buggers here. They're cock-a-hoop."

Reilly grinned at him, patting his Tommy gun. "We just need another couple of days like yesterday, Skipper. That'll do for them."

Rankin smiled at the thought and the boy's wishful thinking. "I hope so, Tim. I bloody hope so."

———

CHRIST, IT HAD *been a long, hard day*. Rankin sat with his back to the wall, legs splayed, helmet on the rubble-strewn floor beside him. It was nearly midnight. He had told Nicholson to rest; Rankin would take the midnight to 0400.

The boys might have finished the day on a high, with delusions of invincibility, but he had not. He couldn't pin down his mood; if anyone had asked him at that moment, he'd have trouble explaining. Optimistic: they had thumped the buggers, good and proper. Pessimistic: it was clear the defence had reached its high-water mark in the effort to regain the airfield. From here on their fortunes must ebb like the tide. Proud and humiliated at the same time, both happy and infinitely sad: proud to have survived a baptism of fire like few others, the equal of that at Gallipoli; humiliated that he'd broken in the field and been brought around by his sergeant. Happy to be alive, he was sad for the many who were not – and for a loss he had trouble putting his finger on.

The watch was quiet, except for those snoring among the ruins. Outside, nothing moved. Looking at the passing stars, he wondered what they were doing at home. Were they glued to the radio? He was desperately thirsty; the well had been hit by a bomb. What was in their bottles was their lot. Dead tired, but not sleepy; that could only be the pills. He also wondered about them.

———

"WHAT HO, BERNARD, have they surrendered then?"

Clutterbuck silently handed him a couple of sheets of signal pad paper.

He read the orders, then turned them over, wondering if he'd missed something. Blank. His empty stomach turned to ice. The CSM's impassive expression provided no enlightenment. Rankin turned the pages over and read the cryptic messages again.

"Bn will withdraw east Platanias R south line Kondomari-Modhion 0430 independent movement. 28 Bn follows. Objective 1000 hrs. Sgnd Leckie DF LtCol."

The second, written in a familiar scribble, read: "D Coy mvmnt under cover immediate cmply Bn order by pltn indpndnt. Objctve E Platanias village. Rpt mvmnt immediate. Sgnd Hamilton OC D/23."

Rankin looked at Clutterbuck, then at his watch: 0455. "It says 'platoons to move independently east of Platanias, immediately',

Bernard. The word 'immediately' is written twice." There was no doubting the meaning. "Withdrawal" in battalion strength ordered by Leckie, to commence at 0430. Hamilton's order was to move as independent platoons "immediate". The time was already past 0430, meaning that "immediate" meant "right now".

"That it does, Mister Rankin."

"But we can hold. We gave them a hiding yesterday." He had to say it. For the benefit of the others, regardless of what he felt inside.

"Our orders say we are not going to, Mister Rankin. A word to the wise, if you don't mind. You're the last platoon on my rounds. Some of the first may already be on their way. You can argue the toss with Jerry if you like. I've done as I was told: delivered the orders. Good luck, Mister Rankin." He stepped back and saluted.

Rankin half-heartedly returned the salute. Clutterbuck made a show of shining the brass badge, pinned above his shirt pocket.

"If it helps, Mister Rankin, Battalion's last number 18 radio went U/S last night. We're out of contact with Force, Brigade, and Uncle Tom Cobley. And, I haven't told you in person, how chuffed I was to receive this, sir. Now, let's move along, shall we?"

Rankin watched him go, then shouted: "NCOs to me, on the double! Mac, run out and get the section leaders, now! Tim, marching order, pack what you can. We're moving."

Orders were issued to the NCOs, who received them blank-faced and angry. Kit to be packed in five minutes, what couldn't be carried to be destroyed. Pickets were called in, rear-guard tasked. Some of the pickets had already seen movement as elements of the battalion pulled out and headed east. The pickets had guessed what was afoot; news spread fast.

The men had plenty to say – their emotions after yesterday's bloodletting still raw. But he had known it when that Junkers turned in from the sea. The Germans committed everything to winning. And they would.

Even the few remaining 75s, firing all day, hadn't kept them from using the airfield. Escaped RAF groundcrew told how they had been made to manhandle disabled and destroyed aircraft out of the way as the shells came down. They reported seeing men deplaning at the run, cargo heaved out onto the dusty ground; the planes' engines kept running while they were reloaded with wounded who were brought up in British trucks. The planes' doors were still open when the pilots gunned the throttles and taxied out in a cloud of choking dust. The stories had spread quickly.

Nicholson had heard the shout for the NCOs.

"Battalion's been ordered to withdraw, Nick, east of Platanias."

Nicholson sucked on his unlit pipe while he absorbed this news. After a long pause, "Not what I was expecting, I must say."

"Thank Christ the Luftwaffe hasn't arrived yet, or Jerry from out front," Rankin said, jerking his thumb in the direction of the airfield. "I hope he's got a bloody sore head." He spread the map on a box top as Lawrence and Johnstone clattered in. Their faces showed they had heard the news. Poring over the map, they saw they were to take a route inland from the coastal road, south of a line between the two villages of Kondomari in the west and Modhion in the east, which would keep them half a mile away from the main road, among the hills and gullies. They would stay away from the main road for as long as possible.

The platoon was ready by 0505. Breakfast would have to wait – the muttering and complaining was furious. Rankin brooked no discussion: all the whys and wherefores were met with, "Orders!" Any further attempt at discussion was rebuffed with a furious, "Orders are bloody orders! I've got mine and I've given you yours. Get on with it!"

Sections withdrew quietly from their positions and fell into a loose platoon marching order, disappearing into the darkened landscape, allowing occasional glimpses of other formations ahead of them. Rankin fell in beside Nicholson as they trudged up the hill behind Dhaskaliana through the groves of trees.

"Sorry about yesterday, Nick," Rankin said. Nicholson looked up and shrugged. Rankin's throat was dry, afraid his outburst had wrecked the easy familiarity they enjoyed.

"Everyone gets a bit overwrought at times," Nicholson said, his expression guarded.

"Yes. You were right to do what you did. We can't afford to let them think I'm a flake."

"You're not a flake. The person you most need to convince of that is yourself." Eventually, in a subdued voice, he said, "I'm sorry I struck you. Court martial offence, striking an officer."

"Administered appropriate therapy to his superior temporarily disoriented by the strain of battle," Rankin replied with a wry smile. "Forget it." They continued in silence.

Rankin glanced at his watch: just after 0600. "I did think we might have held them for a day."

Nicholson searched the empty sky, then turned to Rankin and shrugged. "I ran into a sergeant I know in the Twentieth, yesterday," said Nicholson quietly. "Half their blokes came up the hill to try and get round Pirgos. The Huns used the airfield Bofors guns against them. They did for the three tanks that came up to lead the charge."

"Jesus, I knew it," Rankin fumed. "I'll lay odds that not one of those guns fired a bloody shot during the landings. Poor bloody sods didn't know whether they were Arthur or bloody Martha by the time the Luftwaffe finished with them." Rankin breathed hard, the encounter sharp in his mind. "I'd like to wring that bloody major's neck."

"The one who called you a cocky colonial snot, you mean?"

Rankin glanced at Nicholson. There was the faintest hint of a smile on his face.

"Yes, that one."

They crossed a ridge, keeping off the ridgeline, then strung out into loose marching order again.

"He also told me that Hun parachutists established a stronghold in the prison. Dribbled in reinforcements. Now they control the valley," said Nicholson.

"Christ Jesus," Rankin whispered. "If that's true, they can attack up the valley and cut the coast road. Our way out."

"Said they've been there since day one," continued Nicholson.

Rankin stared at him. Jesus! "Could be a rumour, like the one that said the parachutists were wearing battledress, so we all had to wear shorts."

Nicholson shook his head. "It explains why we're not holding. He also told me the Huns overran the hospital, captured all the staff and patients, and shot the colonel in charge."

Rankin pulled up in mid-stride, staring open-mouthed at Nicholson. "Good God, why would they do that? Take prisoners who can't move. And shoot the doctor? Why the hell would they do that?"

"That's what he told me. Maybe they thought the hospital was something else."

"It was marked, plain as day. You know these rumours, Nick. Mostly bullshit," Rankin replied. "I can't believe that one."

"I'm only telling you what he told me."

They crossed another ridge and continued along the terraced side of the next valley. Two broad terraces, planted in rows of trees, separated by a stone wall about six feet high, made for comfortable walking. It was now nearly full daylight, and they had not long entered the valley when a Messerschmitt 110 roared overhead. The platoon scattered, going to ground among the trees.

The big fighter banked away over the hills and was lost to sight. How long would it take to come back? Petrified, they tried to shrink into the very earth. Rocks and trees suddenly seemed scanty cover against cannon and machine guns.

Anxiously pale under their helmets, the men peered up and searched every quarter of the sky. Hollis was the first to see it as it straightened up away to the east, beyond the end of the valley, then dived towards them. The silhouette grew bigger as it came closer, losing height as it came on. Still a mile away, it opened fire, the distant rattle of machine guns and thump of the cannon heard over the rising roar of the engines. The petrified watchers shrank further into the dry grass, behind the thinnest of tree trunks, and held their breath.

In disbelief they saw the tracers' smoke trails hiss into the valley beyond theirs. The silhouette grew, the fighter's pale blue belly skimmed over their heads as it pulled out of its dive, the noise thundering off the valley's sides. They all held their fire.

As the noise receded up the valley and disappeared, the men tentatively raised themselves, ears ringing, then sheepishly stumbled to their feet and nervously picked up their equipment. Peering up into the cloudless sky, they silently resumed their march.

Sometime later, over another saddle, another engine growled into the valley behind them. Again everyone scattered, instinctively flattening themselves behind a friendly tree or comforting rock. The approaching racket grew louder. Fingernails scratched at the stony soil as each man desperately tried to minimise the target he made. Some anxiously peered out from whatever cover they had found; others were too terrified to look. Everyone except Nicholson.

He stood on the terrace, feet braced, Tommy gun at his shoulder. "Come on, you buggers!" he roared at the oncoming aeroplane. "Come on and make a fight of it!"

Rankin stared at him, eyes wide in astonishment. The plane was nearly upon them, flying level with the terrace. "Nick!" he screamed. The platoon waited for the inevitable hail of gunfire. The monster's clattering approach echoed off the valley walls, coming at them from all sides.

The Tommy gun fired with its characteristic "tock-tock-tock-tock". Only yards away now, the plane came on. Each man desperately clawed at the ground, trying to put something between himself and the machine that must surely end the Sarge's life in a brief, shattering roar. Not wanting to look, but unable to tear his eyes away, Rankin found his throat was too dry to call out again.

The ponderous machine flew sedately past, through the stream of bullets. Sparks and bits flew off the front engine, then off the port engine. The wing tip passed within feet of Nicholson as he stood, firing bullets into the fuselage, feet braced, swinging the gun through an arc as the great beast clattered past. As he watched, Rankin saw holes appear along the side of the cockpit, then a Perspex window starred and became opaque as the line of holes continued down the corrugated metal fuselage. A startled face appeared at a little oblong window and just as suddenly disappeared.

Despite the raucous clatter, Rankin could hear the rattling scrape as the magazine spring on Nicholson's Tommy gun pushed the bullets around and around inside the drum, until each was fed into the gun's breech and coughed out as a fat lead slug, nearly half an inch in diameter, causing another hole to appear in the corrugated aluminium of the aircraft. The line of holes continued past the windows, over the door, and onto the plane's tail.

However, the Junkers 52 flew on as if nothing had happened, its echoes fading away down the valley. Was it trailing a wisp of smoke? It turned left, and vanished from view, leaving a stunned silence behind it.

"Jesus Christ, Sarge! You'll get yourself killed!"

"You and every other bugger!"

Nicholson was still standing, smoking Tommy gun at his shoulder, still braced to confront the next interloper. His shoulders slumped as he lowered the weapon.

"That was my last 50-round magazine."

"On your feet, you blokes," Rankin called into the sudden silence. "We've still got a way to go. We need to put some distance on. Keep a bloody good lookout."

"What on earth possessed you back there?" Rankin asked later, falling in beside Nicholson.

Nicholson sighed and pursed his lips, suddenly seeming older than his years. "I don't know. Something just snapped. They run rings round us, and we just lie in the dirt and take it."

"Well, you certainly picked your target," said Rankin.

A ghost of a smile flitted over Nicholson's face: "Pure luck. Saw the two pilots, clear as day. Lord knows what they were doing, flying down this little valley."

"Probably lost. They would have been shitting bricks when they saw you." Rankin shook his head. "Fifty rounds of .45 calibre … how the bloody thing didn't crash is beyond me."

Nicholson shrugged, eased his pack, and moved the Tommy gun to the other shoulder. "Can't be anything important in them," he said. "More's the pity."

"I don't know about that. That face at the window looked scared stiff. Probably chock full of reinforcements." Rankin whistled. "Imagine the effect of a .45 calibre round once it's punched its way through aluminium fuselage." He smacked his fist into his palm. "Great big fat dum-dums."

"Good Lord." Nicholson stared at him, ashen faced. "Poor blighters."

CHAPTER ELEVEN

The Trek East, 23 May 1941

LATER, RANKIN CALLED a halt in a grove of olives. The sun was already hot as the platoon crossed a road that ran through a cutting on its way down from the foothills to the coastal plain. The olive grove on the eastern side of the road offered shade and concealment. Rankin sat with his back to a tree trunk, chewing German sausage and black bread which Reilly had conjured up from somewhere as he mulled over their position.

Venables crouched down beside him. "Corp wants a word, Skipper. Something on the road up the hill."

"Bugger!" Rankin washed down his mouthful with a gulp of lukewarm water and followed Venables to Johnstone's observation post. Johnstone himself was kneeling behind a tree with the lookout, intently studying the hill above them.

"Dust. Something's moving on the road up there, Skipper," he said, pointing up the hill.

Rankin raised his binoculars to his eyes to see a fine haze of dust drifting off the road and away along the hillside. In the middle of the dust appeared a shadow. He blinked, looked away, and refocused. "Shit!" He strained his eyes, concentrating on the dark smudge. "Could be someone coming round a corner. They don't seem to have got the message about keeping out of sight."

He swept the rest of the hillside with his binoculars, then came back to the road. It was clearer now; two figures out in front, followed by a dark grey centipede. As he watched, the centipede grew bigger, bigger than a platoon.

"Get Sergeant Nicholson, will you, Venables? Bloody good work, whoever spotted this."

Venables returned almost immediately, bringing Nicholson with his German Zeiss binoculars. "I agree with you," he said after studying the centipede for a good half minute. "Huns."

"Jesus." Those nearby were taking an interest in what was going on; Rankin heard weapons being checked and glimpsed rations being stuffed into packs after Nicholson's verdict. "How the hell did they get here? Swinging along like they own the bloody place."

The centipede came steadily down the hill towards them. Rankin rapidly weighed up the options and outlined his decision.

Nicholson, clearly, was not convinced. "Our orders are to keep under cover, not to attract attention to ourselves," he said, face creased by a worried frown.

"It won't attract attention to us, so long as it works," Rankin said. "We can use the stone walls lining the road to stay out of sight."

"We should slip away quietly. As ordered."

Rankin looked sharply at the older man. "And leave the problem for someone else? I don't think so."

"They'll run into strength on the Coast Road, if not before," persisted Nicholson. "Our orders are to get to the Platanias River, quietly."

Johnstone looked away in discomfort.

"And what if they get to the Coast Road and cut it?" Rankin hissed. "Our job is to destroy the enemy, wherever and whenever we encounter him."

"We'd be following orders."

Rankin stared at his sergeant, anger rising. "I'm giving the order. Now get to it!"

After scrambling back down the slope, he quickly briefed Lawrence, then led his section below the fold in the road and back to the western side that they had come from. Rankin positioned himself at the downhill end of the cutting, behind the stone wall that lined the road, with Corkhill and Renfrew next to him. Half the platoon was ranged over the brow of the hill on each side of the road, concealed behind the roadside walls. Unless the Germans sent someone forward to investigate the cutting, they should remain out of sight.

"Skipper, I hear singing," whispered Corkhill.

Rankin's mouth fell open. "Christ! Really?"

Corkhill nodded. Rankin caught a fragment against the breeze. A marching song. "Bloody boy scouts. Keep quiet, for Christ's sake," he whispered to those nearby.

The singing was clearer now. A hundred voices tramping along the road without a care in the world, sure in the knowledge of their own invincibility. The sheer arrogance touched a nerve made raw by yesterday's humiliation. Fury surged through Rankin – with them, with Nicholson, with the whole fucking shemozzle.

The volume rose as they came closer, marching up the rise into the cutting, where the sides concentrated the sound. If he wasn't so keyed up, heart thumping fit to burst, he might have recognised the words of the song or the tune. Jesus, what if Nicholson had been right? What if they muffed it, and got into a bloody firefight? What if the bloody Luftwaffe happened along? They'd been active enough all morning.

The two officers in front of the German column marched into sight. Rankin shrank down behind the wall, bareheaded, terrified they'd look round. "Please, dear God, please don't let me fuck this up!" he silently prayed. Just like at school, before a maths exam. At this point the pair were a good ten to 15 paces ahead. The tail of the centipede mightn't yet be in the cutting. Carefully he pulled the pin from the grenade in his left hand, intensely aware of his sweaty palm and fingers.

Please God, don't let my fingers slip off the arming lever!

His rifle, cocked with safety on, lay beside him. He heard a tiny snick; someone nearby cocking their weapon. His heart thumped in his chest, the blood loud in his ears.

Semi reclining, keeping as low as possible, he was able to see the German officers down the road but hidden from the men opposite him, marching out of the cutting. He showed the pin to Corkhill. Renfrew's eyes were shut tight.

The two officers gesticulated as they marched. What the hell were they talking about that required so much animation? And how come the bastards were not tired? The leading rank appeared from behind the stone wall, helmets strapped to packs, their Spandaus casually slung over their shoulders. They're not even in combat order! *Now, Lawrence, now! What're you waiting for, for Christ's sake? Jesus! What's gone wrong? Jesus Christ!*

His heart was so loud the bloody Jerries must surely be able to hear it. Several ranks of the centipede were in sight now, striding purposefully down the hill. The officers were 20 yards away.

Then, from over the rise, out of sight, the steady chatter of a Bren gun.

Confusion in the centipede! Some began to turn, some stopped; others kept marching, uncertain. They all bunched up.

Rankin drew back his arm, releasing the lever on the grenade; the arming lever flew off with a tinny "ping", distinctly heard in the hushed instant before gunfire erupted from behind the stone walls. He counted his two seconds and threw the grenade into the roadway, already packed with pandemonium. The grenade went off with a crack, along with half a dozen others.

Screams and shrieks, the sounds of shock, panic and agony as bullets and fragments ripped into flesh. Picking up the rifle with his right hand, thumbing off the safety, he jammed it to his shoulder, pointed it at one of the leading officers, who was staring back in shock, and pulled the trigger.

Every weapon the platoon possessed poured a storm of fire into the cutting – the German soldiers had nowhere to run, nowhere to hide, no time even to unsling their rifles. Their song died with them.

The last rounds in a couple of magazines banged out and within seconds it was over. The centipede lay heaped across the road, its order destroyed. The platoon stood impassively, lining the stone walls above the cutting. Fresh clips were thumbed into rifle breeches and automatic magazines were changed; the rattling and pinging loud in the deathly silence. Dust drifted up from the cutting.

Hysterical screaming rent the awful silence. Rankin looked around to see the second officer running in frenzied circles, ranting and waving his Luger in the air.

"God, I had forgotten about him."

"Headless bloody chook," said Renfrew, raising his rifle. Rankin gently pushed it down.

The officer stopped and stood stock still. Like a trapped animal in a panic, he stared at one side of the road, then the other, at the khaki figures standing unmoving behind the stone walls. He stared, unblinking, at the mass of bloodied and stained grey-green uniforms humped in the roadway. The only movement there was an occasional twitch.

Everyone was looking at Rankin. As he raised his rifle, unreasoning rage welled up inside him. Damn the bloody man! Why couldn't he have died, like the rest of them? He bloody deserved to be shot. They'd have to take the bugger with them.

He motioned with his rifle for the man to walk towards Nicholson, on the other side of the road, who was covering him with his Tommy gun. Angrily, irrationally, he wondered if Nicholson had fired a shot.

The officer stood in the roadway, a few yards from his fallen comrade. Turning from Rankin to Nicholson, to the roadway, then back again, his mouth worked silently, like a fish out of water. Understanding crossed his face as he gaped at his command, then he paused and shouted, "Heil Hitler!" as he put the barrel of his pistol to his head and pulled the trigger. A puff of pink floated momentarily in the morning breeze; a puny crack echoed off stone walls.

"Stupid bugger," someone behind Rankin muttered.

From up the road a way came a flurry of gunshots and crack of grenades. Then silence.

"Right, get what's useful, and let's get the hell out of here. If we can't carry it, bust it. As much ammo as we can carry for the Jerry weapons. Let's get to it. Five minutes."

Rankin walked down the slope to the two dead officers. He gazed at them, then stooped and picked up their pistols. The man who had shot himself had fallen so that mercifully only the entry wound was visible, but the glistening stain spreading on the dusty road told its story. He looked to be about 40, hair thinning, tall and lean. The other officer was younger, fair-haired, solid build with a prominent birthmark on his temple beside his left eye. Rankin removed their maps and papers, quickly ratting through their satchels and packs. The numerals on their epaulettes with the green edelweiss motif told him who they were: 85 Mountain Regiment had just lost one of its companies.

"That man was right. You are a stupid bugger," Rankin muttered as he lifted a bundle of letters tied with red string from the older officer's pack. Turning the bundle over, he saw that the envelope was addressed to "Hauptmann W.K. Schmidt" and bore a French postmark: Paris, January 1941. The handwriting looked feminine.

"What have you been up to?" he continued still under his breath as he found another bundle of letters, this one with German stamps, tied with plain string around a tube of foot cream ointment. "Your men should curse you to hell. It's your fault they're all dead, you arrogant fool. You hear me?" Rifling through the dead man's wallet, Rankin found a photo of a serious-looking woman wearing a fur-trimmed coat and hat, posing with two small children. "She's your wife, isn't she, you shit?"

He was startled by a gunshot.

"Who was that? That you, Gardiner?" Nicholson shouted. "Have you just shot that man?"

"Sorry, Sarge. I thought he had a gun."

Nicholson shouted, "You were stealing from him!"

"Jesus, Sarge, keep your bloody hair on. Skipper told us to pick up what we need."

"You don't need another bloody watch, Gardiner!" Nicholson almost screamed.

Rankin looked to Nicholson: *he must be really angry; he never swears*. "That's enough, Gardiner," Rankin called out. "Pick up that machine gun. You can carry that as well as your rifle for a bit. Make sure we've got all the ammo we can carry and let's get going," he added, addressing all of them.

Johnstone reported that a couple of runners had been chased into a house up the road and been dealt with. Rankin nodded; that explained the flurry of gunshots and grenade explosions.

Avoiding Nicholson's eyes, Rankin gave one of the Lugers to Reilly and pocketed the one that the German officer had used to shoot himself. He read the label on the tube of ointment before tossing it to Corkhill. "Add that to your bag of medical remedies, Corky. Hirschtalg Fusscreme – deer tallow foot cream. Good for blisters, cracked heels and bedsores."

Corky smiled. "Bedsores haven't really been a problem, Skipper."

Shouldering their packs, the men got ready to move on. Rankin watched Nicholson out of the corner of his eye; his face was taught, drawn with anger, silent.

The empty feeling in the pit of Rankin's stomach was difficult to identify. It came close to a curious mixture of contempt and sadness. For whom, or for what, he couldn't have said.

———

THEY REACHED THEIR objective before noon. Air attack had become almost incessant during the final stages and as a result Kennelly had suffered a bad cut to his face, caused by a flying stone chip, and Glover was stabbed by a splinter, which penetrated through his webbing and a little way into his flesh. Both insisted on staying with the platoon rather than risk the perilous trip to a dressing station.

They were guided to a house on high ground east of Platanias. Every unit around them had a story to tell; it was hard to discern fact from fiction. 28 Battalion had only just made it in one piece, fighting a rear-guard action all the way. The enemy had been so close behind one of their platoons, they heard, that the Jerries had chased them right to the Platanias River. Machine gun and rifle fire from close range had cost them men as they scrambled up the steep riverbank to safety. The vital bridge had been taken by the Germans using captured RAF trucks, but artillery had shelled them off it. Any of these stories could have been true or none of them. Mention of the RAF, or their trucks, even in rumour, was not well received by men who endured almost constant air attack. In fact, the service was openly scorned for its efforts to the extent there was loud speculation as to whose bloody side the RAF was on.

The enemy following hard on their heels was proof, however, that the withdrawal had been accomplished in the nick of time. Further delay would likely have meant facing an all-out assault, the possibility of being surrounded and cut off. C Company, acting as 23 Battalion's rear-guard in company with a couple of British tanks and Maori carriers, had to fight off a determined German patrol which had snapped at their heels all the way. No more complaining was heard about "handing Jerry positions we should make him bloody pay for".

Rankin's platoon settled into their new positions. At their

backs, to the east, was the picturesque little town of Ay Marina. All whitewash and terracotta on its hillside overlooking the sea, the town was a picture of tranquillity. The Engineer Detachment, whose exploits everyone had heard of by now, was just east of the village. Despite not being infantry, they had taken a heavy toll on the parachutists whose misfortune it was to land in their midst.

The area allocated to the platoon included a substantial whitewashed house with a walled garden, in which they established their headquarters. Rankin sent for Gardiner while the two section commanders and Nicholson sorted out the wider platoon positions. Gardiner arrived as Rankin was discussing their dispositions with Nicholson and the other two NCOs. Gardiner leant against a doorpost and lit a cigarette.

"Gardiner, I hear you've been selling Jerry tablets," Rankin said to him as soon as the others had gone out.

"What's it to you?"

Rankin breathed hard, trying not to show his shock, either at the brazen words or contemptuous tone of voice. "I'm responsible for every man in this platoon, including you, Gardiner. I won't have you selling captured medical stores to the men."

Gardiner moved from the doorpost, an insolently languid movement, and looked Rankin up and down. "From where I stand, I don't think you're in any position to stop me."

"Oh, you don't? Why's that?" Rankin struggled to keep his anger in check.

"You've kept it for yourself. Don't come over all high and fuckin' mighty. You can't threaten me like you threatened old Hamilton."

Rankin studied him. Gardiner exuded sly arrogance. "What the hell do you mean by that?"

"I know you threatened to report him for fucking off in Greece. What about you? You're no bloody better. Taking off with your floozy for a nice afternoon jaunt, leaving the rest of us to take our chances."

Rankin's face flared. "If you have a complaint to make, Gardiner, make it to the proper authorities. In the meantime, I'm telling you, you will surrender any tablets you have to Corporal Lawrence. And you will give him any money you received for selling the stuff. Am I clear?"

Gardiner's eyes radiated pure contempt. He stood still for a moment, regarding Rankin as he might have regarded a lump of excrement. Breathing hard, standing his full height, Rankin couldn't tell if the other man was going to make an issue of it, but then Gardiner insolently flicked his cigarette butt past Rankin's boot, shrugged his shoulders, and sauntered out, mumbling something inaudible. Rankin stared after him, trembling with rage.

———

RANKIN FOUND NICHOLSON in the house's walled garden, his back resting against the trunk of a gnarled old apricot tree. They had barely exchanged a word since the ambush on the road, other than those necessary for the platoon to function. Rankin slumped to the ground next to him, legs splayed out in front of him. Nicholson was ferreting in his small pack for his pipe and tobacco, his Thompson gun propped up against the tree beside him. He looked grey and strained, Rankin thought, face streaked with sweat and dirt, shirt and shorts stained with God knew what. *I must look like that. In my 40s instead of my 20s.*

"I wonder who lived here, until we came," Rankin said, after a long silence, taking in the attractive little walled garden and whitewashed house with its shuttered windows.

"Correction," said Nicholson, leaning back against the trunk, eyes closed, tamping the tobacco into the pipe. "Until *they* came."

Rankin sighed. "Yes."

Nicholson held the match to the bowl of his pipe, flame flaring as he puffed, a comforting blue cloud swirling around him.

"I'm sorry you disagreed with my decision, Nick. I know I spoke harshly. I'd like to apologise."

Nicholson looked at him through his cloud of smoke. "You're in charge. You give the orders."

"I'd prefer you to agree with them."

Nicholson puffed his pipe, but said nothing.

"Anyway, we got here," Rankin went on. As soon as the words were out, he wished he had held his silence. "And they are no longer a threat."

Nicholson continued to smoke his pipe in silence while Rankin pretended to study the house. "I suppose it doesn't really matter to whoever packed up this house in a hurry and left, does it? German bomb or British shell, result's the same."

"War is a catastrophe for the innocent." The sweet-smelling cloud of tobacco smoke wafted up into the branches of the old apricot tree, the spent blossoms of which were swelling into fruit buds.

Rankin decided to change tack. "I need to talk to you about Gardiner."

"Oh, yes? What's he stolen now?"

"Pervitin. The Jerry Benzedrine. He's been selling it to the troops. I've told Lawrence and he'll confiscate the pills and the money."

"This should have been nipped in the bud long ago," said Nicholson, exhaling luxuriously as a bird twittered in the branches overhead.

"I know your views, Nick. I think it's harmless when it's confined to souveniring watches and engraved daggers. Charging the men for military supplies is another matter altogether."

"There we differ," said Nicholson. "These pills: do we know what they do?"

"Help you stay awake, suppress hunger. Keep you going all day and all night."

Nicholson turned his head to study him closely. "I see. Had you taken any when we joined up with the Maoris?"

"Yes. One. To see what it would do."

Nicholson's eyebrows arched and he pursed his lips. "We found that out alright, didn't we?"

Rankin felt his face flare with shame. He hastily took a swig of water and poured the rest over his head, concealing his expression. He leaned back and closed his eyes, heart thumping in his chest. "I won't forbid the men taking something the Jerries issue."

"Why don't our lot issue them, then? Have you spoken to the MO?"

Rankin sat bolt upright, turning to face Nicholson. "Christ, Nick, of course not. How would I even find him? They're bennies; half the judges in the land probably used them to pass their exams."

Nicholson grunted, eyes closed, contentedly smoking. "I wouldn't know anything about that, of course."

Rankin sat silently for several minutes, listening to the birdsong before he tried to restart the conversation again: "We must have marched another two or three miles down the road before the Redcaps poked us in here. Just a stone's throw from 5 Brigade's HQ, I see."

"Yes. You can go and tell the brigadier what he's doing wrong and how he's lost us the war."

Rankin looked up sharply. Nicholson and sarcasm did not go together. The dust-streaked face looking back at him was expressionless.

"I might just do that."

Nicholson took his pipe out of his mouth and wagged the stem at him. "You'd be better off keeping your head down, staying out of the way, not drawing attention to yourself. I would quite like to finish this campaign with the same platoon commander I started with."

"God, now you sound like Boney Anderson."

Nicholson again puffed his pipe.

Rankin shot him a glance. It appeared he was not going to say anything else. "I wonder how this campaign will finish."

"Like the last one. Aboard a boat."

Rankin turned to Nicholson, open-mouthed. "Jesus, Nick. Now you really do sound like Boney Anderson. That's not like you."

"Really. It's not just university graduates who take pills to stay up all night to pass their exams that can see how things are, you know. Even us dumb sloggers can work out what's going on."

Rankin saw how drawn – pinched, even – was Nicholson's face. His eyes were sunken into dark-ringed hollows, skin sallow beneath the grime. *This was the Nicholson who should be an officer.*

"You're no dumb slogger, Nick."

The faintest shadow of a smile creased the corners of

Nicholson's mouth, firmly clamped around his pipe stem. "So, what did you really come to tell me?"

"Johnstone told me Graham ran into a couple more of his friends as we marched in here."

"Oh, no. What unit were they in?"

"Prison detachment, apparently. Mixed guards and prisoners. They've been working for Clive Hulme[11] since the landings, it seems."

Nicholson spluttered. "I don't suppose these men were guards, were they?"

"No. They were in the prison. Prisoners."

"What were they in for?"

"Fighting, missing kit, failing to return from leave, drunkenness, gambling, disorderly conduct … the usual."

"God Almighty," said Nicholson. "You are a sucker for punishment is all I can say."

"Never mind, Nick. We've lost a few of the first lot. Bernard couldn't tell them from a sack of spuds – the company commander even less so. Extra hands will be useful." Looking him in the eye, he continued. "Besides, Nick, if things had been only a little different, and we'd been here longer before the Jerries arrived, I might have been in the prison, awaiting trial on a charge of threatening some bloody British Redcap with a loaded weapon."

"It's not too late, you know," Nicholson said, glancing up at the bird happily singing in the branches above. "Do you know? I think that bird is building a nest. Life goes on, despite the problems of us mere mortals."

---

11 Sergeant (Later Warrant Officer II) A.C. (Clive) Hulme VC, born Dunedin 24 Jan 1911, farmer, wounded 28 May 1941 and repatriated to New Zealand.

CHAPTER TWELVE

Galatas, 24 May 1941

IT WAS STILL dark when Reilly brought a mug of tea and the message: a summons from Clutterbuck to an officers' orders group, to be held before stand-to. Rankin told him to rouse Johnstone but to let Nicholson sleep while he was away. They could all do with sleep. They had retreated several more miles to the east during the night.

The briefing was short and sharp. The battalion was to be ready to move at five minutes' notice, in whatever strength and whatever direction the exigencies of the day called for. They were in reserve, so could be called on by any of 4 Brigade holding the Galatas Front, the Australian 19 Brigade along the Prison Valley Road, or Division itself. Intelligence reports pointed to a major German offensive about to fall upon 4 Brigade. Hamilton's eyes flickered over the group of officers standing in the little room. He appeared tired, skin drawn tightly over his cheekbones, eyes red-rimmed and rheumy, like those of an old man's. *We all look like that, I suppose*, Rankin thought.

"Enemy reinforcements are forcing a gap between us and 4 Brigade, which is under real pressure after hard fighting over the last couple of days." Hamilton glanced at each of them individually as he spoke, and Rankin's attention was drawn to the man's twitching cheek. "The enemy occupies high ground from which it threatens to cut the Coast Road behind us, cutting off our withdrawal route. The General has praised the efforts of the Composite Battalion especially, although he emphasises that all units have done sterling work."

We're all too tired for this, Rankin thought. A gee-up session is going to fall flat. He had just noticed Nellie Robertson was missing. No one spoke. In the absence of any response, Hamilton's nervous tic seemed to ramp up a notch.

"Our role today, as Reserve, is unlikely to afford us the time to rest and refit that a day or two out of the line might normally provide." He searched the little assembly, almost pleading for an ironic laugh. *No one's in the mood, mate.* Rankin noted the Great War expressions: "Out of the line, rest and refit". Thanks to the Luftwaffe, no one was "out of the line" in daylight.

Hamilton continued, outlining the 4 Brigade positions and those of the other units holding the various defensive lines. When he realised the briefing was failing to elicit any response, Hamilton gave up. He handed over to McKenzie, who dealt with a couple of administrative issues and read off the effectives of each platoon. Rankin's was still most numerous, because of its reinforcement before the landings. No one need know about the two unrecorded additions the previous night.

"Morning, Neil. Our fearless leader looks a bit under the weather, I reckon. Pale, drawn, sunken eyes, pallid skin. He looks like a shambling bloody cadaver," said Anderson as they walked back to their positions.

"That's a bit harsh, Boney. We're all a bit under the weather.

And I don't think cadavers are bloody."

"Hah. Fatuous as ever. Still winning in the personnel stakes, I see."

"I think the word you want is 'erudite', Boney. And yes, still entrusted with the hopes and prayers of the nation." Rankin pressed his palms together as if in prayer.

"Yes, well, it's too bloody late for that. Make sure you've booked your place on Jolly Jack Tar's Ferry Service. It'll be standing room only before the week is out, just like last time."

"God, even my sergeant said something similar," said Rankin.

"Wise chap, your sergeant. Mine copped it. And one of my corporals."

"Oh. Shit, Boney. Sorry to hear that. Where's Nellie?"

"Gone the same way." Anderson's expression was loaded with regret and guilt. "My sergeant was leading a patrol, up in the hills. They were on a terrace when one of the boys needed to have a shit – diarrhoea. He's behind a bush doing his business when O'Malley calls out to one of the others to put his bloody cigarette out. Could smell the bloody smoke over the shit. Next minute, there's Schmeissers going off and Jerries all over the place. Sergeant and one other killed, two wounded."

"Jesus. Poor Seamus," muttered Rankin.

"'Poor Seamus' indeed. Didn't kill the fucking smoker, of course. I don't know how many times they've been told: no smoking on patrols. I told him to watch his bloody back. Felt like shooting him myself," Anderson said bleakly. He glanced up at the brightening sky. "Got to go. Keep your head down, old mate," he called out as he dashed off, leaving Rankin staring after him.

———

THE COMPANY WAS directed to a cluster of houses and tall plane trees surrounding a crossroads on rising ground, between the main coastal road and the village of Galatas on a ridge to the south. Rankin's platoon occupied a house with a walled garden and an adjacent stand of planes. The day passed ominously slowly, tensions building as they waited for the expected call for support. A rumour went round early in the morning that 4 Brigade had put Battalion on notice to move as soon as they arrived, but nothing more was heard.

Shortly after midday, a flock of Dorniers followed by screaming Stukas bombed Galatas atop its ridge, about a mile or so away. By mid-afternoon, the noise of battle beyond the village had become not-so-distant thunder. Artillery, mortars, the incessant chatter of machine guns, and continuous rifle fire all merged into a roar that ebbed and flowed, like ceaseless breaking waves. Later in the afternoon, the village was bombed again; the hated Stukas pulling out of their dives, wailers screaming, almost directly overhead.

The men of 23 Battalion peered up from under the plane trees at the murderous crank-winged vultures swooping down onto the smoking carcass of Galatas. The crump of the bombs was felt and heard over the background thunder, the sky filled with the black smoke and thick brown dust of the ruined town so that the sun turned a vivid red-brown.

Their anger increased as they watched in impotent rage. The orderly little whitewashed houses strung out along the top of the hill disappeared from sight, reduced to rubble under its funereal pall of dust and smoke.

Despite the gentle onshore breeze, the bitter smell of German explosives and burning homes reached their nostrils, feeding the anger.

Late in the afternoon, rumours had it that the whole of 18 Battalion's front and the so-called "Russell Force" on the south flank of 5 Brigade's position, anchored on Pink Hill, was cracking under the pressure. Next, they heard 10 Composite Battalion had ceased to exist; the front had cracked. The Divisional Petrol Company and Cavalry, and others like the redoubtable engineers, had been reduced to isolated remnants, fighting for their lives. The few trucks that remained ran the gauntlet of constant air attack to ferry the mounting stream of wounded away to the RAP. God alone knew what conditions were like there. They all prayed silently that they would never have to find out. Then they heard that 23 Battalion's A and Headquarters Companies had been called for and gone to join the fight.

The Luftwaffe had been overhead all day, hounding anything that moved, lining up time and again on the unfortunates east of Galatas. Enemy fighters and bombers roared over their positions, strafing at will, firing at anything seen or imagined. A Messerschmitt 110 thundered up the road and plastered their house and garden with 20-millimetre shells and machine-gun bullets, tearing chunks out of the plaster-covered walls, exposing the stonework and splintering shutters. The only casualty was an old iron bucket left upended on a wall; beams of light shining through the bullet holes danced in the drifting dusty veil.

As the attack continued, the men cowered out of sight, behind whatever cover was available. The all-encompassing noise, shuddering concussions and fear suppressed their hunger so that a swig of water or an occasional barley sugar was enough to wet the whistle between smokes. Anything was better than the taste of dust, explosives and burning houses. Common knowledge held that the chances of surviving a gut wound were much better on an empty stomach; it was better not to eat.

They had to shout to be heard over the background roar and screaming aero engines. A job requiring movement was preceded by a prayer session that would have gladdened the padre's heart. The ever-present threat of sudden death from above was wearing, to say the least. What it was like for the poor bastards directly underneath it, they were happy only to speculate.

Late in the afternoon, men stationed near the track from Karatsos reported a trickle of New Zealanders, some unharmed, some lightly wounded, some unarmed, heading towards the coast. Many were rounded up, shamefacedly claiming they had been overrun, swamped, were the last of their unit, only getting away with their lives by the skin of their teeth. The trickle increased to a steady stream as the sun westered towards the arid hills.

Rumours flew. The line had broken; panic had spread. The trickle became a flood, then a rout. Rumours of the demise of 10 Battalion appeared confirmed by the stream of survivors slinking past. It was said that Kippenberger had been seen running up and down the Galatas Road, brandishing his revolver, threatening to shoot anyone running away, shouting at the top of his lungs: "Stand for New Zealand, you bastards! Stand for New Zealand!" Rumour also had it that the Germans were pouring down the road, slaughtering everything in sight; no, now they'd been stopped by artillery firing into them over open sights; no, the Maoris had charged at them with the bayonet, after a ferocious haka. This was clearly nonsense, as 28 was still in place behind them. Galatas was reported lost. 4 Brigade had been wiped out. Each rumour was more unsettling than the last.

Officers and NCOs, having no better idea than anybody else, could only reassure, cajole or threaten. Orders would be received, they said. They would be told when they were needed, they said. They prayed that this were true, that a command structure still existed capable of calling for them when the time came, contrary to all appearances. The stream of wild-eyed men passing on the road told its own story, and it was not a pretty one.

Orders must come soon. Whether to withdraw or attack didn't matter: they had to do something! Arguments threatened to turn into fights. Friends suddenly remembered past injustices, items lent and not returned. A borrowed cleaning kit could lead to a screaming match.

"Like waiting for bloody exams to start," Rankin said to Nicholson after defusing an argument. "Jesus, I wish we'd just get on with it. Anything would be better than this."

"Don't wish your life away," said Nicholson, looking up from his notebook and putting the stub of pencil behind his ear. "Whatever's coming will be here soon enough. I doubt things will be better."

Smoke and dust continued to rise above the ridges to the west, turning the lowering sun blood-red. The noise of the battle ebbed and flowed on the air currents, a ceaseless, growling roar, sending levels of tension and anxiety soaring. They all knew that they would be called upon to add their own voices to the battle's infernal roar: the roar of the meat grinder.

———

"SKIPPER, MESSAGE FOR you!" McIntyre called out from the house. Rankin ran inside to find him holding the just-delivered flimsy note: "Immed: C D Coys deploy action Galatas rd. A & HQ Coys engaged. Hamilton."

He glanced at his watch: 1820. His stomach turned a somersault before fear turned it to ice. He wanted to be sick. Nicholson was behind him and seeing the reaction on Rankin's face he needed no telling: "Section leaders!"

The whole platoon knew what was happening within seconds. Weapons and bayonets, that had been cleaned, recleaned, oiled and sharpened all day long received a final check. Helmets were tightened, pouches and webbing adjusted and checked, a nervous pee here and there. Some crossed themselves, even though they weren't Catholic, and closed their eyes to quickly implore the Almighty to keep them safe – perhaps, if that was asking too much, to make the end swift and painless. Others felt the urgent need to open their bowels behind the nearest tree while several retched violently.

"I'll take the rifle and bayonet, Tim. You take the Schmeisser." Rankin couldn't look him in the eye as they swapped web kit. Reilly had spent the day sharpening and oiling the bayonet. Rankin looked steadfastly at the ground as he stepped into the trousers of his German paratrooper's smock, did up the zip, and put the web belt, braces with pouches and belt with scabbard on over the top.

"I'd better take the pistol, too, Tim – just in case."

Reilly silently handed the service pistol to him. Rankin looped the lanyard over his neck as he stuffed the weapon in his jacket pocket.

The platoons formed up beside the road, under the trees, in company order, C Company in the lead. Rankin hoisted the bayonet's scabbard on the belt, feeling its weight resting on the hip. He caught Nicholson giving him a look. "What?" Nicholson shook his head.

It was not yet clocking-off time for the Luftwaffe; fighters and bombers circulated overhead even as the sun sank towards the hills. Everyone was aware that a careless glint or unwary movement glimpsed from above could bring them screaming down.

Motion and purpose sharpened the wits. Rankin slipped a Pervitin tablet out of its vial and swallowed it with a swig of water. The two companies, each 80 to 90 strong, hurried up the road towards Galatas, hugging the stone walls and trees lining the road, unsure of what they would find. Astonishingly, they had to make way for two British tanks to pass, leaving thick dust in their wake.

"Christ, Boney," Rankin said to Anderson during a brief halt, "I thought they'd all been scuppered the other day at Pirgos."

"Wonders will never cease." Anderson's flippant words belied the look on his face. "Let's hope they don't break down or find they've got the wrong bloody ammunition this time."

"Well, it must mean that we're throwing everything at it, then," said Rankin.

Anderson turned to look at him as another group of survivors slunk past, avoiding eye contact. "Yes. One can only guess why that might be."

Rankin hurried back to his platoon as the whistle blew to get the men on their feet again. "Boney seems a bit depressed," he said to Nicholson.

The light had faded past the late afternoon softness that normally painted the hills in shadow; the time of day when softening light promised relief from the heat and the pleasant prospect of reflecting on a day well spent, drink in hand. Their day's work was just about to begin, the long-drawn-out wait already forgotten in the clamour of a fast-racing pulse and dust-dry mouth. It would be dark in an hour.

The two tanks had disappeared up the road. Guns on a ridge to the east were firing into or towards the village. As they marched they came across a party of terrified civilians huddled against the roadside stone wall: women, dressed in black, with children; all wide-eyed with fear. Bombed out, presumably – their town shortly to become a battlefield. The soldiers looked upon their pale terror and silent misery. Rankin felt the anger building, in himself and in the men around him.

They halted a short distance from Galatas.

Rankin stopped a subaltern from A Company, who ran past on an errand.

"What's up, Scotty?"

"Christ Jesus, Neil, you jokers are only just in time. It's the real McCoy there. Hot as the hobs of hell. Jerry's in the village. We've got the Brigade Band on one side of us and the bloody Kiwi Concert Party on the other, going at it hammer and tongs. I've been sent back to find an AT gun team. We left ours in Greece. Fucked if I know, frankly, where I'll find one of those. Aussies perhaps."

"Have you, by God. I can help there," exclaimed Rankin. "I want them back, though – no poaching!" He turned towards the platoon and called loudly. "Sutherland, Pringle, fall out. I've got a job for you."

Sutherland cleared the ranks and reported, heavy anti-tank rifle over his shoulder.

"Tub, I want you to go with Mister Scotland here. Where's bloody Pringle?"

"Had to fall out, Skipper, got the trots."

"Shit!"

"That's about the size of it, Skipper.'

"Jesus, not now, Tub. You're going to support the Concert Party, not auditioning for a part in it! Who's loading for you?"

"Blakey." Rankin called him out, too.

"I could actually lend you two AT teams, Scotty, on the solemn promise I get them back. Or Sergeant Nicholson, if I'm detained."

"Fuck me, really? Must be the only platoon in the whole Med with two of the bloody things. I owe you one."

"Two, actually." Rankin called for Smith and his loader. "Any idea what our job is?" Rankin asked.

"Clearing Jerry out of that bloody hornets' nest, I should think. Better you than me. Ta, Neil. Good luck, mate."

They advanced past men slumped by the roadside, heads bent, staring at the ground. Some looked out at the column from under their helmet rims, wide-eyed, slack-mouthed and shamefaced. As they passed, men from his own platoon called out – some gently, most not so – to get up and get going. "Only a bloody girl sits by and watches a man fight!" "Get up, you bastards, get stuck in!" "Get off yer arses, yer fuckin' mongrels! Yer better not still be skulking in a bloody ditch when we come back!" It was not said in good humour. The few who answered all did so in the same flat tone of voice.

The order was passed down the line to fix bayonets. This was it. One of the tanks came clanking down the road, turned behind them, and clattered back towards the village. Several of the platoon recognised the driver, one of their own, through his open hatch. "Learner driver," he called out, grinning, flashing a V sign.

They approached the village, a row of scorched and pock-marked buildings strung out along the ridge. In the middle of the row, the spire of a small church broke up the line of house roofs. The Germans were firing down the road from houses on the village's edge. Planes roared overhead, but in the fading light they withheld their fire for fear of shooting into their own troops.

The light was going as the companies received their orders, huddling behind the stone walls, sheltering from the machine-gun fire. Temporarily commanding the scratch 10 Brigade, Kippenberger strode up the road between the two 23 Battalion companies. The expression on his long, thin face and the purpose in his bearing left no man in doubt as to who was in charge.

He shouted to be heard over the din. "D Company will take the left side of the road, C Company will be on the right, with the two tanks in the centre. Clear out the village. A Company will back you up. This will be bloody. Now get to it!" Simple and direct.

Rankin had found himself beside Hamilton. Perhaps now was his hour! "Good luck, sir," Rankin shouted into a hand cupped over Hamilton's ear. "I had a letter from my father the other day, sir; he asked me to remember him to you."

Hamilton's head jerked back as if he had been struck, jaw dropping. In the fading last light of day his face blanched sheet-white, in striking contrast to the putty-grey of a moment ago. He mumbled something and was gone.

"Good luck, Pyney! Good luck, Boney!"

"You, too, Neil."

Looking at his watch, he noted it was just after eight. He glanced around, seeing faces he did not recognise. The tanks set off, up the gentle slope towards the village about 200 yards away. C Company advanced, first at a walk, then at a run to keep up with the tanks, whose wake was marked by a cloud of dust.

Their own platoons followed suit. They soon found the narrow road crowded; tracers whizzed and cracked, ricochets bounced and sparked off the road and stone walls. The two tanks were firing back, charging into the village. The noise was deafening.

"Over the wall! Off the road!"

The ranks broke into a run. Any semblance of order was lost. Somewhere he heard a haka, followed by a dozen other war cries, school rallying cries, hounds baying for blood. The effect was electric. A glance behind told him that some of the demoralised men, previously slumped by the road or slinking away, had suddenly got their second wind, and were leaping to their feet. Their blood was up.

They charged across the fields and through the orchards, up the slope towards the village. Tracers whipped overhead and around them, cracking the air, thudding into trees, rocks, and flesh. Rankin saw several men slump and fall. As he stumbled over the carcass of a dead sheep, unreasoning rage boiled up inside him. On they charged, across the fields and along the wall beside the road. He lost sight of the company commander and the other platoon leaders. Yelling himself hoarse, his entire being focused on the village, its winking lights and cracking, whining sparks, his only thought was that the bastards were trying to kill him. Yet the rifle was firm in his grip, his hands no longer sweating. Very lights soared above the village. *Germans calling for support, no doubt. Fuck them!*

They reached the first house; the back of which along with the others in the road formed a line of walls and gardens, facing out into the orchards and fields. Running men hurdled the walls, barely pausing in mid-stride, hurling grenades in through the windows. A bright flash, shrieking and yelling, houses stormed from both the main street in front and walled gardens at the rear. Bayonets flashed in the lurid, flickering light.

Flames caught hold. Men screamed. Primal, hideous screams as the blades drove deep into live flesh. The long day of tension and terror, the women's and children's eyes, blank, doe-eyed pools of misery, had keyed the soldiers tauter than piano wires. Movement, attack, action, revenge: it would take more than these German bastards to stop them!

The cry went up from a hundred throats: "Get stuck in!"

Some houses were still occupied by their owners. As the attack began women and children fled into the street, shrieking in fright, adding to the ghastly cacophony. Bombed houses collapsed in piles of rubble and broken timbers spilled into the road and back gardens. Machine guns spat tracer from every angle.

"Keep going! Keep going!" Rankin screamed, pointing the way along the line of houses as men streamed past him. More grenades were hurled; blades flashed red.

German soldiers poured out of the houses they'd been occupying, retreating, leaping the walls and taking cover in the ruins, shooting as they went, running for their lives in panic. Many were cut down as they ran, long blades or heavy butts ending their futile, scrabbling attempts at evasion, at life. The pursuers, firing from the hip, running, yelling, howling like something out of Jack London's *Call of the Wild* let loose, ran on, like a flood in a gorge, sweeping the terrified enemy before them like so much flotsam.

Tracer whistled and sparked off the roadway, thudded into buildings, grenades burst. The attack went on. A flash in a window, a cloud of smoke, a shower of debris, a shriek.

They ran into a lane that cut through the houses from the

"backs" in the fields to the road through the centre of the village. A grenade exploded just ahead, among a group of running soldiers. The flash silhouetted a figure catapulted sideways, helmet flying – one of four men who fell to the ground. Barely 20 yards ahead three Germans rose from a pile of rubble and turned to flee; a burst from an automatic knocked one off his feet. Another hesitated and was engulfed by flailing rifle butts and stabbing bayonets. The third fled, discarding weapon and equipment as he ran. Rankin dropped to one knee and shot him in the back.

"Keep going!" he shrieked. "Keep going!" There was no helping the men who'd taken the full force of the grenade.

The noise was indescribable. Shouting, screaming, shooting, explosions, all merged into a senseless pandemonium. The polished steel on the end of his rifle flickered in the stabbing light like a live thing, thirsting for blood, drawing him on.

A few yards down the street he leapt over a still-smoking body caught in the man-made volcano of a phosphorous grenade: feet and legs gone, burned to a black smear on the cobbles, leaving the torso still clutching its weapon, still wearing its helmet, the stink nauseating.

"Keep going! Keep going! Finish the bastards!"

He ran into a house, hard on the heels of another man, and bounded up the stairs after him. Through the first doorway a German machine-gunner crouched behind his Spandau, framed by a window, firing down the street. His loader, kneeling beside the gun feeding it from a metal box on the floor, spun around, face contorted in terror, then leapt to his feet grabbing for the Schmeisser standing in the corner. The gunner kept hammering away, the roar of the gun in the room and its winking muzzle

313

flash rendered him oblivious to the dangers behind.

"No, you don't, you bastard," yelled Rankin. The loader's hands flung wide as Rankin shot him from the doorway. The gunner, still firing, stayed focused on the street outside until Rankin's companion's hand viciously wrenched back the front lip of his helmet in mid-burst while his other hand flashed across his exposed throat. A dark gout sprayed out over the red-hot gun, spitting and smoking, before it hit the floor. Rankin stared in horror. "Ten years on the boards at the Works, boss," the other man grinned, shouting into the sudden silence. He wiped his blade on the gushing body's shirt.

The wounded loader was screaming, clutching himself. The slaughterman picked up the blood-covered sizzling Spandau and fired a burst, riddling him so that it appeared his jumping, twitching body was dancing as it disintegrated under the impact of 15 rounds a second fired from a foot away, spraying him all over the wall. Rankin's ears were ringing as the man casually threw the gun out through the window when it jammed, its rattling ammunition belt trailing it over the windowsill.

The slaughterman grinned again as he reached past Rankin, picked up the Schmeisser and slung the loader's magazines in their carrier over his shoulder. "Always wanted one of these, eh, boss," he said, patting the gun, before turning and running out.

Rankin ran downstairs behind him, and out into the street. Mortar bombs were falling, back towards the edge of the village. Harmlessly, thank Christ. "Keep going, keep going!" Rankin yelled as loud as he could, waving the running figures on.

Gunfire came from another house on the opposite side of the road. He smashed open the door with his rifle butt and hurled a grenade up the stairs. A flash, a bang, a scream. Rankin leapt up the pitch-black stairs, darkly illuminated by the flickering light coming from an open door. A body writhed on the landing, crying. A dim figure rushed through the doorway. Rankin's bayonet caught him in the side, momentum driving it deep, knocking him off his feet. Rankin's foot got to the landing as the German tumbled sideways, falling over his now-screaming companion. The bayonet flashed, briefly free, and plunged down.

Rankin saw again the sandbags hanging from the wooden frames at Burnham. Beyond each frame, another sandbag lay prone on the ground. The recruits took turns to run up and thrust, first horizontal, into the bag on the frame, then vertical, the coup de grace, delivered to the bag lying prone. Their technique was closely scrutinised by the rheumy-eyed Great War instructor while the magpies chortled in the blue gums above.

"But what does the real thing feel like, Sarn't Major?"

"Like sliding a knife into one of your mother's finest pumpkins, lad, fresh from the garden."

Rankin shut his eyes. The initial reluctance of the blade was quickly overcome, followed by soft resistance. It stopped when it reached the hilt. It was that easy.

He stepped over the body, into the room where a man at the window, who had been firing into the street, turned. Face contorted with horror and panic at seeing the blade, he raised his rifle in an effort to deflect it, but Rankin shot him.

Rankin stepped back over the twitching figures, bounded down the stairs, desperate to get away. At the foot of the stairs a glimmer of light showed from a basement doorway. Levelling the bayonet, he shoulder-charged the partly opened door which gave with a crash, a pile of furniture tumbling to the floor inside the dimly lit room. The pointed tip of the bayonet swung into the room, inches from the face of a shrieking girl, reeling backwards into the arms of her barely visible screaming mother. A small boy lunged at Rankin, a kitchen knife held out in front of him.

"Jesus Christ Almighty! Nea Zilandia! Nea Zilandia!"

He managed to deflect the boy's thrust and avoid puncturing the girl in the same skidding movement. "Sorry! Sorry!" he cried. "Don't go upstairs." Panting with exertion and fright, he backed out through the door.

A cold clammy sweat overtook him. Shaking, he leaned against the wall, sucking air into his lungs. Jesus, I nearly killed a child. Christ. Upstairs, someone groaned and cried out. He drew another long, shuddering breath and stepped out into the street.

CHAPTER THIRTEEN

Galatas, The Town Square, 25 May 1941

THEY HAD REACHED the village square where chaos reigned as tracer crisscrossed the square, sparking and whining off the buildings and cobbles. Khaki-clad soldiers were seemingly running in all directions. The village's handsome white church, the municipal building, the pleasant shade-giving trees, the fountain and the café bar – all wrecked. Other buildings had been bombed, too, causing them to collapse into the streets, while cobblestones had been torn from the ground and hurled about. Rage surged inside Rankin anew.

One of the tanks was stopped in the square, its turret and machine gun pointing up at the wrecked municipal building whose glassless windows were surrounded by bullet holes. A sour smell of burnt mattresses and charred wood drifted across the square along with the resulting smoke. The noise continued; tumultuous, battering, deafening.

Spotting a group of khaki uniforms sheltering behind a pile of rubble and a smashed wooden cart, Rankin dropped down beside them and discovered Mitchell with his Bren gun, Pringle and Meldrum.

"Jesus, Skipper, it's fuckin' hot out there! It could turn a man to drink!" Meldrum yelled, handing Mitchell another magazine. "Jerry's on the roof of that bloody building." He nodded towards the ravaged town hall.

A stream of tracer from the flat top of the building confirmed his observation.

"You alright, Alec?" asked Rankin.

"Bloody unlucky time to take a shit," said Pringle. "I could've been safe behind a nice stone wall with Tub now."

"Seen any of the other blokes?"

"Sarge went that way, Corky and a couple of others went in through the door. Haven't seen them since." Meldrum had to shout into his ear as Mitchell fired another burst at the top of the building. The rounds struck sparks and plaster off the parapet.

Then Renfrew arrived, panting, and dropped down onto the rubble, gasping. He turned over onto his back, and lay there, still panting, safe for the moment from enemy gunfire. "I'm getting too old for this lark, Skipper."

"Nonsense, Colin. We need to get in there and get that machine gun."

Renfrew groaned. Meldrum poked at him with his boot.

"Come on, Col, jump to it. I'll cover you."

"Mitchell's doing that, Mouldy. You leave your magazines here with him and come with me. You, too, Renfrew. We're making for that door over there," he said pointing to the town hall. "Run like hell." He paused, waiting for Mitchell to reload. "You, too, Alec. Cover us, Mitch. Let's go!"

Rankin was on his feet as Mitchell's next burst chattered out, and then he was off, jinking towards the municipal building, trusting to luck that he was not alone. As he ran past the shattered cart, he realised the donkey that had been pulling it was still between its shafts, lying dead.

He was halfway across the square, running past dead and wounded, nearing the abandoned tank when the doors of the town hall burst open. A huge German emerged, holding Corkhill by the neck in one hand and wildly waving his Luger in the other. Corkhill, the smallest man in the platoon, was moving in a macabre, jerky dance at the end of the man's huge fist. As Rankin veered towards them, out of the corner of his eye he saw another figure coming from the side.

The German, wearing a squared-off parachute helmet, which appeared far too small for his oversize head, was beside himself with rage, shouting and yelling, but the noise made it impossible to hear most of what he was shouting. Rankin caught the words "*sende Mause gegen Manner?*". Send a mouse against men? The gun on the parapet fired another burst over their heads out across the square which remained alive with flashes, tracer and running men; the noise undiminished.

The figure that he'd spotted was suddenly in front of him, rifle and bayonet held rigid as it ran at the German. The bayonet slammed into the arm holding the pistol and disappeared, pinning the man to the wall by his arm. Somehow, the bayonet had gone into the wall, causing the pistol to flail uselessly in the German's hand while he ranted at Corkhill, still dangling in the air in the grip of the man's other hand.

The rifleman tried to pull the bayonet out of the solid stone wall but it was stuck fast. "What the fuck?" Rankin heard him shout as he pulled harder and harder, boots to the wall, his whole weight pulling at the rifle. It would not budge. The German, still shouting at Corkhill, appeared not to have noticed either of them.

Rankin saw everything happening in slow motion, loosening his grip on reality, as if he were a spectator at a macabre circus sideshow.

Suddenly the German became aware of the presence of the other two and desperately tried to twist the hand holding the pistol towards the rifleman, who Rankin now realised was Renfrew, all the while yelling at Corkhill who was still held fast in the man's giant fist, choking, hands frenziedly scrabbling at the fingers around his neck. Renfrew continued to pull at his rifle, boots still to the wall, also yelling incoherently. Rankin cursed, knowing he hadn't reloaded but he was too close-in for the rifle with its 18-inch bayonet. In any case Renfrew was in the way.

Renfrew's bayonet had gone through the baggy sleeve of the German's jump smock, rather than the man's arm, and the two men were now in some kind of bizarre embrace, shrieking at each other. Meanwhile Corkhill, forgotten by both, danced maniacally, feet inches off the ground, lips purple, eyes closed, face puffy. Rankin had to bring this farce to a conclusion.

Pulling out the pistol that he'd earlier stuffed into his pocket, Rankin reached past Renfrew, whose head was now only inches from the German's, and shot the paratrooper between the eyes. A look of surprise passed momentarily over his face as the back of his head exploded over the whitewashed wall. Dropping Corkhill, he slumped down although his lifeless left hand, pinned to the wall, still gripped the Luger. Corkhill collapsed, gasping, hands to his throat. Renfrew was in tears of rage, even now unaware of Rankin's presence, as he continued to yell at the dead German to let go of his fuckin' rifle, oblivious of the man's blood spattered across his face.

"Colin, Colin, for Christ's sake, Colin, it's me!" Rankin yelled into Renfrew's ear, shaking him. Renfrew's face turned towards him, eyes glazed.

"Help me get Corky inside, Colin, for Christ's sake. Colin!" Machine-gun fire swept the square, pinging off the tank like flies on a beached whale, striking sparks, whining past inches away, parting the air with an angry crack.

Dropping his own rifle, Rankin grabbed Corkhill by his collar, Renfrew by his webbing, and dragged them both inside the heavy wooden doors of the town hall where he glimpsed a khaki-clad body sprawled across the black and white chess board tiles in a dark spreading pool. A shattering thump sounded upstairs, which was followed by yelling and a machine gun's rattle; the commotion was amplified by the tiled floor and echoed loudly across the lobby.

Rankin lay Corkhill on the floor of a tiny cubbyhole next to the entrance before shaking and slapping him until he gasped a ragged breath. Turning to Renfrew, whose eyes were wildly darting about, he saw that the man was in a state of shock.

"That joker got my rifle, Skipper, he wouldn't let go!" he sobbed. "Corky's had it!"

Grabbing him by his shirt front, Rankin shook him hard. "No, he isn't, Colin," he yelled into Renfrew's ear. "Corky's here!" he shouted, forcing Renfrew to look at Corkhill gasping on the floor. "Your bloody bayonet got stuck in the wall, for Christ's sake, Colin. You look after Corky for me, will you? I'll be back."

Upstairs, the noise of shouting and shooting was still going on. At the front door, he was nearly knocked over by Graham and another two men as they ran inside.

"Jesus, she's a right fuckin' shemozzle out there, Skipper. There's another fuckin' Spandau upstairs somewhere."

"On the roof terrace," shouted Rankin. Another long burst echoed around the lobby.

"C'mon!" Graham yelled. "After those mongrel bastards!" He and the others leaped at the stairs.

Outside, Rankin saw the second British tank trundling down the street, firing as it came, followed by more running men. Another man dashed into the town hall. Hugging the outside wall as he crept along the building, Rankin found his own rifle and picked it up. He stepped over the body of the paratrooper, suspended on one side by the arm still pinned to the wall, and yanked at Renfrew's rifle, but it was still stuck fast. The man's hand was now minus its Luger.

He ran back inside to Renfrew and Corkhill, but it was soon clear that Renfrew's understanding of the situation was fragmentary at best. He was kneeling beside Corkhill, tears streaming down his face, gibbering about him being dead, and it was his fault because that bloke had grabbed his rifle and wouldn't let it go. Graham and the others had disappeared. Rankin told Renfrew to stay with Corkhill and ran up the stairs.

Another khaki-clad body lay sprawled across the first-floor landing which, like a gallery, ran the length of the building, but now ended in a mass of collapsed rubble. Bullets thudded into the rooms, coming in through the windows, splintering doors and woodwork, zipping and cracking across the stairwell, sparking and whining. A shriek from above, followed by a body flying over the banister, told Rankin how far Graham had gone.

Up on the next floor a pair of British boots protruded from a room. Cautiously, Rankin pushed the remains of the door open and peered inside to see the khaki-clad body belonging to the boots lying in a wide glistening pool of blood. Three grey-green

322

uniformed bodies lay near a desk and easy chair like discarded rag dolls, tossed aside by a child in a tantrum. Black viscous-looking puddles on the floor reflected the flickering light. More black stains were splattered up the walls, across a cock-eyed picture of the King of Greece. It was a scene of absolute carnage and had obviously been caused by a grenade.

"Jesus Christ Almighty."

He ran on, up more stairs. The last door led outside to the roof terrace where he found Graham on the floor, face a bloody mask, shirt front slick with blood, head cradled in the lap of one of his companions. A smoking Spandau lay upended beside the parapet, a body sprawled next to it. Another German, an officer by his uniform, sat with legs splayed, back against the parapet, clutching his stomach. Blood ran between his fingers, pooling darkly between his legs.

A third man was shrieking *"Kamerad! Kamerad!"*, hands raised, backing away down the parapet. Two of Graham's mates launched themselves at him, grabbed him by the legs, and flipped him backwards over the edge. The last shriek Rankin heard was *"Nein!"* as he disappeared from sight.

"Bastard threw a hand grenade down below, got Alfie," one of them said in a matter-of-fact tone.

The wounded officer, slumped against the parapet, began to whimper, lips trembling. His breath came in sobbing gasps, drawn through purple lips, contorted face white as paper. The whimper turned to a keening cry, torn from him, despite the effort his face betrayed to contain it. He drew in another gasping, ragged breath and screamed again. Rankin's ears rang with the sound as it pierced its way, unwanted, beyond his very consciousness, becoming the only sound in the universe.

The man holding Graham's head in his lap was shouting something at him, but Rankin couldn't hear a word.

Down below the second tank had halted at an odd angle, not far away. A group of soldiers was clustered around a couple of bodies lying on the ground, trying to drag them to safety amid the flying bullets. The German who had been thrown over the parapet was splayed across the cobblestones, broken.

The screaming near at hand rose to a crescendo, filling the night. Meanwhile, Pringle had arrived on the roof terrace and was trying to tell him something, pulling at his sleeve.

Shaking Pringle loose, Rankin ran to the man and shouted at him. "Shut up, for Christ's sake! Shut up! Will you shut up?"

But the hideous animal-like screams continued. Rankin had once been told by one of the 1939 medical graduates-turned-medical officers that a gut wound, the most painful of all, felt like being burned alive from the inside out; more than any human could take. The man was conscious of nothing but his own agony and the terror of his life leaking away between his fingers, pooling in a dark puddle between his legs. Blood, piss, and shit. His old science teacher had once said that 80 percent of the human body was liquid. And here it was, in all its various forms, gathering in a roof gutter.

"Shut up, for the love of Christ! Shut up!" Bent at the waist, Rankin stood over the man, shouting at him as several more men, one of whom was Meldrum, burst onto the terrace.

Pringle was pulling at his shirt sleeve again, yelling at him. Rankin looked at him blankly, unable to hear him.

"Shut up, for Christ's sake! Stop your fucking yelling!"

The man screamed again, a long, piercing, inhuman sound. Rankin's rifle seemed to leap forward of its own volition, viciously jarring his hands as it did so, causing the long, steel blade attached to it to slam through the man's throat and into the parapet wall.

The screaming stopped and was followed by a brief but oppressive silence. The firing beyond had also stopped so that all of them on the terrace clearly heard the voice calling out down in the square in a very English accent: "Good show, New Zealand! Jolly good show. Come on, New Zealand!" The call might have been at a rugby match.

Rankin tried not to look at the German as he withdrew the blade, but he was drawn by the man's eyes, as they dimmed in the flickering light, became glassy, then accusing, yet sorrowing. His head slumped onto his chest, the hands stopped clawing and clutching as the arms went loose and slipped down by the side of the body. The world had come to a stop, stunned into silence. Rankin looked around to see Pringle backing away from him, horror and revulsion on his face.

One of the men who had thrown the German over the parapet stepped over the officer's body, picked his Luger up off the ground and patted Rankin on the shoulder. "Good on yer, mate. Grazer said you'se a decent coot. Couldn't hear yourself think with that bloody row goin' on."

Turning towards Graham and the man cradling his head, the soldier then turned back to Rankin. With one hand he pointed at the dead officer and with the other held the pistol in the air. "'Sides, that was the bastard shot Grazer in the head. With this."

CHAPTER FOURTEEN

Galatas, After the Battle, 25–26 May 1941

SILENCE. WORSE THAN the brain-battering noise. Dense, like treacle, full of accusation and guilt. But his ears didn't want to work, and his brain felt disconnected, as though he had suddenly been hurled into deep space; a vacuum, cold and empty, devoid of life and humanity. He still couldn't make out what the man holding Graham's head was saying. And Pringle was backing away from him, a horrified look on his face, while Meldrum stood uncomprehending, looking from one to the other, like someone who had just barged in on a conversation no one wanted him to hear.

Everyone was looking at him. What? What had he done? Rankin pushed past Meldrum and ran back down to the ground floor. Noise came back as he ran, his boots clattering on the rubble-strewn stone stairs. Outside, he could hear muted shouting and muffled gunshots. Corkhill was sitting up where Rankin had left him, massaging his neck, pale as a ghost. Renfrew was still a wreck, kneeling on the floor, gibbering at Corkhill as if he weren't there – hands gesturing furiously, explaining that Corky had died; it was his fault, he couldn't save him, then he'd come back to life, but that fuckin' German still wouldn't let go of his rifle.

Peering out through the door, Rankin saw that at last the square was quiet, save for the moans and cries of the wounded. As he crept to the corner sounds of gunfire, the crack of grenades and yelling came to him from somewhere beyond. A pile of German bodies lay in the street, some still twitching and groaning. A number of khaki-clad figures ran across the square, past the pile of bodies and down the dark lane; several jabbed their bayonets into the figures on the ground as they passed for good measure.

"Caught them. Forming up. They've gone on. Jolly good show, New Zealand." It was the same English voice he'd heard from the roof terrace. The pile of bodies must have been a counter-attack assembling. Wrong place, wrong time, too bloody bad. The fight had moved on. He was done in, empty. Mentally and physically. He could go no further. Slumping to the ground, he put his head in his hands and sobbed.

It was Meldrum who found him and dragged him back to the town hall where Mitchell had set up his Bren in a ground floor window.

"I've got him," Meldrum cried as he pulled Rankin inside and lay him on the tile floor. "I think he's hurt."

Rankin tried to protest. Meldrum had put him down only a foot from the body of the man who'd been thrown over the banister. Corkhill came over on his hands and knees.

"Where are you hurt, Skipper?" he croaked. "I'll get the first aid kit."

"I'm alright, Corky. Mouldy's got it wrong."

Corkhill patted him on the shoulder. Fire exploded, a red cloud covered his eyes, and he screamed, a primeval noise he hardly recognised as coming out of his own mouth.

"Jesus, Skipper," cried Corkhill, recoiling in shock.

"See, I told you," Meldrum said in an accusing tone.

They unbuckled his web belt, eased the braces and front pouches away from his chest, and unzipped the German smock. Corkhill pulled the jacket apart, and started to run his hands over him, searching for wetness, blood.

"Shoulder, Skipper. Something's hit you in the shoulder," said Corkhill.

Corkhill started to press against the outside of his shirt. A hot blade seared through his shoulder, forcing another piercing scream from his throat. "Christ Jesus, Corky, what the hell are you doing?" he gasped. No red cloud this time, though. That must be good, he thought.

"Sorry, Skipper, I can feel something in here." Opening Rankin's shirt, he gently probed around the fleshy part of his right shoulder. "It's a splinter," he said, opening his first aid kit and taking a pair of small forceps from a sealed paper envelope.

"I hope you know what you're doing, Corky. Don't make me regret not leaving you to slug it out with that mad bastard ..." That was as far as he got. Corkhill pulled on the end of the splinter, and Rankin fainted.

———

THE BATTALION'S MAD charge into the village had run out of steam somewhere beyond the square. Rumour had it that stubborn German resistance in the schoolhouse, some way beyond the square, had held things up for a while until Clive Hulme, the battalion's Provost Sergeant, cleaned out 60 or so German troops using his customary cunning stealth and a sack of hand grenades. Several hours after the shooting had died away whistles had sounded, rallying the scattered remnants of the platoons. Exhausted, pushed to the very limit of their beings, dazed men stumbled from whatever shelter their battle had ended in, barely comprehending they were still alive.

The road out of the village, back the way they had come, was silent except for the sound of boots wearily tramping, a muted cough and the occasional clink and creak of equipment. Flickering flames among the ruins cast eery shadows, windowless buildings gaped at them like empty eye sockets. No one spoke as they trudged past the buildings lining the roadway. Rankin reprised the earlier scenes in his head, almost from the perspective of a spectator. Although the images were currently tucked away in the farthest reaches of his mind, he knew they would lurk, waiting to spring out and ambush him without notice and when he least expected it. Looking around the dazed and harrowed faces about him, the eyes dull and vacant, he knew he was not the only one feeling this way.

Gunshots punctuated the night as some stumbled across German soldiers, men equally exhausted and terrified, trying to find their own way out of hell. Occasionally, men too tired of killing stepped aside with a gruff, "Fuck off, Fritzy" or "*Verpiss dich, Tommy*". A life spared by a man too weary to take it.

It had cost dearly. Dead and wounded littered the streets. So many officers and NCOs had been killed or wounded that the assault eventually lacked cohesion and direction, breaking down into a series of vicious little fights in which no quarter was given by either side. The battalion commander, Colonel Leckie, had been wounded at the beginning of the action. He had to hand command to Major Thomason[12], who, when wounded himself, handed over to Lieutenant Bond.[13]

D Company's losses reflected those of the battalion as a whole. Everyone soon knew that Captain Hamilton had been hit, gone down in a heap at the head of Robertson's platoon during the charge into the village. Captain McKenzie, the nuggety little Scot, had copped it, felled by a bursting grenade in the street. The boys who had been with him were incensed; they chased the Jerries responsible into a garden yard where they baled them up in a corner, clubbed them to the ground and bayoneted them to death.

The badly wounded, friends and enemies alike, had to be left for the German medical services to take care of them when they reoccupied the village; all parties had to trust that they would be properly looked after. The walking wounded were required to join the defence against the expected counter-attack and no one could be spared to carry injured men. Even as they pulled out, some women and children crept out of their hiding places, bringing milk, bread, honey and water to those too badly hurt to leave.

All except Graham. His friends had refused to leave him behind, instead strapping him to a door ripped from the municipal building and carrying him. An officer who materialised out of the dark ordered them to leave him behind. They told him to fuck off. Huffing with indignation, he disappeared back into the gloom.

As the men moved in a daze through the shattered village, it appeared every house was damaged. Bodies hung from windows,

12 Major H.H. Thomason, born Nelson 9 Oct 1896, orchardist, wounded again 29 May 1941.
13 Lieutenant R.L. Bond, born Adelaide 19 Feb 1908, brewer, 23 Battalion 1940–41 enlisted AIF 1942.

sprawled in doorways, lay thick and clumped across the narrow streets and scattered over piles of rubble. No windows or doors remained intact. Silently passing by, drawing on their cigarettes, the men were gratified to see that German bodies heavily outnumbered their own. Wounded men clutched at them as they passed; some cried piteously, but there was little they could do. Single gunshots sounded from houses and streets, disconnected, scattered, yet everyone knew what they meant. Nothing was said.

A Company remained occupying vantage points in the village, while C and D Companies took up positions on the ridge to the east. The rest of the battalion was sent into reserve behind them. The platoons slipped into their new positions, expecting attack at any minute by an enemy hell-bent on revenge. But the Germans had gone quiet; no counter-attack came. After all, they had the luxury of waiting until morning, when the Luftwaffe could do the job for them.

So the exhausted New Zealanders were left holding their ridge and the village. Small parties and individuals foraged for arms, ammunition, food, water and tobacco. Many volunteered for this ghoulish duty, especially those who had left mates behind in the village, but only a handful could be spared. The night continued to ring with gunshots, the rattle of automatic weapons and crack of grenades. Death wandered singly through Galatas for hours after the mass bloodletting subsided. Foragers, patrols, lone wolves out to avenge a mate or simply out to kill roamed the streets, while A Company rooted out any organised resistance.

A dressing station was set up half a mile down the road, to treat the walking wounded able to get themselves there under their own steam. Nicholson sent Rankin to have his splinter wound taken care of. Men were released by their units in small batches for treatment to avoid having too many away at a time. Despite this, the station was crowded. The number of men waiting perhaps said a lot about how many units had been cobbled together for the assault, or the number of independents who had simply happened along and joined in.

The dressing station was no more than canvas covers strung between trees, with makeshift canvas stools or stretchers for the patients. Light was provided by shrouded lanterns and hooded torches. Rankin joined the queue to be briefly examined by a doctor, who made an instant decision as to what was needed and which orderly was best suited to help. The doctor, as far as he could tell, was no older than himself; his face deeply lined by fatigue and worry, the lines etched into dusty, stained skin the colour of putty, probably like his own. A young man suddenly made old. After examining the scar on Rankin's forehead, he looked in his eyes with a pencil light.

"This scar here, were you concussed?"

"Yes."

"After-effects, dizziness, unable to think clearly, trouble making rational decisions?"

"No."

"What's this bruise on your chest?"

"Winged by a bullet, whacked by a piece of railway wagon."

"Same time?"

"Yes."

Rankin followed the doctor's fingers out to the periphery of his vision, and into his nose, and repeated the six times table from six times eight.

"So what brings you to the Harley Street Clinic today?" the doctor asked.

Rankin pointed to his bare shoulder and the angry red point in his skin. The doctor examined it carefully, then conferred with the orderly in tones too quiet to catch.

After being guided to another stool set up further along the roadside stone wall, Rankin unbuttoned the rest of his shirt and slipped it off, acutely aware of how stiff with sweat, dirt and God-knew-what-else it was. The orderly peered at the wound site with a lens and a pencil light. "It's not all buried under the skin. You're lucky. We won't have to dig too deep for it. This'll hurt me more than it hurts you, mate," he said as he liberally swabbed his whole shoulder with a bright yellow pungent-smelling antiseptic solution. He began probing the splinter and surrounding area with an instrument that looked to Rankin like something a dentist might use. Rankin's intake of breath was sharp; it hurt like hell and tears stung his eyes.

"Here, bite down on this," said the orderly, giving him a wad of cotton sheet to put between his teeth. "Best I can do, mate. No anaesthetic, I'm afraid."

"Jesus Christ." Every exploration brought a new fiery lance of pain, causing Rankin to cry out through the gag. The pain was excruciating, like a knife blade being twisted into the fleshy pad of his shoulder. Screaming and crying into his cotton pad, unable to help himself, Rankin was acutely aware of the stoic silence all around him. Eventually he heard the orderly grunt in satisfaction. "Ah, got you, you little bastard."

The pain was exquisite. He was clammy, cold and sweating at the same time. *This must be like having your nail torn off*, he thought. Then it was suddenly over, and the relief made him light-headed. He spat out the wad of cotton, his jaw aching from the pressure, feeling like he'd just run a mile, utterly exhausted.

"You're a lucky bloke, mate."

Rankin did not feel lucky. Tears streamed down his face, his breath came in ragged gasps, and his shoulder felt as if it were on fire.

"How do you work that out?" he sobbed.

"I've got it out. I hope I got all of it. Looks like a grenade splinter." He waved a jagged sliver of metal, grasped in a pair of forceps, in front of Rankin's face. It was about an inch long and was easily big enough to see, even in the light of the hooded hurricane lamp under the canvas shelter. "It might have still been red hot when it hit you; there's a little burn on your shirt. No blood. Probably cauterised the wound on entry. Hopefully it burnt away any cotton thread from your shirt, rather than packing it into the wound, so it won't go septic. Your shirt didn't look too bloody clean, mate; you should stop cleaning the dunnies with it."

He poured sulpha powder into and around the wound, and then dressed it with a pad held in place with Elastoplast. "Try and keep it dry for a few days. You're bloody lucky it hit you here, and not somewhere more important," he said, nodding at his lap.

"Christ, my shoulder gets more use than my bollocks," Rankin gasped. "That's my right shoulder. Recoil's going to bloody hurt, isn't it?"

"Good way of telling if it's infected or not: it'll get more painful if it is."

"Jesus. Bloody optimist."

The orderly dropped the instruments into a pan of boiling water on a burner that was sitting on a little camp table.

"No steriliser?" asked Rankin, doing up his shirt, wincing as his shoulder burned anew with the movement.

"Are you bloody joking? There's a war on, in case you hadn't

334

noticed. It's a new technique, continuous sterilisation. Just need to keep you jokers from trying to make tea with it. Next case!" he called out, without looking at Rankin again.

———

RANKIN GOT BACK to the platoon in the early hours of the morning, just as orders to withdraw were received.

"My God, am I glad to see you!" said Nicholson, shaking his hand. "Boys aren't happy about being ordered to withdraw. How's the shoulder?"

"Hurts more now than when Corky had a crack at pulling it out. Buggered if I know where I got it. What's been happening here?"

"Quiet. The odd pot-shot somewhere out there," he nodded in the general direction of the German-held countryside, "and occasional flare-up from the village. Mister Scotland was as good as his word, and we have Tub and Smithy back. Got orders to disengage and fall back. Effective in fifteen minutes."

"I see. I'll bet the boys are happy about that."

———

THEY WERE MARSHALLED out of the line and set off down the road – east, towards Chania. Everyone knew what that meant.

"Jesus, we tanned Jerry's arse, good and bloody proper," a voice grumbled.

"Bloody brass don't know their arse from their elbow."

"You can't bloody win by running away."

Rankin let them have their say; they needed to vent their

frustration. It was easy for the men to think that they had knocked the Germans for six; there was no doubt the counter-attack had given the Germans a real caning. The reality, though, was that the enemy had resupply, reinforcement, and air cover, all provided by the Luftwaffe. The British force had none; for all they knew the Germans had already infiltrated in behind them and were preparing to cut the coastal road, their only means of retreat.

The stench of the village was in their throats and on their skin as they marched back down the hill, the way they had come. Everyone was black with soot, dirt, and dried blood. Their clothes were stiff with it, their skin dry, like sandpaper. Those who had tobacco smoked, trying to rid themselves of the sour taste of burnt houses and explosives and the sickly sweet smell of fresh-let blood – to say nothing of the soothing effect of nicotine on frayed nerves. Some were jittery and shaking, barely able to string a few words together; others unnaturally loud and over-confident. By this time, Rankin knew how most of them would react. Even banter and bravado did not mask the quiet, absent moments. The moments they were trying to fix in their memories. Faces of friends they would never see again.

The column resembled a trail of glow-worms getting along the road. Later, there would be no smoking, but not now. Rankin sucked a barley sugar. It was going to be another long night. He ached all over; he was so tired he could barely think. Thirst made his tongue feel too big for his mouth, his throat dry and raw. The fire burning in his shoulder was a constant reminder as the weight hanging on his web shoulder strap aggravated the punctured flesh with every movement.

Reilly was missing. No one had seen him cop it. He had been

with Nicholson late in the piece, but he was missing now.

"He was right beside me," Nicholson fretted over and over. "I don't know what the devil happened to him. Where in God's name did he go?" They were stopped for a rest beside the road while the guides conferred. If they had the means, they could brew up, they'd been told. Rankin never felt more like a mug of tea in his life.

"Nick, you can't be mother to everyone."

"You can talk. What was that all about? Take the boy's rifle and give him your Schmeisser?"

McIntyre handed him a mug of tea, from the dixie boiling on a German cooker. "There's no' many fuel tablets left, Skipper."

"There's no' many of a lot of things, Mac." He waited until McIntyre had retreated out of earshot. "Well, it's my rifle; I should be the one to carry it," Rankin said to Nicholson.

"Hmmph. Actually, being strictly accurate, it's my rifle, but let's not split hairs. You were trying to spare him from using the bayonet. Admit it."

They sat in silence for a while.

"Well, bugger it, so what if I was?" Rankin said angrily, taking another mouthful of tea.

He sat silently, nursing the mug, unable to get the image out of his mind.

"Nick ..." Rankin cleared his throat as his voice had come out small. The tea tasted good. Without milk or sugar, it tasted clean, fragrant even, almost clean enough to wash away the foul taste of the town stuck in his gullet. But nothing was enough to wash away the scene playing over and over in his head: the slumping head, the sliding arms, the bloody throat. He felt like shit. His shoulder hurt, but that wasn't the half of it.

Nicholson looked up, alarmed. "What?"

"I murdered a man. Wounded. I put the bayonet through him."

"Probably did him a favour."

Rankin sharply raised his head. "He was wounded. Someone might have been able to fix him up. He was screaming; I stabbed him in the throat."

"As I said, you probably did him a favour."

Rankin stared as Nicholson took a mouthful of tea. "You've changed your tune."

"War forces you to face some harsh realities. Was he ours or theirs?"

Rankin gasped in horror, stunned. No one knew about Simpson other than Glover. Kenny had never told anybody; he was positive of it. And now he never would: it had been Glover lying on the tiled floor of the municipal building, head bashed in by the same massive maniac who had throttled Corkhill, his body beside the German thrown over the banister. Kenny and Corky had known each other from school days, they drew closer together after Simpson's death. They had dashed into the building together, to run slap into the parachute division's Goliath. To add insult to injury, the colossus had disarmed Glover and killed him with a single blow to the head, splattering Corky in the process, Corkhill had told him in a wheezy, tearful voice.

There was nothing in Nicholson's expression, seen in the dim starlight, to suggest anything behind the question. "Jesus! Theirs, of course. His guts were spilling out in his hands. He was screaming so loud I couldn't hear myself think."

"So, you did him a favour. Why prolong his agony? Besides, you're in charge. You need to be able to think. Our blokes depend on it; they're more important than theirs. Now, that's an end to it. I don't want to hear this discussed again."

"That's not how it seemed, the way they looked at me."

Nicholson got to his feet, saying, "They'll get over it. We'll all do things we're not likely to tell mum about before this is over, Neil. Fact of life."

Rankin stared after him as he walked off. He still felt like shit. He desperately wanted to feel more alive, more human. The hand in his pocket closed over the little glass vial and rolled it between his fingers. He had already taken one tonight.

Regretfully, he let go of the vial and finished his tea.

CHAPTER FIFTEEN

A Day by the River, 26 May 1941

DAWN WAS STREAKING the sky behind the eastern hills as they approached their objective. The coast road had been badly pitted by bomb craters and torn up by strafing. Along its length was scattered the debris of defeat: equipment abandoned and destroyed, newly dug patches of ground topped with a rifle or wooden cross, bodies still unburied.

They smelled it before they saw it; the sickly sweet smell of charred flesh and the sour odour of burning rubber. It wafted in the breeze as they marched up an incline and over the crest of a low hill. Unthinking, one of the men cried out: "Jesus, smells just like the old lady singeing the feathers off the Christmas chook!"

"Put a fuckin' sock in it, you dozy bastard!" chorused a dozen voices.

At this point the road ran through a cutting where, in front of them, they could see the remains of three or four trucks, it was hard to tell exactly, which had been caught in the open. Low flames, still flickering around the wheel rims and in the shattered cabs and engine bays, threw ghostly shadows over the twisted and buckled steel.

The vehicles had been ambulances, or trucks detailed to carry the severely wounded. The canvas covers and stretchers were gone, burnt, leaving the gaunt metal frames as mute testament. The scene was not hard to imagine: screaming quickly silenced by the roaring flames, greedily devouring the helpless cargo, dropping them onto the red-hot metal trays where they had roasted and burned into charred, amorphous lumps. The men marched past silently, each of them no doubt wondering if he'd known any of the unrecognisable, unfortunate occupants. And thanking God he wasn't one of them.

The coast road was choked with personnel and equipment, which slowed them down. The light was already gathering in the east when they crested another rise, where provosts with hooded torches established who they were, and gave them instructions to move to their bivouac for the day. D Company was sent to the left of the road, between the road and the beach, to assemble in a gully. At their backs was the Keriti River, flowing down the valley from Alikianou and under the main road bridge leading to Chania.

Units had started to gather in the area shortly after midnight. Some of 4 Brigade were sent across the bridge to be marshalled into an area south of Chania, already home to the Suda Brigade made up of various Australian and British units.

23 Battalion was dispersed on both sides of the coast road, with its back to the river and the road bridge. On its left, 22 Battalion was gathering, and in their area 5 Brigade established its headquarters. In front of them, facing the Germans, were 21 and 19 Battalions. The provosts had their hands full trying to sort out the chaos of units and stragglers, arriving piecemeal in groups or singly, and head them in the right direction. Inevitably, tempers

were short and voices raised. Finally, Rankin's platoon found its way to a patch of ground they would call home for the day.

The unit dispositions were explained to the officers and senior NCOs by Lieutenant Bond, acting battalion commander, at an officers' orders group before first light. He emphasised that "positions" might mean no more than a scrape in the ground, and even that might be impossible since the ground had not seemed promising when they had walked it half an hour beforehand. Some positions may consist of no more than a sangar, a low wall of hand-placed rocks in front of a man, built as protection for him and his weapon. Not a comforting thought for men expecting attack from the air during the hours of daylight.

They learnt that 5 Brigade now held the front line, with the remnants of 4 Brigade in reserve behind them. The front was established in a rough line from east of Evthymi, their position the day before. That area was now held by 21 Battalion, nearest the coast. The line ran south from the beach, with 19 Battalion (tangled with the remnants of 20 Battalion) next to 21 and 28 Battalions, adjoining the Australians astride the Alikianou road.

D Company's losses forced a reorganisation. Anderson and Rankin lived to lead their own platoons, but at the briefing it became apparent they were the last surviving infantry subalterns. Pyne had either been killed or severely wounded at Galatas. His platoon, presently commanded by his sergeant, was to be amalgamated with the HQ platoon and would be led by Hamilton, who was expected back. In the meantime, it was under Bernard Clutterbuck, along with O'Rourke's platoon. Bernard was the only HQ staff member to survive Galatas; company orderlies, cooks, signallers and clerks had all suffered losses. It was scant comfort that the other side had paid so dearly for them.

The briefing broke up as the pale light of dawn began to chase the stars from the night sky.

"I'm very glad to see you are still with us, Bernard," Rankin said as they walked back towards their positions. Already, the odd pop and rattle of gunfire could be heard from the hills to their front. Troops were still streaming east along the road. They all needed to be under cover before the Luftwaffe arrived. They were cutting things fine, very fine.

"Thank you, Mister Rankin. The feeling is mutual, I assure you."

"I'm very sorry to hear about Captain McKenzie; I had a soft spot for him," Rankin continued, tears pricking his eyes.

Bernard pulled him aside. "I'm aware, Neil – if I may use your Christian name for a moment – that the captain held you in very high regard. Said you'd go far. He interceded on your behalf more than once, when he perceived certain officers may have let prejudices, held for whatever reason, cloud their professional judgement. His biggest concern for you was that you couldn't let sleeping dogs lie. Button it when required, to put it another way."

"Yes, Bernard, I know. It's a bad character flaw. Something happened between that 'certain officer' and my father. I don't suppose Captain McKenzie ever mentioned anything?"

Boney Anderson strode up. "Yes, we'll certainly miss the irascible old Scot," said Clutterbuck. "Best of luck, boys, I must be off."

Anderson stepped aside as Clutterbuck left, then turned back to Rankin. "Did I interrupt something?"

"No, I was just saying how sorry I was that Captain McKenzie copped it."

"Yes, me, too. He should have been company commander.

Yet more proof there is no God, as if we needed it. If there were a God, Dimwitty would have got his permanent posting well ahead of old Mac's."

"Christ, Boney, that's a bit harsh, isn't it? It's been a bloody tiring day. It seems pretty plain we're on the way east. God knows where."

"Yes. That was some shindig, Galatas. Knocked the bugger for six, but there he is, still right on our tails." Anderson's voice sounded brittle.

"I lost that wild driver I was telling you about, among others. Shot in the head. His friends defied orders and carried him to the Advanced Dressing Station over the ridge."

Anderson's shoulders slumped. "I lost another corporal and seven men," he said in a hushed voice. "There's actually fuck-all left of the platoon."

"Jesus, Boney, there won't be anyone left to catch Jolly Jack Tar's Ferry Service if this keeps up."

Anderson was staring at his boots. After a long pause, he raised his eyes. "Keep your head down, Neil."

"Yes. You, too, Boney."

They parted with a handshake.

POSITIONS HAD BEEN scraped as best they could with helmet and bayonet. The ground they had been allocated on the seaward side of the main road was not at all promising for preparing defensive positions. The river ran behind them, flanked by bamboos, trees and reeds. The ridge they occupied was cut through by gullies and broken ground; clumps of bamboos and trees grew in some parts, scattered trees in others, and some of it was cultivated.

"The battalion's in reserve. We're about a thousand yards behind the front-line positions," Rankin explained to the NCOs on his return to the platoon, drawing the positions on the map they had. "Tasks allocated to D Company are to provide support to the 21 Battalion platoons directly to our front if needed," he gestured over the ridge ahead, "and to ensure that the ground between the road and the coast," he pointed north, along the river, "is not infiltrated. We can't let Jerry get between the front-line units and ourselves." The NCOs nodded. "We have the job of patrolling a gully on our right flank," Rankin continued, "which could be used to cover troops creeping up from the beach. I think we can do that with half a section. We're nearest the beach; we'll need to keep the gully watched all day."

The NCOs nodded in agreement. "So much for our day in reserve," said Nicholson.

"It's not all bad," Rankin said. "We can also allow the men down to the river, so long as they keep out of sight. Weapons at hand at all times, of course. No more than half a section at a time."

"Thank the Lord for that," said Nicholson. "My clothes are so blimmin' dirty they could walk to the river by themselves."

"Aah, a change of socks," said Johnstone. "Been frightened to take my boots off in case my socks fall to bits."

"Have we heard from the pair that took Graham to the dressing station?" asked Lawrence.

"No," answered Rankin. "God knows it'll be chaos there. Could take all day."

"The man was shot in the head. You'll be lucky if you ever see any of them again," muttered Nicholson.

Morning stand-to was accompanied by the usual Storches buzzing, trying to place the two opposing armies in the bright morning sun. Pulling whatever cover was available over them, or hiding in the shadow of a tree, the men did not need telling to hold their fire when the little planes with the spindly undercarriage legs came near and the cry went up, "Aircraft! Take cover!"

Breakfast was padded out with captured German provisions scavenged from the dead and wounded of Galatas. Many had not had a decent meal in days, but those with souvenired Esbit stoves who were frying good German sausage and hard black bread were the envy of anyone who caught the smell of it.

———

"YOU GET YOUR head down, Nick. I'll look after things for a bit."

Nicholson raised his head, lids heavy with fatigue. "Are you sure? You're the one who's wounded."

"Just a scratch. I'm wide awake," Rankin replied. "You look like you could do with a decent kip."

Nicholson regarded him doubtfully, grumbled a bit, but took the one blanket which remained and placed it under a nearby tree. Rankin watched him; the man had barely sat down and got his pipe and tobacco out of his pack when he fell asleep. Resting in deep shade, he should be safe enough, Rankin told himself.

Rankin looked at his watch. Lawrence's section, the one nearer the coast, had been given the task of patrolling the ravine towards the sea. He told McIntyre to hold the fort while he went to see the ravine for himself. After putting on his jump smock and web kit, he picked up his rifle and made for the trees and bamboos growing along the riverbank, and their cover from the Luftwaffe.

Some of the spreading plane trees were enormous. Groups from other units were already taking the opportunity to clean themselves and their battered clothes in the river. Deep, slow-flowing pools provided plenty of opportunity to bathe and swim. Again, no one needed to be told to hug the river banks with their overhanging foliage and keep out of sight of the Luftwaffe.

Aircraft were soon constantly overhead, searching for targets. The noise of gunfire coming from beyond the ridge to the west was an incessant reminder of the dire situation, but despite these drawbacks, the day was beautiful enough to make a man forget the disappointments of the last few days.

He found Lawrence preparing to mount his patrol. Lawrence pointed out where he had posted his AT rifle, Bren gun and the Spandau he had, describing each position, what could be seen from it, and how they linked together. They had been signalling using shaving mirrors, and none had reported any trouble. Lawrence considered he could cover the ground with half his section, but before he released anyone to the river he had decided to conduct a reconnaissance patrol of the ravine. The ravine cut the slope in two and was dead ground. Because it debouched about 200 yards from Lawrence's section command post, nothing in it was visible from any of his positions; hence he would need to patrol it.

"I'll just come along for a look-see," said Rankin. "You're in charge."

They set off, seven in all, making their way between trees, clumps of bamboo, and a farm building to the lower end of the ravine. Each time they heard an aircraft, they slipped into cover and froze. Eventually the gully opened before them; a jagged, steep gash running most of the height of the ridge. Rankin studied it from beneath the nearest tree. "Jesus. Half a battalion could hide in there. They'd be bloody invisible."

The gully looked so narrow that in places only one man at a time could negotiate it. Ten to 20 feet deep, rough, filled with scrub, boulders and loose debris, it cut a zig-zag path up the face of the ridge. It would be impossible to see more than 20 yards ahead. "Christ! They could be watching us even now," Lawrence said as he lowered his binoculars.

Making their way up the gully was painstaking work. Boulders and little spurs jutted onto the floor and as they'd already suspected observing any distance ahead was impossible. As they climbed, Rankin expected to encounter a party of Germans coming the other way at any moment. The sky above was a blue slash, framed by the sides of the gully. Rankin's nerves, already stretched taut, began to twang and jangle in alarm.

Halfway up, Lawrence raised his hand; he thought he had seen dust. They took up positions, only able to field a front of three men, cocked their weapons, and waited. Rankin's heart was pounding in his chest, his mouth as dry as the dust underfoot. They were trapped.

They heard them before they saw them. Laughing and talking, scrabbling over rough ground, raising a cloud of dust, a group of a dozen or so men coming down the ravine were surprised to see Lawrence, Rankin and the others rise out of the dirt. The first man came into view, climbing over a dusty rock-fall, scattering stones and making enough noise to wake the dead.

Lawrence, Rankin and the others lowered their weapons but the noisy group pushed past, chattering excitedly, taking little notice of those coming uphill. Rankin found their officer, a captain.

"And who might you be, young man, wearing an enemy jacket?"

"Lieutenant Rankin, sir, D Company, 23 Battalion. This ravine is not secure. We have been tasked with patrolling it against German infiltration."

"Nonsense, Lieutenant. Perfect cover for troops in transit. Can't be seen down here. We're on our way to the river, for a wash and a brush up. Don't hold us up, Lieutenant. We have to get back to the war in a couple of hours." A traffic jam had formed in the gully above them, as more jovial and excited men skidded to a halt in the dust. They began complaining loudly.

"I understand that sir, but the area can't be guaranteed safe from German infiltration –"

He got no further. A Messerschmitt 110 twin engine fighter roared across the gully. Rankin looked up, startled; the aircraft was so close to the ground he could see the pilot's face. He felt, rather than saw, the aircraft bank before it passed out of sight over the rim of the gully.

Rankin looked up the slope, at the wadi full of men, then at Lawrence.

"Get out of here! That bastard'll be back!" He turned towards his men. "We need to get out of here! Now!"

The captain looked at him in surprise. Rankin shouted, "Sir, he'll be back. Get your men out of this gully! Get out of the ravine!"

"Get a grip on yourself, Lieutenant. We're safe in this gully. We're getting on to the river. I'm not letting some gutless wonder get in the way. My men have been waiting a long time for this." He turned his back on Rankin, signalled to the others, and pushed past Rankin, muttering "nut case" as he did so.

Rankin searched the sides of the ravine in panic. He scrambled to the top, hand over hand, using scrubby bushes as handholds, dislodging stones and rocks amid a cloud of dust and dirt. He heaved his rifle onto the edge, grasped a bush on the lip of the ravine, and hauled himself out, heart pounding. In the ravine the captain's troops were pushing past Lawrence, oblivious. The captain was berating Lawrence, shouting at him, telling him to get out of their bloody way, and that his officer was a flake and a bloody lunatic.

"Lawrence, ignore him! Get out! Get out! Get your men out!" Rankin sucked in a lungful of air. "Get out! Get out!" he bellowed.

Slowly, still unsure, some of the others started to clamber up the side of the ravine. Lawrence saw them go, hastily saluted the captain in mid-invective, turned his back on him and started up the gully's side, hand over hand. The captain was shouting at him, demanding he come back. Further down the gully, a scuffle had broken out. As Lawrence and several others reached the top, Rankin ran to them, holding out his hand, pulling them over the lip. Over his shoulder, he saw the unmistakeable twin-engine twin-tail silhouette of the Messerschmitt bank in towards them.

"Run! Run!" he screamed.

He ran along the lip of the ravine yelling for them to get out, run for cover.

He looked towards the oncoming Messerschmitt, to his horror, another was sliding in behind it.

A boulder next to a tree about 20 yards away caught his eye, and Rankin ran for his life. Lawrence had disappeared. The leading Messerschmitt opened fire; the rattle of its four machine guns and thump of its twin cannon echoed off the hillside, drowning out everything else.

Rankin dive-rolled over the boulder and found himself on top of Lawrence. The rattling, booming noise of the Messerschmitt passed only feet above, then commenced its turn, heard rather than seen, away towards the sea. The other aircraft was already strafing the ravine, flying up its length, in its turn. Clouds of dust, punctured by the flashes of exploding cannon shells, hid the ravine from view. Spurts from bullet strikes and cannon-shell bursts marched up the gully in a continuous, clattering, roaring stream. After an eternity, the second aircraft passed overhead and turned away, leaving behind an ominous silence, shrouded in dust.

Rankin was up and running towards the gully. The silence was pierced by a thin scream. Rankin looked into the abyss: the slow-clearing dust revealing a carpet of torn and mangled bodies, hideously wounded. Groans and cries rose from the dirt.

The aircraft cannon and machine guns had showed no respect for rank, age or agility. Explosive shells and steams of bullets had mashed and pulped virtually every living thing in their path.

Lawrence reached his side and stopped dead. "Oh, Jesus, no, Skipper, no, this can't be right." His voice tailed away. The others who had got out of the wadi ran to join them. To a man, they were rooted to the spot. Screams from the ravine died to whimpers. Few cried for help.

"Watch the sky, for Christ's sake," Rankin said.

Rankin glanced over those who had got out: Lawrence plus four of their original six; a clerk named Dalton was missing. There were only four faces he did not recognise; four out of God only knew how many.

Suddenly they became aware of movement in the pit below. Lawrence posted a lookout as Rankin slithered down into the gully, sending a shower of dirt and pebbles ahead of him. The first man he came to was lying on his front, his back a red pulpy mass oozing through blackened dirt and pebbles. He shivered and twitched and although he was drawing breath, it rasped and rattled in his chest, his remaining life measured in drags on a cigarette, which was all he asked for. The next had been cut in two by a cannon shell, mercifully killed outright. Another had been hit in the face; where a moment ago jaw, nose and eyes had been, now was a ghastly, bloody pulp. Stunned, immobile, gurgling, the man somehow still lived.

Rankin recoiled in horror, feeling his face blanch. A coarse gurgle came from the man's throat as he gasped for breath through the hole where his mouth had been. He would drown in his own blood in minutes. Rankin turned away, unable to bear the sound of his impending death, his cheeks wet with tears. With mounting anguish and despair, he searched fruitlessly among the carnage for someone he could help Two more men from Lawrence's platoon arrived. Having seen the Messerschmitts sweep down, they had guessed what had happened. Lawrence sent them to Nicholson with a message asking for help.

There were fewer than half a dozen survivors, several of them uninjured. They had been lucky enough to get behind a boulder or one of the rockfalls that crossed the floor of the gully. None of them were officers.

Shaken, shocked into dumbness, the still-living bore the now-familiar gaunt, haunted look that saw nothing, but saw everything.

CHAPTER SIXTEEN

Rest and Relaxation, 26 May 1941

"JESUS, NICK, THE pilot only had to sit in his bloody seat and press his trigger, then walk his sight up the gully."

Rankin was trying to explain to Nicholson what had happened. He understood it but could barely comprehend it. "Four machine guns, that's sixty rounds a second, plus cannon shells. Christ, if it took eight seconds, that's ten rounds per man."

Nicholson looked at the ground, unable to meet his eyes. "I'm sorry, Neil."

"No. You needed a break. The sheer power … it looked like a giant flail had gone up the wadi, pulverising everything in its path. Blowing rocks apart, bushes stripped to saplings and torn out of the ground. And those blokes. Just bloody lumps, covered in dirt and shit …" Rankin's account tailed away into nothingness.

He was studying a leaf in his hand, turning it over and over, looking to be examining it front and back in minute detail, but in reality not seeing it. "God," he continued, as if talking to the leaf. "He only had to sit in his seat. Pull a few levers and push a few buttons. Thirty-five men dead. Not just dead, destroyed –

torn apart." He looked up at Nicholson, tears in his eyes. "Torn limb from limb. It's not just a figure of speech there in that bloody gully. They'll just have to bury the pieces there." He lapsed into silence. Then, in a whisper, "I couldn't stop it. I couldn't stop it from happening. He wouldn't listen."

"You got your blokes out, Neil. They listened to you. They're alive, uninjured, because of you. You saw what was coming. That's success, that's soldiering. That's being a smart officer. That's what you need to concentrate on." Nicholson wagged his pipe stem at Rankin as he spoke. "You were a success. You can't be responsible for the other man's failure."

Rankin looked at him, wanting to believe him. But not believing. Guilt takes a lifetime to fade.

———

THE DAY WORE on. Nicholson insisted on answering the next call from Johnstone about a German sniper causing a nuisance. "God knows where he came from," Nicholson grumbled, getting to his feet. "You sit still. I'll deal with this. Your turn to sit in the shade and have a rest, after this morning."

Nicholson took Rankin's rifle and telescopic sights, put on the stained and dusty German jump smock and disappeared into the riverside foliage with Johnstone's runner. Rankin propped the Thompson gun against a tree and sat back. He desperately wanted a wash and a shave, but that could wait. McIntyre, the only other HQ section person the platoon now possessed, ran errands and made him a mug of black tea.

The war again seemed a long way off, though it growled away in the background, and periodically roared overhead. It was hard to reconcile the sunshine and peace with what had happened in the morning; he might have imagined it. But the gully was real, filled with its grisly evidence, just down the river.

His eyes closed. He felt himself drifting towards sleep but fought it. He forced his eyes open; it was far too soon after the events of the morning to risk falling asleep.

"Excuse me, Skipper. Can I have a word?"

Rankin looked up out of one eye. "Hello Corky, or should I say, *hallo Maus?*"

Corkhill blushed as Rankin motioned him to sit. "Sorry, twisted sense of humour. Here," he made room against the tree trunk, "take the weight off your feet."

"That story seems to have spread far and wide already." Corkhill was looking sheepishly at the ground. "But I just wanted to say thank you, Skipper." He rubbed his neck. Bruises had started to show around his throat, testament to the size and power of the German's hands. "I owe you my life," he whispered, voice breaking.

"No, you don't, Corky. Just be grateful Colin and I turned up when we did." Rankin smiled. "One to tell the grandchildren, though."

Corkhill turned to face him, his brow furrowed, brown eyes serious. "That's just it, Skipper. How will we ever tell anyone any of this? Who'd believe it?"

Rankin leant his head back against the tree and closed his eyes. "We won't, Corky. No one who wasn't here will understand. There'll be books and medals, speeches, prayers and hymns. Who knows, there might even be a film. But only we will understand. The sight of it, the way the stink sticks in your nostrils so you can still smell it hours afterwards. The God-awful noise. Friends

355

made and lost so quickly you become afraid to make friends ... You've stared it in the face, Corky, and you're still here. So am I. That's all there is to know."

Corkhill lowered his eyes. "I heard you were on a pretty awful do this morning. I'm sorry about that."

"So am I, Corky. So am I." Rankin's vision blurred while bloodied, blackened lumps of flesh swam behind his eyes. He shook himself. "But it'll never un-happen. We need to remember these things happen to us, not because of us. I know you ran into that building last night. You had no idea what was on the other side of that door, but you never gave it a second thought."

Corkhill flinched. "Not really. Kenny ran in first; *he* probably never gave it a second thought. He changed after Billy was killed. Grew somehow, got more confident. Or reckless, depending on your point of view."

"I didn't think he was reckless. But you're right. Billy's death changed him, into more of a leader than a follower."

Corkhill's expression was surprised as he turned his eyes to Rankin's. "I didn't realise you watched us that closely."

"Part of the job, Corky. You've got leadership abilities yourself."

"I don't think I have."

"We'll see. But you didn't come to talk to me about that."

"No." Corkhill took a deep breath as he gazed into the distance. "Kenny ran into the building. I was behind him. We'd only just gone through the doors when that bloody freak stepped out of the shadows, grabbed poor Kenny's rifle by the barrel, swung him so hard against the wall he was half knocked out." Corkhill's lip quivered; he was close to tears. "Then he smashed his head in."

Rankin said nothing. He watched Corkhill struggling with himself, with his memory. He had told Rankin this part of the story before.

He continued in a whisper. "It's my fault, Skipper. I froze. There was nothing up the spout. I just needed to run at him with the bayonet. Kenny would still be here." He choked back a sob. "It's my fault he's dead."

Rankin leaned forward, put a hand on Corkhill's knee. "Corky, listen to me. There's no fault, especially on you. The bayonet's the most primitive weapon we have. It's one thing to shoot a man, either at a distance or close up, but sticking a knife that's a foot and a half long into a man doesn't come easily to a civilised person. It's a terror weapon. You've seen the way they react when they're faced with them. They run away. There's no disgrace in freezing when it comes time to *use* one. Especially your first time."

"But Kenny's dead because of me."

"No, Corky. Kenny's dead because of that bloody Goliath. Kenny's dead because of Adolf bloody Hitler. Kenny's dead because they decided to invade this island. It's no help to anyone to become riddled with guilt. You're not to blame, although I don't expect you to believe me. All of us hang by a thread. This morning fifty-odd men entered that ravine. Two German aircraft happen along. Ten seconds later, literally, thirty-five are dead, only four might survive their wounds, and eleven don't have a scratch on them, including six of ours. We hang by a thread, Corky. Some people might call it God's will. But I think that's bullshit; it's luck. The only thing that might make you live longer than the man next to you is by paying more attention, being smarter, taking nothing for granted."

Corkhill stared at him, clearly not believing what he was hearing.

"You're a good soldier, Corky, and a decent bloke. You're young. Don't let yourself be consumed by guilt for Kenny. He'd be the last person on Earth who'd want that."

Corkhill sat silently for some time. "I still owe you my life."

"I'll be amply rewarded if you carry on being a bloody good bloke. I read somewhere the German champion heavyweight boxer Max Schmeling joined the parachute troops. He's a giant of a man, an icon of the Reich. You, Kenny and Colin might just have killed him. A Nazi champion. David and Goliath."

"Except, Skipper, you killed him."

"I only pulled a trigger. I couldn't have killed him if the things that went before hadn't put us both in that position. It's all a matter of luck, Corky, and intuition, helped along with a bit of training."

Corkhill nodded dubiously, still staring at the ground. Rankin had seen the same expression often enough that morning. He could only hope that something he'd just said would help Corkhill deal with his guilt.

"Tell me, Corky, did Kenny take any of these pills? Have you?" Rankin asked, taking the Pervitin vial from his pocket.

"He had something in a pink and blue tin. Said they helped you keep sharp."

"Did he take one last night?"

Corkhill nodded. "His last one. Took it while we were waiting, when we got the order to fix bayonets. By the time we got the 'go' he was fair fizzing, could hardly stand still. I couldn't keep up with him. In and out of houses, chasing Jerries down the street, over the rubble, it was all I could do to stay with him." He was silent for a minute, before continuing in a small voice. "Then we reached the town hall."

Corkhill eyes were now focused on something away in the distance. Rankin watched him while he struggled to get his emotions under control, then he brought his gaze back to meet Rankin's.

"There's one other thing I'd like you to do for me, Corky," Rankin said. "I'm concerned about Colin. I'd like you to take him under your wing for a bit. Tell him what you've told me. He thinks it's his fault."

Corkhill stared at him for a long time, then nodded. They both stood up and shook hands. "Thanks, sir."

Rankin watched him walk away. "Jesus, you're a bloody hypocrite, Rankin," he muttered to himself.

IN THE AFTERNOON, Rankin sent McIntyre to Johnstone's section to find out how Nicholson was getting on with the German sniper. He returned to say that Johnstone and Nicholson and half his section were away dealing with it, and it was a German machine gun that was making a nuisance of itself, not just a sniper. Rankin gulped but decided to leave Nicholson to deal with it. Interference from him would only signal lack of confidence in Nicholson and Johnstone. Then a runner from Lawrence reported that his section was under increasing pressure on the right flank, dealing with infiltrators who were coming in behind them and from along the beach, sneaking around the right flank of the front-line units.

"Does he want any help from me?" Rankin asked.

"No, Skipper. He said it's under control. The boys are busy. If he needs help, he'll ask for it."

Rankin looked at him. "I'm here if you need me."

"He said to go to the river, freshen up. You had a rough morning."

"Did he now?"

Did they think he was cracking up? The afternoon was wearing on. What was it Nicholson had once said to him? "You can't fight their war for them."

"Bugger it, then, Mac, I think I'll do exactly that. You're in charge. You know where to find me."

"Aye, Skipper, that I do."

He dug into the depths of his small pack, fingers searching for shaving kit and towel. As he pulled them out, an unopened envelope came with it and fell to the ground. Picking it up, he turned it over, smiling at the flowing, precise script. He slipped it into his shirt pocket.

———

THE DEEP POOL was shaded by plane trees lining the bank. Bulrushes grew upstream, and downstream the river widened over a gravel bed where the water rippled and danced across the stones in a shallow rapid. It reminded him of home.

The mood there was relaxed and carefree – at least as carefree as it could be with German troops less than two miles away and the constant rumble of gunfire in the background. Frolicking and splashing were banned, of course, to avoid the attentions of aircraft that occasionally flew up the riverbed and across the hillside. Rankin could see items of clothing hanging among the tree branches, while their owners lay naked in the shallows under the leaves of the protective plane trees, telling tall stories and off-colour jokes.

He washed his filthy clothes in the clean, cool water, reluctantly keeping his bandaged shoulder dry. He would have liked nothing more than to simply lie in the water like a hippopotamus, with only his nostrils above the surface, and let the water wash away the war and block out its sounds. Instead, he washed around the dressing with his remaining sliver of soap. The grime floated off in clumps. As for his beard, it had never been left this long before; his face positively glowed after shaving it. Washed and brushed, with a passing-clean but wet pair of shorts and shirt, he felt renewed.

He wrapped his shaving towel around his waist, realising with a start that he would not have been able to do that a fortnight ago. Picking a quiet spot in the dappled sunlight under spreading branches, he sat down to read the letter that had languished in his pack since the night the mail came.

My Dear Neil,

I do hope this gets to you before Christmas. Summer here looks like being hot. I often think of those far-off days at Castle Rock. They are such a happy memory for me; I hope you think fondly of them too, and that they are a comfort to you on a cold winter's night.

The papers here are full of our "Battle of Britain" boys. Search as I might, I have never seen your photograph among the pictures. They're so grainy, though, a boy's own mother might be hard-pressed to recognise him.

Life here is not without its difficulties. I don't want to bore you, but it's hard to get reliable workers. Mr Wilson has said more than once he wishes he could find another one of you. I wholeheartedly agreed with him.

Tommy's gone to a farm in the Maniototo as shepherd. You know Mr Wilson; he told Tommy he was useless as tits on a bull once too often, and Tommy finally made good his threat to leave. He keeps talking about joining the army, which deep down terrifies Mr Wilson, to say nothing of me. The girls are well. Lily joined the WAAFs and is stationed at Nelson. Betty is working in town for Mr Burgess, the Sheepskin Controller. Very posh she is now! We'll not see either of them back on the farm. You were such a serious young man when you first arrived all those years ago. I'm so glad we all enjoyed some carefree times before this. In many ways, I think of you as one of my own.

I miss our afternoon teas and talks. I hope you haven't taken up smoking! You were always a good listener and patient when I didn't understand. There has been a lot of talk lately about the Japs moving into French Indochina, and threats to Malaya and Singapore. Surely they won't come into the war.

I hope you're safe and sound, and well. I saw Katherine at the station the other day – such a beautiful girl.

Be careful,

Love from Virginia Wilson

He smiled. She had been glorious in that sundress, the first time she'd ridden up the hill to Castle Rock. Those blue, blue eyes; how she'd taken him by the hand, leading him to God knows where. The first time. Was it always in places like this? He felt a sharp twinge of guilt; Dada Grammatico by a leafy stream in Thessaly, Virginia Wilson by the leafy Manuherikia. The sadness the letter brought with it was much more than guilt, he knew. Loss. For a bygone life, a liaison that was but never could be, and one that might have been but barely was.

The low hum of talk drove the rumble of war into the background. The smell of cigarette smoke, the soft rustling of the breeze in the leaves overhead, the heat and dappled sunlight of a Cretan afternoon – all combined to kindle memories of that faraway place and time. Inevitably, drowsiness drifted into sleep.

———

THE SUN TRAVELLED across the sky, the only constant in a world of change. Safe, at least for now, his mind went off in search of happier memories of happier places than the ones he had stored away lately. Voices intruded: laughing, arguing voices, voices that had no part in such a place and time. He mumbled in protest, but they refused to go away. Opening one eye just a crack, he found grinning faces surrounding him. He hastily sat up, face scarlet, grabbed the still-damp clothes from the grass beside him and used them to cover the scrap of towel.

"These manky buggers were laying bets, Skipper," said McIntyre with a straight face. "I told them ta hae more respect."

"Thank you, Mac." He looked around the half dozen leering faces. "Gambling's against regs, you buggers. Do you want me to confiscate the pot?"

Most kept grinning. One of them, possibly the bookie, hastily said, "No, sir."

"Well, piss off then, before I change my mind."

"Sarge came back, Skipper," McIntyre reported. Rankin put on his damp clothes, picked up the Tommy gun, and they walked back to the war. "And auld Captain Hamilton paid ye a visit."

Rankin stopped in mid-stride. "Really? What did he want, did he say?"

"Nah, Skipper. But he seemed a bit agitated: he wanted to know who the hell I was."

"So, what did you tell him?"

"Och, ah told the auld man that ah was attached while we were at that river, Skipper, near the airfield. By the Sassenachs, at yon airfield."

"Good lad. Excellent response. What did he say to that?"

"Och, he just nodded, an' went off."

"I FOUND HIM, Sarge. I had to defend his honour."

Nicholson looked up at McIntyre in surprise. "Did you now? How about rustling up a nice mug of tea." He arched his brows over a quizzical eye.

"Don't ask," said Rankin, flushing pink. "How did you get on?"

"Hun machine-gun team and three lookouts. Took all afternoon. But we got them."

It was Rankin's turn to raise his eyebrows.

"You tell me, and I'll tell you," Nicholson said.

"Bloody McIntyre will tell you anyway. Tell me what happened."

Nicholson sighed a weary sigh. "I wore your parachute jacket and found that grubby balaclava thing in the pocket. Worked my way up behind them while Smith and Mitch and the others kept 'em busy. I had worked out where two of the lookouts were and shot one. Another I hadn't seen popped up and looked up behind, trying to work out where the shot came from. I crawled out from behind my bush and pointed further up the hill. They went back to doing what they'd been doing, and I cleaned the pair of 'em up. The gun team panicked. Smith hit the machine gun, which took half the gunner's arm off, and his number two put his hands up. Not sure why it all took so long."

Rankin laughed as McIntyre delivered two mugs of black tea. "I'm bloody glad to see you back again, that's for sure."

"Now tell me, young McIntyre," commanded Nicholson, "how you saved the Lieutenant's honour."

"Naked as a bairn, Sarge – except for a wee towel, he was." McIntyre proceeded to describe Rankin's dreaming state in excruciating detail. "I could'nae stand idly by, Sarge, now could I?"

Rankin's face was red as a beetroot. Nicholson spluttered into his tea. "I can see that," he said eventually.

"My clothes were drying," Rankin said lamely.

"What's that noise?" asked Nicholson, looking up.

A throbbing, droning noise rose above the background roar of battle. "God, not more parachutists, surely!"

The three of them leapt to their feet, reaching for their weapons.

High above them a fleet of German aircraft passed sedately overhead.

Rankin snatched his field glasses from the branch they were hanging on. "German bombers. Look like Dorniers. Where are they going?"

Seconds later, the ground shuddered and the leaves on the trees shook and trembled. A continuous loud rumble overlaid the sounds of the battle coming from beyond the hill.

Across the river, behind the trees, black and brown clouds rose high into the air. The rumbling continued. More bombers passed overhead.

"Chania," Nicholson said, shaking his head sadly. "Poor beggars."

RANKIN WAS MAKING his late afternoon rounds when out of the blue a dozen or so Stukas appeared high overhead. In a panic, he scrambled into cover, shaking and sweating. He was squinting into the westering sun when the first commenced its dive. The engine note rose, followed by the familiar, hideous wail. Rankin jammed his fingers in his ears and cursed the crews out loud.

The aircraft plummeted, screaming, and dropped its bombs on something not far to the east, towards Chania. The bombs landed with a sickening, gut-churning thump, felt through the very ground he was sitting on. Every shrieking dive brought back terrifying memories. It was all he could do to sit still, under a bush, his arms tightly hugging his knees to his chest, rocking backwards and forwards, gibbering like a child, until after the last one had flown away.

Shaken, he arrived back at the command post, where he was met by McIntyre whose grin stretched from ear to ear. "Skipper, look what the cat's dragged in."

Apprehensive, still shaking, and feeling cold and clammy, he found Nicholson standing over three men, one with his head swathed in bandages.

"Good God, I didn't expect to see you again in a hurry," Rankin said, extending his hand. Graham moved to stand up, but Rankin motioned him to stay sitting. Graham's head resembled that of a mummy.

"Head too dense for a Jerry slug," one of his mates said.

"Bloody oath," muttered Graham. "Be right as rain in a day or so." He could barely move his jaw, was slurring his words badly and even in the half light of dusk, the visible parts of his face were mostly vivid purple and very swollen.

"Have you been discharged by the MO?" asked Rankin.

"No, he hasn't," said Nicholson, none too kindly.

"Well, he sort of has," said Potter, who'd made the earlier comment about Graham's head, grinning as he lit a cigarette. "See, the hospital was packing up, moving on. Walking wounded told to make their own way; some badly hurt blokes put on a few trucks they scrounged from somewhere. The even worse ones had to be left behind. An Aussie doc and some orderlies volunteered to stay with them." He passed the cigarette to Graham, who somehow found the gap where his mouth was located. "Grazer reckons he can walk. We decided to come back here rather than head to some shit-festering hole called Stilos or somethin'."

"Yeah, besides, knew you jokers could do with a hand. Might still be a scrap or two yet," said the third man, Duncan.

Graham nodded, inhaling smoke.

Nicholson looked at Rankin, his unhappiness patent, if unspoken.

"Don' worry 'bout me," Graham said in a whisper. "I won' get in ya way, Sarge," he said, turning his head with an effort towards Nicholson. "I got a real score to settle, now, though, by Jesus."

"I'm not worried about you, Graham, I'm worried about the bloke who has to look out for you," said Nicholson.

"We'll do that, Sarge," chorused the other two. "We'll make sure 'e don't fuck things up any more'n usual."

"You got shot in the head, for God's sake," Rankin said. "How can you not be dead?"

"I went for that Jerry, he put his little pop gun up, and it went off 'ere," Graham whispered hoarsely, indicating a spot in front of where his ear must be. "Broke me fuckin' cheek bone, but the bullet went up 'ere and over the top of me 'ead, an' stopped over 'ere somewhere," he indicated a point on the other side of his head, above the other ear. "Bastard nearly scalped me. Doc said I was lucky I was wearing a tin 'at: could've taken me scalp an' all me 'air off otherwise."

"Didn't knock any bloody sense into ya, though did it, Grazer?" laughed Potter.

"Gave me a bloody 'eadache, that's for sure."

"That get-up gonna make you stand out like a bloody ferret in a henhouse, Grazer. Can't wear yer tin hat, we'll have to put yer ugly swede in a sack!" Duncan hooted.

"Hang on a moment, I've got something that might do the trick," said Rankin, picking up the German parachute jacket and fishing in the pocket. "Here, it's a bit grubby. Sergeant Nicholson has been using it to confound and confuse the enemy. Might just do the job." He tossed the paratrooper's balaclava to him. "Jerry's likely to shoot you if he catches you wearing it, though," added Rankin, "and Captain Hamilton's likely to order a court-martial for wearing enemy uniform."

Nicholson shot him a filthy look.

"You'd be in good company, Graham," Rankin added with a smile.

Graham managed to get it over the dressing and pulled down the face mask.

"Jesus, Grazer, you could've done with that when you was robbin' banks for a livin'." Potter fell into hysterics at his own joke.

Graham made to swing at him, but pulled up short, wincing. "If me scone didn't 'urt so much, I'd clock ya one, ya cheeky bastard."

"It's good to have you back, Graham," said Rankin, laughing, avoiding Nicholson's withering glare.

CHAPTER SEVENTEEN

Nocturnal Rendezvous, 26–27 May 1941

"AS YOU KNOW," Hamilton informed the assembled officers of the battalion in the temporary battalion headquarters, "4 Brigade in front has been hard pressed, as have the Australians to the south. The Germans have been infiltrating all day and our chaps have been called on to deal with them. This will get worse after dark. Command considers that present positions cannot be held for another twenty-four hours, as was the original hope." Hamilton was now the most senior officer in the battalion still on his feet. Temporarily in command, having taken over from Lieutenant Bond, he delivered his briefing under a scrap of salvaged camouflage netting fixed to a tree by the river. The sun was low on the hills; the battle to their front had subsided and the low-flying Messerschmitts had mostly gone home.

His nervous tic was operating at full strength. "A full five-ticker", Anderson had dubbed the way the side of his face jerked and spasmed when under stress. His voice had lost its timbre, and his eyes flickered everywhere, except to engage with his officers. On top of this, one of his knees was immobilised by a thick bandage, while his head was wrapped in another.

Evidently, thought Rankin, his elevation did not sit easily on his shoulders.

"We must be prepared to move tonight. A line is to be formed west of Suda, at the junction of these two converging roads, here," Hamilton said, pointing to a Y-shaped road junction on his map. "Units must keep close together to guard against infiltrators and snipers. 5 Brigade will hide up in an area along the road between Suda and the 42nd Street turnoff. Your areas will be allotted by staff on the road. Rations have been dumped near the main bridge on the Chania Road, and you are to help yourselves as you pass. There may be ammunition available on the road near the Main Ordnance Depot. Take what you can carry. Understood?"

All in the audience nodded, then relaxed. They were not holding the front, then.

"We are now under the operational control of Suda Area, commanded by General Weston, Royal Marines."

Rankin felt an elbow jolt his ribs, hard enough to make him grunt.

"Do you have something to say, Mister Rankin?" Hamilton rasped, avoiding his eye.

"No, sir. Honoured to be under RM command, sir. I formed a strong impression of the effectiveness of RM leadership when I was stationed on the Tavronitis, sir."

Anderson coughed, supressing a guffaw. Clutterbuck glared at them both.

"I'm pleased to hear it. Battalion expects the confirming and execution order from General Weston to be passed on by Division at any moment."

The briefing broke up following discussion of details about

who should move where and when. The platoon commanders returned to their positions as the light faded.

"You almost landed me right in it again, you chump," Rankin said to Anderson as they sat under a bush, waiting for an unseen aircraft, which must surely be the last Luftwaffe sortie of the day, to bugger off. "In front of the whole battalion."

"Sorry, mate. I remembered your heated description of the inimitable Marine Major. 'Mad Dog Martinet' may have been one of the politer epithets, I think."

"Yes. If Weston's even got twice the tactical nous Major Martinet had, we're in deep shit."

"So we are already, old boy, or has your sunny day by the river prevented you from noticing?"

"Bugger off, Boney. Clutterbuck gave us a very evil look. After he took the trouble of warning me."

"Warn you about what? It's obvious, the powers-that-be have come to the realisation that Crete cannot be held. Next stop the beaches, and Jolly Jack's Ferry Service."

"Warned me not to get on old Dimwitty's goat. Hamilton said nothing about evacuation."

"Didn't have to, old boy. When you're invited to loot the quartermaster's stores, as much as you can carry, no forms in triplicate, it's all over."

———

THE "MOVE IN five minutes" order was relayed by CSM Clutterbuck at 2315. Rankin was told to bring in his northernmost section, nearest the beach, and then move south along the riverbank towards the bridge, gathering the rest of the platoon as he went.

The company was to take up positions on the opposite bank.

"Very well, Bernard. We've received the confirming order, then," said Rankin.

Clutterbuck stiffened. "You know very well we have not, Mister Rankin. Orders confirmed by Brigade."

"Hopefully someone knows where we're going, Bernard," Rankin sighed.

Rankin took the familiar path down the river to the first picket protecting Lawrence's flank and passed on the message himself. A few minutes later, Lawrence counted off his men as they marched silently by.

"That's the last of them," Lawrence said, as they both turned to follow. "Been all quiet, Skipper. Nothing since dusk. Place could be swarming with Jerries, mind you, but at least they're doing it quietly. Probably all in bed by now."

Lawrence and Rankin followed the rest of the section along the river bank towards the road. There was no talking, just an occasional clink or a grunt as someone stumbled in the dark. McIntyre had Rankin's kit ready, and along with the three recent returnees, they set off to pick up Nicholson, waiting with Johnstone and his section further up the river. Soon afterwards they combined with Anderson's platoon and made their way to the road bridge. Approaching the bridge, the leading element stumbled into a bomb crater, still stinking of high explosive. They soon came upon another; shattered tree trunks and branches obstructed the track.

Rankin caught a low noise: an unfamiliar hum or a drone, which rose and fell, similar to the noise near a beehive. As they approached the bridge, the noise got louder, accompanied by grumbles and complaints as the platoon stumbled and clambered through the dark, devastated landscape. Soon, low yellow lamp-light shone through the gaunt, leafless branches from underneath the concrete road bridge.

"CSM's going to have someone's guts for garters," he said to the black shadow in front of him.

"Jesus, Skipper, come and have a look at this," Johnstone's voice called from ahead in the dark as they swung up towards the roadway.

A honey-coloured glow shone out from under the bridge, illuminating a throng of civilians. Rankin scrambled down the bank to find Anderson and a number of NCOs standing stock-still among a larger group, staring at the scene. The banks of the river beneath the bridge were covered with black humps. Cretan men, holding hurricane lamps aloft, searched among them, yellow light playing across the scene. Black shadows jerked and leapt across the still forms and up onto the arch of the bridge above, every shape irregular and outlandishly oversized.

Rankin recognised the sound now for what it was: grief. The black humps were black-clad female bodies. He saw now a pale blotch was a face, a white stick a leg. Their menfolk searched among them for any sign of life.

A shriek accompanied the identification of each victim, followed by a blood-curdling howl. Despair, grief from the belly, piercing the heart and tearing at the soul. A lifeless body clasped to the breast of its finder, its cold face covered in kisses and washed in tears. The outpouring of grief, the keening, rising and falling, transfixed the passing soldiers. Unable to help, they stared in unhappy silence. Rankin looked around. The warm glow cast by the lamps showed that the knowledge that they had been impotent to prevent this sat heavily on the men's shoulders.

Eyes bleak, mouths set, hurt and anger was written across their faces.

"The bastards. The utter bastards," Anderson murmured. "There must be forty or more, women and girls. All dead. And there's worse: underneath the grown-ups are the little ones. They were trying to protect them." His voice fell away, lost in the burble of the stream and the ululation of despair all around them.

Rankin felt like an intruder: a rubbernecker at a bus crash.

"There's not a mark on them," Lawrence whispered. "It's like they all lay down, covered the kids, and then just went to sleep."

"Blast," muttered Anderson. "It must have been blast. Those fucking Stukas."

"Jesus Christ Almighty."

They looked at each other. Tears shone in Anderson's eyes while Rankin felt his lip quiver. Not far away, Nicholson had tears running down his cheeks. Lawrence stood speechless, eyes glittering, Johnstone motionless; the two platoons silent, still.

"They must have come here to shelter from the bombing in the town," whispered Nicholson.

"Only to run into those fucking Stukas," Anderson muttered.

"Fucking war," Lawrence added.

———

RANKIN LOOKED AT his watch again. Time to go. The last of the Divisional Cavalry had passed through nearly half an hour ago, giving the thumbs up as they crossed. They had been the last troops on the western side of the river, according to the timetable, and as far as anyone knew. The watchers, who had lain patiently in the dark across the river, on the enemy bank, listening for

374

sounds of infiltration and movement, splashed quietly back to the eastern bank. Nothing had been heard. NCOs silently got their men up, they shouldered their loads, and quietly set off.

Gaining the road, D Company turned towards Chania and Suda. The road was bomb-scarred and cratered; no light shone except for burning vehicles and buildings. Guides provided by battalion or division stumbled and fell into the bomb craters, swearing bitterly, along with the leading rank of their charges.

After negotiating one such group of overlapping bomb craters, Rankin heard raised voices from up ahead.

"But there's no one out there to relieve," he heard Hamilton say. Rankin recognised the exasperated tone only too well.

"We have our orders, Captain, from General Weston himself – to take up positions occupied by the New Zealand and Australian units."

"But they've all moved out, Major; we are the last. We were holding the bridge as rear-guard. There's no one beyond the river except the Germans."

The reply was inaudible. Rankin heard the muted order to resume the march, followed by the tramp of boots on the gravel road. A column of soldiers marched past; hard to tell in the low light, but from the way they moved, and the look on their shiny faces, they were fresh troops, not dirtied and wearied by days of hazard and hiding. And fully equipped. Not the ragtag bunch the New Zealanders had become, half of them armed with captured weapons.

"'Ere, step aside, boyo, they've called for the real men, now, don't you see?"

"Enough of yer chopsing, Kiwi, mitching off when there's

work to be done! They've called for us – Force Reserve, us."

"You're going the wrong way, mate. Everyone else is going the other bloody way! Including the Jerries."

"You've got your compass upside down, see, boyo. Comes from standin' on yer ruddy 'ead all the time, doesn't it now?"

Rankin watched in mounting disbelief as company after company marched past. How could anyone be so bloody stupid? When they had passed by, the last cries rang out of the dark: "Lechyd Da, Kiwi! Cymru am byth!"

A clear rejoinder rang out. "You're fucked, Taff. Give Adolf our love."

"Who the fuck was that? What friggin gabble were they talking?" a voice asked loudly in the resounding silence that followed.

"Welsh," answered Rankin.

"Poor stupid bastards. They're a fuckin' goner," the voice replied, speaking for everyone as they got to their feet and shouldered their loads.

———

THE GUIDES LOST their way in the confusion of the pitch-black night and narrow lanes, finding themselves instead in rubble-choked streets on the outskirts of Chania. Flames leapt and crackled, shadows danced and jumped as they clambered over the ruins of houses and past the bodies of their occupants, past vehicles under fallen bricks and timbers, some still burning. A donkey cart lay shattered, the owner's vegetables strewn across the road. Dogs howled. It was like a scene from Dante's *Inferno*.

Townspeople picked over the ruins of their lives, looking for something to save, or searching for someone beyond saving. A woman sat in a doorway to nowhere – wide-eyed, silent, rocking back and forth.

The voices from the ranks grew louder, audible over the crackling flames and howling dogs. First the dead women under the bridge, now this: "Why, for Christ's sake? What have they done to deserve this?"

The anger rose; Rankin could feel it in the air. "Fucking bastards."

"Jesus Christ, just wait until I lay my hands on one."

They'd all wandered through the old town in the balmy days after they first arrived, marvelling at the merchants' houses, Venetian lighthouses, Ottoman palaces. The narrow streets' history imbued the town with character, reminders of the conquerors down the ages, fascinating and awe-inspiring for men from a country whose oldest building dated from the 1830s.

Stone and plaster had been no match for what fell on them. Fires spread quickly in the narrow lanes, hiding the sky behind the rising clouds of smoke. The smoke of the burning town joined that of the burning ships, oil and stores from Suda Bay, which had spewed into the air for days.

"Wanton, deliberate destruction," murmured Nicholson.

"Fucking bloody murderers," cried a voice from the ranks.

––––––––

23 BATTALION WAS shown into position, behind the other battalions of 5 Brigade, about 0400. It was difficult to tell in the dark, but it appeared that they were to the rear of the Maori Battalion, with other units mixed up on both sides of them. As the light grew,

an impression of surrounding olive trees and thick undergrowth grew with it.

"What's this place called, then?" asked Blake.

"42nd Street, apparently, Blakey – like the musical film," replied Nicholson.

"Rum do, naming it after a song and dance show. Hey Mouldy, you can frighten the Jerries into surrendering with your little pink frock, mate."

"Fuck off, Blakey," replied Meldrum indignantly. His eyes lit up as he spotted Renfrew carrying water bottles. "Now Colin, here," he continued in a superior tone, "he could give Jerry an ear-bashing on the evils of fornication and too much bare leg in the films. Lowering moral standards in today's misspent youth, and all that." Meldrum called out as Renfrew passed. "Hey, Colin, did you know this place is called 42nd Street? Loads of dancing girls with legs up to their armpits, just over there."

"Knock it off, Mouldy," said Corkhill.

"Sort yourselves out, boys, before the Hun does it for you," Nicholson called out. "The place is named, apparently, after some British engineers who worked here. Now, get going."

Orders at company level were sketchy. It was unclear whether they were in reserve, whether the units in front of them were the front line, whether they were to hold these positions and for how long, and, if there was a covering force out in front, who it was and where it was.

"We definitely passed a Welsh battalion going the other way," Rankin heard Hamilton telling an officer from the battalion staff. His puzzled reaction did not augur well.

Their own platoon was dispersed among the trees and scrub. As the light grew, features of the landscape became clearer. Before the Luftwaffe's clocking-on time, troops mingled to see what had happened to friends and acquaintances in other units that they may not have seen for weeks.

Rankin was standing apart, under a large olive tree, watching Nicholson and the section leaders organising the dispersed positions for their sections and placement of their heavier weapons. Orders, apparently hastily sent from Battalion, had just been received confirming the road would be held and the 23rd would move up if the line were attacked.

"What-ho, Neil. Left it all to your indomitable sergeant again, I see."

"Hello, Boney."

"What's the matter with you? You sound glum this fine morning."

"I can't get that bloody bridge out of my mind. Then the town; smashed to smithereens."

"Yes. More dead Greeks. Why carpet bomb the place? Doesn't make any sense."

"Just because they can, the bastards. Makes you wonder if we're doing any good here."

"God, that sounds like something I might say. You know as well as I do: 'ours not to reason why, ours but to do and die', to misquote Tennyson."

"I suppose so. 'Into the valley of death rode the six hundred.' Apt to our present situation. Perhaps better as 'Into the valley of death strode the six hundred'."

"More of a limp, really – half dead with worn-out boots. Hello, who's this?"

Rankin looked up to see a figure in a raincoat appear through the undergrowth. He seemed to be on his own and wore a battered British peaked cap, which appeared several sizes too large for his head, pulled low to shield his eyes. The cap bore a Royal Marines badge. Both subalterns got to their feet.

"Who the hell are you and what are you doing here?" the man asked in a clipped English accent. He looked about, taking in the men scraping holes for themselves. His bearing and demeanour exuded seniority, and a haughty inability to suffer fools.

"Lieutenants Anderson and Rankin, D Company, 23 NZ Battalion, sir."

He appeared not to hear. "What are these men digging in for?"

"Er, we're the reserve behind the troops manning the 42nd Street line, just over there," Anderson replied, raising his thumb over his shoulder.

"Who gave you orders to be here? You're bloody fools to stay here. You should be on your way back." The stranger gestured towards the rising sun.

"Brigade, sir. 5 NZ Brigade, Brigadier Hargest."

"Uh. Where's his HQ?"

Both shook their heads. "Sorry, sir, we have no idea, sir. Our company commander is just over there, though; we could take you to him."

"Waste of bloody time talking to him. You're bloody fools if you stay here, is all I can say," he repeated, and stalked off.

Both were left gaping after his spare frame shrouded in its raincoat as he disappeared back into the undergrowth.

"Christ Almighty, who the hell was that?" Anderson burst out.

"Judging by the Royal Marines cap badge, that may have been our commanding general, Weston," replied Rankin.

Anderson stared at him. "You've got to be fucking joking."

Rankin shrugged. "You can't say I didn't warn you," he

smirked, relishing the unaccustomed feeling of getting one back on Anderson. "If it weren't so serious, it might be funny."

"I'd better go and report this to the Old Man. He's never going to believe *you*."

"I'll lay odds he won't believe you either."

CHAPTER EIGHTEEN

42nd Street, 27 May 1941

"WELL, WHAT DID he say?" Rankin eagerly asked Anderson later that morning.

"Wanted to know if you'd put me up to it. When I told him that we both saw him, and that's what he told us, and he couldn't be arsed talking to Hamilton, he nearly had a fit. Said he hadn't forgotten the charges pending against you and I'd be with you if I didn't stop peddling such bally nonsense."

"Ha, ha. Told you so."

————

RANKIN CHECKED THE time. Nearly 1100. Such positions as could be dug or prepared with what they had available were ready. Breakfast had been improvised from whatever the men had brought with them, or traded on their walkabouts, and the men who had missed out on being able to wash the day before were detailed off to join a throng of men from all units at a couple of wells and a tiny stream nearby.

Clutterbuck arrived, making his rounds of the company.

"Unnaturally quiet for the time of day, Bernard," Rankin said, gazing at the clear blue sky. "Not even a visit from Egbert this morning."

"You can be sure the buggers are brewing something," he replied. "The captain reports you claimed to have had a visit from the Area Commander earlier this morning."

"Indeed, Bernard. Wore a Marines cap and a raincoat. Could have been a flasher, of course. Looked a bit battered, like he'd been wandering all night, looking for lost sheep. Wasn't interested in talking to anyone other than us. Told us we're bloody fools to stay here. We thought it discreet not to mention the Welsh battalion we passed in the night, going the wrong way, apparently under the General's orders."

"God, you are full of it, Mister Rankin."

"Well, sorry to disillusion you, Bernard, but that's an exact and full account of the encounter. You can ask Boney. How's Captain Hamilton's battle injuries?"

"Jesus wept," Clutterbuck replied, peering into a nearby thicket, as if to verify Rankin's story. "Oh. He tripped over a rock charging into Galatas. Bunged his knee and knocked himself out. I am going to talk to Mister Anderson."

Clutterbuck stalked off, leaving Rankin staring after him.

———

"PERHAPS THE HUNS haven't worked out we've left them to it," said Nicholson. He puffed on his pipe. "Where on earth were the Welsh going? Had nobody told them we were to withdraw?"

"Jerry's probably enjoying Welsh rarebit for breakfast. I told you what our commanding general told Anderson and me this morning. Wearing a flasher's mac, wandering around in the bush all alone."

Nicholson turned to him angrily. "You don't know it was General Weston."

"No, Nick, that's true. But he had British general officer written all over him, topped off with an extra helping of senior-service arrogance. If it wasn't him, it was someone on his staff. Regardless, he had no idea we were here or what we're here for."

"We need water," said Nicholson, changing the subject. "Should be able to get everyone their fill today from the wells here. At least everyone managed to pick up a ration box or two, even if it's only hard tack. I got the corporals to distribute the ammunition we picked up at the dump, though it didn't go far."

"Yes, not a lot left for tail-end Charlies."

A rumbling roar went up nearby, followed by the unmistakeable tearing rattle of a Spandau machine gun. A black cloud towered above the olive trees. A clatter of rifle and Bren fire broke out along the line.

"Bugger them! Not again!" cried Nicholson, knocking out the tobacco in his pipe and stuffing it into his pack.

The men were on their feet, grabbing their webbing and weapons as they rushed forward through the olive trees to line the roadway.

"Here we go again!" Rankin shouted to the laggards, picking up his web harness and rifle, running up to join the others.

The road ran through a sunken lane between scattered olive trees on both sides. The side facing the Germans was topped with an earthen bank. Soldiers were kneeling or lying behind the bank, firing into the trees beyond; at what, Rankin could not tell. Several mortar rounds landed beyond the earth bank. A hullabaloo arose on their right, a noise like the roar of a crowd at a football match, heard even over the background gunfire.

"Jesus Christ!" The Maoris manning the front rank suddenly rose to their feet, fixed bayonets, hurdled the bank and disappeared at the run, yelling and shrieking as they went. They were followed by the next rank, and the next, seemingly without orders.

Screaming and shouting rose up and down the length of the road; the noise grew into a continuous roar, blotting out individual sounds. Men from other units, singly and in groups, rushed forward out of the olives, crossed the road, and launched themselves over the bank.

His own men were yelling, unheard over the tumult, running for the bank, fixing bayonets as they ran. There were no orders. Rankin had no means of stopping them, even if he wanted to.

A cry went up amongst the olives: "Murdering bastards!"

It was answered: "Into them!"

Rankin fixed his own bayonet as he rushed across the road.

Over the bank on the other side the scene was like a silent movie. The noise was such that individual sounds had no value; leaping the bank was like leaping into a continuous thunderclap of gunfire and explosions, an ear-splitting hurricane of sound. Dust and smoke drifted through trees and across open spaces. Men ran, firing from the hip. The first rank had gone to ground perhaps 50 yards from the road, firing at grey-green figures coming toward them; some of them had gone to ground also, and were firing back. The next khaki rank simply ran past the men lying prone, and straight at the Germans, only yards away, bayonets flashing. The first rank rose as a man and hared after them.

The Germans hesitated, got to their feet, and broke. Many were too slow to realise what was coming, to get on their feet, to run. They were overwhelmed by the surging wave of khaki. The grey line wavered, shivered, shock waves rippled out from holes punched through it. Stephen Crane's *Red Badge of Courage* came to Rankin's mind; he had read that book a dozen times as a boy. Good Christ, now he was living it!

He had not gone a hundred yards when a grey uniform rose out of a bush only to be swatted aside by a rifle butt wielded by the man charging ahead of him. Running at the writhing figure, which screamed as it tried to hold its shattered wrist and forearm above the dirt, Rankin drove his bayonet into the man just below his rib cage, baulking at first, momentum then driving it deep.

"Like a knife into one of your mother's finest pumpkins, lad, fresh from the garden."

As the point rammed up through the man's liver and lungs, it drew from him an audible gasp, followed by a spray of bright red blood and froth from his mouth. He looked about the same age as Rankin, his blue eyes registering in turn surprise, betrayal, and finally cloudy death. Another man close behind Rankin took a turn at stabbing the German in the gut as he ran past, shouting "Fuckin' bastards!" before racing forward.

Rankin extracted the blade from the man's body and ran on. Out of the corner of his eye he saw two khaki figures chase someone into a bush where, cornered, he faced his pursuers, hands outspread, only to be hoisted bodily off the ground, spitted on the end of both rifles like a stook of wheat on a pair of pitch forks.

As the Germans realised that falling in the path of the onslaught meant certain death, they hastily abandoned packs and weapons. For many it was to no avail as the pursuers, including Rankin, were gripped by a feral, primal savagery that was fed from those around them as they killed without mercy. The advance carried them forward hundreds of yards and while the noise was still appalling, it now comprised yelling, screaming and howling rather than gunfire; sounds made by humans but not human. It was a scene from hell: the noise of machine guns and mortars fell away, the killing was done with blade and butt, pole and knife. Hands raised in surrender evoked no charity; the first swift lunge of a bayonet was often followed by several more.

A shallow depression hid a dozen or more German soldiers until Rankin and the others were practically on top of them. Their sprawled disposition veiled the manner of their death; they looked for all the world like they were attending to their duty, lying in cover, weapons at hand. Yet the hurricane that had passed over and consumed them where they lay had not been kind to them. Rankin recoiled in fright at first glimpse, instinctively stabbing the man prone on the ground. As he withdrew the blade, it occurred to him that everyone who had passed this way already had done the same.

The drifting dust obscured one primitive scene only to open on another. The faster the Germans ran, the faster the chasers went after them. Days of endless air attack, lack of sleep, constant fear, hunger and thirst, overlaid with fury all combined to suddenly erupt as a primordial whirlwind, the brunt of it borne by the unfortunates who had stumbled into them that morning. Powered by an exhilarating mix of adrenaline, revenge, release, the contagious madness of the crowd, the imperative to kill was paramount. Many of the bodies on the ground were stabbed and stabbed again in the frenzy of men running past, prescient enough to remember lessons from the battle's early days, when corpses miraculously rose to toss a grenade or shoot their mate in the back.

Rankin came across Corkhill and Renfrew standing over the blood-covered body of an older man, perhaps 30 or so, whose grey-green uniform bore a senior NCO's insignia. "Murdering, godless men," muttered Renfrew. "By thy works the Lord shall know thee and smite thee down." He looked down at his blood-stained hands and crossed himself. Rankin glanced from him to Corkhill, who gave him a wan smile, then pulled at Renfrew's sleeve, before the two of them ran on into the olives and scrub. As Rankin followed, a machine-gun crew leapt to their feet from behind a bush, overtaken perhaps by the pace of the charge and too slow to join the hasty German exodus. Lowering his rifle, Renfrew ran full tilt into the first man who doubled over, screaming as he hit the ground. Corkhill caught the second in front of an olive tree, the impact of his bayonet so hard that it ran the man through and pinned him to the tree. Corkhill freed his weapon, and the man toppled to the ground, face down, shrieking in pain. But the sound ended when Renfrew stepped forward and plunged his own bloodied blade into the man's back, ending the hideous racket. "You're not grabbing my fuckin' rifle again, you godless bastard!"

Renfrew raised his head to Rankin, panting hard, a wild, manic light in his eyes: "Just like Burnham, Skipper. If the old RSM could see us now, he would know his words fell not on the stony ground. The unjust are reaping what they have sowed."

"Christ, is he always like this?" Rankin asked Corkhill.

"Since Galatas," Corkhill confirmed.

Now deep into the German rear area, in relatively open ground with a covering of olive trees and scattered bushy undergrowth, Rankin noticed the mortar and machine gun emplacements, manned only by the dead, that dotted the landscape. The ground was littered with upended tubes, overturned guns pointing at odd angles, abandoned bombs, ammunition, helmets, packs, and personal weapons. Bodies lay everywhere: propped up against trees, scattered across and under scrubby bushes, some barely recognisable as having once been human – all cast aside by a terrible tornado that had slashed and bashed everything in its path.

Rankin came to a body hanging grotesquely over a tree's lowest branch. Somehow the man still lived, although half his head was caved in so that one eye was resting on its cheek. An arm hung by a thread, dripping blood.

"*Wasser, Wasser*," the wreck of a man murmured pathetically as Rankin dragged him off the bough. Wearily studying him, Rankin mulled over how many times he had been thirsty. The enemy soldier's single eye squinted at him, cloudy and dull. He appeared to be young, fit, perhaps good-looking, judging from the side of his head that wasn't a morass of blood. Rankin sat down and leaned against the tree, realising he was desperately thirsty himself. He had run his course; gone as far as he could go.

"*Wasser, bitte*," came the plea from the distorted mouth, shattered teeth visible behind torn and bloody lips.

"Fuck off," Rankin said gruffly, dragging his own bottle from its web carrier. "You're too far gone." The German twitched again, repeated his plea.

Rage unaccountably welled up inside Rankin, rage that would not lie still. "Ask one of those Greek women under the bridge!" Rankin shouted. "I'm not wasting my bloody water on you!"

The single eye followed him, but the shattered mouth was silent. Rankin leant back, closing his eyes, holding his bottle to his own mouth seeing in his mind torn lumps of human flesh in a ravine, the soft light and harsh grief-filled braying under a bridge, the haunted dark pools of despair in the eyes of a Greek woman rocking back and forth in an empty doorway. Then there were earlier images. Kenny Glover lying on a tiled floor, his brains splashed over the walls and poor Corky's shirt. Jesus, he could barely remember Billy Simpson's face, but he remembered the burnt-black hole in his khaki greatcoat. The water tasted of bile.

Opening his eyes, he turned to the German. "Where are they now?!" he shrieked at him. "Where are they now?! You've fucking smashed them! Everything! Don't you ask me for water, you bastard shit!"

The eye showed no comprehension, only pain. "*Wasser*," the mouth burbled through its mask of blood.

"Fuck you and your bloody water!" Rankin leapt to his feet, enraged, dropping the water bottle. "I'm not giving you any of my fucking water! *Kein Wasser! Verstehen Sie?*"

The eye stared, accusing.

"Fuck you!" he screamed and drove his bayonet through the man's chest. Again and again, irrational, hating, until exhausted, drained and empty, he fell to the ground, landing on his hands and knees beside the patch of wet ground where his water bottle lay on its side, and burst into tears.

Later, much later, Rankin would probably recognise this feeling as grief; grief for the tiny, shrivelled walnut which now occupied the cold black void once home to his soul; grief for the death of God.

The sound of whistles intruded. Somewhere voices called, rifles banged, and machine guns chattered. Staggering to his feet, he picked up the empty bottle and his rifle and turned back the way he'd come. As he walked away, he felt the dead German's solitary eye, glassy and lifeless, watching him leave.

––––––––––

THE WILD CHARGE had pushed the Germans back close to a mile in places; the return across the battleground was, by comparison, slow and sombre. There were khaki casualties to recover, but they were outnumbered by the German dead. Wearing the stylised green edelweiss emblem of a Mountain division, and the numeral "141", they lay thick on the ground. Judging by the evidence, the 141st Mountain Regiment had ceased to exist.

By now the adrenaline and herd effect that had carried them forward – invincible, indestructible, killing everything in their path – had evaporated, leaving the men with a hollow feeling. The sickly sweet scent of death, spilled blood and shit filled the air. Rankin had not noticed it until now, but it hung thickly in the air. A slaughterhouse could not have smelled bloodier. There was little stink of high explosive or smokeless powder; death had been delivered the old-fashioned way – man to man, slashing, stabbing, and clubbing. As they walked, they could also smell their own bodies, rank with expended fear and sweat, sweet with someone else's blood. It was an odour that, once experienced, could never be adequately described. Or forgotten. Already, the corpses were humming with clouds of flies. Crows cawed, drawn by the heady scent of carrion, and they could hear the sound of stray dogs howling.

Passing through the Maori position, Rankin saw a tall figure he recognised talking to an NCO. "Why, Captain Royal, I'm very glad to see you again, sir."

Royal turned around, frowning, then his face lit up with a smile. "Lieutenant Rankin, I believe. The same to you." To the corporal, he said, "Lieutenant Rankin, 23 Battalion – the Pakeha

Maoris, Corporal Ransfield." Ransfield's shirt and face were sprayed with blood from breast pocket to hairline; he stared silently at Rankin, his expression bleak.

"Your chaps have rocked them back on their heels, sir, well and truly. Given us all a breathing space," Rankin said.

"Not just us, son. The Aussies kicked it off and everyone got stuck in – including you, I see." He glanced meaningfully at Rankin's own shirt. "They'll be back, have no fear of that."

"Yes, sir." Rankin felt flat. He had no idea what to say next. He felt Royal's eyes boring into him.

"Real fighting, man to man, takes practice." Royal's expression softened. "Fighting like warriors, son, you need to keep the grip on your taiaha firm." He demonstrated, using his staff. "Thrust at his body. When he sidesteps, clout him around the head, knock him off his feet; finish him with a thrust to the throat and the liver." He brought the imaginary spear around at head height, danced to one side, and thrust downwards. "That's how it's done, eh Corporal? The SMLE rifle tipped with eighteen inches of steel may not be the real thing, but it's a good substitute. See that your men clean and oil their bayonets, Lieutenant. You never know when you will have need of them again."

He must have read the expression on Rankin's face. He laid a hand on his shoulder and spoke gently. "Look, son, we've grown up with our korero, stories, of warriors and battles fought this way. Small children listening, spellbound, in the marae – to the kaumatua telling their histories. Many traditional kanikani toa – dances with the spear – act out these battles. We learn them as children, playing with sticks. But ritual dance is one thing; taking a man's head off and being sprayed with his living blood is another. There is no dishonour in finding this distressing."

Rankin nodded blankly.

"We are a proud people, a warrior race. But we are not savages, despite what Lord Haw Haw says. The fact that we are good with the bayonet and fighting close in, man to man, reflects our history – our cultural heritage, as you might say. It doesn't mean our men enjoy gutting another human being any more than you do. The Good Book tells us all life is sacred." He looked at the ground for a moment, then raised his head to look Rankin in the eye and smiled; a broad, beaming smile. "But it does no harm to have your enemy scared shitless when he learns he's up against you. When he's ready to run at the first flash of a blade in the morning sunlight, you have the upper hand, the psychological advantage. Remember that, Lieutenant: one haka, and he throws down his weapon and runs away. That is the power of the taiaha."

———

RANKIN FOUND HIS way back to the platoon post where he heaved a sigh of relief to see both Nicholson and McIntyre had returned before him and were sitting under an olive tree. He propped the rifle up against the tree and slumped to the ground.

"Are you alright, Neil?" asked Nicholson. Rankin opened his eyes to see Nicholson examining him, his face unable to hide his concern.

"I could ask you the same. You look a bit haggard yourself."

"I'm not hurt. Not on the outside, anyway," Nicholson said quietly, as if to himself, pulling his pipe from his pack. Then louder, he responded to Rankin. "God, if I ever deserved a smoke, it's now. Cover the stench from over there." He nodded over his shoulder. "Bloody charnel house. Be stinking to high heaven tomorrow."

"No, I'm not hurt," Rankin said.

"Och, let me clean yon weapon for ye, Skipper," said McIntyre, getting to his feet and reaching for the rifle. Rankin looked at it, and for the first time realised the blade was stained with blood and gore, the hilt of the bayonet and muzzle of the rifle thick with a congealed black ooze, clustered with flies.

"No! No! McIntyre, leave the bloody thing alone!"

McIntyre froze.

"Let the boy do it, Neil. There's nothing he hasn't seen or heard. Let him clean it for you, for God's sake."

Rankin stared at Nicholson. Nicholson stared back at him, then turned to McIntyre and nodded. Mumbling to himself, eventually Rankin looked up at McIntyre, "Plenty of oil with the elbow grease," he instructed.

As McIntyre took the rifle and moved towards his mates Rankin heard several muffled oaths as the men talked among themselves.

"Let them talk, Neil. They have to get it out of their system," Nicholson said. "Besides, doesn't do any harm to have them reminded occasionally of what a hard nut they serve under."

"If they only knew," murmured Rankin.

———

"ALRIGHT, BOYS?" ENQUIRED Clutterbuck. It was early afternoon, and 23 Battalion's platoons had resumed their positions scattered among the olive trees and undergrowth behind 42nd Street, in reserve.

"Fine, Bernard, thank you," said Anderson. "What brings you out on this fine day? Jinking between the showers of Messerschmitts?" he continued in a brittle voice.

"Checking our status, on behalf of Captain Hamilton," he replied.

Anderson and Rankin looked at each other, but said nothing.

"It's been a busy morning," Clutterbuck went on, eyeing them with a meaningful look.

"We might have bought ourselves a bit of time. Jerry's gone silent," Rankin sighed. They reported their effectives – casualties in both platoons had been surprisingly light considering what had taken place. "I hope Jerry still feels that way when it's time to move on." Rankin's voice faded away as he spoke.

"Yes. And I must say, you two, for all the piss-taking you do," Clutterbuck said briskly, "this morning you and your platoons – in fact all the platoons – carried out a fine display of good old-fashioned soldiering. The old RSM would have been proud of you all."

"Well, thank you, Bernard," Anderson said. He turned his head away, his gaze distant. "It's a bugger of a thing, you know. It takes control – there's no stopping it. Until you run out of steam, then it tips you off a cliff. All you want to do then is blub your bloody eyes out."

Rankin looked at him, astonished. So did Clutterbuck, who recovered first: "And so it does for all of us, Mister Anderson. Just as it did for the old RSM in his day on the Somme. Good luck, boys." Clutterbuck came to attention, saluted them both, executed a smart about-turn, and marched off.

Rankin caught the early afternoon sun sparkle off the moisture in his eye as he turned away.

———

DURING THE AFTERNOON, the Luftwaffe seemed hell-bent on making up for the infantry's ignominious defeat earlier in the day. Despite the sound and fury, nothing fell near 23 Battalion. A despatch rider leaving a conspicuous trail of dust behind him attracted the attentions of a gaggle of Me 109 fighter aircraft, which brought the men to their feet, albeit under the foliage and out of sight from above. Each time one of the planes lined up behind him, ready to engulf him in a torrent of bullets and cannon shells, some sixth sense prompted the rider to scoot off the road and into the trees. The unofficial bookies rapidly adjusted the odds of his survival while the excited yells from the bystanders increased in volume and pitch with each successful evasion, so much so that the first many soldiers knew about the lone rider was the noise of shouting coming down the road with each fighter's pass. Just as it seemed his luck must surely run out, the Messerschmitt chasing him at that moment waggled its wings and pulled away.

As the winners rejoiced and the bookies lamented the paucity of ammunition carried by an Me 109, the despatch rider disappeared behind his cloud of dust, unscathed and oblivious of the fortunes riding on his fate.

Later in the afternoon D Company was called upon to clear the little village of Tsikalaria, where Germans had been observed, which lay behind and above the 42nd Street line, up the slope rising to the south. If the enemy occupied the village in strength, they could harry the defence's rear; their continued presence could not be tolerated. The village was cleared in a short, sharp action, notable for the discovery of a British wet canteen store in a basement. The contents were eagerly liberated and distributed among the dry and dusty throats lining "the Street".

Rankin's platoon was tasked to participate in the assault. Afterwards he told Anderson that he had "just gone through the motions" – there in body but not in mind. It was only after he sent a case of gin to Rangi Royal, along with a note acknowledging that he'd been "saved by the power of the taiaha" that the fog cleared and his mood improved.

CHAPTER NINETEEN

Chaos and Suda, 28 May 1941

TOWARDS DUSK, THE officers were called to a Battalion briefing where Hamilton, who was the most senior man still standing, acted as Officer Commanding. Boney Anderson had been temporarily elevated to OC, D Company; Clutterbuck and Rankin were each to oversee the remnants of an additional platoon commanded by its senior surviving NCO; while Lieutenant Bond had reverted to his own company to make good some of the deficiency of officers there. That the temporary company commanders were junior officers spoke volumes of the officer availability throughout the battalion. The new appointees needed no introduction.

"Orders from Brigade," Hamilton began tersely, after announcing the changes in responsibilities. There were no congratulatory remarks, no "job well done", no mention of the village clearance, or even, for that matter, of the spirited performance that morning. There was very little even about their present situation. No doubt Hamilton's knee prevented him from taking part in the wild charge from 42nd Street, but it surprised Rankin that Hamilton had not assumed the credit for Tsikalaria since he had given the order to clear it.

"We must withdraw further to the east," continued Hamilton. "Brigadier Hargest has ordered this withdrawal on his own initiative, not waiting for orders from General Weston, who is apparently now in command of all troops and temporarily out of contact. Undoubtedly these will come."

The statement passed without comment from the audience. Rankin caught Anderson's eye; perhaps this was the reason for Hamilton's discomfort. Absence of communication from imperial command lent credence to their report of the vagrant in the raincoat.

"We are to make for the Sfakia road, beyond Suda, where the road rises into the mountains. Our objective is Stylos, a mile or two south of the junction. Companies holding the front will disengage and withdraw from 2100 onwards. D Company as reserve will cover their withdrawal." He looked up from his notes, almost defying someone to mention they were again the force rear-guard. "D Company will withdraw from 2300. All units must withdraw leaving the enemy unaware." He looked around the small audience, then fixed his baleful gaze on Rankin. "Can you do that, Mister Rankin? Withdraw all the way to the Sfakia road without attracting attention to yourself?"

"Unreservedly, sir."

The briefing broke up as a Messerschmitt howled low overhead, disturbing a flock of loudly cawing crows across the road.

"Ha, I'd laugh if one of those pricks ran into a bloody crow," Anderson said as they walked back to their positions. "And splattered himself all over the countryside."

"Murder. A flock of crows is a murder."

"How very appropriate. So, now we know. It's Sfakia port we're bound, to join the ferry service."

"Did you notice?" Rankin felt an unreasonable surge of anger. "No praise for the boys' efforts?"

"Well, he has serious battle injuries, Neil. No doubt we're lucky to still have him to guide us."

"Bernard told me he tripped over a rock and banged his head running into Galatas. Knocked himself out of the attack."

Anderson stopped and stared at him, mouth gaping. "Oh, dear God."

Back at their positions, the hum of conversation and cheery clink of bottles in the surrounding bush was punctuated by the rattle and bang of machine-gun and rifle fire, leavened with the crump of mortar bombs. Enemy probing the front line had increased as the afternoon went on.

"Sounds like the bloody Jerries might make getting out of here difficult. At least the boys can enjoy our little windfall," said Anderson.

"Speaking of windfalls, I forgot to congratulate our new company commander," said Rankin. "Hail to the chief!" After a pause, he asked, "Why did the old bugger pick me out for a sarcastic comment?"

"Yes, company commander. And I won't be tolerating any of your seditious nonsense, Rankin." Anderson's stern glare was belied by the gleam in his eyes. "Making meaningful eye contact with me when Old Thunderguts was talking about the British General wasn't at all tactful."

Rankin chuckled.

"I wonder if his faith in the British military classes has been rattled at all yet," mused Anderson, lips pursed as he scratched his head.

"I bet the blokes in his platoon are pleased to be rid of him,"

Rankin said. "First saddled with poor old Nellie, then him. Nicholson heard he refused them any beer from the loot we found in Tsikalaria." Rankin smirked. "Doesn't mean they didn't get any, of course."

"Hah! The trading ability of the ordinary soldier. I should think plenty of valuable loot's been offered up for a few bottles," said Anderson. "The going rate's probably about two Lugers and a Schmeisser for a bottle by now."

"Yes, the rarity factor for German weaponry is much reduced." Rankin stopped in a gap between two trees and gazed out over the morning's battlefield. "I don't envy whoever has to clean this place up," he said idly, gesturing across the road.

"The poor bloody locals, I suppose," Anderson sighed. "Or POWs, poor bastards. There'll probably be no shortage of them, judging by the fuck-up we're making of this. Generally speaking."

"Ha, ha. That's no way for a company commander to talk about his commanding general!"

"TIME TO GO, Neil. They're all ready and waiting."

Rankin looked at his watch; it was after 2300. Swinging his rifle over his shoulder, he stepped out from under the tree and joined the others as they slunk away into the darkness from the positions they had occupied since evening. The afternoon had become progressively more dangerous as German gunners and mortar crews crept back onto the ground contested only by the carrion eaters across the road. From there, they laid down sporadic fire through the lanes between the olives, particularly targeting the approaches to the wells.

"Fixed lines," Rankin said, as a burst of tracer hissed between the olives only 30 yards away. "Let's hope they stick with Teutonic dependability and don't try anything too adventurous, like raking the whole area."

"The Maoris had trouble getting their men grouped up to go. I hope Bernard's all right," Nicholson said.

Mortar bombs were terrifying; they could come whistling down from nowhere, burst in quick succession, then move on, catching the unwary out in the open. No one was safe, even those in a decent scrape. In the late afternoon the Germans had tried a couple of frontal assaults, aimed towards the right-hand (Australian) end of the line, nearest the Coast Road. The German line of advance took them across the New Zealand front, although hidden in the trees, until they broke cover and charged the Australian line. The Australians had seen these attacks off with a spirited "offensive defence", which involved running headlong at the attackers and vigorously applying the bayonet. The Germans did not linger; each charge was repulsed, with many of the terrified survivors fleeing across the open ground in front of the New Zealand positions. The withering fire from behind the earth wall added to the humps lying among the trees.

Once darkness fell, the German harassment diminished until it was largely confined to machine guns firing along fixed lines. Nevertheless, they had taken a steady toll of casualties during the late afternoon and evening. Trucks scrounged from somewhere managed to evacuate the less severely wounded; the serious cases once again would have to be left behind. Everyone's nerves were badly frayed by the time it came to vacate their position.

The embankment above the road was thinly held by Clutter-buck's element of two platoons, who occasionally shot at shadows to keep the Germans' heads down. The usual wise crackers stayed quiet – saving themselves, perhaps, for what lay ahead. The beer had provided a welcome interlude on an exhausting day, but evening came with the knowledge that another long night lay ahead. Over the mountains, however, lay the Royal Navy – and the chance of evacuation. No one needed any more incentive to march through the night. No one wished to dwell on the alternative.

Rankin and Nicholson kept the platoons close as the company crept through the olives, making for the road behind the Australian positions. They prayed their absence went unnoticed by the other side, and in the event they reached the road without mishap. Anderson's platoon was halted along the roadside as Rankin's two platoons came through.

"Keep on to the junction, Neil. Don't let them stray off the road."

"Have you seen Bernard?" Rankin asked Nicholson, the last man out.

"No, not a sign."

"You go on, Neil. We'll pick up Bernard and be right behind you," said Anderson with a confidence Rankin was certain he did not feel.

Rankin and Nicholson pressed on. Making their way along the road, not sure if they were being flanked, or outflanked, by Germans patrols moving parallel to them, they came to the paved road that led to the military establishment at Suda Bay, with its engineering workshops and stores warehouses. At this point the pace increased to almost a canter. Rankin looked at his watch: midnight. The last of them must have left 42nd Street to the Germans by now, surely.

Suda was visible from miles away, its burning buildings and

ships acting as a beacon. A large oil tanker had been burning for days, spewing thick black smoke several thousand feet into the air. Bombing had wrecked both the army's and navy's shore facilities, sending tons of supplies up in smoke or to the bottom of the harbour. The human cost of the defeat soon became all too apparent. A rabble of base troops clogged the road, shambling along, pushing and shoving, panicked beyond reason. They had only one thought in mind and one word on their lips: Sfakia.

"Dear God," Nicholson said loudly during a brief rest stop. "You blokes, keep hold of your gear!" he roared over the hubbub. "Or it'll be gone in a flash." He turned to Rankin. "Despatch riders ride in pairs, you know: one to carry the message, the other to stop the bike from being pinched."

"Base wallahs and pen-pushers," Rankin marvelled, as a gaggle of voluble Cypriots pushed past. "That lot'll be from the docks, probably."

"No use to man nor beast," Nicholson fumed. "Light-fingered buggers, the lot of 'em."

NOT FAR BEYOND the base they came upon a melee of leaderless men, shouting, shoving and gesticulating wildly on the roadside. Rankin pushed through the group to find the source of the fracas.

"Organised units only," the Redcap shouted at the mob, pushing them away.

"Having trouble here, Corporal?" Rankin looked hard to see if it was the same corporal he had encountered on his arrival on Crete. Fortunately, it was not.

"Organised units only, sir. One tin and a half dozen of biscuits between five men, sir."

"That'll cause grief," Rankin muttered, wondering why it wasn't a packet a man until they ran out.

Nicholson shooed away a group of supplicants, menacing them with his Tommy gun. They were pleading with the MP in an unknown language. "Damned foreigners," he muttered. "God knows where this lot come from."

"Palestine," replied the corporal, watching the stores clerk hand the rations out, pushing another group away.

"I'd be getting on, sir, if I were you," the corporal said to Rankin. "Could be Jerry aircraft about, and the fires around here make a plain target."

They did not need to be told twice. The stream of humanity moving towards the junction thinned out somewhat as they put distance between them and Suda. Rankin and Nicholson kept the platoons tightly bunched, marching as fast as they could, pushing their way through the leaderless herd like an icebreaker through pack-ice. The road soon deteriorated, bunching the leaderless rabble into the middle.

A Bren carrier stood at the junction with the Sfakia road. Brigadier Hargest and his brigade major stood in the road, checking the elements of the brigade through. Rankin reported, and the major called over his shoulder, "Here's the first of your lot, Alex."

Hamilton limped out from behind the carrier. "Ah, Rankin, good work. You're the first of D Company. Have you seen the others?"

"Not since we left 42nd Street, sir. CSM Clutterbuck's element was rear-guard, and Lieutenant Anderson passed us through while he waited for them. We heard no significant firing after we left, sir."

"Good work, Rankin, good work. Carry on. You'll pass through a roadblock a half mile or so up the road: manned by the Maoris and a British unit."

They swung off up the hill where the going immediately got tougher, the road poorer. The men started to breathe harder, sapping breath for talking. Rankin smiled in the dark; no doubt Hamilton's good-humoured remark and encouraging tone had been entirely for the Brigadier's benefit.

Not far inland from the junction, the road passed over a small bridge where they were challenged by a Maori Battalion guard.

"Which company are you from? Who's your commanding officer?" Rankin asked the corporal in charge of the bridge party.

"B Company, sir. Captain Royal."

"Give him my compliments when you see him. Tell him my taiaha is still held firm."

The corporal looked puzzled but was called away to deal with a fight between groups of stragglers.

CHAPTER TWENTY

Stylos, 28 May 1941

THE ROAD CONTINUED to rise steeply, the going still harder. Coming at the end of an already exhausting day, the hill required little thought from the men but mindless plodding, almost sleep-walking. Requests to smoke were refused; they had been told at the junction and at the bridge that German patrols could well be in the hills to the west of them. Rankin reached for the vial in his pocket and swallowed one.

They passed a village uphill and to their right, where troops were digging in. and then, after a particularly hard slog, they crested the hill. Pale in the starlight, the road sloped down into a broad valley. Dozens of pinpricks of light dotted the valley floor and lower slopes looking like fairy lights.

Rankin reacted swiftly. "Christ, what's that?" Calling a halt, he sent for Nicholson. Meanwhile, the roadway quickly filled with groups of curious onlookers peering over shoulders to see what the soldiers were doing, trying to scrounge something to eat or drink. Nicholson, at the rear of the column, harshly shooed them out of the way.

Through his binoculars Rankin could see that the road descended into the valley and followed a stream for some distance, before crossing the broad floor of the valley. Another river flowed from the foot of the mountains on the far side. The fertile-looking plain, between the hill they were standing on and the mountains proper, was planted with orchards and fields. The magnified image in his lens showed that many of the trees were burning, accounting for the strong smell of woodsmoke. But what had set them on fire?

At the sound of an aircraft engine, a panicked cry went up: "Take cover! Aircraft, take cover!"

The roadside came alive as people bolted into the bush and behind rocks. Nicholson roared at their own men to hold fast. A flare burst bright in the distance, wobbling and floating in the heavens. Shadows swayed and teetered in the harsh unnatural light. The platoon slunk into the shadows and froze.

"How's the new boots, Terry?" Rankin overheard Blake ask Cameron nearby.

"Not bad. Better than the buggers I had before, I reckon," Cameron replied.

"Where'd you get those, then? My bloody boots are starting to come away from the soles," Meldrum said.

"Yeah, bloody Indian boots. You'd think they'd be made for Indians, be used to this sort of malarky. My missus'd be taking the buggers back to where she bought them if this is all the fuckin' wear you get," said Smith.

"Yeah, but you don't normally eat, sleep and shit in them, Smithy, now do you?" said Duggan.

"Done fuck-all sleeping," grumbled Smith. "Not a lot of eating, either."

"Shut up the pair of yous. Where'd you get new boots from, Terry?" repeated Meldrum.

"Swapped 'em. Bloke in the Maori Battalion had four pairs tied round his neck. Said he'd picked them up from the stores depot."

"What did you have to trade, for Christ's sake?" asked McGeorge. "Did he have any spare ciggies? You should've got some more cigs."

"That's the joke, see," said Cameron. "I gave him a half dozen of that captured piss."

"Fair go," said Meldrum. "For only one pair of boots? He saw you coming, mate."

They all guffawed until Nicholson told them to put a sock in it.

"Jesus, Terry, he could'a chucked in a coupl'a packs of fags," McGeorge despaired.

In the distance gunfire rattled and explosions thumped.

Infinitely slowly, the flare lowered and steadied, casting regular shadows, until it finally faded and went out. It seemed to take an eternity. The naked exposure brought Rankin out in a cold sweat.

A mile or so of easier walking brought them to the bridge over the larger river on the other side of the valley, and Brigade staff. They had reached Stylos, they were told. Here the men could rest and have something to eat and there was water in the village, off the road to the right. They were directed to 23's area, near the stream.

Most immediately slumped to the ground, footsore and beyond tired. Too exhausted to be hungry, many simply sat down and fell asleep. Nicholson cajoled parties to fill water bottles while he posted sentries.

By now it was well into the small hours, but there was still no sign of the rest of the company. Rankin lingered near the bridge, fear rising; the others must surely come in soon. Where had that shooting been? It was all somehow going wrong. Time ticked by, agonisingly slowly. Men continued to tramp up the road, some turning into the village, others continuing uphill. He could hear the river burbling underneath the bridge and murmuring voices that occasionally turned into the raised tones of an argument. As he paced back and forth, troops on foot kept coming up the road. He even heard several motors grinding their way up the hill in low gear.

Too wrought-up to sleep, he kept conjuring up disasters. Eventually, above the low buzz of voices below, he heard a guide instruct someone from 23 Battalion to go to their right, above the bridge. "The first of your lot came in more than half an hour ago," he informed them.

The new arrivals looked as weary and worn as Rankin's had been on arrival. Anderson himself gazed at the slope with hatred, as if it were the straw which would break the camel's back. "Where the hell have you been?" Rankin almost shouted at him.

"Jesus, keep your hair on. I didn't know you cared so much."

Rankin felt a surge of relief, which left him weak at the knees. "Sorry. I've been imagining all sorts."

"Well, a Jerry patrol did make contact as we came through the junction. A couple of companies of Maoris and some British unit saw them off, but the buggers are close behind."

Just then a carrier came clattering up the road and halted not far away. Hargest and the major climbed out and helped Hamilton down. Several brigade staff hurried over to Hargest, who disappeared with his major, leaving Hamilton stranded.

"You're the company commander, you'd better go and give him a hand," Rankin told Anderson. "I'll see to putting your blokes in near ours."

Shortly afterwards, Clutterbuck's group came in, and Clutterbuck joined Rankin and Nicholson.

"Apparently, a truck brought rations up here after we passed Suda," Nicholson told Clutterbuck. "I don't wonder; it was a right shemozzle down there, all those thieving foreigners," he added with feeling.

Clutterbuck raised his eyebrows. "Don't ask, Bernard," Rankin said, "but it seems a lot of these base types have no idea of proper procedure when it comes to forming an orderly queue."

Anderson returned as the new arrivals' water parties and ration details were despatched. "It looks like quite a few of them have just dossed down and gone to sleep. Any idea where we are?"

Rankin looked at his watch: nearly 0400. "No. I was thinking the same thing. We should go and have a look."

Rankin picked up his rifle and Anderson slung his Tommy gun over his shoulder. "We'll go and have a shufti before the sun comes up," Anderson said to the NCOs. "You hold the fort."

Away from their hearing, he said to Rankin, "Are you alright, Neil? You look a bit jittery."

"It's these bloody Bennies the Jerries issue. They keep you awake alright, but they don't half make you jumpy. 'Fizzing' is how I heard one of our blokes describe it."

"I've seen them," said Anderson. "Boys brought a couple of the little bottles in and I sent one off to the MO. Of course, it's all gone to shit since, so God alone knows where he is now."

"They heighten the senses, keep you awake, but let you down with a hell of a thump," replied Rankin. "Then you need to take another. Not sure they're good for you. Stronger than any Bennies I ever took when I was swotting."

"Jesus." Anderson looked sharply at Rankin. "No wonder you passed all your exams first go, you bloody fraud."

"I caught one of my blokes selling them to the troops."

"Ha. What did you do about that?"

"Confiscated the money and pills, told him not to."

"Hmm. I'm sure that gave him a dose of the frighteners."

They walked towards the hills west of the village; there were no pickets beyond the village itself. Following the contour of the hill to a point where they could just make out the river debouching from its gorge, they were aware of the bulk of the White Mountains looming above them, blotting out the sky to the south and west. To the east, a glimmer of dawn was lightening the view across the plain. They made themselves comfortable on a rocky promontory overlooking the river.

"Christ, I'm bloody tired," said Anderson.

"Here, try one of these," said Rankin, holding out his vial of tablets. "It's four o'clock in the morning, you've had no sleep, and we're going to climb a fucking mountain in the morning."

Anderson hesitated, then took one, washing it down with a swig of water.

"Funny thing, Neil. When I helped old Dimwit into the HQ, he asked me if I'd ever met your father."

Rankin sat up straight. "What did you say?"

"Well, I don't know why, but I said yes, I had. Several times. I don't know why he asked me. There was something in his voice. He sounded odd."

"I said to him, just before Galatas, that I had received a letter from my father, and that he asked to be remembered to him."

"Jesus. What did he say to that?"

"No time to say anything, but he looked like he'd seen a ghost, and soon after he tripped over a rock and banged his head."

"Jesus," Anderson repeated.

"It could even be possible that it's thanks to him I was born."

"Remind me, what was your old man going to pot him for? If it *was* him."

"Falsification of patrol reports. He'd found a roll of Jerry wire they kept hidden in no-man's-land, then cut lengths off it to bring back. Proof they'd been over to the Jerry wire. Patrols never lost a man, very popular with the blokes. And the brass."

"Bloody hell."

A flicker of movement caught Rankin's eye.

"Christ, Boney, what's that down there? There's something moving, in the mouth of the gorge."

"Probably a goat. Don't change the subject just when it's getting interesting," Anderson said, hauling his glasses out of their case. "Jesus Christ! You're right. On the riverbed. Fuck! Jerries!"

"Go back and sound the alarm. I'll keep them busy."

"We need to get up on top of the hill behind us!" Anderson cried, scrambling to his feet.

Rankin rested the rifle on a boulder, snapped on the telescopic sights, and set the range for his guess at the distance, 450 yards.

There were half a dozen dark forms on the riverbed now, very hard to see in the half-light through the lens. From the gestures they made it was clear that more were coming down the gorge. Aiming at the leading man, who he hoped was the officer, he pulled the trigger. The resulting flash lit up the whole sky, the deafening report rolling and rumbling around the hills. His next shot felled a figure carrying something, then a flash and bang from the riverbed was immediately followed by a whack and a wicked whine. Time to go!

Dodging behind trees and rocks, he forced his legs to go upwards. The hill was steep, desperately steep, and as he struggled

413

higher, he heard Anderson's whistle and shouting in the distance. The buggers had set up a machine gun on the riverbed; bursts of tracer whistled up the hillside. Out of the corner of his eye, between his panicked gasps for oxygen, he could make out dark shapes running from the gorge, heading for the hill.

Breath rasping in his throat, lungs and legs burning, Rankin hauled himself up, over rocks and between the scrub. He'd had to sling the rifle over his back in order to free his hands, the slope being so steep in parts he had to use his hands and knees to scramble over rocks and scree, ignoring the resulting cuts and scrapes from the rough surface. And while the sparse scrub offered cover, he was making so much noise they must surely hear him in Suda. His stomach rebelled at the sudden effort, threatening to heave its contents over the hillside; he told himself it was a good thing that it contained nothing but water and bile.

The slope eased; he was nearing the top and he could see the stone wall that ran across the summit, only 20 feet away. His breaths came in hoarse gasps, legs in agony. Stumbling the last few paces, he was shocked to see a head wearing a soft field cap, then a body, appear beyond the wall.

The light was slightly brighter up here, which allowed him to see the expressions of surprise, disappointment, fear, then anger pass across the man's face. His Schmeisser hung across his chest on a strap around his neck. Jesus Christ, Rankin! Mountain troops!

There was no time to unsling his rifle. The man moved both hands to his own weapon; in a moment it would be pouring a torrent of bullets at him. The pocket of Rankin's smock slapped his thigh heavily, reminding him of its contents. His hand dived in and came out with the Luger. Thumbing off the safety, he used both hands to bring it up to chest height and fire it at the German, who was only 20 paces away. In his panic and heaving exhaustion Rankin emptied the eight-round magazine, and the man collapsed.

Yelling and shouting came from both sides. He crouched behind the wall as a bang in front of him sent a chip flying just a few yards away. Feverishly, he dropped the pistol and hauled the rifle over his head, shaking with fright and effort. The target would not steady in his scope, but the few shots he fired sent them diving for cover. They kept coming, though, knowing he was on his own.

Then there was the sound of boots and heavy breathing behind. Corkhill, thank Christ! Corkhill needed no telling: his rifle was up at his shoulder, firing at the shapes breaking cover and advancing up the slope. Several more khaki-clad men arrived, including Clive Hulme, who sat astride the wall, firing down the hill. The sheer weight of fire from the rock wall sent the enemy scurrying for cover.

Rankin emptied his magazine, then sat with his back to the stone wall, gasping for breath.

"Jesus Christ, that was close."

———

THE FIRING WAS getting heavier. Rankin looked at his watch: 0950. They had been at it for hours. So far, and to the best of his knowledge, the Germans had been beaten back from the hilltop three times; once by the skin of their teeth. Some men managed to get out far enough to the left flank just in time to prevent a German machine-gun squad getting across the wall and outflanking the whole position. More troubling, a mortar had been set up somewhere down the hill and so far it had defied all attempts to put it out of action.

Across the valley, several trucks ventured out of the western hills and stopped near the Sfakia road bridge across the stream. To Rankin's fury, they included British RAF and army trucks. Boiling angry, he sent for Sutherland and Smith.

"There's a shepherd's hut along the wall a bit further," he yelled at the gun teams above the racket when they arrived, streaming with sweat and out of breath, having dragged their 35-pound rifles to the top of the hill. "You'll have to do someone else's fucking job for them. Shoot up those trucks across the bloody valley."

Sutherland and Smith looked at him wide-eyed.

"What the fuck are you waiting for?" Rankin shouted.

Protesting loudly, Sutherland and Pringle hauled the mammoth rifle to the stone shelter and set it up in a window space. Smith found a gap torn in the wall by a mortar bomb. Rankin watched the RAF's .50 calibre tracer rounds drop into and about the trucks, three quarters of a mile distant, scattering the enemy nearby, and managing to set one truck on fire, then a second.

No sooner had flames flickered up from the second truck than an explosion erupted 20 yards out in front of the shelter, showering it with rocks and clods. Another landed a dozen yards closer.

"Get out, Tub, get out!" Rankin shrieked.

Sutherland and Pringle bolted through the door, unhampered by the rifle. The next mortar bomb landed on top of the hut and blew it to pieces, burying the Boys rifle under the rubble.

"Jesus," said Pringle, looking back at the dust rising from the wreck of the hut with relief. "Just when we were getting the hang of it."

CHAPTER TWENTY-ONE

The Road to Perdition, White Mountains, 29–30 May 1941

"I SAY, WHY don't you chaps take the weight off your feet while your men get water at the spring?"

Rankin and Anderson raised their heads to look at the speaker, a serious-looking young man wearing a British uniform and leaning over the bougainvillea-laden balcony railing of the pretty villa.

"Intelligence Officer, B Commando, Layforce," he called out as he came downstairs to shake each of their hands in turn.

"Ah," said Anderson. "Yes, the Commandos. We've heard of you. Passed through some of your chaps down at the junction last night."

Rankin frowned at Anderson through his blinding headache. Chaps? Really?

"Yes," the Commando continued. "Given the rear-guard I'm afraid. The boss is not at all pleased. We're an offensive unit, you see – nothing heavier than a Bren gun. You've just come from Stylos, I gather."

"Yes," said Rankin, gritting his teeth against the searing fire behind his eyeballs. "Rear-guard action, cost another three from my platoon."

"Foiled a Hun attack, though, and got away," Anderson added hastily. "There was quite a do down the road where your chaps were. Saved when a couple of Matildas turned up out of the blue."

Rankin looked at him again: Foil? Hun? Do? Where was all this coming from?

"Yes. I heard about their adventures."

"We only just got away," said Rankin. "Some of your blokes and half a company of Maoris charged into the Jerries' rear."

"Oh, I see."

"Disorderly, you see. Attack from behind – not what they expect. Confounded them, luckily for us," Anderson said.

Rankin stared at him, wondering at what point he had been propelled into some alternative universe.

"We're the last, you see," Anderson continued blithely. "After us cometh the Hun. Sorry if we've kept you waiting."

"Oh, not at all. Punctuality is a virtue of the bored, I always think."

"Nice billet you've landed here," said Rankin, hoping to bring the conversation back to Earth. They were standing on the villa's shaded marble terrace, surrounded by cascades of bougainvillea that flowed over the balconies and balustrades. Its perfume vied with that of the jasmine in the scented air. Outside, a profusion of pink and white oleander trees grew in the sunshine.

"Babali Inn. The Pantes Springs are the last before you ascend to the summit. The boss thought it would make a good Brigade HQ. How long have you chaps been on Crete?"

"Since the beginning of May," said Anderson. "It was quite

charming for a couple of weeks."

"Some of our chaps found yesterday very trying," responded the Commando. "Dive-bombed all day. Didn't stand up to it well. We arrived on the twenty-sixth; bit of a shambles really. We understood you still held the airfield. We had the devil of a job finding anyone who knew what was going on."

There was a call from outside; the water parties' bottles were filled.

"Ha. Well," said Anderson, "if you see a chap wandering around wearing a battered cap and a scruffy raincoat, he's probably General Weston, the man in charge. Give him our regards." They shook hands and Anderson went out.

"What did you say your name was?" Rankin asked, extending his hand. Serious dark eyes bore into his own, giving him the oddest feeling of being catalogued, like a specimen that had been described, carded, indexed and filed away.

The other man swept an errant lock of dark brown hair from his forehead with the open palm of his hand. "Waugh, Evelyn Waugh[14]."

A corporal showed Rankin out. "Have a nice chat with our Mr Wuff, did you, sir? Quite the card is our Mr Wuff."

———

"JESUS, BONEY, FIRST you're sucking up to him in a bloody faux accent, then you're calling the general a wanker," Rankin fumed.

———

14 Capt. E.S. Waugh, born London 28 Oct 1903, Intelligence Officer 'Layforce'. Royal Marine Commandos, journalist and novelist (*Officers and Gentlemen*, Chapman & Hall 1955 deals with Crete), best known for *Brideshead Revisited*, published 1945).

"Judging by the corporal's name for him, I don't think all's sweetness and light there."

They were plodding up the hill in the midday heat, single file on each side of the road. Rankin's head hurt abominably.

"What makes you say that? First class chap, I thought," Anderson replied with a smirk. "Anyway, if it gets back, they'll just think it was you."

"You're lucky it's too bloody hot to shove you over the bank, you prick." Rankin jumped to one side at the sound of an approaching motor. "Look out, here comes the Brigadier."

Hargest drove past, shouting to the troops to keep going, keep together, keep to the sides of the road, and keep separated.

"I must say," said Rankin after the carrier had passed, "his retreat's rather better run than his advance."

"Fucked if I know how you keep together and keep separated at the same time," grumbled Anderson.

The heat became intense causing them to suffer agonies of thirst. The water bottle each of them carried on their belt had to last the whole day. Separated into platoons, lacking sleep, footsore and hungry, the men found the unrelenting gradient became a battle of will for each and every step. Heads down, shoulders drooping under their respective loads, one foot in front of the other they continued to plod upwards, taxing legs that had already given of their utmost in the wild scramble at dawn. The climb soon began taking its toll: some men's feet were bleeding in their boots while others found their clothes, stiff with dried sweat and dirt, chafed to the extent that in places their skin was rubbed raw.

Formed units were forced to elbow or push their way through the rabble of unarmed and disorganised base troops, picking up the stragglers from kindred units to add to their own as they went. All around them, the morale-sapping detritus of a defeated army littered the roadsides: discarded equipment, abandoned packs, officers' valises, and possessions – precious, no doubt, up to the point that exhaustion on the part of their owners forced them to be jettisoned. Abandoned vehicles had been pushed over the side of the mountain when they ran out of fuel, or the radiator had given up the unequal battle against the heat. However, the crocodile of misery noticed little of this, certainly not the astonishing views that opened up as they climbed ever higher. Each man's span of concentration was limited to his personal battle to keep one foot ahead of the other.

The struggle proved too much for many. Some sat at the side of the road, head in hands, while others lay among the boulders and scrub off to one side, unable to go on; pathetic figures exhausted to the point of indifference to their own fate. Sadly, these casualties provided opportunity for the baser aspects of human nature to flourish. The weak, unable or beyond defending or protecting themselves, were looted of anything of value: food, cigarettes, water, gear.

Rests were curtailed to five minutes – no longer – to reduce the danger of men falling asleep and being left behind. On top of that, officers and NCOs had to watch both front and rear of their columns to make sure no one fell out or slipped behind. Even so, some staggered up the road propped between two companions; others carried two rifles to allow a mate a lighter load. And there were those who simply found the load too great. There were a number of tearful scenes in which exhausted men were forced to abandon a friend that had hitherto been carried in a blanket or on a makeshift stretcher.

The noise of an aeroplane caused a wave of panic to ripple along the line. Shouts of "Aircraft! Take cover! Aircraft!" were heard, causing an ill-disciplined stampede of humanity for the roadside rocks and tawny scrub into which it magically vanished, accompanied by curses and profanities from those already in occupation. The disciplined groups held to the road edges, waiting for the danger to pass, before resuming their march. Later, Rankin could only remember one encounter with an aircraft on this particular day; a lone Messerschmitt 109, flying vertically up a gully, whose pilot waved cheerily as he rocketed over the road and disappeared. For all he knew, it could have been a hallucination.

Via Dolorosa: the name rang in Rankin's head. For him it was a road where the next footstep was more pain-filled than the last, where the next blind corner simply led to another, and each summit gave view of one yet higher. The road illustrated human nature stripped bare.

Almost beyond caring or comprehension, the column of exhausted men reached a blasted pile of rock and rubble at which point the road completely disappeared. A guide tasked with showing the retreating troops the way across the obstacle told them an over-enthusiastic engineer had triggered the demolitions protecting the pass over the summit, effectively the gateway to the town of Vrises. The detour added only 200 yards to the day's tally but took hours to cross as much of it had to be accomplished on hands and knees, resulting in bleeding knees, scraped elbows and ripped hands. The engineer responsible would have learned much about his parentage.

THE TOWN OF Vrises had been reduced to a pile of red-brick rubble. The inhabitants had fled. and the new arrivals soon found that the poles used to lower and raise the buckets in the village wells had disappeared, along with the buckets. The wells themselves were surrounded by jostling, thirst-crazed mobs of men who had made the climb and were desperate for water. Among them the story was oft repeated that the Germans had used Greek civilians and POWs to shield their attacks on the Maoris and commandos defending the junction at the foot of the mountains. The telling and retelling added to the mindless panic among the rabble of disorganised troops and considerably increased the anger of the soldiers belonging to formed and still functioning units, for whom it might not be too late to exact a little retribution.

Nicholson, beside himself with despair, raged at the mob, calling them "those damn thieving foreign buggers, not a grain of sense between the lot of 'em!". Lowering bottles, helmets and tins into a deep well at the end of a rope consisting of rifle pull-throughs, equipment straps or string was nerve-racking and time-wasting enough. And when the jostling and shoving by the ill-disciplined crowds, desperate for their turn, caused the vessel to be upended, spilling its precious contents, tempers blazed.

Nicholson posted an armed guard while the platoon drew the last of its meagre share, which threatened to shoot "any idle bugger who comes near and doesn't form a proper line!". Rankin ignored the ensuing uproar, which simply aggravated his already parched throat, raging headache and painful jittering behind his eyes. In the end, some bottles were filled and some thirsts partially quenched.

"God almighty," Smith erupted furiously, after gulping half his allocation. "There's no bloody petrol for trucks, 'cos some

423

bloody coot's poured it all in here."

"Eau de benzene, Smithy, vintage 1941," Sutherland said. "Make even the padre's sermons go with a bang."

"Typical bloody army," Duggan added. "Never knows its arse from its bloody elbow."

"Hey, Sid," Blake called out to McGeorge, "don't strike a match on the seat of your pants, mate, or you'll blow your arse to kingdom come." McGeorge's angry answer was lost in a chorus of guffaws.

They had been promised a long rest, but the first inkling that the promise would be broken was not long in coming. The ready-to-move order was received late in the afternoon while they were still trying to find uncontaminated water.

The comatose were kicked awake, and struggled up onto aching legs and feet, hoisting equipment before marching out in order. Rankin, barely able to focus his eyes, fell in beside Nicholson.

"We've looked for Gardiner everywhere," Nicholson fumed. "Damn the man, nothing but trouble."

"He must have gone with the group that couldn't keep up."

"He didn't go with my permission. Or yours. He's a damned deserter. Graham at least had good reason; he could barely stand when he got here. Gardiner was still on his feet."

Rankin looked sideways at Nicholson. Always black and white, his attitude now came with a bitter edge; the result, no doubt, of the days of hard fighting with little or no sleep or food. "Probably terrified of losing his loot – or getting caught with it," Rankin said.

"Serve him blimmin' right. It wouldn't have happened if you'd made an example of him in the first place," muttered Nicholson.

"We've had this argument before; stealing personal effects is not the same as taking their gear. You know that very well."

"No, I don't know. What's the bloody difference? Dead men don't need watches! He's probably sold what he's stolen. He's actually been useful lately, surprised me in fact."

Nicholson shot him a look. "The road to perdition is paved with good intentions. I expected more from you, I must say."

Rankin swallowed the urge to hit him and they tramped on in brooding silence.

If they thought the worst of the climb was over when they got to Vrises, they soon found out that the route to this point had been merely a ghastly foretaste of the steep climbs, hairpin bends, and switchbacks to come on the road that climbed up the side of the White Mountains proper.

Reaching the final pass in the pitch dark, more dead than alive, they were ordered to take up defensive positions. These needed to be improvised, dug with whatever was available on the steep slopes above the road.

The flow of stragglers and the steadier tramp of formed units withdrawing over the pass continued all night on the road below. The rest of 5 Brigade passed through 23 Battalion's cordon and continued towards the evacuation beaches, accompanied by the stream of human flotsam that represented the remainder of the defeated army.

———

"I TELL YOU, Blakey, she must have been a film star. Looked like Veronica Lake, only she was yabbering away in Greek. She was some looker." The voice belonged to Cameron.

"You've been out in the sun too long, mate. Whoever heard of a blonde Greek?"

"I'm telling you; I saw them with my own eyes. In a truck, going south."

"Now I know you're bloody dreaming. They must've been Jerries if they was in a truck."

Rankin was shaving early next morning. A couple of hours of rest had diminished the headache and he was at least able to see his reflection in the mirror and control his hands enough not to shred his face. As he listened to the men, he noted there was still life in some of them – despite the circumstances – judging by their conversation.

"Did you hear Wilf's done a runner?"

Rankin stopped scraping the razor and listened.

"Yeah," said Blake. "Dumb bugger. He owes Harry a fiver. Never paid him out."

"Left me in the shit as well. I'll have to carry the fuckin' ammo for the Spandau now, as well as the sodding gun."

"Give it to Tub. Smart bastard blew his bloody gun up."

AS IT TURNED out, not all the British transport on Crete had been destroyed or was in German hands. There were trucks south of Vrises, and limited service was available to the end of the Sfakia road. In the morning water was miraculously trucked up to Rankin and his men. It came in a novel assortment of large glass carboys wrapped in wicker panniers or in earthenware amphorae. The carboys had apparently previously contained wine, and the amphorae may once have been filled with milk or yoghurt.

Whatever, the vessels took some careful handling to make sure they did not fall and smash.

Rations were sparse: a couple of tins of bully between six, and a packet of biscuits per man. Ribald comments flew about the army, its catering ideas and the ability of their teeth to deal with biscuits you could use as roof tiles.

Rankin sought out Lawrence to ask if he knew anything about Gardiner taking off.

Lawrence looked up from examining his feet. "He came to me yesterday; said he had dysentery. I said he might have the trots, but he was no worse than half the blokes."

"Do you know anything about him owing Harry Bloxham a fiver?"

Lawrence averted his eyes and his shoulders slumped. "Sorry, Skipper, I thought I could sort it out. It was about a bet. Bloxy's been putting the hard word on him for his money. He offered to pay him with stuff he had and Greek money, but Bloxy wouldn't take it. Wanted his fiver."

"I see. Did Harry threaten him?"

"He might have clocked him one."

"Shit!" Rankin swore under his breath. Perhaps Nicholson was right. Perhaps he should have made an example of Gardiner to tone down the betting. It was so ingrained, even that might have caused a riot.

"Terry will need a new loader for the Spandau."

"Brian volunteered when he heard Gardiner had taken off, Skipper," Lawrence replied.

———

DAYLIGHT REVEALED THE full extent of the deficiencies of their position, causing Rankin's mood to deteriorate as the heat rose, concentrated between the walls of a gorge which acted like an oven. Despite the water they had received, everyone was thirsty, which was made worse by the salty tinned beef. Few had husbanded their water ration and saved enough to soften their biscuits and slake their parched throats. Many couldn't deal with even the paltry ration of biscuit they received.

Early on German patrols were seen in the distance. The stream of evacuees had already dried to a trickle, but everyone understood that there would be no more coming by that route. Later in the morning, a Junkers 52 appeared and dropped a string of parachutes over the German positions. The comments that this provoked ranged from the light-hearted to the nearly treasonous. Apparently refreshed and resupplied, the Germans resumed their probing until, in the afternoon, a vigorous firefight developed.

Orders had been received to begin sending sections back from 1730 hours onwards. Anderson's timetable dictated that the last section of Rankin's platoon would disengage at 1930. Disengaging was not easy with the Germans pushing forward and firing across the ground they would have to cross. They had to run the gauntlet in ones and twos, each man making a mad dash for a protective bluff as the bullets zipped and whined off the rocks about him.

At last it was Rankin's turn to scramble across the open ground and through the cutting. Pursued by bullet strikes and whistling ricochets, he charged through the gap in the rocks to safety, where a haven of peace and tranquillity unexpectedly opened out before him. The flat, green plain at the foot of the hill appeared to be completely surrounded by steep slopes rising above it. It was like looking into the crater of a large, verdant volcano from the top of the rim. The soft afternoon glow illuminated whitewashed farms, red-tiled roofs, and green-and-yellow strips of cropland and orchards which stretched across the flat land to the steep hills beyond.

The Germans were dissuaded from following hard on their heels by an artillery barrage, which poured 25-pounder shells down on top of them. To the fugitives, the Plain of Askifou looked like paradise itself.

CHAPTER TWENTY-TWO

Askifou Rendezvous, 30–31 May 1941

AND PARADISE IT was. Burning thighs and calves could rest. There was a well that was still intact and surrounded by undamaged plane trees which provided as much cool water as anyone could wish for, hidden from the prying eyes of the Luftwaffe. Out of harm's way, for the moment at least, the men enjoyed an infectious holiday mood as they lazed in the gentle evening light.

Rankin was starting to feel better. His headache had receded, he had slaked his thirst, and the pain behind his eyeballs and his jittery hands had calmed considerably. The green and fertile-looking countryside reminded him of home. As often happened in a relaxed moment between the bouts of madness, thoughts of home inevitably led to wondering what his loved ones were doing, what news they might have had of the battles in the last few days. How long would it take for the telegrams to start arriving? God! He told himself angrily that he could not afford to think along these lines and forced himself to turn his attention to the last leg of the journey: the night march down to the beach. After what they'd been through it would be like a moonlit stroll through a pleasant park. The scent of the jasmine growing over the crumbling remains of a nearby wall and the oleander bushes alongside the track to the well were nearly overpowering in the evening light as dusk fell.

He was abruptly shaken from his reverie when a messenger arrived and called him to a briefing where he found Hamilton and Anderson huddled together in one corner of a ruined building. A tarpaulin had been secured to the walls, giving the impression of a poor man's camp, whose only adornment was an unlit hurricane lamp standing on a pile of bricks. Rankin glanced at Anderson, who avoided his eye. Hamilton, sitting on a folding camp stool, did not get up.

"Ah, Rankin, there you are. Do sit down," Hamilton said looking up from the papers in his hand in answer to Rankin's salute. He brusquely waved towards a pile of broken masonry opposite him. Anderson stood and shuffled from one foot to the other. Rankin swallowed hard, but the lump in his throat refused to budge.

"Your platoon remains one of the strongest in the Battalion," said Hamilton, not waiting for Rankin to sit. The bald announcement sent a surge of apprehension through Rankin. "The Brigadier requires you for a special operation. Independent action, vital job – should be right up your alley."

Rankin looked from one to the other. "I see, sir."

"The road to Sfakia descends from here, the Plain of Askifou," continued Hamilton. "There is a fear that the Germans may parachute reinforcements onto the plain to disrupt the evacuation."

Rankin's apprehension mounted. "I see, sir," he repeated while internally, he was verging on panic.

Hamilton's eyes darted around the forlorn scene, as if to make sure no one else was listening. "The Brigadier has passed us orders of the utmost importance. A mobile Air Ministry Experimental Station, set up to give early warning, is located near the western edge of the plain. It is absolutely imperative that this does not fall into German hands." He paused, bent forward, and fixed Rankin in the gaze of his pale eyes. "You, personally, will ensure that it does not, Rankin. The station is to be destroyed and the operators evacuated. If you cannot evacuate them safely, you are ordered to shoot them." Rankin gasped. "They must not fall into German hands, any more than their equipment. Do you understand?"

Rankin had taken an involuntary step backwards. "Shoot them?"

"Yes, Rankin. Shoot them."

Rankin felt the colour drain from his face. He looked from Hamilton, whose eyes glinted, to Anderson, who shuffled nervously as he looked at the ground.

"I see, sir. I wish to request such an order in writing, sir."

"Of course you do, Rankin. I expected nothing less." Hamilton reached into the pocket of his shirt, and withdrew a page torn from a signal pad.

Rankin scanned the signal form. Headed "Utmost Urgent: Top Secret", it was signed by Freyberg himself and counter-signed by Weston. So, he must have turned up somewhere, Rankin thought bitterly. He read for himself that "... he was to use any and every means at his disposal to prevent – repeat prevent – under any circumstances, the operators falling into enemy hands."

"I see, sir," he said, once more, folding and pocketing the order.

"Lieutenant Anderson will hand you such maps as we can provide, showing the location of the station and the route to the beaches. These have been drawn by Battalion staff. Battalion has only one map of the area and cannot give you an original. Good luck, Rankin. You will *not* let us down." He leaned forward again, chin jutting, eyes glittering in the low light. He glared at Rankin for a few seconds. "The importance of this was impressed upon me, as you may discern from your written orders," he hissed in an icy tone.

Rankin stepped forward, returning Hamilton's stare. In the evening light he felt the man's malice radiating from him and saw something he had seldom seen in Hamilton before: triumph. Hamilton continued to sit, his eyes fixed on Rankin's. "Sorry, Rankin, my injuries prevent me from getting up. Good luck." He waved airily as Rankin took a pace back, came to attention and saluted. "I'd get cracking if I were you, to get there before it's completely dark. They won't come in the dark."

Outside, Rankin rounded on Anderson. "What the fuck was that all about, Boney? Nowhere do those orders say to shoot the buggers!"

"'All available means', Neil."

"You know as well as I do, that if I shoot them, they'll deny the order ever meant that and I'll face a murder charge. And if I don't, I'll be court-martialled for letting them fall into enemy hands!"

"I'm a witness, Neil."

"Well, you can fucking well make a written declaration sworn under oath on the battlefield in face of the enemy as to what you heard him say. You're no good to me as a witness if you're fucking well dead."

"Jesus, keep your hair on. You only have to go a couple of miles, fetch them off a hill, and whisk them down to bloody Sfakia."

"Yes, and hope like hell they don't drop another bloody parachute division on top of us, for fuck's sake!"

———————

"I'VE FALLEN OUT a couple whose feet have packed up," reported Nicholson when he returned to the platoon, all of whom were happily relaxing under the trees by the well. "Transport's being organised for the sick and wounded."

"That must make about sixteen effectives, counting me. Apparently, we're the largest platoon in the battalion," Rankin said, seething with anger, turning his head away from the rest of the troops so as not to be overheard.

"Seventeen." Nicholson replied, raising his eyebrows.

"It seems we've got one more bloody job to do before we leave," said Rankin.

"I see," said Nicholson, looking crestfallen. "What?"

"Rescuing some clowns off the top of a mountain," Rankin fumed, spreading out the hand-drawn map. "Here is Ammoudari," he said, stabbing the village with his finger. "A track leads from there to this point here, labelled Point 1350. Jesus Christ! That's its height – in metres."

"Let's hope they're not sitting on the top, then," Nicholson said dubiously. "They must be very important."

"Bloody Air Ministry Experimentals. Too secret to let them fall into the wrong hands, apparently."

"Oh," Nicholson replied, the implications clear from the way his shoulders sagged and jaw dropped.

Rankin broke the news to the platoon. It was not well received.

"Well, look at it this way, boys," he said, trying to put a light-hearted spin on it. "It's two or three miles tonight, a quick canter up another couple of miles tomorrow morning, tidy things up, and then down to the beach and away. I have been guaranteed that we will have priority to the ships because of the importance of our mission."

He had been guaranteed nothing of the sort, but they needn't know that. They needn't know, either, that they might be ordered to shoot the men they were meant to save.

There was more than the usual grumbling as they shouldered their loads, but at least they had seen that water was plentiful and the wells on the plain had not been vandalised by the mob or tainted with petrol. In addition, they had been issued a special ration of a tin of bully between two, and two packets of biscuit each.

As the walking was easy, flat, and the productive-looking fields and landscape smelled of mown grass and honeysuckle, tempers among the men improved dramatically.

It was all but dark when they stumbled into a platoon from 18 Battalion, under the command of a corporal, coming the other way. "Where the fuck are you lot going? Er, sorry, sir. Rare to run into an officer these days."

"I might ask you the same thing, corporal."

"Anti-parachute duty, sir. Tin-pot wee place called Ammoudari. Our orders were to stay until 1900 hours. We're headed for the assembly point."

"Jesus Christ," fumed Rankin, after they had passed. "Why didn't they send a message to them to do the job?"

"Perhaps our brigadier was the only one the General could find."

"Very bloody likely. At least they'd heard of the track."

They marched on in silence, Rankin's doubts and misgivings growing with every step.

––––––––

AMMOUDARI TURNED OUT to be a cluster of half a dozen houses around a tiny church and a well. As they had arrived in the dark, most of the men simply sat down beside the track and fell asleep under the trees. Sentries were posted, but it was the devil's own job to wake men for their watch, and for them to stay awake during it. Rankin could not get the interview with Hamilton out of his mind. The baleful eyes, glinting with triumph, his relentlessly severe demeanour … the man exuded a malicious and hate-filled aura. It was patently obvious that he never expected to have to deal with Rankin again. Not in this life, at least. Rankin, overcome by exhaustion, eventually fretted himself into a troubled sleep. He awoke from several bad dreams, thankful each time to hear the sonorous breathing of others and the gentle rustle of leaves overhead.

First light was accompanied by tinkling goat bells and the inquisitive stares of the pint-sized herder.

"Do you know where the *angloi antres* are?" Rankin asked him.

This was met by a torrent of excited Greek and a lot of wild pointing; the boy's coal-black eyes lit by a big smile. As well as "*angloi*", Rankin thought he heard "*michano-kinito*". Something mechanical?

A black bandana tied over his head, along with baggy shirt and breeches and bare feet gave him the air of a junior pirate. Rankin found himself dragged by the sleeve to a cart track leading from the village. At the junction the boy poured out another torrent of words, with more excited pointing and wild gesticulations. He was joined by a small girl, who didn't say a word, but tugged at the boy's clothes until he gave up, with evident reluctance, and returned to his goats. Rankin gazed along the track to which the boy had pointed; it led in the right direction. To the south and west, between them and the coast, the White Mountains reared up, seemingly vertically, out of the bowl of the plain.

Most of the platoon could not recall when they had last eaten a hot meal. But now plentiful water allowed for mushed biscuit mixed with corned beef to be turned into hash, cooked on German cookers under the cover of the trees. Bottles were refilled from the village well. Rankin allowed only four men to go to fill them, in an attempt to hide their numbers from any hostile observers, but anyone watching could have counted the bottles.

The path led them to the edge of the plain, the limit of cultivation, then into the barren hills. They were soon back in a moonscape of dry scrub and rock, so familiar from the climb from the coast. It did not take long for the heat to rise and the sweat to form as they climbed higher, finally losing sight of the village altogether when they rounded a bluff and struck off cross country away from the plain. A vista of rising peaks, scrub and pine trees opened before them. The bush and scrub that densely covered the slopes became sparser as they climbed higher. Deep ravines and gorges cleaved their way through the wild, uneven ground.

Skirting around the side of the second peak, they marched across a shallow valley. In a dust-filled hollow they found the impression left by the tread of a pneumatic tyre. Rankin allowed himself to breathe easier; perhaps, by some miracle, they were indeed on the right track.

Climbing ever higher, the rough trail led through a narrow gorge carved into the hillside. It opened out, and in the far distance they saw the sea, deep blue from this height. Corkhill motioned them to halt and listen. Something was humming, he reported. Not far on, they cautiously rounded another bluff, weapons ready, onto a flat plateau.

"Halt! Who goes there?"

Rankin overcame his surprise and laughed out loud. "Nobody actually says that."

A timid-looking young soldier in khaki rose from behind a boulder, and shakily levelled his rifle at them.

"Here, go easy with that, son, in case the bloody thing goes off. Point it away if you don't mind."

"W-what are you doing here?" the young man asked. His shirt bore RAF flashes.

"Rescuing you, by the look of it," said Rankin.

Rankin and Nicholson sent two pairs of sentries back into the canyon they had just traversed to keep watch, then continued to the AMES camp. A four-wheeled trailer housed the station itself, another contained the receiving equipment and interpretation centre, and a generator, roaring loudly, and ancillary equipment filled the third. All were dotted around a relatively level area and hidden under camouflage netting laced with branches torn from the scrub. From a distance they matched the scattered bushes and trees. The area ended in a cliff overlooking a deep gorge.

"Turn that bloody thing off!" Rankin shouted at the man in charge, a young RAF corporal who introduced himself as Phillip Montgomery. The man almost collapsed in tears; whether of fright or relief, Rankin could not tell.

"We've been sent up here to ensure this lot is destroyed, and then escort you down to the evacuation beach," Rankin announced loudly. It was clear nothing had been destroyed or prepared for destruction on the crew's initiative.

"Our officer, Flight Lieutenant Burgin, went with a driver in the truck down to Suda three days ago, and we haven't seen them since. Then the sergeant fell over a cliff yesterday, and he's in a bad way." Montgomery shook as he relayed the story, looking close to tears, on the verge of panic.

"Is this thing still working?" Rankin asked, pointing at the nearest trailer. He yanked open the door and stared at an incomprehensible array of grey-painted cabinets. An operator, wearing headphones, sat with his back to the door, twiddling knobs and peering at a round black screen with a green squiggle travelling across it.

Montgomery gulped and nodded.

"Well, shut it down – now – and start smashing it up so that we can get the hell out of here. The Jerries aren't far behind us."

Montgomery looked terrified. "I can't destroy the equipment. It's too important."

"It'll be bloody important, alright, if it falls into Jerry's hands, I can tell you. I've got my orders, Corporal."

Montgomery hesitated, torn.

"Come on, Phillis, for Christ's sake, let's bust it up and fuck off out of here!" urged one of the airman-operators from the door of the trailer, none too gently.

"Get the power off, and shut the bloody thing down," Rankin ordered the operator, over Montgomery's head. "Robbie, you work out how we're going to get these bloody trailers over that cliff. Nick, find Corky and get him to take a look at the sergeant.

Montgomery, do you have manuals or records that we need to destroy?"

Time flashed by as they hurried to get the equipment prepared for demolition and remove evidence of the true purpose of the camp. As well as the trailers, tents hidden under camouflage netting provided accommodation and the mess. Montgomery told Rankin that the transmission aerial was on a bolted steel frame set up between some boulders higher up the hill,

When he heard Lawrence ask what they were doing away up here Montgomery replied that the equipment had managed to track shipping in the Strait at night, although the purpose of the set was to provide early warning of aircraft. Rankin gathered, from the way he spoke, that the experiments had yielded results that had surprised them.

Meanwhile, Corkhill reported that the sergeant had suffered two broken limbs and a head wound and was barely conscious. He also suspected internal injuries and probably fractured ribs. Without proper medical attention, he wouldn't live long.

They dislodged the transmission aerial from its mounting with a couple of well-placed hand grenades and dragged it to the edge of the precipice. The trailers had to be man-handled and roped out of position; then, with steering wheels locked, pushed and levered to the edge of the cliff. They went into the abyss with a satisfying sound of crashing and splintering.

While they were pushing the last caravan to the edge, they heard in the far distance the ominous but familiar buzz of a Storch. Rankin's heart sank – was it looking for them or just looking? Either way, it meant the German army could not be far behind. With strength borne of desperation and fear, the last trailer was levered over the edge just as the last pages of documents went into the petrol-fed flames. What was left behind would show there had been a camp here, but hopefully not its purpose.

It was already mid-afternoon, far later than he wished, when the job was done. Sweating with the heat of the sun and exertion, the men picked up their loads. There had been some good news. The camp had most of a case of .303 ammunition and a Lewis gun for anti-aircraft defence. Six of the ten men had rifles; but whether or not they knew what to do with them would remain to be seen. And they had proper food: tins of vegetables, meat and vegetable stew, even tinned fruit. After lunch, sumptuous by recent standards, what could not be carried on tired backs and weary legs was punctured and sent over the cliff.

Keeping an eye out for the Storch, they retraced their steps along the track to the village, carrying the wounded sergeant in a stretcher fashioned from a blanket and canvas slung between two sturdy tent poles.

———

AS THEY APPROACHED the final bluff before the descent into the village, Rankin gazed across the relatively sparsely covered hillside. It would be a terrible place to get caught in the open. His watch said 1645: still five hours of light. Enough, surely, to get back to the main road and down to the evacuation beach before midnight.

Searching the sky away to the north and west, he missed the leading section suddenly go to ground as it approached the bluff. Rankin's stomach did a somersault as panicked airmen threatened to bolt. Hand signals that had sent the trained men to ground off the track had triggered their flight reaction, restrained only by the NCOs' hissed orders and rough hands of the troops. Rankin hurried to Johnstone at the front of the column as the RAF personnel sheepishly slunk into cover.

"Company – in the village, Skipper," Johnstone reported, gesturing through a bush beside the path. "I thought we should know who they are before we show ourselves."

"Fuck!" Rankin muttered, his insides in turmoil. A khaki-painted truck was parked near the church. No one was visible. "Shit!" He needed to get a grip of himself. "Seen anyone?" He raised his binoculars to his eyes.

"No. Just the truck."

"Shit!" Rankin swore again, examining the truck through his binoculars. "Looks like a bloody RAF 15-hundredweight Bedford, roundels on the bonnet."

"Could be the officer on his way back, I suppose, Skipper."

Rankin snorted. "Yes. It could also be a platoon of flying bloody elephants." He examined every building through the lens. "They're either searching the village or coming up the track after us already." A man sauntered out from one of the houses and stood beside the truck. "Yes, bloody Jerry. No doubt about that." Another appeared and the two conferred.

Rankin turned his binoculars to the mountainside, but nothing moved. Johnstone nudged him, pointing to a dust trail coming from the north. "Another truck. There may be more, hidden by the dust."

The map Rankin had been given showed a track from Point 1350 crossing the uppermost reaches of the ravine beside the camp, then over a saddle and down into the next gorge. This ended in an arrow to the sea, and "Evacuation". It had looked like two to three miles from the camp. The length of the gorge was not marked.

"Bugger them. We'll have to use the alternative route to Sfakia," he said, thoughts tumbling around in his head. "You keep six men and take up the rear-guard, Robbie. We'll head back to the RAF camp as fast as we can. There's a goat track from there around the top of the gorge, which leads to the next ravine. If we get separated, make for there; it leads to the beach."

Johnstone nodded. Keeping the bush between themselves and the village, they backed around the bluff.

CHAPTER TWENTY-THREE

The End of the Road, 30–31 May 1941

RANKIN AND THE main body had reached the top of the gorge that the map portrayed as leading to the beach. It was 1800: the sun would set in another in two and a half hours. Johnstone had not yet caught up with them, but Rankin could not wait for ever. The gorge looked quite wide at this point but appeared to narrow rapidly and deepen. They had to be on the beach before the evacuation was called off, sometime after midnight.

"Go at least another mile with the Erks, Nick, to a point you think is defensible. Take the Lewis gun and Smithy with the Boys rifle; I'll keep Lawrence's Bren and the Spandau. I'm relying on you to keep them from panicking," he said jerking his head in the direction of the RAF technicians.

Nicholson looked doubtful. "I know," said Rankin. "I've already divided my force, now I'm doing it again. I don't see another way. If we haven't turned up by dark, keep on going. This gorge is supposed to lead down to the sea, to the evacuation beach."

"What will you do?" Nicholson asked in a worried voice.

"Join you, if we can."

Rankin gnawed at his knuckles. Lookouts, who should be able to see anyone approaching, were hidden around the position. Searching through his binoculars, he saw what appeared to be a track on the other side of the ravine, but it could have been a trick of the light and it was obscured by bushes. Shepherds must wander these hills with their goats, but you would be lucky to see anyone coming 200 yards away through the scrub and stunted trees. They heard nothing: no gunfire, nothing to indicate that Johnstone had run into trouble. With his heart thumping in his chest, he decided to wait until 1830.

————

"IT'S TIME, SKIPPER," Lawrence whispered, tapping his watch.

"I know." There was no sign of Johnstone. They could wait no longer. "Bring in the pickets; I'll get them on their feet."

They set off in extended single file down the gorge, following in Nicholson's footsteps. Discarded equipment littered the track. Others must have come this way; Nicholson would never countenance jettisoning any equipment until it was the only option left. What had been thrown away ran the whole gamut of army issue, except there were no weapons. That was something, at least. The sides of the gorge began to close in as they descended: it felt like being in a terrestrial submarine, slipping slowly below the Earth's surface into the underworld. They marched alongside a chattering brook, which in less fraught circumstances would have made good company. A little further on the ravine threatened to close over their heads altogether. It would be dark down here well before sunset, he realised; there would be no dusk.

They had been going for half an hour when they came across a clearing dotted with a few stumpy pines and stopped for a rest. Proof of the hasty transit of the remains of a panicked army lay everywhere. The clearing was dark and ominous, the ravine all but closed in around them, magnifying the noise of the burbling creek. The air, scented with pine, was cool. Rankin shivered.

They had only just stopped when tail-end Charlie, at the uphill end of the clearing, whistled. Rankin's heart leapt into his mouth: Johnstone? Or the Germans?

"What the fuck took you so long?"

"Keeping your arse clear," came Johnstone's terse reply. Rankin could have kissed him. "They're not far behind, Skipper. Hard to say how many; could be a platoon or more."

"How much time have we got?"

"Fifteen, twenty minutes. Half an hour at the outside."

Rankin looked about. Downstream, the clearing ended in a bluff pierced by a rocky canyon, the sides of which rose steeply above the clearing and were well shaded. Upstream, the slopes opened out somewhat.

"Quick, Robbie, dump your heavy gear behind that bluff," he said, pointing to the downstream exit from the clearing. "Get your Bren up that slope, fast as you can. Morry, yours up this side. Corky, scarper down the track, find the Sarge. Cameron, behind a rock with the Spandau, block the exit. Don't fire until they're on top of you!"

Rankin dropped his own pack with the others and scrambled up the slope behind Johnstone's squad. It was steep, the going hard. Rocks slithered and clattered into the gorge, making enough noise, surely, to wake the dead. More skin came off already grazed knees and elbows. What if it were more than a platoon?

Even a platoon could make trouble among evacuees on the beach. But what if it were a company? Or more?

They pushed along the slope as they climbed, extending past the little clearing. Each man picked his spot, behind a boulder or bush, clinging perilously to the hillside. Johnstone's Bren gunner was lying at such an angle, his number two had to hold him by the ankles to prevent him sliding into the canyon.

As they waited, Rankin felt as much as saw the others shuffling for better positions, relieving bodies hastily thrown down onto the hard, rocky ground. He was jittery with nerves, the tension excruciating.

The first German cautiously appeared 50 yards up the gorge, checked the entrance to the clearing, and signalled behind him. Several more appeared and while they searched the clearing, more emerged on the track. Rankin's eyes were by now well accustomed to the low light enabling him to count 26 of them. Every muscle tensed, he hardly dared breathe while he prayed that none of them would look up.

One of the Germans picked something off the ground and called out to the others. Rankin assumed the rest must all be in the clearing now, as no additional soldiers had come through the upstream gap into the clearing for at least a minute. Another man, probably the officer, hurried forward to take whatever the other held out, and turned it over in his hands, talking all the while. The others milled about, poking and prodding at objects on the ground until the officer called out at which they all straightened up and the leading men moved towards the clearing's narrow exit. Rankin located the machine-gunner; infinitely slowly, he worked him into his sight.

The vanguard was only yards from the rocky gap, its members

shifting their loads, taking a drink, talking, making their way back into patrol order, as they moved onto the track.

Without warning Cameron's Spandau fired. Tracer streaked across the clearing, whined and sparked off rocks. The sides of the gorge burst into flame and the resulting noise immediately boomed back, concentrated by the rocky slope, like a physical assault, pummelling ears and body. Rankin barely felt the first recoil, grunting in satisfaction as the gunner collapsed into the grass, before moving the sight to another figure.

Targets wilted into the grass in rapid succession as the storm of fire came at them from all angles. There was no hiding. Rock chips flew, dust rose into the pine-scented air.

"Cease fire!" a voice bellowed from the narrow exit. Nicholson!

In the clearing, a man lifted himself unsteadily to his knees, dropping his rifle and raising his hands towards his head. In his sights, Rankin could see his mouth working.

The shot boomed out, the man splayed backward, the echo reverberated around the cliffs. It seemed to take minutes to fade away completely.

————

"AND WHAT WERE we going to do with a bloody prisoner?" Rankin asked heatedly.

"Hand him over at the beach," Nicholson replied through clenched jaws.

"We don't even know there is a bloody beach!" Rankin hissed back.

"Your orders–"

Rankin's anger threatened to boil over. What did Nicholson

know of his bloody orders? "Yes, my orders! My orders don't allow for prisoners. I'm sorry if that doesn't fit with your sensibilities, but that's the fact. It's not up for debate."

Turning away, Rankin called for the NCOs to get the men to reclaim their kit and get going. Silence fell over the gloom in the clearing, giving it a menacing, oppressive feeling as the men picked up their packs and checked their weapons. Still without saying another word, Rankin led them into the gorge, towards the sea and the Royal Navy.

The further they went; the more Rankin's apprehension grew. Surely to God they must be nearly at the beach. Surely, they should have run into a patrol by now. At least a picket, thrown out to hinder the Germans. The beach should be crowded with evacuees. Where in God's name was everyone?

Coming to another narrow chink in the canyon, literally only yards wide, Rankin saw the sky ahead, through the narrow defile. Pushing past a rocky bluff, he passed through the rocky jaws and the light shining through the widening cleft in the rock drew him on. He stepped out of the dark, into a place flooded with the soft, golden glow of evening. Further on, whitewashed houses stood honey-coloured in the golden light. Beyond them, he had his first glimpse of the sea: deep blue-green water, a bay enclosed by honeyed cliffs.

"Where in God's name is everybody?" Rankin stammered, feeling his panic mounting.

Weapons at the ready, the men behind him slowed to an uncertain shuffle. Closer to the buildings, they now saw what the golden evening light had previously hidden: the walls of the whitewashed houses were scorched and pock-marked; collapsed buildings and trees stripped bare by blast lined the streets. Bomb craters were everywhere and as they approached, they came upon the first bodies, khaki and civilian, lying together in the street.

Nearer to the waterfront Rankin caught a glimpse of wrecked boats and a landing craft smouldering in the water just off the gravel beach. A voice, sounding very drunk, called out from a building on the front, which might once have been a beachside taverna: "You're too late, mate. They've all pissed off."

Rankin looked about in disbelief, tears welling behind his eyes. That could not be right! Had Hamilton known this all along? Or had he, Rankin, made a ghastly error? Had he led them down the wrong gorge?

"Jesus Christ Almighty," he whispered.

What happens next?

This book concludes with a great deal of unfinished business for Neil Rankin and his companions. Has Rankin finally been outwitted and sidelined by his superior, Captain Hamilton? Can Rankin save his mission and prevent them all having to sit out the war in a prison camp? Can he repair his fractured relationship with Sergeant Nicholson?

The next book in *The Rabbit Hunter* series with the answers to these questions – and much, much more – is due for publication in 2025.

Historical Notes

I have endeavoured to accurately portray the Battle of Crete through the eyes and experiences of the fictional characters in this book. The New Zealand Division was deployed to Greece in March 1941 as part of a British Empire force to support the Greeks. After the invading Wehrmacht overran the mainland, most of the survivors were evacuated to Crete, including the New Zealand 23 Battalion and its D Company of which Rankin's fictional platoon was a part.

Generally, characters in the book with the rank of captain and below are fictional, whereas those with the rank of major and above are based on the actual participants. Captain Rangi Royal, commanding officer of B Company, 28 Battalion, is an exception. I have endeavoured to be as accurate with my portrayal of Captain Royal as with all other actual participants.

The book is as historically accurate as I can make it. The battle unfolded for the soldiers who fought it, on both sides, largely as I have described. There was a real "Platoon on the Tavronitis". Drawn from 21 Battalion, it was commanded by a Lieutenant H R Anderson from Dargaville. Sadly, Anderson was killed on the morning of 20 May and the platoon was led by Sergeant Gorrie for the rest of the day.

The time sequence reflects the facts. Writing the story brought home to me the sheer physical and emotional drain of the battle. The second part of the book, the withdrawal, is 10 days of almost continuous hard fighting by day and marching by night.

Some events, such as the stick of paratroopers descending into the broken bamboos, may seem the product of an unnecessarily ghoulish imagination, but they are based on fact. Both of Rankin's ambushes are also based on fact, as are the battles at Galatas and 42nd Street. Even the official history records one veteran's comment to the effect that the troops had a lot of "bayonet work" on Crete, which was unusual in modern war, illustrating how much of the fighting on the island was at very close quarters. Pervitin was real; millions of tablets were issued to German troops in the campaigns prior to Crete. It was also available over the counter and purchased by parents for their sons serving abroad.

My aim is to project the reader into the person of the central character, to know what he knew, to see what he saw and to feel what he felt. Only the reader can judge whether I have achieved this aim. Any errors or failings in the telling of this story are mine alone.

The fictional characters in this book are entirely the product of my imagination. They are not based on any person, historical or otherwise, and any resemblance to any person, living or dead, is purely coincidental. This is particularly the case with Captain Hamilton, who bears no resemblance to the real commanding officer of D Company, 23 Battalion.

While the battle was a clear defeat for the Empire troops taking part, it was not one-sided. The German airborne troops suffered such casualties they were never again used in a major airborne assault. The losses of aircraft (over 350) were never made good and were sorely missed at Stalingrad 18 months later and during the Luftwaffe's efforts to supply the army in North Africa.

The New Zealand official history (*Crete, New Zealand in the Second World War 1939–45* by D.M. Davin, published in 1953) gives the following casualty figures for the forces engaged:

	Killed	Wounded	POW
Britain	806	264	6972
Australia	272	507	3102
New Zealand	671	967	2180
Total	1749	1738	12254
Germany	4000	2600	17

Notes:

1. These figures do not include Greek combatants or civilians, who paid a high price for defending their homeland.
2. Losses at sea during the evacuation are estimated at another 260–300 soldiers; Royal Navy losses during operations around Crete are estimated at over 2000.
3. Of the 4000 Germans killed, the New Zealand history estimates (based on German records) that 2500 were killed and a further 500 wounded in the initial landings.

Acknowledgements

First and foremost, I wish to thank my wife Niki for her continued patience and fortitude during the time it has taken to write these books. My hope is that you think the result worth all the blank stares and vacant looks over the years while I have been away in Neil Rankin's reality.

A fabulous family holiday on Crete in the late 1990s meant the children also were subjected to car trips to out of the way places on very hot days while I endeavoured to explain why I wanted to see the very large German war cemetery on top of a hill overlooking Maleme Airfield, which, at the time, was operated by the Greek Air Force. That hill has a central part to play in this book, where it is known as Hill 107. We also visited the British Commonwealth war cemetery on the Akrotiri Peninsula. Both are beautifully kept; you cannot help but be moved by the ages on the headstones.

Details of the landscapes and places we visited were stored away until 2003, when Dianne Brown and the Aoraki Polytech fiction writing course gave me the impetus and encouragement to start putting the kernel of an idea into words. Ross Parry and Steve Tillyshort read early drafts of the book years later, providing valuable input and giving me the confidence to continue. Later still, Fred Cookson, chartered accountant of Opotiki, read the exchange between the fictional Rankin and the real Captain Rangi Royal (pages 391–393) for which I am indebted to him.

Chris Else of Total Fiction Services provided insightful professional guidance, including introducing me to the phrase "the psychology of soldiering". Authors tend to live inside the heads of their characters; writing the battle sequences was exceptionally difficult and had a profound effect on me. I have endeavoured to reflect this in the central character's reactions.

Eventually the draft got to the point where Matthew Fulton (The Book Editor) and Renée Lang, of Renaissance Publishing, were able to turn Rankin's story into a book.

Thanks, too, to Alicia Sutherland and Chris Saxton of Saxton CA Ltd for printing the proofs for me.

To all of the above, my heartfelt thanks.

About the Author

Chris Worth was born into the lucky generation. A generation that avoided the necessity of facing first-hand the dislocation and tragedy of war. We were raised by parents who wished for their children the things that had been denied to themselves. Brought up in Dunedin, Chris became a chartered accountant, joining the firm of Coopers & Lybrand in 1974. He went to London on his "OE" in the early 1980s before returning to Christchurch with Niki and moving to Dunedin in 1987. In 1996, now with two daughters, the family packed up and moved to Russia, where Chris was a partner with Coopers & Lybrand (later PricewaterhouseCoopers) in the Moscow office. This second OE lasted six years, and the family returned to New Zealand in 2002.

Chris has always had an interest in the Second World War, and in writing. The two came together between 2004 and 2021 while Chris worked part time as a contract practice reviewer for the Institute of Chartered Accountants in New Zealand. The result is *The Rabbit Hunter* series of books.